Praise for Lost Girls

'*Lost Girls* is remarkable and compelling. But, more than that, it is a novel that goes some way towards reinventing the literary ghost story' *The Times*

'This is one scary book . . . you'll want to keep all the lights on as you read this one' *Independent on Sunday*

'Think *The Shining* mixed with *The Sixth Sense*. A truly scary ghost story that will have you turning the pages late into the night' *Maxim*

'A remarkably fine debut novel . . . *Lost Girls* has an atmospheric menace that is all its own' *Time Out*

'*Lost Girls* is a hugely impressive and utterly compelling thriller that mixes the ghostliness of Wilkie Collins with the plotting and courtroom drama of John Grisham . . . moody, thought-provoking and altogether remarkable' *Independent*

'It's hard to say exactly what kind of tale Pyper has told, but there's no doubt that he has told it brilliantly' *New York Times*

'This is an excellently written novel, brilliant in its evocation of an atmosphere which, at first mildly sinister, progressively thickens and darkens' *Evening Standard*

'Part enigmatically atmospheric ghost story, part hard-edged thriller, *Lost Girls* usefully cracks a number of moulds'

Scotsman

Andrew Pyper was born in Ontario, Canada, in 1968. He received a BA and an MA in English literature from McGill University in Montreal, as well as a law degree from the University of Toronto. He is the author of several bestselling novels, including *The Guardians* and *Lost Girls*, which won an Arthur Ellis Award. To learn more about Andrew and his writing visit www.andrewpyper.com

By Andrew Pyper

Kiss Me (stories)
Lost Girls
The Trade Mission
The Wildfire Season
The Killing Circle
The Guardians
The Demonologist

Lost Girls

Andrew Pyper

An Orion paperback

First published in Great Britain in 2000
by Macmillan
This paperback edition published in 2013
by Orion Books,
an imprint of The Orion Publishing Group Ltd,
Orion House, 5 Upper St Martin's Lane,
London WC2H 9EA

An Hachette UK company

1 3 5 7 9 10 8 6 4 2

A CIP catalogue record for this book
is available from the British Library.

ISBN 978-1-4091-3887-7

Printed and bound in by CPI Group (UK) Ltd,
Croydon CRO 4YY

The Orion Publishing Group's policy is to use papers
that are natural, renewable and recyclable products and
made from wood grown in sustainable forests. The logging
and manufacturing processes are expected to conform to
the environmental regulations of the country of origin.

www.orionbooks.co.uk

For Leah

*Terrible experiences pose the riddle whether
the person who has them is not terrible.*

—*Nietzsche,* Beyond Good and Evil

Prologue

An afternoon following a day so perfect that people can speak of nothing but how perfect a day it has been. At least these people, sitting in canvas folding chairs on the small cleared beach of a lake in a country where summer is only a brief intermission of winter, watching the sun begin its setting with reverence and sunburned fatigue, making music with the ice in their drinks and feeling that this—ownership of a good place near water and trees and out of sight of neighbors—is more true and real than anything else they could hope for their lives. One of the men rises to tend to the barbecue and the air is filled with the promise of lighting fluid and burning fat. It is not yet dusk but mosquitoes rise from the unmowed grass and drift up into the willow limbs as bats burst out from under the cottage eaves to swallow them. More drinks, more ice—*clinkety-clink*—the rising gush and sweep of a woman's laughter at one of the men's mumbled stories. A feathery lick of wind swirls among them, through their legs, cooling the sweat at their necks. Before them the lake flashes with reflected light but steadily darkens just below the surface, turning the afternoon's clear blue to a purple coagulation of silt and weeds—the color of frostbitten lips, of blood left to dry on the blade.

First a girl and then a boy come out through the cottage's screen door and the people by the lake turn to wave lazily up at them, having almost forgotten that they are here as well. The two stand together in bare feet and tans, whispering, the boy telling the girl things about their parents that make her throw her hand to her mouth. He is in his early teens and she a half-year younger, but they have known each other and days like this before, time spent behind the backs and under the dining room tables of the grown-ups. Everyone is pleased that the two cousins get along so well and take care of each other so that the adults can imagine themselves, for the time they're all up here, as young and untroubled and childless.

As the man at the barbecue lays the slabs of meat upon the grill, the boy and girl walk down to where the others are sitting and ask if they can take the canoe out for a while before dinner. There's no disagreement from the parents, although one of the women makes a joke about how "cute" it is that the two of them have such a "crush" on each other, and this starts a mocking whoop from the man who isn't tending the barbecue. They've all been through this routine before. The boy and girl know that this is what their parents like best: drinking a little too much and making remarks about experiences that have passed to a comfortable enough distance that they can now make fun of them, dismiss them even, like first love. So in response they say nothing directly, although the girl mouths *ha ha ha* at her mother to note that the joke stopped being funny a long time ago.

They pull the aluminum canoe out from under the dense scrub of sweet gale and leather-leaf which marks the end of the property and, sharing a look, throw the life jackets back under. Slide the hull down to the beach and over the narrow stretch of pebbly sand which screeches against the metal. The girl is at the front and the boy at the back (or bow and stern, as the boy's father keeps telling him). This is their usual arrangement. The boy is strong and has a practiced J-stroke, which comes in handy when the girl gets tired and he has to bring them in on his own.

"Kissin' cuzzins!" shouts the barbecue man, who was not in on the earlier joke. The girl's mother looks back at her husband and states his name with exaggerated severity, shaking her head as if to say, *He never gets anything!*

"What? What?" the barbecue man asks, shrugging, looking to the other man with a *Who can figure women?* look on his face, and they all laugh again, because for them this is the way men and women are like together when things are good.

The girl squeals as her feet sink into the weedy mush that lurks just off from where the sand stops, then steps into her position with two athletic swings of her legs. With a final push the boy kneels in the back and puts fifty feet between the canoe and their parents' laughter in three strokes.

"Wanna go to the island?" the girl asks. This is the place they usually head for. It has a high granite point rising up out of the tree cover from which you can see almost half of the lake's inlets and jetties. It's also where, at the end of last summer's Labor Day weekend, the two cousins made out for the first time.

"No. Let's go to the beaver dam."

"That's far."

"*That's far,*" he mimics, which she hates, because he's good at it.

They turn away from the island, which lies a half-mile straight ahead of the cottage's beach, and toward the mouth of an unnamed river beyond it.

"I don't want to go home," she says without turning.

"What do you mean?"

"I want to stay up here. For the summer not to end."

"But it *does* end. It gets cold, the lake freezes over, and there's no TV."

"I don't care. It just makes me sad that we can do this, now—all this stuff together—and soon I'll be back home and you'll be back home, dealing with all the dickheads at our schools and whatever. It's just shitty, that's all."

"I know."

"And I miss you. I mean, I know I'm going to miss you."

"Yeah, I know."

"I wish—" she exhales, but doesn't continue. The boy knows what she means, and that she is a girl full of wishes.

As they near the beaver dam she pulls her paddle in and turns around to face the boy. Smiles, tilts her head back to absorb the last heat of the day's sun. The boy studies the galaxy of pale freckles that crosses her chest and clusters in the space above her small breasts. Her hair, red-brown in winter and blonde in summer, falls straight back and reaches down almost to the water. She makes a low moaning at the back of her throat and stretches her legs out in front of her, wriggling her toes until he quietly brings his own paddle in and grabs them.

"And these little piggies got barbecued!" he cackles, and the girl screams, famously ticklish. Then she comes forward and kisses him.

"Kissin' cuzzins," she says.

"Wait. Let's get to shore first."

The boy maneuvers them in the last twenty yards to the river's mouth, into the reeds, tapegrass and coontails. Once he steps out onto the shore he takes the girl's arm and half guides, half lifts her to where he stands. As their feet sink into the softness of the river's edge the smell of rot rises out of the ground, the decomposition of fish and slug and frog.

"Ugh. Stinks like shit!" the girl shrieks, though the boy knows it isn't that, but the stink of dead things.

"They're getting ready to eat."

The boy squints back across the water at the miniaturized figures of the adults, who are now ambling up to the picnic table and fetching more drinks. Once they leave the sunny spot by the lake they disappear into the shadows, just as the boy and girl, if you were to look for them from where the adults had sat, are concealed by the lengthening darkness.

"Should we go back?" the girl asks.

"Are you hungry?"

"No."

"Then we'll take our time."

They sludge along the water's edge to where the beaver has blocked a narrow point in the river with twigs, fallen tree limbs, even a found section of hockey stick, all held together by dried mud. The boy walks a few feet out onto the dam and extends his hand for her to follow. Beneath his feet the passing water sucks and gurgles, the meshed-together wood creaking under his weight.

"No! Get off! It's the beaver's house!" the girl calls to him with a mixture of protest and delight.

"C'mon. Don't worry. It's abandoned. It's gone somewhere else now, so it doesn't matter," the boy lies. He knows nothing of beavers or which mushrooms can be eaten in the woods or how to tell compass directions from the stars, but he tells the girl stories about all of these things.

"Really?"

"Yes."

"Promise?"

"Promise."

The girl takes his hand and steps up beside him, close

enough that he has to circle his arm behind her back to prevent her from falling in. Her breath, sweet-smelling and spicy as cinnamon, warms his neck.

"C'mere," he whispers, although she can move no closer. Then he lowers his head and kisses her, moves his tongue inside her mouth and his hands to her hips to hold her in place. They have kissed before, but this summer things have been different. They felt different. But one thing that's the same is that when they kiss he keeps his eyes open and she closes hers. He likes this almost more than the smooth invitation of her lips. To watch her eyelids come down like sleep so that he can watch her pleasure without being seen himself.

When they pull apart they hold each other still for a time, stand without speaking, each listening to the other's shallow breaths. In the single moment of their silence the dusk has begun its advance. From the blackening trees behind them lights appear, pinpricks of color. Without a word, the boy and girl watch them emerge, fireflies flashing through the branches and high grass. Hundreds of flickering communications moving forward from the woods.

"It's like they're *talking* to each other," the girl says.

"It's beautiful. Nice." The boy counts to three in his head. *One Mississippi, two Mississippi, three Mississippi.* "C'mon, let's get back in the canoe. It'll be more comfortable."

The boy turns and picks his way back from where they have come and when he steps off the dam he wonders if the beaver is out there in the woods, watching them.

"Let's go!" he shouts back to the girl, and she turns to follow. When she meets him at the canoe she climbs in first and then he pushes them off, his feet making a foul suction-ing sound in the mud as they go. Without speaking they slowly paddle around the river's mouth, watching small pike, rock bass and tadpoles flash through the water at the disturbance of their wake. Then the boy directs them out into the open lake and, once they reach the middle, stops and pulls the paddle in. Watches the perfect stretch of her back, the soft crease of skin at her sunburned neck.

"Hey," the boy says, and the girl turns to him, placing her paddle next to his.

"Hey what?"

"Hey, you look amazing. Here, in the light."

The boy moves forward, steadying the canoe with his hands on the sides. Then he kneels before the girl, cups her face in his palms. "Amazing."

He kisses her hard and she makes a sound, an indeterminable sigh of submission or resistance, and his hands move to her hips, lift her up and place her down again below him without removing his mouth from hers. As his fingers go to work—pulling, pressing, positioning—he holds his mouth over hers to keep her from speaking. But eventually he has to pull back to arrange his own body into the right angle, and when she opens her mouth it's not to say *Don't* but "Please," her voice constricted with panic. She asks him to stop without calling him by name—just *please*—for to the girl he was no longer her cousin but something else, a wild, rabid thing, like the bear she'd once seen frothing and wailing down by the landfill before the provincial police shot it through the skull.

"Don't move. You'll tip it," the boy whispers. But she doesn't want to move. What she wants is to lie so still it makes him stop. So she closes her eyes, stiffens her back straight over the jabbing aluminum ribs of the canoe's hull and imagines herself floating on the perfect line between water and sky. But still there is his breath, his strong fingers, the weight of his thighs pressing down on hers.

For a moment the boy stops and she opens her eyes to see him scrabbling with the clasp on his shorts and the zipper below it. With a grunt he falls back and pulls them down, ripping the seam and kicking them off his feet onto her chest. Then he comes forward again and brushes his mouth next to her ear.

"C'mon," he whispers. It's all he can think of to say. *C'mon, c'mon, c'mon.* He wishes she were different—older and inviting, like the faceless women of his imagination—not this girl with bony hips and a face he knows too well pinched up in fear. He doesn't want this. He wants a dream. So he closes his eyes, fumbling with himself, and just as this and the sway of the canoe and the blooming heat within him begin to feel more like what he wants he is awakened by her screams.

He tries to shush her but she screams even more, banging the sides with her fists and slamming her heels into his back. The screaming doesn't stop even after he pulls back from her and tells her it's O.K., it's over, he's sorry, he won't try it again. Checks over his shoulder in the direction of the cottage to see if her sounds have brought anyone down to the beach but he can't tell, his view blinded by the lowering sun. When he turns his head back again the girl is struggling to stand up, one hand waving in the air and the other pushing down on the side. The shadow of her cut against the dim sky, looking down at him with both recognition and horror. Then, in the same moment—in the same half-moment—that she gets to her feet the canoe moves into a fluid spin that pushes them both below the water.

Cold.

It's the cold that shocks the blood in their hearts and cramps their muscles as soon as they begin thrashing for the surface. The boy keeps his eyes closed but reaches up, searching for the overturned canoe and soon finding it. With a single pull his head breaks through into the air and he takes in a hungry gasp. How long had he been down there? Five seconds? Long enough to make his chest ache. For a time he holds his arms over the slippery hull and simply breathes. Then he remembers the girl.

Calls her name once, but doesn't shout it.

Nothing.

No sound but the lapping of water against his shoulders. Where was she? Both of them good swimmers but she better than he, faster and with far greater endurance. She should have been beside him, spitting water in his face, or a hundred yards off kicking her way to shore. But she wasn't. The boy knows he has to go under to find her, but it feels so cold down there, only a few feet below the surface. A difference of several degrees between armpits and toes. It's the cold that frightens him.

The first time he goes down only a few feet before twisting back up, eyes closed against the imagined sight of bug-eyed snakes and glowing, tentacled jellyfish. Gnashes at the air.

On the second dive he takes as large a breath as his lungs will allow and flutters down against his own buoyancy, eyes still closed, hands reaching before him. Then he feels her. Not any actual part of her body, but the vibrations of her struggle radiating out through the water. Down, further down. The burning in his chest now descended to the bottom of his spine, numbing his legs. When he begins to feel the muscles in his jaw ache to pull his mouth open he tells himself to turn back but nothing obeys and he goes two strokes further yet.

And finds her arm. Slides his hand up and bracelets her wrist with his fingers. Then he kicks like hell.

But the girl feels heavy, heavier than she should, as though attached to a sack of wet sand. A dozen sacks of wet sand. The pain that comes with the lack of oxygen now a bell tolling in the boy's head but he doesn't let her go, pushing against the weight with the last of his strength until his free arm knocks against the underside of the canoe.

Even with the leverage of his fingers locked around the hull's edge the girl is still too heavy to bring up with him. His shoulder strains, his toes brush through her hair but she moves no further. Then he feels a tug. A sharp force from below her which nearly takes him down too. Then another.

It's not that the girl is too heavy for him to pull up. Something else is pulling the other way.

With the third tug she's gone.

The boy pulls his head through to the light, counts to two and goes under once more. *One Mississippi, two Mississippi.* This time, when he's down as far as he can go and moves his arms out to feel for her, there's nothing there.

He tells himself not to do it, that it will be too horrible and do no good, but he does anyway. He looks.

What he notices first is that the opening of his eyes also opens his ears, because it is only then that he hears his cousin's scream. Then he sees her scream, her gaping mouth blowing a diminishing stream of bubbles up toward him before breaking soundlessly at the surface. But as she runs out of air her scream becomes something worse, a moaning inhalation of the lake's purple weight. Eyes a wild white, blonde hair now black as oil, writhing out from her head like eels. Fingers grasping up toward the light, at him, at anything, but when they stop they are frozen into gnarled fists.

She goes down fast, but he remembers all of this.

Not sinking but pulled. That's what he sees. His cousin pulled down from the last snaking shafts of sunlight into the black, into the blind, cold depths.

PART ONE

One

There is nothing more overrated in the practice of criminal law than the truth. Indeed it's something of a trade secret among professionals in the field that the facts alone rarely determine the outcome of a trial. What's overlooked by the casual observer is the subtle distinction between the truth and the convincing of others to accept one of its alternatives.

Allow me to make reference to current events:

Later today I'm expected to complete the defence's case in a sexual assault trial where the facts are clear and they all disfavor the position of my client, a Mr. Leonard Busch. To make matters worse, counsel for the prosecution is as skillful, determined and ambitious as yours truly. A constipated-looking young woman whose eyebrows form a piercing "V" when she speaks and whose every word vibrates with accusation, qualities which contributed to the splendid job she did in her exam-in-chief of the complainant. When the tears started in the middle of the girl's recounting of the night in question my opponent stepped helplessly toward the witness box, levered a vicious glare at my client, and shushed the girl with, "It's alright, Debbie. You don't have to look at *him*," while at the same time stabbing a trembling index finger at my man Lenny. It was a beautiful move: theatrical, maternal, prejudicial. The effect was so damaging that I was tempted to leap to my feet and make an objection against what was so obviously a purely tactical maneuver. But in the end I

remained seated, met the prosecution's eyes with what I
hoped was a look of indignation and held my tongue. It's
important at such moments to remember one of the first
rules of successful advocacy: sometimes one has to accept
small defeats in the interest of capturing the final victory.

But victory for Mr. Busch (and more importantly for his
lawyer, Bartholomew Christian Crane) did not appear to be
an imminent outcome of the trial. In fact, as the Crown's
evidence was paraded plainly before the court, the prospect
of an acquittal seemed a fading likelihood unless our defence
could come up with an ace. Nothing short of a miracle would
do, judging from the set faces of the jury who, although
thoroughly screened to exclude socialists, feminists, and
those who believed O.J. did it, knew a *bona fide* creep when
they saw one. So as I blink my eyes open to the abusive light
of a Toronto August dawn I search my mind for a savior for
the otherwise doomed Leonard Busch.

And nothing comes to me. But this is not unusual, given
the time of day. The left ear buzzes, the right ear hums, my
brain tickling the nerves at the back of my eyes. Roll my head
from side to side and let the whole mess slosh around. It's on
occasions like these (i.e. the beginning of every day) that I
thank God I live alone, for the fact is I find it difficult to
tolerate close contact with others under the best of circumstances, and utterly impossible before nine. This may have to
do with my particular habits and addictions, or it may not.
But no matter if I've been drinking the night before or
sipping herbal tea (if I ever *have* sipped herbal tea), I have
woken with hangover symptoms every morning since I started
practicing law. That was five years ago. And just as the butcher
endures his bloody aprons or the garbageman his stinking
fingers, I have learned to live with it.

I raise myself stiffly from the white expanse of a singly occupied king-size bed and scuff over to the kitchen counter where, piled into a crystalline white anthill, my inspiration sits. Reduce its mass in two sinus-burning whiffs and with this I am able to swiftly conclude that the only chance Leonard has is Lisa, the accused's eighteen-year-old girlfriend.

Leonard Busch himself is fifty-two, barrel-chested, butter-nosed, and the owner of Pelican Beach, a nightclub located in a former auto parts warehouse stuck beneath the cement buttresses of the Gardiner Expressway next to the harbor. It's one of those hangar-size places that boasts "co-ed" beach volleyball in February, wet T-shirt contests in April and Ladies Night every Tuesday (a free rose and half-priced tequila until midnight, at which point the "ladies" are in generally good enough shape to be hauled back to a stranger's futon). Leonard ran the whole vile affair from his office suspended above the d.j. booth with mirrored windows overlooking the seething dance floor. It was there that he conducted his business, where "business" means the counting of receipts, the consumption of Ballantine's on the rocks and the inter-viewing of girls seeking waitress positions. Early evidence from a number of them indicated that Leonard took these opportunities to ask questions of dubious purpose ("Are you wearing any underwear right now?") and to squeeze bottoms in the interest of determining the applicants' qualifications.

All of these details, however unseemly, were not of any particular concern to me. But Leonard's fondness for plying certain female staff with liquor, taking them for early morn-ing drives down to the docklands and heaving himself on their half-comatose bodies was substantially more troubling from a legal perspective, especially given that one of his dates came forward the next day and insisted that Leonard Busch, her employer and friend ("At first I thought he was kinda sweet"), had taken his pleasure with her without her consent. Indeed, as she testified, she would've been unable to voice her permission even if she'd wanted to as her brain had been made so mushy with booze she could only slap her palms against his back and try to remember the names of the teddy bears in her old bedroom at her parents' house.

Shower, shave, stick a hastily assembled margarine sandwich into my breast pocket for the rare moments that hunger visits, and head up Spadina and over Queen Street to the courthouse. The air is unseasonably chilly but I only half notice, concentrating instead on the approach to take with dear little Lisa. More stupid than the prevailing standard among mall-vixens of her vintage, she was not only foolish enough to be Leonard's sole long-term lover, but to be *in love* with him as well. Attended every day of the trial, finding a place in the back row and trying to make eye contact with her beloved every time he rose to be shackled and led away to his cell. Initially I thought the girl might be a potential asset to our case, but when asked about it, my client dismissed the idea.

"Forget it. She's fuckin' nuts. Besides, my wife don't know about her," was Leonard's exact phrasing.

It wasn't clear to me how Mrs. Busch would be more upset over the disclosure of a mistress than the conviction of her husband as a rapist, but I said no more about it.

Until today. When I arrive at the court I descend to the basement holding cells, shake my head at Leonard and voice my suggestion through a hole in the Plexiglass wall between us.

"We got anything else?" he asks.

"Not a thing."

"Then talk to her. But I dunno what she could say to help. I didn't even see her that night."

When the court convenes the judge begins by asking if I'm prepared to deliver final submissions. I advise him that I require a brief adjournment to make a final survey of the defence's evidence before concluding the case. The judge orders us all back following lunch. I have three hours.

After the few courtroom spectators mill out into the hallway I snake up behind my prey and, bending low enough for my nose to be filled with the lemon styling gel of her perm-crinkled, bleach-yellowed hair, whisper an invitation for her to follow. Without a word she steps behind me to an interview room at the end of the hall where she sits and I lock the door with an echoing *clack*. Shuffle over to the chair opposite hers and settle myself in its cup of orange plastic.

"I'm not going to waste any time here, Lisa, because frankly we don't have any time to waste," I start with a beleaguered sigh. "Can you appreciate that?"

"Yes, Mr. Crane."

There is a tingle of pleasure with her voicing of "Mr. Crane." (I am still young and vain enough to enjoy the sound of my surname spoken by others.)

"Then let me tell you that I'd like you to be the final witness in this trial. I'd like you to tell *your* side of the story, Lisa." Inhale deeply. "That Leonard *couldn't* have committed the crime of which he is accused, because he was with *you* on the fourteenth of August. That's what I'm asking you to do for me."

"But I can't say that."

"Why not?"

"Because it's not true."

In one movement I stand, kick my chair back and send it sliding over the waxed marble floor into the wall behind me.

"You can *say* whatever you want, Lisa! Let me show you." Lean forward over the table so that my face is all that she can see. "Open your mouth."

"What?"

"Just open your mouth."

The mouth opens.

"Now, say 'This whole thing is my fault.'"

"No—he—"

"Just *say* it!"

"This whole thing is my fault."

"Lovely! And therein lies the lesson of the day: it is possible to tell a different story from that which we know."

I move back from the table and cross my arms in my football coach pose, the whole time holding the girl's black-pupiled eyes in mine. "And *you're* going to say he was with you that night. That he drove you down to the docks as usual, that you had sex in all the usual positions until around three, at which point he drove you uptown and dropped you off a couple blocks from your house as per usual."

"But that's not true," she attempts, voice cracking wide open. "Mr. Crane, that *didn't* happen. Not that night."

Then the tears start, a shaking torrent, and I know I've won. In my experience, tears are a strong sign of a mind willing to be changed.

"You've forgotten your lesson already, Lisa! Listen to *me* now." Move forward again so that the closeness of my voice cuts off her sobbing. "I wouldn't want you to make a very big mistake because you failed to appreciate the *seriousness* of the situation, so let me make this extremely clear. We—you and

I—are going to save Leonard's life. Because if Leonard goes to jail, he will die."

I allow a slight smile now, a suggestion of my full and sympathetic understanding. "You do love Leonard, don't you?"

"Yes," she nods. Blinks.

"And you want to have a life together with him?"

"Yes."

"But you can't have a life with him if he dies in prison, can you?"

"No."

"And you know that right now you're the only person in the world who can save him, don't you?"

"Yes."

"Then there's only one thing to do. And *you* have to do it, Lisa."

She's drying up now, dragging her nose along her sleeve. The steely glare of purpose fixed in her eyes.

"O.K.," she says.

"Good girl. Now, Lisa, let's get this story straight."

Having been granted permission by the court to call a final "surprise" witness (the judge had little choice, given the risk of an appeal if he denied me), I summon Lisa to the stand. As instructed, she has reduced the redness in her face by applying a damp cloth to her cheeks and has steadied her carriage with the half tab of Valium I supplied her with at the end of our interview. Moves forward from her seat in the back with concentration, one foot at a time, raises a hand and swears on a leather King James to tell the truth, the whole truth, etc., etc. Peers down at me, all big eyes and lipstick. The jury leans forward. *A surprise witness,* their faces say. *What's she going to say?* I'm not sure myself.

"Tell us what you want to say in your own words," I instruct her softly. "Just tell the court what really happened, Lisa."

And then she does it. A clear chronology, point by point, blow by blow. Even better than as rehearsed, as she ends up throwing in a few details which lend greater specificity to the tale, including my personal favorite, "Leonard had a tough time getting it up that night because one of his kids had strep throat and he was really worried."

Can a traumatized, frightened, confused eighteen-year-old lie like that under oath in a court of law? With a little push and some coaching, she certainly can. She can introduce reasonable doubt into the minds of jurors who previously had none, deliver freedom to a man who otherwise had no right to it. All of this just by opening her mouth and using the magic words.

Of course I understand how this sort of thing gives rise to the concern that my role in these proceedings shows a lack of ethics. And how then an argument could be made in sharp response, the one that lawyers always make to justify assisting the guilty for a fee: that everyone has the right to be presumed innocent in a free and democratic society, and that every opportunity must be afforded the accused to meet the charges made against him, etc., etc.

But I will not make such an argument. Not because I believe it to be false, but because philosophy makes no difference and truth is none of my concern.

In short, to appreciate the meaning of Leonard Busch's victory you need not trouble yourself with "principles," however you may understand such a prickly term. So too can you stay well off the foggy moors of "honor," "mercy," 'justice," whatever.

All you need to know is this: I *won*.

TWO

Law firms always have two names. For example, the one which I'm a member of is formally known as Lyle, Gederov & Associate. But its name among defence lawyers, court clerks, judges, bike couriers, repeat offenders and Crown Attorneys who work in this town is Lie, Get 'Em Off & Associate. The suggestions of the name are clear. It is also clear from the record of its success that Lie, Get 'Em Off & Associate is among the finest criminal law firms in the country. And there're only the three of us.

Categorically speaking, criminal lawyers are known as the freaks of the legal profession (who's ever noted the eccentricities of a real estate or tax solicitor?), and Graham Lyle, law school gold medalist, oft-mentioned potential appointee to the bench (perennially rejected as too "risky") and $375-an-hour leader of his field, is freakier than most. An excitable, octave-spanning vocal range, and a face so defined of bone, gentle of mouth and long of lash it is difficult not to be disturbed by its prettiness. Add to this a flair for fashion which runs to pastels, chunky jewelry, cravats and polka-dot bow ties, along with a habit of calling his scum-of-the-earth clientele "darling" or "sweetheart," and you have Graham, a raving queen whose superior intelligence, Peter O'Toole good looks and pure wickedness put him in a different league from the rest of the competition. More to the point, I *like* Graham. As advocates we are of the same mind. I often recall what he told me at the close of my first solo trial after I'd misled the court on the prior criminal record of my client, a deception which led to his acquittal. "There are no such things as lies," he said, leaning back in his chair and giving me a wink. "There are only misperceptions."

Graham Lyle's partner, the other freak of the place, is Bert Gederov, a second-generation Russian immigrant who has somehow retained a threatening hint of his ancestors' accent. His body—hunchbacked, broad-assed, arms swinging from his shoulders like sides of pork—is the physical manifestation of pure hostility. Even in moments of relative calm his face conveys an impatience and brutality which has assisted in winning him case after case before "pussy judges" at the expense of "dumb-shit Crowns."

For whatever psychological reasons, Bert Gederov is the sort whose primary means of social interaction is intimidation. What's truly impressive, however, is that he manages to inspire fear in others through his mere presence and only rarely through actual exhibitions of viciousness. He speaks little outside of the time he is paid to, and when he does it is to utter obscenities and crushing insults at the most vulnerable subject available. Recall the bully from your school days. Remember the shuddering of the bowels, the sudden slackness of the facial muscles, the lung-seizing paralysis the sight of him could inspire? Yes? You're now one step closer to knowing Bert. Still, although he is cruel, misogynistic, racist, flatulent, and nauseating dining company, Bert is a lawyer for whom I have nothing but the greatest respect.

As for the "& Associate," that's me. And here I am, staring at myself in the Barristers' Water Closet mirror having washed off the sweat smeared across my cheeks by Mr. Busch's grateful lips. Turn a little to the left, a little to the right, check the profile out of the corner of my eye. Conclude that I'm not looking too bad, particularly when you consider the few hours of sleep I've had over the last five of my thirty-three years. But I can also acknowledge that time is beginning to show: grey in the face, premature grey at the temples and sides, grey clouds drifting into the blue of my eyes. A lot of grey about me these days, but that's fine. Gray suits me. And I'm thinking that very thought as the beeper at my waist erupts to inform me that I've been summoned to an emergency meeting at the boardroom of Lyle, Gederov, and that both partners are to be in attendance.

As I walk the short distance north from the courthouse to the office on University Avenue, my face warming in the reluctant sunshine, my mind mulls over the last part of the beeper's small screen message: WE'VE GOT THE LOST GIRLS. Graham's touch.

I'd heard of the case listening in on the chat in the court cafeteria (defence lawyers pay the kind of attention to news of homicides that corporate lawyers do to the fortunes of the Dow Jones). Something about two fourteen-year-old girls who'd gone missing a couple months earlier and were now presumed dead. Police were said to have "encouraging leads," which meant they had their man and were just buying time to accumulate enough physical evidence to make an arrest. Somebody had passed me the newspaper while we were waiting for the judge to return from lunch and on the back page of the front section were side-by-side pictures of the victims, the kind of bland, backgroundless portraits taken for high school yearbooks. Just two missing teenaged girls captured in a flat frame. The sort of thing you see in newspapers almost every day: smiling, chins raised, careless.

When I enter the small boardroom at the office I'm met

with a wall of cigarette smoke previously passed through Bert Gederov's lungs. Somewhere in the haze I see Graham rise and wordlessly indicate the chair I am to take. He's wearing a purple suede blazer and his school tie, faded by years of repeated wearings. Bert is jacketless, his sleeves rolled up, and judging from the war-torn state of the ashtray before him he's been waiting here a while.

"Took you fucking long enough," he says without looking up.

"Sorry, but they tend not to adjourn court whenever a beeper goes off."

"Little prick—"

"Gentlemen!" Graham cuts in, arms open and pleading. 'We have business—quite *startling* business—to attend to."

I take my seat, pull a blank legal pad out of my briefcase, ready a pen above the page. Bert pushes his chair from the table and lets his head tip back in exaggerated boredom. This is to be Graham's meeting. He begins by tossing the day's *Star* over the table at me.

"You've seen?" he asks.

"Not really."

"You must have heard of those missing girls up north?"

"I've heard."

"Well, the local constabulary arrested a man last night, and he has since retained our firm for his defence."

Graham, who up to this point had been standing, now settles himself into his chair. With a wave of his hand more appropriate if it came from royalty passing in a gilded carriage he attempts to clear the air of smoke, but it does no good. Bert, pretending not to notice, belches forth another sulfurous cloud like some nineteenth-century coal incinerator.

"Which of you is taking it?"

"Kind of you to inquire, but we'd like *you* to handle it, Bartholomew. It's yours. Bert and I discussed it early this morning and we thought, 'This is a career maker.' You know what I'm saying? We thought, 'This is the one for our boy, Bartholomew.' Hoorah!"

Graham titters and circles his hands in the air, palms out, like a flapper doing the Charleston. Then his face contracts again into a mask of mock severity.

"It has all the makings of a classic. The media have made starlets of them already—they've taken a very strong *What-is-the-world-coming-to-when-these-little-darlings-go-missing?* angle on it. And the English teacher as the accused is perfect for the Humbert Humbert poeticism of the thing. Well, with all of this obvious promise I can tell you that Bert and I were both slobbering over it like dogs. But no, we decided it was time to give you a turn at the bitch's teat."

Graham beams at me over his clasped hands like a schoolboy who has just completed his multiplication tables in prize-winning time. Bert lights another cigarette and coughs up something large-sounding, considers spitting it somewhere, then, not finding a waste basket within range, swallows it back down to the tarry depths from whence it came.

"Did he do it?" I ask.

"Who?"

"Our guy."

"Name is Tripp. An unfortunate moniker for an accused murderer, I admit. And yes, I suspect he did it. I mean, they've *all* done it, haven't they?"

"What I'm asking is, did he do it *beyond a reasonable doubt?* In short, Graham, am I going to get fucked on this?"

At this, Bert makes a sound in his throat which could be either a grunting effort toward laughter or an attempt to dislodge a new obstruction from his windpipe. At the same time, Graham gasps in theatrical surprise.

"*Language!* Bartholomew! *Language!* To be truthful, there's lots of circumstantial physical stuff connecting Tripp to the girls, yes. And he has taken a behavioral turn for the weird of late, apparently. But nothing too *too* unusual: nasty divorce with the missus a few years ago where she got to keep the kid, followed by some fairly curious preoccupations including cut-out girlies from the Sears pajama section plastered all over the bedroom wall. And he is not the most coherent conversationalist one could hope for, particularly for a *professeur d'anglais.* But it isn't *charm* we demand of our clients, is it Bartholomew?"

I slide my chair back from the boardroom table and stand before Graham, in part because I intend to turn and get myself a cup of coffee from the cabinet behind me and in part to get the height advantage on the tricky bastard. Don't take my eyes off him as I pour and lump and stir. And the whole time Graham meets my gaze as Bert sets a new personal record by lighting his third cigarette within four minutes of my arrival.

"So that's why you and Bert don't want it," I say, taking them both in through the gloom. "Dead little girls. And the teacher did them in to sniff the panties. No alternative suspect, no alternative theory, no alternative alibi. That's why you're giving it to me. It's dirty, ugly, and unwinnable. Plus, he probably couldn't *afford* either of you. So you'll take the professional credibility kick for handling the famous client while skimming the margin between what he pays you and you pay me."

"Bartholomew! Your suspicious streak is showing! *Really!* No, no, no. Not at *all.* I should have told you earlier. You see, there's a very nice thing about Mr. Tripp's circumstances you haven't yet heard," Graham almost giggles, and then it's his turn to pause. "There are no *bodies*. No photographs of pale limbs in tall grasses. Not a single nasty snapshot of bruise, cut, or purple lip to titillate the court. Six weeks of helicopters, *woof-woof* police doggies and weepy search parties of concerned citizens shuffling through the trees, and nothing. No bods to keep the lonely coroner company."

"No girls, no case," I say, calculating with a sugar cube between my fingers. "Even if they prove he had intent, if there aren't dead bodies they can't establish the *actus reus*, and they need both. Am I right?"

"That would appear to follow at first blush, although I suggest—"

"Did he confess?"

"No. He's a muddle-headed fellow, but not so stupid as to tell the truth to the police."

Graham grins up at me with his ashen face of blue eyes and fastidious wrinkles that somehow fixes him in a state of permanent childhood. Bert smokes. They're waiting for me to say yes. But I'm not going to. I need my first murder to be a winner, and if these two are handing it to me there's got to be something wrong with it. We work together; they're my mentors and only friends in the world, but they'd far sooner screw me than each other.

"No," I say, and touch lips to coffee.

"No what?"

"You can keep it."

"Faggot," Bert spits.

"No, Bert, that's your partner. Maybe you can't see for the smoke. I'm the guy over here trying to cover his ass."

"Fucker fuck!"

"Boys! Boys! I must say for the record that I resent both of your comments." Graham shakes his head in false injury. "And as for you, Bartholomew, it's *not* a loser file, you *are* ready, and I've advised Mr. Tripp to expect you in Murdoch the day after tomorrow."

I attempt to read their faces but it's impossible, their features shrouded in thickening smoke. For a time nobody moves. Then it's Bert, his voice a low, territorial growl.

"You want to keep your job, you take this file."

"That's it?"

"That's it, pally boy."

"Well if you're going to be so *sweet* about it, Bert, then I guess I accept your offer."

Graham throws his fists into the curdled air.

"Good! I'm *so* pleased! We'll—"

"But I have to do it alone."

"Alone? Well now, you really should consider that dividing some of the work would only assist—"

"No dividing, no assisting. On my own. Completely."

"I *do* like this attitude! Very eat-what-you-kill. *Grrr!*"

Bert pulls his chair in and places his thick hands on the table, drills his eyes into my forehead.

"I'm leaving now," he says. "Call us if the newspapers get too hot on you and I'll handle them from down here. Other than that, any shit you create is your own. And when Graham said this was a career-maker, he forgot to mention it could also be a career-breaker. Therefore, I strongly advise you not to fuck up."

He leans back again and grabs his cigarette from its brief resting place on the table's edge. I note that his words qualify as both the kindest and most effusive he has ever uttered to me.

"Thanks for the confidence. Now if you'll excuse me, before I pack my bags I think I owe myself a night of self-congratulation. Didn't I mention? I won the Busch trial today."

"Well done, Bartholomew! You'll have to tell us all about it sometime."

Graham's head is down and he's already sliding the Tripp file over the table at me. Bert stabs his half-finished cigarette out in the grey dunes of the boardroom ashtray, lifts his gut with a wheeze and leaves without another look.

When Graham is finished handing everything over he carries himself to the door, his head perfectly still on delicate shoulders, but hips swinging in their sockets. Then he turns back to me and reveals one of his vampire smiles.

"May I suggest that if you plan on engaging in any carousing, you do it tonight. Things may get a little hectic for you over the next while."

"No doubt."

"So, care to join me for a bite? I know a perfect place not far from here."

"Don't bother, Graham. I know a perfect place of my own."

"Of course you do."

He steps forward once more to where I sit, throws a hand out to me through the smoke now twisting up the air vent or lingering in blue pools in the ceiling light sockets. We shake hands: two formal pumps, his grip—as always—firmer than mine.

"Good luck, my boy," he says, releasing me and sliding back to the door. "And *enjoy* it. I'm sure you'll find that there's *nothing* like your first homicide."

Three

With tie loosened and Tripp file stuck under my arm I walk out into the purple light of early evening and direct myself east toward the noise and tawdriness of Yonge Street for a victory drink. Victory for today, and the prospect of a more dazzling victory in the weeks to come. My first murder trial. And so long as no bodies turn up, the chances are good that I can manage to spare Mr. Tripp the indignities and stigma of long-term incarceration. I'm pleased with myself, and even more pleased after I've vacuumed the extra generous line of Great White Hope off my desk before leaving. Things are looking up.

I like strip bars, and of the many of this fine city The Zanzibar is my favorite. It occupies this position for no special reason other than it's exactly the way a strip bar should be. My law school friends and I used to come here after exams or for birthday piss-ups, but while those guys have all gone on to sensible marriages and four-bedroom Victorians in neighborhoods renowned for their alternative-education elementary schools and low crime rates, I've become a regular at the place.

What I like is the padded front door that seals off the interior from any trace of natural light, the always startling first appearance of a room appointed with women in various states of undress in place of paintings or potted plants, the air a mixture of beer mold and coconut oil spread over passing breasts and thighs. I even like the men, pathetic and despised, *knowing* they are pathetic and despised, offering up foolish portions of their wages to the waitress, talking to the girls before a table dance and imagining themselves as wealthier and better-looking than they are, the kind of men these girls might want to be with for free.

I like the young-looking ones. Their pouting shyness, teacup breasts and *Who, me?* eyes. Girls' school tartan skirt and close-fitting white blouse. Off they come in teasing slow motion, leaving her standing as though before her mother's bureau mirror, index finger hooked on lower teeth and her other hand tracing over the smooth discovery of her body. Bad girls. A parade of *faux* teen naughtiness beneath the black stage lighting that hides the crude truth of blemishes, stretch marks and scars. This is what I come here for, why I put my money down: to be free of this world of women and live again, for a time, in the world of girls.

"Something to drink?"

The waitress is an impatient hag who's been here forever and who doesn't bother to get to know any of the regulars for fear of having to use more than the few words she is obliged to in order to do her job. I like her, too.

"Double rye with ginger on the side."

She walks away without acknowledging my order and I look past her at tonight's offerings. Very California these days. With the summer always come the bleached bikini babes, tans burned onto skin through repeated sessions under the lamp, spherical implants high and unmoving. Soon the leather will return though, the biker fantasies shipped down from Montreal to meet the demands of the Christmas office party season. But I'll keep searching for my little girl.

And find her. There, dropping a lemon into her Coke

over at the bar. From this distance and in this light she could be sixteen, fifteen. Not a day over twenty, at any rate. I give her a little two-fingered wave as though making a bid at an auction.

"Hi," she says when she comes over, lowers her eyes flirtatiously. Good. She's acting the part as well.

"Hello there. Would you care to dance for me?"

"O.K.," she says, looking around as though to make sure her teacher can't see her. Then she pulls over one of those plastic stands they use to dance on and sits on it.

"I'm Deanna."

"I'm Barth."

"You're a very handsome man, Barth."

"And you're a very forward little girl, Deanna."

She giggles and raises herself as the d.j. fades out the Aerosmith and "slows things down a bit" with the lounge saxophone intro to "Careless Whisper" by George Michael. I down the first rye in two gulps without adding any ginger as Deanna picks open the buttons on her blouse and shimmies out of her skirt.

Behind her the waitress turns my way with eyes hooded by years of distaste followed by further years of boredom. Raise my finger to order another round, and on it goes: another ten-year-old top-40 song, another set of stretches and thrusts, another round. Throughout I am silent, everything still but my eyes.

She keeps going, turning and stroking and bending in cycles until another song ends and the d.j. comes over the sound system praising the dancer who's just finished her routine on the main stage: "Oh *y-eah*! Gentlemen, let's hear it for the lovely *Roxanne*! Oh yeah! Rox-*anne*!" Deanna pulls back from my chair and stands limply on her pedestal.

"Another?" she asks.

"No, I don't think so. Thank you."

Ask how many songs she's danced for me and, as usual,
I'm startled by the size of the number. I pay her and include
an excessive tip. It is my habit to leave excessive tips in strip
bars.

"Thanks," she says, tucking the money into the zippered
pouch she carries with her. Then she pulls her underwear
back up, clips on her skirt, shrouds her breasts beneath her
blouse and steps down from her stand. She is as before,
another stripper in a girls' school uniform, but with enough
age now showing beneath her eyes and at the corners of her
mouth to make her current act almost laughable.

"Have a great night," she says as she leaves.

"Have a great life," I say, slipping, having meant to use
the same words she had.

Once outside I stand on the street for a time, close my eyes
and absorb Yonge Street's Friday night cacophony of chant-
ing panhandlers, vomiting drunks, hip-hop thudding over
hysterical speed thrash out the windows of refitted Jettas and
Civics. The air a humid cloud of sugary perfumes and jock
deodorant wafting off the packs of high school kids in for the
night from the suburbs. Breathe all of it in and let its ugliness
fill my lungs. It occurs to me (not for the first time) that it's
sometimes good to stop and remember that you live in a city
and envision what that entails: a clotted intersection of lives
all set on different trajectories, each one indifferent to the
other. There was a time, I think, when this kind of observation would have left me melancholy, but now it brings a
certain comfort. The satisfaction of a suspicion confirmed, an
idea buried inside yourself long enough to fossilize, its mark-

ings now permanently etched. When I open my eyes again to
the yellow bath of neon in the street I step to the curb, raise
my arm and hail a cab to take me home.

I say "take me home" but where I live isn't a home at all
but a "space." That was the way it was described in the full-
page ad that ran in one of the weeklies soon after the
building was re-zoned for residential use from its former
function as a textile warehouse: COME AND DEVELOP
YOUR OWN WAY OF LIVING IN ONE OF OUR SPACES.
Not "condos" or "units," not even "lofts." Vacant, off-white,
ahistorical, pre-personalized space. I was immediately drawn.
Down I went to the block of rust-dirtied brick at the south
end of Chinatown and bought a space of my very own the
same afternoon.

Up in the freight elevator to the top floor and down the
wide industrial hall. It's late, I'm tired, there's plenty of work
to do tomorrow before heading up into the barrens. But I'm
starving for another line, and as the door swings open I head
for my stash nestled among the ceramic nectarines in the
fruit bowl without turning on the lights. Spill out a serving
and up it goes. Only then do I turn on the lights and think:
How few things I have. There's a sofa under the broad window
which frames the compact bundle of downtown office towers,
a composite portrait of my graduating law school class,
Swedish-designed, buttonless stereo (rarely used, all music
having become grating sometime in my late twenties) and
one wall of bookshelves containing the textual souvenirs of
my education. No art, flowers, rugs, mirrors. Every time I face
the opportunity of acquiring such things I ask myself why
and, having no answer, move on, unburdened.

There's one photograph though. Unenlarged, tucked
into a dollar-store black plastic frame. There, on the bare

coffee table, facing the corner so that an observer must stoop to make out the details: my parents, caught in a balance between posed smile and laughter, arms around each other's waists, standing before a setting sun the color of a Singapore Sling. I keep meaning to put it away, tuck it on a shelf in the closet or maybe just turn it even further to the wall to lessen the directness of the angle, but then I forget, so that I'm always surprised by their faces shining back at me. A happy couple moving into the middle years of accomplishment without visible hints of regret, baring to the camera the familiar faces of strangers. The sort of picture that comes with the frame when you buy it.

I walk over to the window and open one of the glass panels wide enough to let me stick my head and shoulders through. Below, the street is a river of headlight and brake-light crosscurrents, the air swirling up in warm gushes sharpened by the rotten fish and vegetables piled high in boxes in front of the Chinese markets a couple blocks north. Close my eyes and inhale. It used to make my stomach turn, but now it's almost welcome. A signal in the atmosphere to let you know that you're home, back in your proper space.

PART TWO

Four

I can move fast when I want to. Lift myself up to the heroic heights at which my working life takes place. This state of being goes by a name which carries the resonance of a philosophical concept or historical epoch: Billable Time.

But this transition requires a little help. Most opt for the coffee and doughnut approach, but as coffee holds some antagonisms toward my bladder and doughnuts leave a suspicious film over tonsils and gums, I prefer a line or two of reasonably priced but honorably cut cocaine. This involves some embarrassment to admit even to myself, as more than a few years have passed since this particular narcotic was the hippest in town. Call me old-fashioned, but coke just suits my go-get-'em, 80s temperament. And in the end, the entire matter of which drug is coolest is ultimately beyond rational criticism or debate. Who can argue with tried and true physiological addictions?

With me, I never have to wait for a birthday or anniversary—it's breakfast in bed every morning. Two lines taken off the bedside table and the day opens up before me, burns through every vessel in my head and washes cool bleach down the back of my throat. Everything at once electric and numb, a sense of purpose pulsing through tissue and tickling over skin. And along with all this a yearning to sing. Don't even hum in the shower (and fake it every time I have to stand for the national anthem) but there it is, a balloon of song rising up from a fist of hot muscle in my chest. Sometimes, if I happen to pass a mirror at times like these, I can see myself as one of those grinning lunatics from a Technicolor musical who's always on the verge of abandoning speech in favor of expressing themselves through rollicking chorus numbers instead. Not joy but a feeling that's somehow suggestive of the word: the fish hook "j," startled "o," the raised hands of a blissful "y." Even now I know it's nothing more than the word itself though. For surely if it was the real thing you'd be too busy being joyful to imagine how it might look printed on heavy bond paper under the office letterhead.

I'm up. Pull back the bedsheet, peer down the neglected but so far—praise God!—still flat expanse of stomach and slouch over to the nectarines for another line. Then another. And then (only after a moment's balanced consideration) one more for the road.

I pack, pick a few things up at the office (dictaphone, tapes, laptop, color markers, yellow pads—lawyers' friends all) and swing down to the car rental place near Union Station to set myself up with some wheels. Normally, it is advisable practice to confirm the price of such items with one's client, because in the end he's the one who faces the numbers under "Disbursements" on the fee statement. But seeing as Mr. Tripp is unavailable at the moment, I don't see the need to be nitpicky with the professional procedure on this particular morning.

"Compact, Mid or Full?" the guy at the counter asks once he's got my essentials tapped in.

"Anything bigger than Full?"

"You want a limo?"

"No, although I suppose I *should* be thinking about booking ahead for the prom . . ."

No smile from the guy. Then I remember: for the rest of the world, the coffee and doughnut is already wearing off.

"Whatever you have in the Full will be fine."

"We got a Lincoln Continental that's clean."

"A clean Lincoln. Splendid."

The sign at the side of Highway 400 appears for 69 North and I steer the big car onto the off-ramp, jelly around the curve that sets it on a new course. The way of the weekend pioneers heading up to their vacation properties, rich but preferring to go by the name of middle class, over-leveraged, under stress, a family. And today an entire generation of children moving into adulthood sharing little but the memory of blazing Friday afternoons, carsickness, the view from the flip-up backseats of station wagons. Peeling off at the exits marked by signs for lodges alternately named after long-gone species of tree and Indian tribes. But not today. Everything clamped shut the morning after Labor Day as though from annual news of approaching plague.

For the first while I share the highway with pickup trucks, occasional semis hauling gravel, farm machinery lumbering along the shoulder. But as the organized fields of corn, beans and dozing cattle yield to outcroppings of rock, bogs coated green with algae and undisciplined acres of thorny under-brush, the road thins of even this traffic, narrows to two lanes, and leaves me alone. I push the speedometer up to 70 m.p.h. with the idea that increased velocity might move the land behind me more efficiently, but it makes no difference. The engine remains virtually noiseless, and the passing trees roll by in steady blocks interrupted every mile or so by an overgrown lane to mark the line between properties. The deeper I press the gas pedal the less I'm passing through the landscape and the more I'm moving into it, sinking with every curve into its ragged texture.

Something's different up here.

The brush creeps up to the orange line that marks the boundary of the road and reaches across as a territorial challenge. Lone fenceposts push up from the earth like bent thumbs. Occasional signs giving directions to marinas, campgrounds and private side roads that are no longer there. Then even the signs become difficult to see as bugs begin to kamikaze the windshield, obscuring my view with their yellow guts. On go the windshield wipers and I squeeze off a couple good sprays of washer fluid, but there's something in the insects' blood that resists easy removal and I'm left to peer ahead through a smudgy haze of horsefly, dragonfly and moth.

Of course on a map it all looks the same: a vast white space marked by a couple of rail lines, watercolor dabs of small blue lakes, jagged veins for rivers throughout. But when you get here the map might as well be a child's crayon drawing. The lines are imaginary, nothing relates. You can't see the lakes or rivers from the highway, and you don't believe a train would have any business passing through such a place.

No matter where you start from, north is always so close in this country. Almost any exit taken off the main highway along Lake Ontario after the heavy industries, warehouses and nuclear power stations have passed and in only a couple of hours it's all over you. A place where the ratio of altered to unaltered space gets shifted dramatically in the latter's favor and there is little more ahead than an interminable expanse of humanlessness. Despite patchy settlement and the logical plotting of county lines the north communicates to those traveling through it what it probably always has: there is good reason why most people on this continent hug the ocean, lakeshores or riverbanks, for those are places where someone might have a clue where they are.

Of the true character and magnitude of nature I know nothing, of course. I recall novels and poems fed to us in high school which involved lonely settlers and their wives, the difficulties in building a log cabin, and the eventual freezing to death of the protagonist. This, I believed throughout my schoolboy career, was the single plot and full extent of Canadian Literature. And so too of nature. For Barth Crane is no adventurer. At least not of the compass and pup tent variety. Fresh air inspires nothing in me but suspicion and quick fatigue. A city slicker born in a country where the cities are few and far between.

But here I am anyway. Only a couple hundred miles north of where the six-lane artery from Toronto ends, from well-lit service centers and towns with hotel and restaurant chains large enough to have network TV commercials and American head offices, from the bedroom communities where the commuting middle class has staked its claim, wrestles with the mortgage, and in the evenings haggles over which of the thousand satellite channels to watch for that particular half-hour—two hundred miles from the world lies the north. And I don't belong.

The only indications that forest might soon be giving way to an outpost of civilization are the two or three roadside stands that begin to appear, clapboard rectangles wedged into the trees: one for blueberries, one firewood, one earthworms, all closed. The area had long ago been touted as a future destination for wealthy Torontonians once the four-lane highway was extended north as promised by a provincial government ousted four or five elections ago. However, after some bean-counter pointed out the cost of the project and its unlikely benefits, the extension was never undertaken. Those wealthy Torontonians not already in possession of family summer places either stayed put or ponied up the dough to get their foot in the Establishment door in Muskoka, having wisely decided that five hours was too long a drive just to smell pine sap six weekends a year.

Still, there must have been a few who took the bait, for there, stencilled onto a slab of wood resting against the town sign that tells me where I am (MURDOCH—pop. 4400—GATEWAY TO THE MID-NORTH) and the local service clubs (Optimists and Rotary only) is the now-belated greeting, WELCOME BACK, SUMMER PEOPLE!

"I am not a summer person," I say out loud as I pass at a speed that most would consider improper for a town populated by young pedestrians, seniors and pets. "I am a man for *all* seasons."

I search for lodgings. The first candidate is the Sunshine Motor Inn on the edge of town. Comfortable enough looking in a homely, anonymous way, but currently suffering from "renovations" which consist of a pickup truck of yokels knocking down a wall in the reception area and hammering a bar in place on the other side to make way for what the owner winkingly promises will be the town's new "meeting place." It's immediately clear that the future of the Sunshine lies in providing shelter to adulterous middle-agers for the half-hour they require to complete their blubbery poundings. While this type of market repositioning doesn't trouble me, the shriek of circular saws and the grunted profanities of workmen does. On the way back to my car I seek the advice of one of the hammer-holders who appears to be acting as foreman (sporting a shirt and the fewest tattoos) as to alternative accommodation.

"You stayin' in town?"

"Or as near to it as possible."

"Well, the only other hotel round here is The Empire. But nobody stays there but the peelers."

"The owner's family?"

"They're no family. Peelers are strippers, man."

"Ah! How do I get there?"

"Downtown. Across from the old Bank of Commerce."

"I'm not familiar with it, but I'm sure The Empire's marquee will be a sufficient beacon."

This brings a smile to the foreman's lips, or what may be a smile. A brief exposure of blackened gums before he returns to his work.

The Empire Hotel. I like the sound of it, its suggestions of local history and color. The former jewel of the county with a once distinguished tavern on the main floor and high-ceilinged rooms above, one likely containing a bed that was once given the business by some duchess or prince visiting the colonies as part of their regrettable royal obligations. Every Ontario town has such a place, and most have either gone pay-by-the-week or been gutted and drywalled into bingo halls. But with a name that Protestant, that splendidly Victorian, that naively overreaching—*The Empire Hotel*—how far could it have declined during the region's intervening decades of brief boom and prolonged bust?

The Empire Hotel sits at one end of Murdoch's main thoroughfare, Ontario Street, and the County Court House at the other. Between them there's a coffee shop with floral curtains halfway up its grease-coated windows, a used bookstore, used children's clothing store, as well as a pawnshop called All Things Used!, two women's hair salons (the Glamor-ette and Split Enz), a closet-size barber shop, an army surplus place, a butcher and a baker (but no candlestick maker, alas). A third of the windows are empty, and many of these seem to have given up hope of occupation, barren even of FOR LEASE, RENT or SALE signs. I've always taken this as a sure indication of a local economy's health. When the real estate brokers stop trying to sell it, it's pretty much all over.

When I reach the end of the street I lean over to the passenger window and confirm I'm at the right place from the electric blue letters that round the corner of the building, with THE EMP facing Ontario Street and IRE HOTEL over Victoria Avenue, all with bulbs inside them strong enough to illuminate the snaking trails of rust descending from each of the "E"s. A small marquee screwed above the entrance to the bar on the south side announces: COM NG EVE TS—GIRLS! FRI AND SAT. None of the usual mention of "dancers" qualified as "beautiful" or "exotic." Perhaps this is simply because the girls of The Empire Hotel are neither beautiful nor exotic. Nor do they dance, as that word is commonly understood.

The building itself is a four-story whitewashed affair whose plainness is offset by some copper detailing over the main floor windows (roaring lions before fluttering Union Jacks and, behind them, EST. 1904) as well as a series of stone gargoyles set along the rooftop's edge. Not the standard depictions of growling mastiff or sneering gremlin either. These are clearly human, faces sculpted by a stonemason whose wonky craftsmanship is apparent even in the grey light of dusk. All male and bearded in the ministerial, turn-of the-century style of early immigrant Brits. From this I surmise that these are the heads of Murdoch's founding fathers. Yet their expressions are anything but noble. It's impossible to tell if it's the result of intended caricature or the mistake of limited artistic ability, but each of the heads seems to bear its own unique threat or perversion. Eyes halfshut in drunken lasciviousness or bulging in madness or terror. Mouths held tight as though keeping a secret within or opened wide with a pointed tongue lolling out.

I park the Lincoln on the street before the front door and stand for a moment with my head craned back, taking in one head and then another. It's as though their expressions change while I look at them so that when I turn from the second back to the first, eyes that were open have closed shut, or from the fourth back to the third, a tongue extended that had previously been licking lips. A blur of movement just beyond the peripheral range of what I can see. It's a common sort of illusion, I suppose, but real enough that I have to force a laugh and lower my head to street level again to rid myself of it. But no matter what I tell myself as I pull my garment bag and briefcase out of the trunk and step up to the door, I don't look up.

The hotel lobby is lit by a single oversize chandelier fitted with a half-dozen of those fake gaslamp bulbs, so that one has to peer for direction and footing through an orange fog. The next striking thing is the smell. Something distinctly geriatric ward about it: a combination of damp linen, bean soup and the sting of chemicals wafting out from the stack of deodorizing pucks that sit at the bottom of the men's room urinals.

Andrew Pyper

To the left is the padded black leather door to the bar and above it a screwed-in sign with fancy script: THE LORD BYRON COCKTAIL LOUNGE. GENTLEMEN'S ENTRANCE. From the other side of the stuffing and wood comes the sound of music, or at least certain wavering vibrations which never move above or below the middle range—the sleepy murk of elevators, waiting rooms and department stores. On the right is an open archway to an unlit room that, judging from the streetlight that finds its way through the salty grease of the front window, was at one time the parlor. There's a fireplace (now enclosed by splintered plywood), and a large mirror over the mantel that sends back a picture of me standing in the lobby. Faded, sickly, a smudge of paleness fixed over the dark background. A yellowed newspaper photograph discovered in an attic trunk.

I step up to the reception desk and bring my palm down on the service bell. No immediate stirrings, and for a time I stand and wait, staring into the pattern of complicated vines bulging out from the velvet wallpaper. It's as old and smoke-stained as everything else but isn't dreadful, probably even an admired extravagance when first plastered up fifty or sixty years ago. In fact the only thing that seems to belong to the present decade is the bottom-of-the-line computer which sits behind the desk and displays a blue screen unblemished by text. Beside it a quarter-full coffeepot sitting on a hot plate, islands of turquoise mold floating on its surface.

Ring the bell again. This time there's the sound of crumpling tinfoil from the back office, and then a man with papery skin and a bald head mapped with burst capillaries steps out into the dull marine light.

"What can I do you for?" he asks, the inside of his mouth caked with sandwich residue.

"You can do me for a room. Something large, with generous natural light. And quiet, if you can manage that."

"They're all the same. 'Cept for the honeymoon suite." He lifts his eyes to mine, but there's nothing in them.

"It's got a TV, phone, separate shower?"

"Ever been in a hotel room that didn't?"

"Well, in Europe . . ." I begin foolishly, but the blankness of his eyes remains set. "The honeymoon suite sounds like just the thing."

I register, pay for the first night (I'm not asked how many more may follow), take the key and directions from Mr. Hospitality, and ascend a set of stairs marked by a brass plaque with GRAND STAIRCASE on it in raised letters, though now not so much grand as unnecessarily wide. Turn right and all the way down to the end, unlock the door, kick it open, flick on the bedside lamp.

It's big. One could certainly say that about it. Bigger than the standard. Right on the corner too, so that each exterior wall has its own window overlooking its own street, as well as a semicircle of glass between them and a ledge wide enough to sit on. The smell of vegetable oil and burnt beef, moisture stains blotched over the ceiling, furniture of a sufficient age and ugliness to be sold at "antique" prices in the city but which in this room showed only their age and ugliness. All of that and still not bad. Unimaginable what set of misfortunes would ever bring present-day honeymooners to spend a single moment in such a room, but for Bartholomew Christian Crane, long-resigned bachelor and aficionado of the seedy, not bad at all.

Sometime in the dead of night the phone at the reception desk downstairs starts to ring. It's one of the old ones with a real tin bell inside, and the sound it makes carries up the stairs, down the long hallway and through the heavy bedroom door without any muting of its volume.

Four rings, five—doesn't that zombie who checked me in have anyone work the desk overnight? Six rings, seven—who the hell would be calling an empty hotel at this hour for so long? No doubt some long-suffering wife of a regular at the lobby bar attempting to locate her gin-soaked lesser half.

With each ring I'm pulled closer to consciousness, although I resist opening my eyes. But by the time ring number fifteen finishes I take the Lord's name in vain, pull on socks and pants, slip over the hardwood floor to the door and step out into the hallway, ready to go down and rip the phone cord out of the wall. But for a time I only stand there. Arms crossed, cool drafts breathing against my back.

I must have risen too quickly everything suddenly prickling and light, a black ring closing around my eyes. Throw out my hands for balance and almost touch the walls, the hallway constricting around me like a swallowing throat. A clicking sound that is my tongue wrestling for words that have dried away.

In the middle of the nineteenth tolling it stops. Echoes in the perfect quiet until it's replaced by the whisper of dust balls scuttled across the floor by the sour air blown out from under every door.

I remain there for a time, pretend that I'm ready to slide down the banister and throw the fucking thing out onto the street if it starts up again. But it doesn't, and eventually the cold forces me back to my room. Pull up the covers and wish for sleep. Eyes held shut, listening to the imagined footfalls of the old hotel.

F i v e

It is an unfortunate fact that the largest and most handsome building in Murdoch is its jail, the whimsically named Murdoch Prison for Men. The original building, set in a green cleft next to the courthouse, is a modest but dignified red brick block with oak doors and a marble cornerstone marking its inauguration by some Lieutenant-Governor or other, as well as the date, July 16, 1897. Since then several additions had been made to the rear, and the structure moved within its high walls down a long slope to the edge of the creek that runs through town.

Its history was obvious enough. Over the decades, with each quarry closing, and the ongoing confirmation that a tourist market was never to be, a sympathetic provincial government would construct another cellblock and expand the region which the jail was designated to serve. These days one of Murdoch's greatest boasts was that it had criminals bused in from far and wide to serve their summary terms or await trial. And while other small town jails across the country were being shut down in favor of new, computer-managed institutions, Murdoch's would go on with the job assigned to it at the end of the nineteenth century so long as the people who lived in the woods up here continued to do bad things.

This will be Thomas Tripp's home for the course of the trial no matter what I have to say, as those accused of first-degree murder are statutorily denied the right to a bail hearing. And it's just as well as far as I'm concerned. I like my clients in jail as a rule. I do what I can to obtain bail, of course, but if I fail I'm always a little relieved, for this way I know where to find them, and can thus avoid one of the primary challenges of conducting a criminal trial: locating your client.

Inside, the Murdoch Prison for Men looks like every other jail—waxed hallways, pale green paint over floor, walls and ceiling, barred gates where doors would otherwise stand—except older. Including the guard with blushing nose and alcoholic cheeks set upon a comically Irish face who takes me to the interview room and asks en route, "Up from Toronto, are ye?"

"I am."

"Where ya stayin'?"

"The Empire Hotel."

"The Empire, eh? Nobody but drunks stay there."

"That's fine. I'm something of a drunk myself."

He swings around to shoot me a quick look. But he's a man whose career has been built upon the efficient dispatch of wiseasses, and he doesn't miss a beat.

"Think yer man did it?"

"It would be inappropriate for me to comment on that. Besides, with all due respect, it's none of your fucking business."

"Quite so, quite so."

Before he opens the door to Interview Room No. 1 he pauses to smile in a way that is either an expression of friendliness or a practiced mask meant to hide something far more uncongenial.

"Well, I can tell you this," he says. "Everyone around here thinks yer man quite a strange one."

"The last time I consulted the books, being a strange one wasn't illegal."

"That may be. But taking little girls away sure as hell is."

"Thank you so much. Now that you've clarified the law for me, could you just do your job and go fetch my client?"

He meets my eyes for a moment, makes a horsey sound with his nose, but opens the door.

"You just make yourself comfortable," he says before closing it, which, it is immediately apparent, is exactly what he says before closing these doors on everyone.

Who knows whether the guard takes his time bringing Tripp in because he's busy with other matters of legitimate urgency or is savoring the opportunity to give me the finger from the other side of the one-way glass, but it's nearly a quarter of an hour before he returns with my guy.

"Thomas Tripp, meet Mr. Crane. Mr. Crane, Thomas Tripp," the guard says formally, standing between us with hands extended as though to bring us all closer together in the way of old friends.

"Thanks. But I think we can get along on our own now," I tell him, gesturing for Tripp to sit down, but he doesn't move.

"I'll be back in twenty minutes," the guard says.

"Look, I'm permitted as much time with my client as I require, as both you and the warden are well aware, and—" I start, and would continue (my appetite for laying into gnomish quasi-officials sufficiently whetted) but he stops me by raising his small palms in surrender.

"Quite so! Quite so! Take all the time you need, Mr. Crane. Just you knock whenever you're through."

He skips out of the room with something near a click of his heels—suddenly the sprightly leprechaun—and leaves

Tripp standing in the same position as when he was brought
in, seemingly unaware of the negotiations going on around
him.

"Please sit down," I tell him, once more indicating the
seat on the other side of the table. Once more he seems not
to hear.

"Mr. Tripp, you'll soon learn that I'm an unconventional
sort of lawyer, open to almost any innovation in protocol,
with the sole exception of conducting interviews with those
who insist on standing while I'm seated. So please, for my
benefit, won't you sit down?"

"You're my lawyer?"

"Didn't your local counsel, Mr. Norton, confirm this with
you? It was upon his recommendation that you have retained
the firm of Lyle, Gederov for your defence. I'm their associate, Bartholomew Crane, although I urge you to call me
Barth."

"Ah yes," he says with a flare of recognition. "So you're
to be my winged monkey, are you?"

"Is that how Mr. Norton described me to you?"

"Not exactly."

Neither of us says anything for a time until I conclude
that the responsibility of carrying out the niceties is to be
borne by me alone.

"Well, for what it's worth," I say and extend my hand,
which snaps him out of whatever spell had been placed over
his motor skills. He gives me a firm, if somewhat moist
handshake.

"I'm Thom Tripp," he says, and finally slumps into the
opposite chair.

"Well, I've reviewed your file, Mr. Tripp, and—"

"Thom."

"Thom, yes—thanks—reviewed your file and now I need to talk to you about your view of things. You offered no statement to the police, which was wise. But what I need now is all the background stuff, anything you feel is relevant. Especially what you think the Crown may already know that I may not yet know, if you see what I mean."

He looks at me and breathes through enlarged nostrils, as though he requires more air than his nose was originally designed to accommodate. His file gave his age as forty-two, but I would have put him a few years older. Not because of the usual evidence of baldness, grey hair or wrinkles (his skin is smooth and his hair, although thin, covers most of his scalp and is more brown than anything else) but from the sticky weariness of his eyes. Aside from this one might even say he has an air of youth about him, a schoolboy-turned-school-teacher precision to his features along with the eager, craning effect of a head sitting a little too high on top of his neck. But the eyes show something else, a white space between sagging rims and irritated lids onto which time has projected itself. Not the face of a handsome man, but there's a neatness to the mouth and wide brow that suggests he probably pulls off a pleasant appearance in photos taken from at least ten feet away. This, I would guess, is the minimum distance required to diminish the dark grief smeared around his eyes.

"You want to know if I did it," he says abruptly, the big nostrils opening wide to release a long gust whistling up from his lungs.

"Glad you brought that up. I should let you know right off that all communications between you and me are privileged, and as such are not admissible in court. That's on the technical side. On the practical side, I don't *need* to know if you did it. And as for my *wanting* to know, if I had to express a preference, I don't think I do. In my experience such things rarely make a difference."

"Such things?"

"The truth, as it were."

"So you don't care if I'm the one or not?"

"Mr. Tripp, a good part of what you pay me for is to remain singleminded. Caring would cost considerably more."

For a moment he holds himself as though caught by an unexpected flashbulb explosion—eyes peeled back, breath held—and absorbs the words that hang between us.

"Maybe I'm the one who needs to know," he says finally.

"Well, unless your two former students show up with some additional information, I would have thought that you're the only one who does."

That's when the tears start. A series of transparent globes coursing over his skin with such speed that in a single moment they begin to drip steadily from his chin onto the table's surface. What's most strange about this performance is that he doesn't apologize. Doesn't wipe his face with his sleeve or turn his head away.

"Well, that's fine. You don't really know," I start, slapping at my jacket pockets to find that I've forgotten to pack my Kleenex. "That's O.K. In fact, that may be good. We can get on without that information, so let's not worry about it for the moment."

"Not worry about it. No."

He smiles at me briefly. But maybe not, the parting and closing of his lips so swift that it may have only been an exhalation of air, although that job appeared to be ably performed by his nose alone. What's more certain is that the tears, so sudden and gushing a moment before, are now gone, leaving only two dishwater stains down his cheeks.

"Can we go on now, Mr. Tripp? Thom?"

He inhales.

"You were the girls' teacher, yes?"

"I taught English."

"For how long?"

"A year. They were very bright."

"Oh?"

"Not the best grades in the class, but pretty close. They were *interested*."

"In what?"

"Books, poetry. Stories. Good Lord, they were even interested in what *I* had to say!" He laughs at this obviously old and tested joke with a determined effort.

"And they would come to see you after class for extra help?"

"They didn't need my help. They were just *interested*."

"But on the day they disappeared—did they come after class to speak with you then?"

"Which day?"

"The day in *question*, Mr. Tripp."

"Which day of the *week*?"

I gage his seriousness in this, but his face is unchanging, so I check the file.

"It appears it was a Thursday."

"Then yes, because the Literary Club met on Thursdays. That was when we'd talk."

"So on that Thursday, after you got together to talk, did you go for a drive?"

"Drive . . ."

"To the lake. Did you take the girls to Lake St. Christopher?"

He lifts his eyes away from mine and up to the ceiling,

blinks into the anemic fluorescent light as though in brief prayer. The stubble on his exposed neck like a clearcut of timber viewed from the air. But when he brings his eyes back there's a narrowed concentration, the effort of memory.

"Do you want to know something funny? I wanted to live in this place ever since I was a kid," he says, suddenly breezy. "Back when my family used to come up from the city in the summers. I thought that one day when I was old enough I'd move here and live on that lake in my own little place forever."

"I see. But what—"

"Just one of those cheap, rickety-as-all-get-out sort of vacation cottages. You know the ones? Nothing much at all. It's always a little embarrassing, isn't it? The things you wish for when you're young."

"I wonder if we could—"

"And then comes the real world. Flattening everything in its path, handing out the just desserts. So I end up living alone in a bachelor apartment in the ghost town down the road, teaching literature to students who can't read the back of a hockey card. This is what happens to children's dreams, Mr. Crane."

"That's too bad, Thom. It really is. But for the time being I'm just wondering about you and the *girls* and the lake."

"The girls."

"That's right. Did you take them up there that Thursday?"

"They always talked about it."

"Going for a drive?"

"About the lake." He sweeps his knuckles over his lips. "They liked stories."

"That's fine. But what I'm looking for here is a sequence of events starting, oh I don't know, say, from the *beginning*, and going to the *end.* To your drive to the lake, if there *was* a drive to the lake."

"A regular water rat, that's what my mother called me. I was such a good swimmer."

"How about the girls? Were they good swimmers too?"

He presses his lips together so tightly they disappear altogether except for the bloodless white crease they leave halfway between nose and chin.

"There's not much . . ."

"Not *what?*"

". . . not much I can say without . . ."

Then the tears again, a splashing deluge that falls onto his face but affects no other part of his body. No shaking shoulders or trembling lips. It's as though they arrive for reasons that are either unknown to him or so well known he has ceased to supplement them with any other expression.

"Please, Mr. Tripp," I say, pushing back the impatience rising in my voice. "It's apparent that you're under a great deal of stress. But frankly so am I, and you're not helping very much. If I'm to act for you, there are some things I need to know. At the moment, I don't have much: girls went missing on Thursday, May the twelfth; a fruitless search over the course of the following weeks; warrant issued for your apartment and car a couple weeks later which yielded cut-out catalog pictures of girls in pajamas on your bedroom wall, muddy pants in the laundry hamper, muddy shoes at the door and a few bloodstains in the backseat. Two months later you're under arrest. There's an *outline* of a story there, and certainly a whole number of potential *inferences,* but I think it needs some fleshing out, so to speak. Don't you?"

Sarcasm may not be the best approach under the circumstances, but the truth is I'm finding Tripp more recalcitrant than the usual. Clients are rarely forthcoming at first and even more rarely articulate, but if this guy's la-la-land routine is as intentional as I suspect it is I have to let him know I'm not convinced. So I sit for a time with pen poised over notepad and wait. Count to thirty in my head and wait some more, although I lower my eyes for the next thirty because I have the feeling that if I got into a staring match with this guy I'd lose. And in the end he wins anyway.

"O.K, Thom. Let's try just yes or no. Did you drive the girls *anywhere that* Thursday?"

"It's not me you want to ask."

"There's nobody else to ask, is there?"

"They always told me what to do."

"And they told you to drive them to Lake St. Christopher, is that it? They wanted to go?"

"I don't know what they wanted. I just . . ."

"Just took them there?"

"Always talking about it. 'What about the lake, Mr. Tripp?' Those two! 'Tell us about the lake.' I had a choice about it at first. And then after a while it didn't matter."

His voice isn't a whisper, doesn't travel as whispers do, but is so soft I strain for every word.

"There are some things you can't fight, Mr. Crane."

"By 'things' I take it you mean 'urges'?"

"I mean the will of others."

"Are you telling me—are you *trying* to tell me that there's another party involved here? If so, I need you to tell me now. Give me a name."

The tears have been stemmed once more, but Tripp's head now hangs down to meet his chest and his arms have fallen inward so that he takes up as little space as he can, as though he would pull his entire body up into himself and disappear if he could.

"Whoever it is, you can't help them now," I continue, keeping my voice even. "It's time to think of yourself, Thomas. And I can help you—we can help each other—if you just give me a name."

He wriggles his shoulders as though invisibly bound. His blinking irregular, accelerated. An audible smacking of eyelids sounding out an unreadable code.

"Can you hear them?" he whispers.

"I can hear you and me and an inmate barking for a smoke down the hall. What else are you referring to?"

"They change."

"Change?"

"From one to another."

"Well, that's the basic structure of conversation, isn't it? An exchange between more than—"

"They talk to *each other*."

"Mr. Tripp. Are you trying to suggest to me your suitability for the defence of insanity? If this is your plan, you need not pretend with me. I'm your *lawyer*. It's essential that you realize we have shared interests. Now, if you prefer the idea of lifelong hospitalization to the possibility of lifelong incarceration, you just tell me how you'd like me to go about it, and we'll—"

"I can *hear* her!"

Tripp pulls himself up, leans across the table and hisses this at me, his face a mask of goggle-eyed desperation. Hands gripping the edges of the table hard enough to turn his knuckles an instant white, shoulders braced as though in anticipation of a physical blow from behind. And now bigger than I thought, as though another, larger man was swelling within his skin. Slithering pulses down his neck.

There's something about this new turn to his perform-ance that gives me serious pause. An urgency I didn't recog-nize at first, a sharp edge that could cut through whatever lay before him. Fear. But a fear that could be translated into other extremes. And just as these possibilities begin to cloud together around him he retreats back into the depths of his chair, his eyes returning to their usual appearance as two undercooked eggs. The room turns cool again. He's my man Tripp once more, an equal mixture of timid schoolteacher and confused child.

"Her?" I ask. "And what 'her' would we be speaking of?"

"I don't care if you believe me."

"Nor do I, Mr. Tripp."

I stick my bare notepad back into my briefcase and rise to knock for the guard.

"I urge you to consider the seriousness of your situation," I say to his back from the safe distance of the door. "Perhaps the next time we speak you'll have come to appreciate the fact that I'm on your side. That I'm the *only* one on your side."

The guard's rubber soles squeaking down the hall to let me out.

"A strange one, I told ya," the leprechaun guard says as he walks me to the front doors, but seeing as I have to agree I end up not saying a word.

S i x

As I walk through the two hundred yards of downtown Murdoch to The Empire I'm thinking that Tripp should count himself lucky. Unless something nasty bobs to the surface of Lake St. Christopher over the next few weeks there's still no evidence that anyone is dead. Pictures of girls in undies ripped from the Sears catalog and pinned up on the accused's wall show a depraved loneliness and suspect libidinal preoccupations, but hardly murderous intent. And the bloodstains in Tripp's car—they could be anybody's. As for the muddy shoes and pants, you can't cross the street up here without treading through something soft and brown. Add it up and all you've got is circumstantial will-o'-the-wisps and nothing more. So what if Tripp is an uncoachable loony who'll bring about utter disaster if he ever gets within twenty feet of the stand? All I require is for Mr. Weird to sit there nice and quiet and keep the waterworks in check. We've got the law on our side.

"How're you doing today?" the concierge greets me as I step into the front hall. I squint over in the direction of the voice and find his slouching silhouette behind the desk, his teeth chipped piano keys in the dark.

"Is there something you want to tell me, or is that just your way of saying hello in the unnecessary form of a question?"

Cups his jaw in a toothache pose.

"Well, now you ask, I guess I'd say a little of both."

"Then tell me."

"Got a couple messages here I took for you over the phone."

"Let's see them."

"I'm not sure you're gonna—"

"Give me the fucking messages, if you don't mind."

"Don't mind at all. Just that they weren't those kind of messages."

I slide forward over the carpet until my shoes thud against the front of the desk.

"What kind were they?"

"Prankster stuff. Kids. Girls mostly, funny enough."

"Hilarious." I lay the back of my hand down on the desk. "So what'd they say? You write them down?"

"No, sir."

"Why not?"

"Didn't ask for you in particular."

"Why are you telling me then?"

"People know who you are. Who you'd be working for."

He says this without an edge of criticism. He says it without anything at all.

"Get names next time," I say. "I'll lay charges."

"For what?"

"Uttering threats."

"I didn't say nothin' about threats." The skin of the concierge's head glows in the blue from the computer screen.

I step back to go up the stairs, but pause at the bottom.

"How many?"

"A good few."

"Oh yeah? Well, after this, don't bother letting—"

"Not a word."

The concierge looks up at me and shakes his head blue black, blue black, across the line of shadow and light.

By the time I shut the door and glance out the window at the day's intestinal clouds I'm having doubts. Not about the thinness of the evidence against Thommy Boy, but about the soundness of the whole no-bodies-no-murder thing. I *think* I remember some law school prof in a cheap suit (no help—they all wore cheap suits) stating that no murder conviction had ever been obtained in Canada without the evidentiary assistance of the victim's discovered remains. But the voice of Graham Lyle nevertheless singsongs through my head as it always does when the necessity of legal research raises its pernickety head: *My dear Barth, didn't your mother ever warn you about hanging your hat on loose pegs?*

So I pull out the laptop, hook up the modem to the phone beside the bed and connect with the Canadian Criminal Database through which, thanks to the monkish work of some law school drop-outs stuck in a suburban basement office, every single reported case in the nation can be reviewed at a cost of $320 per on-line hour. A little dear, I suppose, but far handier than having to schlepp the firm's library up to this wasteland or call down to Toronto to have a paralegal pull together a memo which, in the end, is invariably wrong.

The afternoon gradually darkens in the space outside the computer's screen as I scroll and click through the cases summoned by my search terms, variously arranged: "homicide," "remains," "evidence," "*actus reus*," "discover(y)." By the time I have to turn on the bedside lamp to see my fingers it appears that my original assumption was correct. And then I come across *R v. Stark*. I read the whole decision before exhaling, a pain in my head like two birds pecking their way out at the temples.

The facts annoyingly similar to those at hand. A teenaged girl goes missing in rural northern Ontario and the police boil the suspects down to one Peter Stark, the father of one of the girl's school friends. He admits that he picked her up in town, but says he dropped her off at a gas station after he bought her lunch because she wanted to make a phone call. However, when Stark returned home at the end of the day his wife recalled his having mud and leaves stuck to his clothes. They never found the body before the trial, but the Crown proceeded against Stark anyway with little more than muddy jeans. Then he made his big mistake. In the court's holding cells just before the trial was to begin he bragged at length to the fellow who occupied the lower bunk about how he'd raped the girl and then used an ax on her afterwards to ensure she wouldn't tell, and then dumped her somewhere in the middle of the Manvers Township swamp. Although he stuck to his gas station drop-off story at trial and the police never managed to uncover the body, Stark was convicted and sentenced to life.

I close the laptop and fix my eyes on the halo of mist around the streetlight swaying outside the window. What does Mr. Stark have to say about the present case? Nothing good. But there's one fact missing in Tripp's situation that still clearly distinguishes his from Stark's: he hasn't con-fessed to anything. And so long as Tripp remains isolated in his bug-eyed state he isn't likely to reveal concrete details of the crime to his own lawyer, let alone the guy across the hall.

Nevertheless, there's one thing about today's discovery that is quite unavoidably bad: although they certainly help, it appears that bodies are not necessary to put a man away for murder after all.

Seven

The next morning finds my head buried in the complicated tunnels of my garment bag. I'm not feeling so hot. Not true—I'm in the grip of a death fever, I'm black leather in the sun, I'm a kettle boiled dry on the stove. And there it is, my home away from home tucked into the plastic bag designed for carrying shoes. Zip back the zipper and pull it up into my arms, give it a teary kiss as though a hard-won trophy. It even looks like a trophy: a silver thermos of burnished aluminum, roughly the size and shape of a nuclear warhead. Enough coke to entertain 150 movie producers and their dates for an entire night, a volume carrying a street value equal to an only slightly used Japanese sedan. Screw off the cap and spoon a line out onto the bedside table. Without sitting up I wrench my neck into an angle that enables me to accommodate the procedure, and with an efficient snuff (I snort only when drunk or subject to an especially monstrous craving, and almost never before noon) the day begins. Everything you need and then some. A witty conversation resumed within yourself, a Gene Kelly spring to the step, two inches added to your height. A nearly perfect simulation of what I can only assume to be hope, fluttering and shy in my chest.

"Good morning, Mr. Crane," I say to the paint-bubbled ceiling, but my voice sounds distant and thin through the air of the room. In fact it seems the entire hotel absorbs all sound but that which it creates itself. The chattering of the windows and muffled yawning echo for long moments, while a spoken voice is immediately drawn away.

Slip boxers off into a ring around my feet, step over to the bathroom and crank up the hot water. But for a while there's nothing but a thundering expulsion of icy white.

"Don't do this to me, *goddammit,*" I say to no particular person or deity, but something must be listening, for the water instantly becomes steam and my finger, which a second before was turning blue, is now pulled back a blistered red. Just as the burn's first flash of pain arrives I manage to turn and stick it under the tap in the sink. Take the opportunity to check myself out in the mirror, my face already fogging over at the edges. The glass is old, its surface spotted black where the silver has been chipped away, and the reflection it returns isn't quite right. Accentuates the shadows in a way that turns the circles under my eyes into bulging pouches and deepens the few wrinkles at the edges of brow and mouth into withering cracks. Pull back a bit and force a smile. Still a little bleached and inflated, but nothing to be alarmed about.

In fact I could say I'm not bad looking, but that's what all good-looking people say of themselves, hedging their bets behind the double negative of "not bad." So to avoid this false modesty I should simply say that I think I'm good-looking, in a certain way. The way of preppy boyishness, good posture and self-congratulatory smiles. Something in the way of the Kennedy boys in their early thirties (more Jack than Bobby). I have even been told this by others, although I think the likeness is fairly subtle, more an interpretation of aura than a description of physical detail. I've spent enough time in front of mirrors to know that I don't look like Bobby or

Jack, not really, but I admit the three of us might have stood comfortably next to each other in some school portrait or Cape Cod snapshot. It's that look of satisfaction and easy purpose carried within a single strand of DNA that is in turn bundled in with the other strands which predetermine the less important factors like intelligence, integrity and foot size. That's why people say I look like a Kennedy when I only *remind* them of a Kennedy, for in fact there's more of the prematurely debauched Irish rugby player in my face than the shining American aristocrat.

I circle my palm over the glass surface and wipe my face back into focus. So what, specifically, does the mirror say these days? Good things mostly, although good things in a state just prior to—or in the beginning stage of—the decline from young man firm to middle-aged sag. Beneath this, however, the fundamental elements resist and, for the most part, prevail: pronounced cheekbones, organized white teeth (apparently self-cleaning), hair that looks better tousled than combed, thin as a homework excuse and tall as an undertaker. Even from adolescence I recognized that mine was a build made for dark overcoats.

But the distinguishing flaws, the markings of "character"—let's not forget them, either. There's the Crane nose: too wide and crooked as a boxer's. Not a pretty thing to situate in the center of a face but suggestive of a tough-guy history which I've had occasion to be glad of. Thin lips more cobalt than crimson, eyes blue enough to go by violet. Brows turned up slightly at the corners to indicate vulnerability or, more likely, mischief. And a couple of things just plainly unfortunate: smallish ears whose tips pixie up and away from the sides of my head, a restless Adam's apple that leaps and dives the length of my neck. But before I can go too far down the list of aesthetic regrets the mirror steams over again, leaving only a wavering shadow deep within the glass.

I turn off the cold at the sink and do the same to the hot at the tub, the water now up to within a foot of the edge. While showers are my preference as a rule, seeing as I'm freezing my ass off I decide to step in and have a bath instead. It's one of those old, lion-clawed, heavy-duty porcelain units installed when they built the place. And it's deep. So for a time I lie there with eyes closed, absently whispering the opening lines of the only thing that I've ever memorized from beginning to end:

> *My heart aches, and a drowsy numbness pains*
> *My sense, as though of hemlock I had drunk,*
> *Or emptied some dull opiate to the drains*
> *One minute past, and Lethe-wards had sunk:*

Keats. Had to recite the whole thing for an undergraduate English class taught by one of those old-school profs who still believed that speaking the words aloud was essential to catching the full force of their poetic meaning. Maybe he was right; I wouldn't know. He was certainly pissed off when I asked him what a "Lethe" was when I was done. Apparently the question was more properly phrased not as what but where, as it turned out Lethe is the river of forgetfulness which runs through the underworld. "Perhaps you have drunk too deeply from its waters yourself," the old bastard scolded me in front of the class, but gave me an A on my reading as I recall.

I loved the words. I loved their sound and suggestion and rhythm, but could live without having to think too much about their meaning. It's likely that this passion, or some lesser form of it, was inherited from my father. A professor of comparative literature, although I never knew what he compared to what. The Romantics were his specialty—Keats, Byron, Shelley and other flowery sorts—but his text of principal interest was my mother. He read her and re-read her, coveted her like a rare first edition, his affections singular and exclusive. In my limited set of childhood memories he strikes two distinct poses. The first has him sitting at his desk preparing a lecture or fussing over an essay, in either case not to be interrupted. It seems I needed only to consider approaching the sliding oak door to his study before there would be my mother's sharp whisper behind me, "Your father is *working*!" The other is a picture of him reaching to embrace my mother, his face loosened into an expression of unseemly satisfaction for a grown, married man.

Of course I was too young myself to recognize how much he loved her (in the sense of how much more than other husbands loved their wives) but in the following years, whenever I've bumped into someone who knew them both back then, I've been told over and over that while he was a committed teacher, he was a devoted husband. Always the same adjectives used to describe the same occupations. In fact I came to understand the distinction between the two through this common observation others made about my father. One can be committed to any number of things. But when it comes to people, devotion requires attention to only one.

In the years since, I've come to see the two of them held together in a kind of orbit. Each connected to and moving about the other according to some superior, intricate power. And somewhere on the periphery there was me, passing them at a distance, related but secondary as a moon.

> *Darkling I listen; and, for many a time*
> *I have been half in love with easeful Death,*
> *Call'd him soft names in many a mused rhyme,*
> *To take into the air my quiet breath;*

We were a family of three. But when they died together in a car accident at the end of my fourteenth summer, the family part was gone. I required farming out. It was my wish to be sent to boarding school and the sympathetic but preoccupied circle of uncles and aunts in charge of my care were more than happy to oblige. Somewhere along the line there were friends, books and a handful of clever, scandalous pranks, all now difficult to recall. It wouldn't be an exaggeration to say that the better part of my remembered adolescence was spent staring out the window of a third-floor dorm room at Upper Canada College. The smell of burnt margarine hanging in the stairwells, the salt of lights-off ejaculations buried in every mold-speckled mattress. And this: on my seventeenth birthday I was given a mint-condition yellow MG convertible. It remained in the parking lot until the following year when I put a classified ad in *The Globe* and sold it to a recently divorced Lawrence Park orthodontist. Nobody asked what I did with the money.

There's more—there *must* be more—but from the first two decades of my life there are few details I can call on. A stuffed zebra with button eyes plucked from its head. *Charlie's Angels.* The wrought-ironed, duplexed streets of the city leaning down to the lake. A broken collarbone from running into the goalpost looking skyward for a long-bomb pass. It seems to me now that my childhood was more a prolonged setting of mood than a sequence of actual events, like the music the orchestra plays in a darkened theater before the curtain is raised and you're required to start paying real attention.

Although I was alone I don't remember being lonely. Never popular but respected from a distance in the way that derisive, slightly feared young men can be. And so when I went to university when the trust fund finally kicked in after I turned nineteen there wasn't the usual cast of mentors to advise me on what course of study to take, and I had no strong inclinations of my own. It must have been some kind of subconscious tribute to the old man when I signed up to major in English when it came time to register. Four years of British verse, French theory, American novels and all around me girls morphed into talking panthers I dared not speak to. Then law school, for all the usual reasons: legitimacy, money, a safe reservoir for undistinguished intelligence. But it turned out to be far more compatible than I imagined, my passion for words finally married to an indifference to truth. For me, law school was the discovery of religion, albeit a godless one, with its Latin prayers and shifting, manufactured convictions. Belief the weight of the air in your lungs.

Of course not all of my classmates experienced their legal education the same way I did. Many even arrived with declared intentions of "doing some good out there" or "making changes from within the system," but there was much less of that kind of talk by the time graduation rolled around. And it was a good thing too, the rest of us having found the spectacle of diminished moral ambitions rather embarrassing and sad, like watching a man with a wooden leg take dance lessons.

Then the purchase of suits and the dailiness of practice and all of my classmates drifting away into marriage or property or the pursuit of expensive, rarely indulged hobbies.

Whether due to my suspicious bachelorhood or success in releasing unpredictably violent offenders back into the world, I am no longer asked to their late-bloomer weddings, house warmings or—if such things still go on—cocktail parties. Although occasionally curious, I miss none of them. I assume all of us are happy in our ways.

> *Adieu! adieu! thy plaintive anthem fades*
> *Past the near meadows, over the still stream,*
> *Up the hill-side; and now 'tis buried deep*
> *In the next valley-glades:*
> *Was it a vision, or a waking dream?*
> *Fled is that music:—Do I wake or sleep?*

Eight

After I've shaved and thrown on a shirt I sit on the edge of the bed for a minute, the heat of my skin escaping out into the chill of the room which lingers despite the sunlight that slices in through the windows. Pull out my leather agenda and study the series of empty days leading up to the trial. The pre-trial conference for disclosure of any remaining Crown evidence is scheduled for tomorrow morning, but today's still wide open. I riffle through the loose-leaf appendices of the police report and pull up the already wrinkle-worn map of the county, spread it over the bed. There, in a meandering line of radioactive yellow highlighter, is the course of the accused's drive from Georgian Lakes High School to the side of Fireweed Road where his 1990 green Volvo station wagon was parked and the victims allegedly removed to be taken down to the water.

It's not a short drive. Judging from the map, five miles as the crow flies but probably closer to eight when you consider the snaking private road Tripp would have had to take through the woods and around part of the lake's coiled shoreline. And then, once he'd parked, to somehow pull the two girls down to the water—that must have taken a while, too. How did he manage it? If he'd sedated them somehow, it was too far to lug them over his back. (Tripp isn't small, but he's no hulking woodsman either.) And if he hadn't knocked them out one way or another, they must have followed him either willingly or under threat. But couldn't at least one of them have pulled free and ripped off into the woods when his attention was on the other for a moment? If it's as long a walk as it appears on the map, the implication of an unused opportunity for easy escape may be of assistance to the defence's cause. And seeing as Tripp is unlikely to be of any help in providing topographical descriptions himself, there's nothing for it but to follow his tracks on my own.

I fire up the Lincoln, pull a U-turn and head back up toward the courthouse. A left at the second of the three sets of lights and into the blocks of staunch brick homes with paint peeling off the eaves and trees planted too close to the front windows. An Ontario town. Whether clustered at the meeting of concession roads on the flat land nosed into the Great Lakes or blasted through the pitching rock of the Canadian Shield, all of them built on the shared assumption that one must always start with straight lines. Grid patterns. County borders designated by surveyors' measurements instead of the creeping accidents of lakeshore, escarpment or creek. And all but a few people meant to live on the even blocks set inside phantom town limits, residential streets finally melting into endless gravel roads or weedy culs-de-sac at the edge of bullfrog swamps. Order thrown down on the land like an unmet challenge, fenced backyards and rect-angular playgrounds plotted out in the hope that dignity and history might follow.

And Murdoch no different from the rest. In fact some-thing classical about it, the humility that comes with all failed experiments. Shingles flapping off the roofs to be replaced with smearings of tar. Uncertain-looking houses with nylon curtains permanently drawn in the upstairs windows and a single porch light packed tight with moth wings. Above the main street storefronts the by-the-week apartments where the whiskey bachelors peer down with faces you can never clearly see, as though a ghost or a minor character in a complicated dream. Below them, the good citizens of Murdoch scuffing by. Hard-working if there's work to be done, honest if asked directly, skeptical of good fortune. People not so much friendly as prepared to help if called upon.

At the end of the street there's the high school, the brick a dirty yellow instead of the houses' dirty red. Nobody outside except a couple guys in Guns 'n' Roses T-shirts, energetically smoking as though it might make them warm. At one of the classroom windows a teacher points at a map of Europe, the heads of her students hung low from note-taking or sleep.

I check my watch. 9:37.

Left at the lights and right at the courthouse and then out of town on the main highway north which follows the shore of Georgian Bay, although now, even with most of the leaves off the trees, it's still too far off to be seen. I keep an eye out for signs but still come to the turn almost too late to make it: LAKE ST. CHRISTOPHER, RIGHT 50 YARDS. The Lincoln leans off onto the crunch and bump of the single lane that quickly disappears, behind and ahead, into the trees.

The map calls it Lake St. Christopher, but it used to go by Fireweed Lake. At least that's what the couple of hand-painted direction signs nailed onto roadside pines still call it, erected in the days before some poet at the Chamber of Commerce changed its name. From what I can tell Fireweed Lake is more appropriate though, for instead of the dramatic rock formations or clear, sandy beaches which dignify many of the other settled lakes an hour or so to the south, this one could claim only a slow and soggy decline into the reed-ridden muck. It's a big lake with limited road access and plenty of cheap land surrounding it, but the same could be said of a hundred other lakes up here that don't suffer the blight of duckweed, quack grass and floating green algae as this one does. And then, after forty or fifty brake-pumping turns, it's there before me, a glimpse of reflected cloud between an entanglement of brown trunks.

The road rises, falls and jerks, occasionally exposing the entrance to a cottage driveway marked by some cutesie name burned into a hunk of driftwood. Mayonnaise Manor, Monarch Point, Bucky's Palace. But there aren't many of these, and the spaces between them are dotted with realty signs crippled from the rot setting in at their bases. The map is spread out beside me on the passenger seat and I pull over to trace the final part of Tripp's path. A red dot to mark the place where he supposedly stopped, halfway around the circumference of the water. If the lake runs about three miles from end to end and three-quarters of a mile across at its midsection, and judging from how far I must have gone already, I've got to be pretty close. But it seems I have to continue on another quarter of an hour before, with the cresting of a final steep incline, the woods on the right are set off by the yellow plastic of a police line fluttering over the road.

Roll down the window and suddenly my ears are filled with a high-voltage hum. An orchestrated layering of clicks and gulps and tweets that together is louder than the car's engine. *Over here.* All society of nature calling out to each other, to itself. *I'm over here.*

It's beautiful. Even I can recognize the beauty of it. But

as it goes on it becomes increasingly mechanical in my ears. A primitive, poorly lubricated machine producing some hard and common product, and soon all I can hear is noise.

I turn off the car and step out onto the road, look down into the woods in the direction I know the lake to be but it's not visible from here. The map showed that at this point the road wandered from the lake and left a wide margin of land between them, maybe a quarter-mile of exposed rock of a size only retreating glaciers could move. All things considered it would seem an impractical place for Tripp to stop: no cottages nearby to give rise to the concern of potential witnesses (even if anyone was up here at this time of year, which they apparently aren't) and from this starting point the walk down to the water would be an unnecessarily prolonged pain in the ass. Why here? Did he come this far out of nervousness, choosing caution over convenience? Or was the nature hike part of the fun?

Step onto the pulpy bed of pine needles and leaves which gives off the damp odor of living fibre turning into something else. Clouds of flying things enter at collar and sleeve only to explode from their own gluttony, leave dark smears over the backs of swatting hands. The going is slow. But despite the absence of any clear markings, the path is obvious. The grey rock faces shift to one side as I pass, the thorny branches arch high enough to let me through.

When it finally comes the water takes me by surprise, a sudden levering out that laps up to the rim of the rock I stand on. A foot below on either side is the marshy beach, which is less a beach than the meeting of earth, weeds and runoff the color of mustard left too long out of the fridge. There's no way you could jump in without getting covered in it, without legs sinking into the softness of whatever collection of half-dissolved things it was that settled on the bottom. How could Tripp have deposited the girls here without having them float in the exact spot he'd left them? There wasn't enough current in this place to shift a fallen branch six inches, let alone take two loads of 120-pound human being out to the middle. Did he get in there up to his armpits himself, swim out a bit to where it got deep? That would explain the first one maybe, but not the second waiting patiently on the rock for Tripp to paddle back and send her off the same way. And what if he had to carry them down—

My thoughts are cut off by the idea of a sound just behind me. Turn, but there's nothing there. A rush of blood past the eardrum. A lick of wind sounding as a whispered name.

I jump off the rock and land funny on the pebbles below, the bolt of pain from a twisted ankle shooting up to my crotch. Then I'm rolling to the ground with both hands gripped around my sock while some woodland rodent chatters down at me from the network of trees overhead. Wait there on the poking stones for the throbbing to pass to the point that I can get to my feet. But there's the voice again. Blown thin through the clacking branches. Not a name at all but the first call of alarm, startled and high.

Lift myself as much with arms as legs and hop back up to the path. Wishing I could move a little faster but both the hill and my useless ankle hold me back. Although I know there's nothing but the water cut off by the trees behind me I don't turn around, keep my eyes on my feet stubbing over roots and stone, the wind now a distant laughter in the remaining leaves. By the time I reach the Lincoln and scrabble for the keys in my pocket I'm surprised by the choking tightness of my lungs.

84 Andrew Pyper

The road is too narrow to turn around so I'm forced to reverse to the first cottage driveway and on the way I scrape the passenger side past a fencepost that, with a sound like clicked fingers, neatly lops the mirror clean off the door. Watch it scuttle down into the ditch, sending back a glimpse of my own blanched face. Consider stopping to pick it up but my foot doesn't move from the pedal. Add it to Mr. Tripp's disbursements.

It's only on the main highway back into town that I check my watch. 11:42. Nearly two hours from start to finish.

When I get back to the honeymoon suite I pull out a blank legal pad with the intention of taking down a physical description of the crime scene to help with cross-examination somewhere down the line. But nothing comes, and instead I find myself writing the heading SPECULATIVE HYPOTH-ESES at the top of the page and beneath it the following three theories:

The first would suggest that Tripp is in fact a man possessing remarkable (however hidden) physical strengths as well as extraordinary patience in carrying out the transport and disposal of his victims.

The second theory admits some degree of voluntariness on the part of the girls, who perhaps up until the final moments were under the impression that they were on a field trip out for an inspirational gazing over still waters.

The third theory is that he had some help.

Nine

After a breakfast of toasted bagel discovered deep inside the pocket of my overcoat I head back up to the courthouse for my conference with a Mr. Goodwin, the Crown Attorney assigned to the trial. I'm feeling a little sluggish, having limited myself to only a single line of wake-up coke, but the fatigue seems to come from a different source. Since arriving in Murdoch my sleep has been degraded to a series of five-hour toss and turn marathons. Waking lacquered in sweat or balled-up in shivers, eyes opening at the imagined scrape of the window lifting open. A rattling breath joining my own in the dark room.

I make a mental note to buy pills.

When I find Goodwin's office I take a second before entering to finish a heaving yawn and guess at what sort of opponent I'm about to meet. "Never heard of him," Graham had e-mailed back when I'd asked if Goodwin was a known quantity. "They assign the weird ones up there."

And he is weird, if being startlingly fat satisfies the definition. A peony-faced water retainer jammed behind a desk occupied by neatly arranged columns of documents. He's still straightening them carefully from top to bottom when I come in, fingers rolling down their sides as if sculpting pottery on a wheel.

"Hay-lo, you must be Bartholomew Crane. Pete Goodwin," he says, his mouth sounding as though there's something in it but there's not, just his thick tongue banging up against the inside of his teeth.

"Good morning, Mr. Goodwin," I say, and try at a brisk smile. There's a moment when a handshake is mutually considered, but because it would be a stretch for me to reach him across the broad desk and because his position there appears more or less permanent, I simply take a seat.

"So, this is it?" I nod toward the fondled papers.

"That's right. Of course, you'll have to review all the materials in whatever detail you deem fit, but I thought in the meantime I might provide you with a summary. The main highlights, as it were. By way of courtesy."

"Sure, yes. Courtesy. Give me your best shots."

Goodwin pushes his chair back and stands, revealing his full immensity. Panting a little, he takes a black marker from his jacket pocket and begins to make point notes on the white presentation board on the wall behind him. His mouth a puncture flapping out from the top of a hot air balloon.

"First, there's the fruits of our search of Tripp's apartment. Not sure if you've seen the place—it's your standard one-bedroom above the corner store at Brock and King—and pretty tidy when the police arrived. Your typical single guy setup, I guess."

"Was he always that way?"

"Tidy?"

"Single."

"I would've thought you knew."

"No, I don't. That's why I'm *asking*."

Goodwin pauses as his brain registers my sarcasm, but for the moment he does nothing more than file it away.

"Tripp was divorced three years back. We've provided a list of witnesses, among whom are people who knew him before and after the split who will testify as to the terrible strain the whole thing put on him. Stopped calling friends or going out, noticeably distracted at school staff meetings, diminished performance in the classroom, things like that."

"So he was depressed. The wife left him. Is that considered unique up here?"

"Not on its own. But he didn't just lose his wife. The man lost his family."

"What family?"

"Well, his wife left in something of a hurry—I really would've thought you knew this—and took their daughter with her. Then a prolonged custody hearing over the girl, Melissa I think her name was. Is. A real backstreet brawl, I understand. And it got personal. Tripp accusing the wife of sleeping around and the wife accusing Tripp of becoming obsessive over the daughter, constantly taking photos of her, not letting her play with other kids, that sort of thing. So one day she just packed up and took the girl with her."

"Still, I don't get—"

"There's a bit more to it, Mr. Crane." He smiles uncertainly, little teeth huddled beneath a glistening lip. "Melissa was only ten years old when she left, and the accused's only child. That's bad enough. And then a year later he lost all his visitation rights after she told her mother that Daddy wanted her to bring her big suitcase and passport next time because the two of them were going to go on a long trip. Mother went to court, changed address, got a restraining order and all of a sudden Tripp's totally out of the picture. After that, he dropped everything and kept to himself. Except for some of his favored students, of course."

This last bit isn't meant as provocation, you can tell just by looking at the basset hound arc of Goodwin's brow. But I clear my throat threateningly anyway to let him know I've taken notice.

"Next on the list are the photographs of the accused's bedroom that show the catalog pages he'd ripped out and plastered over his wall," Goodwin continues, adding a long dash and PICS to the list on the board. "All girls, aged ten to eighteen. And as the photographs indicate, Tripp selected pages showing their subjects in underwear, pajamas or revealing sportswear."

"Revealing *sportswear*, you say? Oh *my*. What else?"

"The other evidence from the apartment was a pair of brown dress pants found in Tripp's laundry hamper, covered in dried mud from the cuff up to the shin. We have a witness, a colleague of Tripp's at the school, who will testify that she recalls these pants being the same ones he wore on the day of the girls' disappearance."

"Mud. Well, well, well."

I raise my eyebrows to show how little I'm impressed so far, but Goodwin again pretends not to notice and keeps himself focused on the labored push and slide of the marker over the white surface.

"Next up is Tripp's car," he goes on, actually drawing a picture of a station wagon, complete with spoked hubcaps and door handles. "Once impounded we discovered half a dozen small bloodstains on the backseat. We believe that these will be sufficient to yield a large enough sample for DNA testing, and so we've gone ahead and sent a section of the upholstery down to forensics in Toronto for a run-through along with hair samples taken from each of the girls' hairbrushes. We expect the results back shortly—they're really getting better and better at these things, aren't they?—

although, in the event they *aren't* available, certain arrangements can of course be made to adjourn for a period . . ."

Then I lose him. Not *him* actually, but his words. In fact my attention turns more closely to the man himself. There is a particular aspect to Goodwin's obesity—a posture, perhaps even an aura to it—that compels one to stare and await disaster. By "disaster" I mean either embarrassment of the first order (a popping of shirt buttons, a pastry slipping out of a jacket pocket and splatting, jelly side down, onto the floor) or something worse, the spontaneous regurgitation of the past twelve hours' consumption or the final explosion of his overworked heart. When he stands I can't resist calculating his dimensions, thinking of his very being in terms of so many hundred cubic feet or comparing his belt length to the width of living rooms. Even when he's seated it's a struggle to do anything but watch him and his heaving movements as he bends forward to take notes or dig around for his pen, the flesh of his face folded over itself like a partly disassembled tent. While I have known body size of his type to work to the advantage of other lawyers who have managed to harness the authority of the jutting belly and bulldoggish ferocity of the triple chin, in this man it suggests only ineptitude.

But more. His fatness tells a story. On Goodwin's pink layers and crimson cheeks is written the history of a man who once believed that when he'd reached a certain point of accomplishment in his life, when he could stand knowing that his own words represented the voice of Queen and country, that then, after years of schoolyard mockery and half-concealed giggles over his shoulder, he would be taken seriously. But here he is, finally, and nothing has changed.

I don't know any of this for a fact, of course. But his

body told me just the same, as clearly as if his biography were written on the vast fabric of his suit. However, while Goodwin presents a pitiable picture to the world, there is little pity in me as I wait for the hand that rests too heavily on the back of his chair to flip it over and send my opposing counsel's rice-sack ass to the floor. He's on the wrong side of the proceedings for pity.

"Thank you for that informative presentation," I begin when Goodwin has found his chair, pushing my totally blank legal pad into the middle of the table for him to get a good look. "But I have some questions."

"Go ahead," he swallows.

"First of all, what's the evidentiary basis for your obtaining the warrant to impound Tripp's car?"

"We were investigating the possibility of—"

"I don't care what *we* were investigating. I'm asking what you put before the justice of the peace to get him to sign an order to search my client's car. Do you understand the question?"

"I *understand*, Mr. Crane. And the short answer is tire tracks."

"What tire tracks?"

"At the crime scene. The ones left at the end of the road on Lake St. Christopher are consistent with the size, wear and brand variety tread on Tripp's Volvo."

"Tire tracks are *not* what you'd call scientifically precise, are they?"

"They were good enough for the j.p."

"They must've been. But we'll see how that stands up before a judge who actually holds a law degree. And let me remind you that your reference to the location of the tire tracks as the 'crime scene' is desperately premature. No bodies, no crime, no crime *scene*."

"You're free to call it what you like, Mr. Crane."

"Thank you. I think I'll call it horseshit then, if you don't mind, because I don't see a single good reason for the police to have been searching the end of that road for tire tracks in the first place. Why there? Why, in a county with 172 prime locations to ditch bodies, would the bright sparks of the Murdoch O.P.P. detachment all head to the one place?"

Goodwin presses his lips together, pushes the color out of the skin around his mouth. "A collection of reasons," he says finally.

"I'm curious."

"Well, Tripp used to spend his summers on St. Christopher for years, so he would know the area well. That's for starters. Next, his car had been seen up there once or twice driving around in the months prior to the girls' disappearance. But more importantly, it was simply the first place people around here thought to look. The woods are thick, the water's deep. And there're stories."

"Stories?"

"Bad things that happened, years back. And you know how people can turn old facts into new tales."

Goodwin tries at an embarrassed laugh, brings the pads of his hands together in a single smack of flesh.

"I know all about turning facts into tales, Mr. Goodwin. And I'm beginning to see that you and the police up here are enthusiastic amateurs at it."

"Now, there's no need for—"

"You said 'bad things.' What kind of bad things?"

"I'm not sure of the particulars. A drowning, I think. And now there's a ghost story to go along with it."

"Beautiful. So are all the cops up here gypsies or something?"

"I'm not trying to—"

"Regarding the search of Tripp's apartment: there was no journal or diary found? No half-finished letters?"

"No."

"Just the muddy pants and catalog pinups?"

"That's right."

"And both easily explained, wouldn't you say? Lonely father seeking comforting images to remind him of his only child. A lonely father who *also* lives in a town of wall-to-wall mud, particularly after the big spring thaw?"

"Perhaps, but I think—"

"And no weapon found?"

"Nothing yet."

"No bloodstains or anything gruesome in the laundry hamper?"

"No, just—"

"Just the bloodstains in the Volvo. I know. Now, *assuming* you get a readable result on the DNA analysis, I ask you, what do you propose to match it *against?*"

Goodwin raises a corner of his mouth slightly to reveal starshaped dimples cratered high in his cheeks.

"Perhaps I neglected to mention," he says, mouth still raised, "that in addition to the bloodstains in the back and the hair taken from their hairbrushes at home there were also a number of hair samples found in the car, apparently emanating from two distinct sources: one dark, one blonde, both long. Not Tripp's. We've sent these out for DNA tests as well, and if the hairbrush hair matches the hair found in the car, or if the hairbrush hair matches the bloodstains—well, I think at the very least it would go a good way toward proving their presence in the car."

"Big fucking deal!" I'm shouting now. "Nobody's *denying* their 'presence in the car.' Who *cares* about their 'presence in the car'? The elements of the offence of first-degree murder, Mr. Goodwin, involve establishing that a planned and deliberate homicide has occurred. Girls with long hair having nosebleeds or picking scabs in the back of their teacher's car falls a little short, wouldn't you say?"

Then Goodwin does something alarming. He sits forward (as far as this is possible), his face a shiny Macintosh, his upper lip dancing in the involuntary way that signals the onset of either frustrated tears or violence. But neither come. Only his voice, struggling for calm.

"Mr. Crane, this is a *pre-trial conference.* It is meant to assist in defining the issues of trial, thereby to expedite procedure. It's *not* an opportunity to practice your closing submissions, nor am I a witness obliged to sit through a test run of your cross-examination strategy. I'm pleased to answer your inquiries, but I find your argumentative tone extremely inappropriate."

Then he sits back again. The redness (at least the additional redness) drains from his face and his upper lip is released from its seizure.

"Quite right, Mr. Goodwin," I admit, vaguely impressed by the big man's performance. "I'm aware that what you call my *argumentative tone* can sometimes get the better of me. I suppose it just wouldn't let me sit here, having appreciated what I take to be the full extent of the Crown's evidence, without pointing out its woeful deficiencies. Sometimes my *argumentative tone* overwhelms me when a client of mine has been charged with the highest criminal offence known to our law on the basis only of catalog pictures, muddy slacks, a haunted lake and crossed fingers on the outcome of what will in any event be inconclusive DNA results. For this, I apologize."

I rise at this point, collecting the stacks of papers left on the table and sticking them randomly into Goodwin's accordion file, now mine. But I can't help noticing at the upper extreme of my vision a wet-looking grin moving across the fat man's mouth.

"You think I don't *wish* I had more? I know darn well the limitations of my case, Mr. Crane."

I direct a mocking snort at his "darn well," but once again he continues as though he hadn't noticed.

"There's a difference between you and me, Mr. Crane. And it's likely not one of the differences that's already occurred to you. The thing is, you want to win this case because it would be doing yourself a service. I want to win because I believe Thomas Tripp is guilty. Everyone in this town knows it. He tried to steal his own daughter once, and when he couldn't do that, he stole someone else's."

"Very nice, very—"

"And you know what *else*?" He raises himself from his chair in a single movement of surprising agility, extending his arm in my direction at the same time. "I believe you know this yourself."

"You can't tell me what I believe."

"No, I can't. But I'll ask you this. Next time you have a talk with your client take a good long look into his eyes and tell me he didn't do it."

The meeting's over. His hand, puffy and spotted white, wavers before me. When I finally take it he gives my own hand a long, dry squeeze.

It's ridiculous how some small, totally inconsequential things can come to drive you nuts. But what bothers me about this handshake is that it's my hand that's slick with moisture when it should be his. It's my sweat that is wiped from the fat man's hand onto the front of his cheap pants.

Ten

The Murdoch Public Library is located across the street from the courthouse in what used to be the manse of St. Andrew's Presbyterian Church, a dour, cracked plaster affair that epitomizes the town's no-nonsense Protestant aesthetic. Who knows where the minister lives today (perhaps tucked away in the basement and dusted off once a week to deliver a sermon to his diminishing, blue-rinsed congregation) but what used to be the dining room, sitting room and even the kitchen of his residence are now clotted with book stacks, a couple of study carrels next to the windows and, in the place where the stove and sink used to be, a bearded man with alarmingly dark eyes seated behind a wooden desk shuffling index cards. When I approach I note first that he and I are the only ones in the place, and second that he's not seated at all but standing, and is a man who, given the benefit of the doubt, may be estimated to reach the height of four-foot-six.

"Can I help you?" he asks in a voice deeper than would seem possible for a man his size, plush and tranquilizing as a late-night d.j.

"Hope so. I understand that you have a newspaper here in town. A weekly?"

"*The Murdoch Phoenix.*"

"Indeed. I was wondering if there're back copies of it on microfilm, or if you have it on-line?"

"Neither, I'm afraid. But we do keep a pile of them in the Periodicals section. It's the pantry to your left."

A glance in that direction reveals a room the size of a walk-in closet off the kitchen with a foldaway table, battered oak chair, and on the shelves around them, yellowing editions of the local paper.

"I see. Well, would you mind if—?"

"Not at all." He gestures a babyish hand at the chair. "Can I ask if you're conducting any particular type of research?"

He has stepped out from behind the desk now and placed his hands on his hips in a let's-get-down-to-business pose. Something in the bemused crinkle at the corners of his mouth communicates intelligence, and the directness with which he meets my eyes (head held back in a way that appears oddly natural, given the sharpness of the angle) leads me to suspect he's not snooping, that his interests are wholly professional.

"What I'm interested in, to be precise, are news stories having to do with the lost girls."

With this he remains perfectly still for a nearly uncomfortable length of time. Then, briefly, a smile appears and recedes into the fur of his beard.

"Then you'd be Bartholomew Crane," he says. "I'm Doug Pittle. We ran a story on you in the last issue."

" 'We'?"

" 'I,' actually. Aside from being Head Librarian, I'm also Publisher, Sales Director and Editor-in-Chief of *The Murdoch Phoenix*. I hope you don't mind the publicity, but it's nothing too terribly inflammatory, I assure you. In fact, I think you'll find that the *Phoenix*—that is, *I*—have taken a more balanced view of the case than even the Toronto papers and considerably more than the television news, needless to say."

"A profile? Where did you get my bio? As far as I'm aware, I'm not yet listed in the *Who's Who*."

"I'm a researcher, Mr. Crane. It's amazing the things you can find if you look in the right places." As he speaks he guides me to the pantry and pushes the door half-closed to provide a level of privacy as well as a flow of oxygen into the tiny room. "If you need any help, I'll be here until we close at six."

"How did you—"

"It's a small town," he says flatly and retreats back to his desk.

Before I get started I wonder at how Doug Pittle so smoothly resisted a prolonged exchange and at the same time left me with the impression that further conversation would come later. No doubt he had himself a long experience of living among the damaged goods that constitute the better part of Murdoch's population, and he knew that, in time, another like himself would have to eventually seek refuge in the one place where they could be surrounded by the calming presence of books.

So it is that I find my nose stuck in the crimpled pages of the May 17th issue of *The Murdoch Phoenix*, when the girls were first reported missing. The initial story ran as a front page blurb noting that two local students had not been seen since the previous Thursday (the *Phoenix* was published every Tuesday) and that, the girls being close friends, it was suspected by police that they'd most likely "run off for the weekend." The next issue featured two pictures of the girls, the same yearbook portraits published in every paper in the country. Smiling, floral Sunday-best dresses, side-by-side, blanketing the top half of the front page. One light-haired and dimple-chinned, the other dark and freckled, blue eyed both.

The story below told of how the police were now of a radically different opinion from that of the week before, how search teams were being arranged throughout the area, how Armed Forces helicopters were brought in to run aerial patterns over a hundred-square-mile grid, and how two senior O.P.P. homicide detectives had been assigned to the case to "explore potential foul play scenarios." In the weeks that followed stories chronicling the frustrated search appeared on every front page, and never failed to include a vague quote from the detective in charge ("Every avenue of investigation is being pursued," and, later, "It's true that we are now treating the case as a homicide, although of course we remain hopeful"). Then, during a heat wave in the week following Labor Day which registered the highest temperatures the town had experienced since 1937, Thomas Tripp was arrested and charged with two counts of first-degree murder. The police weren't releasing anything to the press that wasn't already known: the girls were last seen after school that Thursday getting into the back of Tripp's car, both wearing white summer dresses, and that authorities were now "marshaling the full extent of the evidence for the Crown." At the bottom of the page a small photo of the accused inset at the lower left-hand corner, a face carrying the bewildered look of those who have suddenly found themselves in serious trouble.

Having read through every story from the beginning to the present ("Tripp Hires Prestigious Toronto Firm for Defence") I bring the entire pile out of the pantry and stand it on a table next to the library's lone photocopier. After an hour of holding my head over the machine's blinding flashes I amass an inky heap as thick as a nineteenth-century Russian novel.

When I'm finished Pittle stands, moving around to lean against the shelf that holds the magazines—*Time*, *Popular Mechanics*, *Maclean's*—all neatly labeled and untouched.

"Can I help you with anything else?"

"Maybe you can. Do you have anything in the way of a local atlas or history? Something that might provide a kind of general overview of the town?"

"You're a historian as well then?"

"Not at all. I just like to know what I'm dealing with."

"You mean *where* you're dealing with," he laughs, dark as coffee. "I know just the thing."

He slides around the corner into the stacks and in a few seconds returns with a large, apparently untitled hardcover book.

"*A History of Northern Ontario Towns*," he announces. "Compiled by Murdoch's own late Alistair Dundurn, honored World War II veteran, amateur historian and, in his later years, well-known eccentric who walked the town's streets talking in a language known only to himself. Remember him myself, although he died just a couple years after I arrived. Found him frozen solid in the middle of a snowdrift beside the doors of Our Lady of Perpetual Help after the big blizzard of '84. Everyone thought it was a funny thing, his choosing to impersonate an ice cube outside of a Catholic church, being a die-hard Presbyterian all his life."

"Sounds interesting," I say, meaning not the book but the way its author died.

"Some of it is," Pittle says, meaning the book.

He holds it out to me and it instantly shrinks in the transfer from his hands to mine.

"It's got a good chapter on Murdoch in there," he says critically. "Histories both official and unofficial."

"My thanks. I guess I should haul all this stuff out of your way now, though. What do I owe you?"

"Well, I don't imagine you've counted all those copies, and I'm certainly not about to, so why don't we just call it even. And as for the book loan, consider yourself an honorary member of the Murdoch Public Library. Or perhaps more a visiting scholar."

"That's quite a designation."

"It comes with one condition."

"Yes?"

"When it's all over—the trial I mean—you agree to give me an exclusive interview. A few remarks for *Phoenix* readers."

"Agreed," I say, and sticking the heavy wad of paper and book into my leather document bag, walk out the library's front door and back down Ontario Street through a bitter autumn rain that, although varying in its intensity, has been falling since the day I arrived.

Back in the honeymoon suite I take out the copied articles and arrange them chronologically over the bed. Then, without an idea in my head, I take the rest of the afternoon to tape them all in this order to the wall next to the desk, the dresser, the window frames and then, standing on a chair, in a series of lines beneath the wood moldings of the ceiling around the entire perimeter of the room. When I'm finished I consider the fruits of my work and marvel at its pointlessness, at the way I've voluntarily made an ugly room even uglier. Put together like this, the smudged print of text blends together so that only the yearbook photographs and banner headlines ("No Sign in Search for Local Girls," "Our Little Sweet One: A Father Talks," "Lost Girls' Teacher in Custody") stand out. It's as though the walls themselves now disclose a tale of their own, pushing through the layers of insulation and plaster. A story told largely without words, and the few that could be seen acting only to provide different titles to rename the same recurring image. Although the girls' smiles are unchanging, their intimations are subtly enhanced as I walk around the room, transformed from something innocent to ironic to tragic to, by the end, a mocking ambivalence.

I wasn't aware of their names until now.

Of course I'd seen them typed out on police reports and witness statements and in every news story I'd read about them but, my mind on other things, they failed to register as *names*. The personality of the words ascribed to faces, the language used to translate people into paper.

Krystal McConnell.

Ashley Flynn.

Names of the times. Borrowed from soap opera characters of prominence fifteen years ago who have since been replaced by spiffy new models: the social-climbing *Brittany* now an unscrupulous *Burke*, the generous *Pamela* a refitted, urbanized *Parker*. But when Krystal McConnell and Ashley Flynn were named deep in the heart of the 80s the thing was cuteness, feminine delicacy raised to an aesthetic paradigm. Pink cotton perfumed with designer fragrances. A belief in the transformative powers of positive thinking, spring water, German-made automobiles and avocado. Brand names in banners beneath made-up family crests, galloping polo ponies and green reptiles embroidered over every heart. And everyone named according to a particular version of the pedigree fantasy. *Ashley*: transplanted Southern privilege, a destiny lying in sorority mixers and a marriage of health club memberships, state-of-the-art appliances and night courses in *nouvelle cuisine. Krystal*: light refracted through the grooves and crests of fancy cut glass, a fragility tempered with the Eastern European heartiness of an imported K.

I look again at the grainy pictures on the wall. Pointillistic dots in varying degrees of light and dark that blur up close but magically assemble into faces as I pull away. Ashley and Krystal were their names. And that, at the moment they obligingly smiled at the corny joke told by the school yearbook photographer, was what they looked like.

Eleven

Three days of wading through police notes and warrant documents, of prepackaged ham sandwiches purchased from the corner store beneath Tripp's apartment a couple of blocks away, of sleeping in the desk chair and listening to the rain tap-dancing on the eaves. Three days of working alone and Barth Crane could use a little entertainment.

"Evenin'," the concierge says to me when I reach the bottom of the Grand Staircase.

"Good evening. Any messages?"

He lowers his head either to check for notes that may have fallen to the floor or to give me a better view of his vein-mottled baldness. When he rises again he squints at me through the lobby's gas lamp gloom.

"Nope. Nothing but—just more of the same."

"Fine. If I get any serious calls, could you have your staff please refer them to my room?"

"Staff! Ain't no staff but me!"

He makes a clacking sound against the roof of his mouth that one immediately wishes one had never heard.

"Well, I suppose that explains why the phone was left ringing off the goddamn hook the other night."

"What's that?"

"Nothing. Thanks so much for your help."

"Not a worry."

Then he lowers his head once more in what I can only

take to be a bow of some kind, but I prevent myself from looking again at his awful scalp. Instead I turn and pull open the door to the Lord Byron Cocktail Lounge, stepping into an even greater darkness than the one I'd come from.

At first, the only appreciable light emanates from the small stage at the far end of the room, and even this is of the purple fluorescent kind known only to strip bars and adolescent basement bedrooms. At the moment, however, the stage is empty, and after my eyes adjust I see that most of the bar is empty as well. There's a table of four beards in lumber jackets slumped around a table of half-consumed pitchers, three loosened ties with rolled sleeves spotted around the stage, and what I assume to be one of the dancers sitting at the bar in a transparent blouse and bike shorts, her impossibly long blonde hair hanging stiffly down her back as though the plumage of an extravagant nineteenth-century hat. In the background the muted rumblings of cheesyjazz, a barely recognizable "Little Girl Blue."

Acquire a double rye and ginger and take a table near the stage but well off to one side against the wall where the darkness is almost complete. For a while nothing happens, and nobody seems to mind, not even the lumber jackets who look the sort who wouldn't stand for excessive delays in the delivery of entertainment. I finish my drink and raise my arm to the barman for another.

Then, without the usual P.A. introduction and change in music that signals a new dancer's arrival, a young woman takes the stage and immediately drops her slip to the floor. She's blonde as well but unbleached, and judging from the taut smoothness of the flesh at the back of her thighs and under her arms, could be no more than twenty years old. But as she dances it's impossible to get a good look at her because of hair so loosely feathered it shrouds most of her face. The kind of hair one finds on those embarrassed by a scar or spotty skin, yet the few glimpses she offers suggest she's as likely pretty as not. Moves without interest in her movement, fingertips running down over her ribs and stomach as though checking for dust. Hips swaying a little too slow for the music so that she's always a halfbeat behind, hands now squeaking up the brass pole at the side of the stage. Raises her arms above her and the whole of her body, slender and pale and high, is clinically displayed.

When she finishes the audience applauds dutifully but without the usual whistles or howls, which I assume is out of either boozy distraction or respect for her tender age. She bends down and picks the gauzy white slip up off the floor, lets it fall over her shoulders. On her way to the bar I wave to her to join me and she brings me another drink as well as one for herself.

"Like the show?" she asks when she sits, places the fresh drink she's brought for me down beside its two empty friends. Her skin egg-yolk yellow inside the thin fabric.

"I did indeed, thank you. I feel much better now."

She makes a hollow sound at the back of her throat in place of laughter. Even up close I can gain no better view of her face, and she keeps herself a little turned from me to make sure of it. But her body leans into the table, a leg sliding forward to make contact with mine.

"You want me to dance?"

"In a minute maybe. How about we talk a little first. You live in town?"

"Not exactly. But I know *you* don't."

She moves her head so that it's now at a different

indirect angle from before, but as she does she exposes a
flash of teeth from behind the veil of hair.

"Oh, so you must know me pretty well, do you? Let's see
then. What's my name?"

She laughs, once.

"No? It's Barth."

I extend my hand to her but she doesn't take it. Instead
she pulls her feet up beneath her on the chair and rocks
back and forth distractedly to the music, which has now
changed to a heavy metal ballad from the 70s that I can't
quite place. And then over the girl's shoulder I see the older
blonde take the stage and immediately begin to squeeze her
pendent breasts together and glower at the four lumber
jackets who respond with a couple beery hoots.

"Don't you have a name?" I try again.

"Call me whatever you want."

She leans forward, close enough that her hair brushes
against my cheek, and I notice that it has no smell. That she
herself gives off no powder or perfume or sweat.

"But I know you," she whispers.

Something in her voice moves me back against the wall.
Maybe it's only that she doesn't speak like all the other
dancers with their little girl or smoky madam routines. She's
so new at this she's still using her own voice.

"So it's *that* obvious that I'm from out-of-town?"

She nods, and her hair shifts like poured honey.

"Is it the clothes? Or wait a second. You saw the story on
me in the local paper. There must have been a picture, too.
That's it, isn't it?"

She says nothing to this but rises, bending down at the
waist when she's on her feet. Once more she moves her head

in a way that briefly exposes a smile, a narrow row of too-small upper teeth.

"Going already? You haven't even danced for me yet."

She laughs again, this time cracking out so loudly I expect the whole room to have noticed, but when I glance behind her all eyes remain on the stage. The girl places her hand briefly on top of mine and sends a dull shock up my arm that holds me there, waiting for her to let me go. And when she does she leaves the idea of her touch over my skin—dry as paper, bird bones and muscle strings within—long after she withdraws. Moves to the bar, her spine a slippery semi-colon under the cheap lingerie. Says something to the barman and leaves by way of the door marked LADIES' ENTRANCE.

I finish the drink she brought in a swift gulp, pretend to watch the finale of the other blonde's routine. The lumber jackets hollering, then transfixed and silent for the moment of lowered panties, hollering again. Her body a blue-lit phantom, a photograph come to dollish life. The men watch her. Fixed to their seats, eyes held open to the small miracle of remembered desire.

Except for me. Eyes moving between my drink, the glowing bottles behind the bar, the closed door of the LADIES' ENTRANCE. Trying to recall when I'd last been with a woman. Years. Not since university, and God knows even then only rarely and without success. It's hard to discern with any precision when impotence turns from a lack of desire to incapacity. Having consulted neither shrink nor urologist in my own case, I can only guess. For me, there was never repugnance, only a flat indifference. Women could still charm and allure, but the third requisite response—the stirring mechanics deep down where it counts—was never forthcoming.

I haven't been with a woman in years because I know that I cannot. Cannot because there would be no rewards for her and I'm too old for new shames. But tonight with this girl there was something. The swift, passing shiver of physical longing. A pooling of warmth in the lower back, neck loose, toes curling up within the leather privacy of shoes. The need to reach out to another met by the discipline to sit still, everything left in an almost painful balance. For the time she sat near me I wanted only to diminish the air between us, pull her hair aside and stroke my knuckles over her face. I wanted only this, but at the same time wanted only for her to leave me and these feelings alone. For with this there came also an apprehension. Not of her exactly, but of seeing and touching more than I could bear.

Twelve

Early the next morning, inspired by six hours of semi-adequate sleep and a larger than usual nasal breakfast, I decide to drive back up to Lake St. Christopher for another look around before taking on the day's more pressing tasks. Outside, the rain comes down in silver curtains. Cold enough to draw the blood away from fingers, toes and face within a minute of stepping out the door. If it gets this bad up here at the end of September, what cruelties will December bring? I make a mental note to check out the army surplus store down the street and stock up on thermal long underwear.

Then I'm in the car, head buzzing, heat cranked, crunching onto the white-frosted stones of Fireweed Road. Rain syrups down the windshield, thinks about turning to ice before the defroster's warm breath decides the matter for it. Bringing the Lincoln to a stop in the squishing mud that has blurred the pattern of boot prints and car treads clearly visible just days ago.

But I'm not here to take the same route down to the water as before. Instead, there's a path that begins where the road ends and heads around the far side of the lake. Rain turns to mist as it bounces off the cover of pine needles and black ash boughs above. The air is quiet, and the turning leaves around me—yellow and red and an almost unbelievable gold—are uninterrupted for long stretches by any building, signpost or litter. In fact I have to walk a full twenty minutes around the far end before spotting the first cottage, a shabby clapboard box that wouldn't pass for a garden shed in certain Toronto backyards. Look in its windows expecting abandonment but instead finding definite signs of life: a loaf of bread beside a knife on the tiny kitchen's cutting board, the embers of a fire in the brick hearth, an unfinished mug of coffee holding down the sun-yellowed page of a crossword puzzle magazine. Beyond this I can see straight through and out the window at the front which takes in a view of the water and the few road-accessible cottages on the far shore.

"You make a habit of putting your nose up against other people's glass?"

An old woman's voice behind me. Not a day under eighty judging from the wrinkled erosions mapped into her skin, shoulders collapsed at her sides. There, standing at the top of the slope next to a woodpile I hadn't noticed on the way in. Her tone is disapproving, pitched up through the grinding sand in her chest. But she takes me in with a squint that softens her a little, adds a scornful humor to her face, blotched and fuzzy as a bruised peach. The accent is the same as the others up here—clipped and tight—but beneath it there is also the slight rise at the end that I've heard before in those who've grown up in Scotland, the north of Ireland or one of those damp, peaty places.

"I'm not a snoop by vocation," I answer. "But I do apologize for—"

"Names first. I'm Helen Arthurs. Widow of Duncan James Arthurs."

I wonder for a second if I'm supposed to recognize the dead husband's name, but seeing as I don't, I make no mention of it.

"I'm Bartholomew Crane. Just to explain, Mrs. Arthurs,

I was walking along this side of the lake for the purposes of an investigation of sorts—"

"Bartholomew Crane, you say?"

"Call me Barth."

Shifts a little inside her bundled layers of knit sweater, windbreaker and scarf. Then she slowly pulls the folds of her neck out of the encasement of her clothes, a turtle's head emerging from its shell.

"But tell me now, Mr. Crane, what are you really doing up here at a quarter to eight on a rainy bugger of a morning?"

"You know something? I'm not quite sure myself."

I smile up at her as charmingly as I can, hoping she'll simply stand aside and let me go. But she does nothing of the sort.

"I'm here on business."

Nothing.

"I've been hired as Thomas Tripp's defence attorney, if you'd like to know the truth."

"Oh I *always* like to know the truth, Mr. Crane." She laughs now, though her stance is unchanging. "Now, speaking of the truth, there are some things about that whole business you may not know."

"Oh yes?"

The squint returns. Puts one hand on a tree trunk next to her and the other on her hip, gives me a good looking over, lingering on the mud-caked dress shoes and loosened silk tie of black and emerald stripes.

"I'm *sure* of it," she says. "But if you ask around here you won't get much help. They all think the teacher's the one. If you ask me though, I'd say it isn't exactly so."

"That's encouraging. But you know, I really should be heading back."

Neither of us move. Odds are the old lady's clueless, her brain softened by too many years spent alone in the empty woods, or maybe just by too many years, period. But you can never be sure. There's always the possibility that she had her bird-watching binoculars on the day in question and saw something that may be of help to old Thom Tripp. Nothing for me to do but try to grease her wheels by stepping forward to rest my foot on a protruding root halfway up the incline.

"Mrs. Arthurs, it's been informative, truly, but I must—"

"Don't you want to hear?"

"Hear what?"

"What I think happened to your missing girls."

"They're not *mine*. In fact—"

"I think they're in that lake there."

She sticks the hand on her hip out in the direction of the water, but her fingers are too crooked with arthritis to indicate any point in particular and their wayward pointings take in everything before her at once.

"Well, that would seem the most likely suggestion," I say, now a little closer to her than I would like. "But the police have conducted extensive searches—scuba divers, underwater sensors and the rest. And nothing, I'm afraid."

"I didn't say they're ever going to find them."

She holds up her chin in a gesture of triumph and the loose folds of skin that enwrap her neck are drawn tight enough to show the bulging pipe of her throat.

"You beg the question, Mrs. Arthurs, so I'll ask it. How do you know that's where they are?"

"Because it weren't your man that took those young girls

away, although God knows he may have had some hand in the business somehow." She flicks her hand dismissively through the air before her. "No, it weren't him, if you ask me. It was the Lady."

"The Lady?"

"That weren't her real name, of course. It's only because nobody had a bloody clue what to call the wretched thing that we all got to speaking of her as The Lady, or The Lady in the Lake, though there's not many alive today who'd remember her as she was then."

She's setting me up. Without even an invitation inside for a cup of coffee and lump of bread she's going to go ahead with this tale of hers no matter what evasions I might attempt. And the tough old bird has got me stuck here, nodding at her to continue.

"She was barren, you see," she says now, voice lowered as though there was a risk of being overheard. "At least they *made* her barren, so she couldn't have no more."

"I'm sorry?"

"Gave her a hysteronomy or whatever they call it. But that was only salt in the wound for her, you see, because they did that *after* they made her childless. Had her little ones taken from her, on account of a mental hospital not being a fit place for a mother to bring up children. So the doctors or the government or whatever—they took her kids away, and were never seen by their blood mother again. At the time there were some who said it was the taking the kids away that made her go strange. Some others say it was the operation they went ahead and did on her. But *I* say she was damn crazy to *begin* with."

"So where is she now?"

"Oh she's of no use to you, Mr. Crane. She's been good and dead for fifty years now."

The old lady juts her chin out at the lake and I involuntarily turn, as though she's got something right there in her sights before her. But there's only the grey surface of the water, pocked by rain.

"Nobody knew what her real name was, you see, because back then all the crazy people were just put away and nobody much cared about why or where they came from. It was 1945, the war not long over and all the boys back home, and she just showed up in town one day, a bag o' bones with her hungry kids holding her hands, like they'd just come back from the war themselves. Christ knows, they probably had."

A swipe of a knuckle under her nose wipes away a dried stalactite hanging from one of her nostrils. Her face now gone pale—was always pale except for the splatter of liver spots the color of tea stains on linen.

"Now, people tried to do her a good turn at first, you understand. Got her to do housekeeping work if they could afford to pay her, but it never worked out for one reason or another. Mostly I suppose because she didn't talk proper English to nobody. And she never told a soul her name nor those of her wee ones. Like she knew and wouldn't say, or had forgotten altogether. And of course there was her *behavior* to think of too."

"Behavior?"

She peers into the rain that falls between us, pulls tight the scaffolding of lines inscribed over her forehead and empty cheeks.

"Indecency. Lived like a gypsy. Camping out in the woods here. And when they bathed, they'd just go down to the water without a stitch on and wash themselves right out there in plain sight. In the middle of the day. Starkers."

"And this—"

"Was a terrible *temptation*, of course. Word got out. Boys back from the service started coming round to watch her stand there washing herself on the rocks. And she'd turn around slow so's they all could get a good long look. She *knew* they were watching, sure as day. And so who could be surprised when our boys—some of them married men—started visiting her at night. None left disappointed, is what was said. And we couldn't let that go on in addition to everything else, could we?"

I say nothing to this, but she must take it as solemn agreement, because she draws a racking breath and continues with renewed volume. Behind her, something scuttles away through the leaves.

"Well, there wasn't anything for us to do, was there? We had those poor kids of hers to consider in the long term, you see. So we got her put away at Bishop's Hospital up the road there, which isn't a real hospital at all, it being nothing more than where the old folks with no family were put and some of the boys that came back not quite right from the war. And which would've been alright if she hadn't busted out."

The old woman coughs once and sends a pearl of spit tumbling through the air at such velocity that my ducking lunge comes a full second too late.

"'Twas the winter after she was put away that she went and escaped and she was *still* nobody, not a name under God she could go by," she goes on. "Just this poor thing with the wind ripping up her hospital gown and only the blue cotton slippers they used to give them in there on her feet. And when she fell through the ice of that lake there after she'd run away, there weren't a funeral or nothing like that, because any family she would've had around here weren't admitting to belong to her. A woman who went around for a week in a freezing cold March, cooing at the little kids from town while they were walking to and from school, trying to get them to come back with her into the woods, come for a nice walk with Mommy. For that's what she said, using the few words she could say proper. You see what she had going on in her head? But of course none of us cared a whit about that, did we? Our first concern was to protect our own children. Keep them from this creature who wanted nothing but to take them away."

"Mrs. Arthurs, I really must be getting—" I start, but a drop of rain that lands directly in my eye cuts me off and for a moment Mrs. Arthurs is washed away in tears. When they clear I see that she now struggles to hold back her own.

"There was nothing else for it," she goes on finally. "And so it was that my own Duncan along with some of the other men in town got together and went into the woods—these woods right round here—to find her out. Hunt her down. And when they came upon her they found her lying in the tree trunk she'd made as her bed, talking to herself like the madwoman she was. Well, the men had a meeting right there among themselves and decided that instead of taking her back to the hospital where she'd just get out again, they might as well go ahead and put an end to the matter."

"An end to *her*, I take it."

She glances out at the lake again, nods once as though answering a question distinct from my own.

"But she was fast. Faster than any of them expected. Chased her all the way down out of the bush and onto the ice that was breaking up under the first days of spring sun, though all the men had the sense to stop at the bank. Stood there and watched her, just like I did, for I'd heard all their whooping from up here and come down to see for myself. All of them there—the bank manager and the fellows who ran the town stores and the ones who worked the quarry—all the men of Murdoch watching her out on the middle of the ice. We could see it was cracking, the water bubbling up dark around her feet. But that wretched woman, do you know what she did? Turned round to us and gave us a look. Just gave us this long *look*, you see, and opened her arms out wide like she was bringing someone to hold to her breast. She did all that, which was terrible enough, and then she does something worse. From the black hole of her mouth she lets out an awful cry. Hateful and mournful all at once. Truth was it got to a point we were all left wishing for the ice to break through and swallow her up just to be rid of the *noise*. And then finally it did, and down she went. Just kept crying out with her mouth wide open until the water came up and flooded it closed. But the last thing we saw of her—and we all saw it, I know, despite the distance she was at—the last thing we saw was that *look*. And I can tell you now, sure as Christ, there weren't nobody who saw it who had any doubt that woman had something monstrous in her heart."

She smacks her lips closed, presses them white.

"That's quite a story, Mrs. Arthurs."

"'Tisn't a story."

I take another step and pull up my lapel to combat the cold that's now reached below my skin to the bones. Only now does the old woman move aside to let me pass.

"A question," I say when I'm standing beside her at the top of the slope, surprised to find that on even ground she's not much broader than the trees around her and little more than half my height. "Why do you believe The Lady in the Lake has anything to do with this? I mean, you have to admit, the likelihood—"

"Do you have any children of your own, Mr. Crane?"

"No, I don't."

"Ah, well then," she says and shoos me off with a wave of her hand. "*You* wouldn't know then, would you?"

"Know what, Mrs. Arthurs?"

"What a mother or father will do."

I head back into the trees, leave her to collect whatever wood she'd require to cook her dinner, to her crossword puzzle and view of the weed-choked shore. It isn't until I've found the path again that I call back to her.

"About The Lady. How many children did she have?"

"Two girls," the old woman shouts through the trees. "Isn't that a pickle?"

Thirteen

When I get back to the hotel I open the binder marked WITNESS INTERVIEWS and scribble Helen Arthurs's name at the top of the first page. She is, after all, the first person who'd spoken to me about the case, not to mention the first to provide me with an alternative theory outside of those I'd already come up with. Unfortunately for Thom Tripp, that theory involved a woman who'd been dead for over fifty years rising out of the lake and taking her victims back down with her. Not the sort of thing that meets the credibility threshold of the dimwits of a typical jury, let alone most senior members of the judiciary. Nevertheless, I end up transcribing the whole of Mrs. Arthurs's quaint rural myth in as much detail as I can recall. An hour later I've filled twelve handwritten pages, having thrown in a few supplementary details of my own for the hell of it. When I'm finished, however, I realize the morning's totally shot and I haven't yet performed a minute of useful work for my client.

The list of potential witnesses Goodwin provided me with is composed almost entirely of those who can only support the Crown's case and do no good to my own. Not surprising, given that there's only three people who can speak directly of what happened that Thursday in May: two have disappeared and the other appears to be in the process of losing his mind. So, more to avoid continuing the labored review of documentary evidence than for any other reason, I start to call some of the victims' school friends to see if I can arrange an interview.

The first four numbers yield only startled mothers explaining that their kids are in school, each of them demanding, "Who *is* this?" I take to hanging up before responding. And I'm about to give up altogether when I reach Laird Johanssen, who doesn't sound much surprised to hear from me at all.

"Taking the day off from school, Laird? All your friends are in class."

"Half days. I'm in the gifted program. Only have to show up in the mornings." Then, matter-of-factly, "And I don't *have* any friends."

We arrange to meet at the Make 'n' Bake doughnut shop near the school. A concrete and glass cube on the corner with a yellow fluorescent light inside so powerful that it glows from two full blocks away even during the day. Outside, beside the newspaper boxes and orange waste bin buzzing with wasps, a half-dozen girls pull their heads back from a whispering circle to watch my approach. Two pierced nostrils, four bleach jobs, all wearing lipstick the color of a fading bruise. I pass them and reach the door, pull back against the spring that holds it closed, and in this sluggish imbalance between inside and out I hear one of them whisper *fucking scum.*

I should turn and say something in response, and nearly do, but the door is now fully open before me and I step inside without a glance back. Still, I know they stay there and watch me squint inside against the glare of orange plastic tables and stainless steel coffee machines until I find a seat next to the hallway to the toilets. Watch me through the glass wall, whispering together a plan.

Inside, the place is crawling with other kids skipping class in order to pursue more fruitful enterprises such as smoking and constructing sentences which repeat the word "fuckin'" as often as possible. I recognize Laird immediately though, moving through them to where I sit, bringing with him his mug and honey cruller cradled in a sheet of waxed paper. I know it's him although he wears the same pea-green army jacket favored by his colleagues, his hair the same greasy medium-length disaster. But there are certain clues that give him away: oversize head, painful cluster of pimples at the top of each cheek and glasses so heavy they slide down to the edge of his nose despite the best efforts of their wearer, who stabs his middle finger at its bridge with a maddening frequency. It appears that old Laird wasn't kidding about not having any friends, for as he approaches my table he is completely unacknowledged by the other chain-smoking snifflers.

"Laird?"

"The one and only."

"Thanks for agreeing to meet," I say, and slide a five-dollar bill over the table at him. He looks at it a moment before stuffing it in the breast pocket of his jacket originally designed for carrying grenades.

"Nothing much better to do," he says.

I watch him count to four while pouring a broad stream of sugar into his coffee.

"I understand that you were in the Literary Club with Krystal and Ashley," I start, and measure a half-teaspoon of sugar into my own.

"In a way, yeah. I mean, we *were* the Literary Club. Just the three of us. And Mr. Tripp. But I never really went after the first few meetings, so it was more just them."

"Why'd you stop going?"

"I dunno. It was boring, I guess. And they were sort of into it, talking about books, the characters they liked most and all the *metaphors* and *symbols.* You know? I couldn't care less about that poetry shit."

"So why'd you join?"

"To hang out with Ashley and Krystal."

"You were friends with them?"

"I told you, man, I'm not friends with *anybody.* But they were O.K. They were a lot smarter than most, and definitely smarter than any of the other hot girls at school. But nobody was really friends with Ashley and Krystal except Ashley and Krystal, you know what I mean?"

"So they were pretty close then?"

"Like sisters, man. Better than sisters. Sisters without bitching over who took the last tampon or whatever."

I glance over Laird's shoulder and see the circle of girls still there outside the glass, guessing at my words.

"What about Tripp? Were they close with him?"

"Depends on what you mean. They'd talk to him, yeah, but that's about it. They were pretty much the only ones who *would* talk to him after he got all zombied out or whatever. But they weren't in love with the guy or anything."

"You think *he* was in love with them?"

"He thought they were pretty cool, I guess. I mean, they were the only members of his little club, which was the one thing he seemed to care about. But if you mean a *sex-love* sort of thing, I have no idea. But I wouldn't blame him if he did."

Slurps at the coffee in front of him and pours more sugar into what remains.

"Do you know if Tripp ever took them to Lake St. Christopher before the day they disappeared?"

"Doubt it."

"Why?"

"Doubt they'd want to. Everybody's scared shitless of the place, man. Especially girls."

"Why would they be scared?"

"Because they knew."

Over Laird's shoulder a kid throws a match into an ashtray piled high with crumpled napkins and in a second it's sending up high spits of flame. But the girls outside the door don't move their eyes away from where they're set.

"I'm sorry. What did they know?"

"That there was some bad shit that went on up there a long time ago—like *history*, this old babe who eats kids or something—and now there's all kinds of stories. Everybody believes at least one of them."

"Yeah? Which one do you believe?"

"I believe them all, man."

Laird smiles and it reshapes his face in a way that makes me hope he never finds anything amusing ever again.

"So, you're saying that you think Ashley and Krystal would never volunteer to go up there?"

"Not unless they were with fourteen other people all stoned on some shit that made you totally fucking fearless, I'd say no."

I look past Laird again to see the girls outside now pulling closer together, a single body blocking the way out.

"Fine. New question. Did you ever hear Ashley and Krystal talk about running away?"

"No. Not that they'd tell me."

"What about Tripp? Did he ever say anything to you about them?"

"Not really. My brother had him for English like three

years ago, and he was supposed to be really into all the great classics of literature and *teaching* and shit. But that was before. By the time we got him he was just walking around half-asleep or something. So no, I wouldn't say he was much of a conversationalist."

"Did you ever see Tripp and the girls together with someone else? When he'd drive them home after Literary Club meetings, for example. Was there ever a fourth person?"

"Not that I saw. Just those three, him up front driving and the two girls in the back. That was the way they always went. I thought maybe that's because he didn't want anyone to think he was trying anything creepy, you know. But maybe not. More likely they just wanted to sit together in the back."

Looking at me through the glass. Eyes held open and so black with mascara they appear as a line of empty sockets poured full with oil.

"You O.K., man?" Laird asks, his own eyes magnified and squinting into mine.

"Fine and dandy."

Fine and dandy?

"You just look a little—"

"It's all the smoke."

"Uh-huh."

"So. Were they popular?" I ask, forcing myself to focus on Laird alone.

"Oh yeah. Guys wanted them and girls wanted to be like them. But I don't think Ashley or Krystal gave a shit one way or the other. Still, you should've seen when they called an assembly in the gym at the beginning of term and the principal got up and told everyone that the school was undergoing a *mourning process*—man, the whole place broke down. I've never seen so much hugging and crying and snot in one place. Mostly the girls, right, all of them pretending that they were best friends with Krystal or Ashley. It even got kind of competitive."

"How do you mean?"

"Like everyone's going around with these just-add-water personal *memories*, like 'Krystal told me this big secret once' or 'Ashley said me and her would be best friends forever' and other crap like that. For the first fifteen minutes everyone was sad, and then they all had to be the *most* sad of all. It got so bad they brought in like half a dozen shrinks to calm everybody down. Guys too, and some of the teachers even. Everybody saying how much they knew Tripp was the type, saw it coming a mile away, somebody should have done something. All of it such shit."

"Thanks, Laird. I'll leave you to your doughnut."

I tuck my notepad back into my case and pull my legs out from under the table to leave but the kid raises his hand for me to wait.

"I brought this along," he says. From his backpack on the floor he pulls out a crumpled folder and lays it on the table. Then he sticks his hand in and slides the bundled contents halfway out: a collection of handwritten notes with either ASHLEY or KRYSTAL printed at the top, clippings from the school paper with the names of the girls highlighted, photographs of them talking together in front of an open classroom door or kicking a soccer ball between them at the front of two lines of other girls in lime-green gym shorts, all taken with instant, develops-before-your-eyes film.

"I thought you might want to use this."

"What is it?"

"I dunno. A collection of souvenirs, I guess. It's all about them. I started out collecting things separately, one for

Krystal and one for Ashley, but it didn't work out because they were like a team really, not individual people. You know how some girls can be like that?"

"You collected this stuff yourself just on these two?"

"*No,* man. That would be weird." He shakes his head, and the glasses slip down to the very precipice of his nose. "I keep a file on *all* the hot girls."

I push the papers back in the folder, the barren light of the doughnut shop too garish for their inspection. Or maybe it's only that I don't want the girls at the window to see me lingering here with the school nerd and flipping through his masturbatory archives.

"Can I keep it?" I ask, already tucking the folder into my bag. At the same time turning to look behind me down the hall. Yes. A back door.

"Sure, man, it's yours. I don't have any use for it any-more," Laird says, and throws the last nugget of cruller down his throat. "I mean they're both dead and shit now, right?"

Fourteen

The next night I enter sleep easily for the first time since arriving in Murdoch. Amazing really, what one evening free of the white stuff will do. Within seconds of pulling the covers up I'm off into that nearly forgotten zone of solid nothingness, all thought and image and word emptying out and I'm gone . . .

Until the tin bell of the front desk phone brings me back. One, two, three rings, the echo between each hanging in the air and then diminishing, promising it's all over, that in a moment the last trace of sound will be absorbed into the ceiling—and then another, more insistent than the one before.

I pull on the boxers, suit jacket and socks lying on the floor next to the bed and go out into the hallway where the ringing seems to come from more than one source, out from under the doors of neighboring rooms and through the air vents above and below. This time I'm definitely going to pick up. And when I'm done telling the caller which particular circle of hell to go to, I'm going to deep-six the thing out in the woods where it can make all the noise it wants and keep the slugs awake at night.

Slip down the hall to the top of the stairs, my head lowered to watch my footing in the sparse light of the wall lamps, and take the first steps down. The gaslight chandelier below dimmed to a useless flicker, dark sliding up the walls below. The air clotted shadow in my mouth.

And stop halfway down. On the step below, another's leather shoes. Stand there for the length of an entire ring and the trace of it that follows before looking up.

"We meet again."

It's the peeler from the Lord Byron Cocktail Lounge, the young one from the other night. A glimpse of smile as she turns her head to me.

"Again. Yes."

Another ring before I realize that I must look ridiculous, padding around a hotel in nothing but blazer and paisley boxers.

"I was just coming down to unhook that goddamn phone," I say, hands searching for pockets that aren't there.

"Someone must want to talk to somebody pretty bad."

"Must be."

She doesn't move.

"You stay in the hotel?" I say. "To do your work?"

"I have a room."

We stand there for the duration of another ring, then I squeeze myself flat against the banister to move past her.

"It's bad luck," she says. "Crossing on the stairs."

"I don't have much choice."

"You could go back up with me."

Then she takes my elbow and we ascend the stairs together, leaving the phone still ringing at the desk below. At the top she guides me down the hall to the opposite end from the honeymoon suite, unlocks the door to her room. Slightly smaller than mine, but the window just as tall, its pane lifted open and the night's rain blowing in.

"Your window's open," I say, but she pretends not to hear. Directs me over to the bed where, sitting on its edge, she pulls herself out of her loose cotton sweater and skirt and lies back on the rain-soaked sheets. Despite the hard bites of water against her body she remains still, legs outstretched and arms haloed around her head. Skin nubbled with a layer of sand, pale as talcum. All of it washing away to expose an emerging web of ochre veins.

It doesn't occur to me to leave. To do anything but throw my jacket off, step out of my underwear and lie next to her on the bed. But even in the few seconds it takes me to reach her the air has grown colder. The rain now spraying over the entire room, the walls, the length of our bodies.

"Shouldn't we—" I start, but her kiss cuts off my words. Her strength surprises me, and although I don't resist I know that if I tried I couldn't pull myself away from the arms that lie over my back, fingers linked together at the spine. Her limbs chiseled bone over my skin.

But something's happening.

Without her hands leaving my back or any movement of my own I'm inside her, and she slides beneath me in the growing puddle the weight of our bodies has created on the bed. Even when she rolls us both over the edge of the mattress, splashing into the half foot of water collected on the wooden floor beneath the window, I can't push her back or rise up to meet her. Raises herself at the hip and a shaft of muddy streetlight casts across the side of her head. The smile still there, jagged and glistening.

I try to shout something but when I open my mouth it fills with the water that has risen further and now washes over chest and shoulders. Stay below as long as I can and then summon the strength to come up again, but each time I try to break through the water has risen higher. The only sounds are the crash of rain and, from somewhere above, the peeler's laughter. Swallowing the water out of the air and the last ache of bubbles from my lungs and—

The phone.

I'm up. Eyes open but not taking anything in. Two sounds filling the room: a hoarse gasping and, from the floor below, the ringing of the front desk phone. Back in the honeymoon suite, in my bed alone, the windows closed against the light rain outside. A pain like a splinter of bone caught in my throat, but awake.

Pull the sheets back and slip on the paisley boxers, blazer and socks that lie together on the floor. Slip over to the door, down the hall. The only light below coming from the gaslight chandelier which leaves a small orange circle on the faded carpet.

"Could somebody pick up the goddamn phone!" I shout down, although I'm certain there's nobody there.

Let it ring another three times before I can move. Before I can pull myself down toward the orange light, telling myself there's nothing in front of me. That there's nobody there who I wouldn't have seen or heard by now.

When I reach the bottom I move around the railing and squint the phone into focus, its black rotary dial staring back at me with a startled oval for a mouth. My own mouth hanging open as well, too small to take in the sudden need for air. The phone in its circle of light shrinking as though I'm being lifted away into the empty rooms on the floors above.

Another ring that brings me back. Then my own shattered voice.

"Hel-*lo*?"

Nothing on the other end, the line violent with static.

"Listen, can I ask you something? Do you know what time it is? No? I'll tell you then. It's fucking *late*, that's what time it is, and if you—"

"*I know you.*"

A woman's voice, faint beneath the crackling interference.

"Who is this? You want me to have this traced? Because I won't hesitate—"

"*I know what you like.*"

"Yeah? Well, then you know I like *sleep*, and that you're interrupting it right now, so why don't you call up somebody else?"

"*You like them young, don't you?*"

"I'm going to go now. You hear me? So if you ever want to call here again, I suggest—"

"*Don't you? Don't you like—*"

Slam the receiver down hard enough to make the bell inside ring. But it doesn't start again. She doesn't call back.

It's only after I've hung up and am standing with both hands clinging to the edge of the front desk that I recognize the voice. The peeler from the hotel bar the other night. The one from my dream with the long hair and skin a powdered white.

Fifteen

It's four days until I venture out again, and when I do it's to visit the home of the presumably late Krystal McConnell, whose parents have consented to be interviewed by yours truly. This came as more than a little surprise. Generally speaking, the victim's family doesn't like to have anything to do with defence counsel for reasons that don't require mention. In this case, I suspected the odds would be even more acutely against me, given that Goodwin's file showed the McConnells to be high-ups in the congregation at Immaculate Conception and described in almost every news story as "community leaders." I took this to mean the kind of people who were first to set the match to books they'd wrenched from the hands of school librarians because they contained the word *damn* or scenes involving adolescent hands rising to adolescent breasts beneath angora sweaters. Further, from what I had gathered from my reading of *The Murdoch Phoenix*, Mr. McConnell was acting as spokesman for the victims, furnishing the press with tirades about the "many masks of Satan," the hellfire awaiting Tripp in the afterlife, and the despair of living under a government that showed no intention of bringing back the death penalty.

The McConnells live in a massive Tudor rip-off on the street which, judging from the other dozen monstrosities which hunker on both sides of its length, is the address of Murdoch's elite. They're not new constructions; the ridged

brickwork and Victorian gables suggest their having been
slapped together sometime in the first quarter of the century.
Perhaps then they were handsome, even majestic residences
for the few that made money on the plundering of the town's
surrounding rocks and trees. But that doesn't save them
today from the intervening decades of infrequent paint jobs,
the insurrection of gardens which have long since become
thickets, the replacement of natural wood siding with aluminum. The McConnell place has fared somewhat better than
others, its facade composed of a knobbly white stucco which,
as I pull into the driveway, looks freshly clean through the
dripping autumn colors of the front yard maple. McConnell
himself, who opens the door before I have the chance to
touch the doorbell, looks clean as well in creased navy slacks
and grey cable-knit sweater pulled over his pregnant belly.

"Mr. Crane. Come in," he says, extending his arm out
across the front hallway but failing to meet my eyes. He
makes no move to take my coat, so I'm left with no choice
but to leave it on.

"May I say first, Mr. McConnell, how sorry I am for your
loss. As strange as it may seem coming from me, I can
only—"

"Perhaps the living room is a better place for discussion."
He steps behind me, looking up and down the street before
closing the heavy front door.

McConnell's money came from fixing cars. Three service
stations now bore his name, dotted along the main north-
south highway through the county. McConnell's Auto Stops
had managed to corner what was left of the market just by
sticking around, moving in whenever one of the remaining
big name franchises went under and could be picked up for
a song. And as he leads the way to the back of the house and

bids me to take a seat in an overstuffed recliner next to a fire too large for its hearth, one can see the former mechanic in his scuffling walk, bearish shoulders, the loose shiftings of his ass. He gives the impression of being a man who, having ascended to the pinnacle of employer from the trench of employee, didn't take with him any special sympathies for those who now toil in the grease below him.

"I don't want to take up any more of your time than necessary," I begin, pulling a notepad from my case and smoothing it over my knee. "My questions, I assure you, are of a general nature only."

"Yeah? Well, I got some questions too."

He's standing with his back to me, looking out over the backyard carpeted with fallen leaves. His voice isn't angry— not yet angry—but there's a tightness in it, an effort to control its tone so that he can make the points he's listed in his head. How could I have thought that his voice over the phone suggested something else, like shyness?

"What sort of questions?"

"How about 'Why are you trying to keep the man who killed my little girl out of jail?'"

He turns now and looks at me directly for the first time. If it weren't for his standing silhouetted so hugely against the window and the heat of the blaze next to me made worse by the thick insulation of my overcoat, I could handle this better. As it is I'm suddenly woozy, an ominous tingling at the tip of my nose. My stomach barks.

"With all due respect, Mr. McConnell, my client's guilt hasn't yet been determined."

"Oh yes it has. By *me* it has. By my wife and family it sure has. By God Almighty, that man's guilt has been determined alright."

Something, either a long-distance drop of spit from McConnell's mouth or perspiration falling from my brow lands on the bridge of my nose and trickles down to where it is no longer felt. My eyes stray to the side, to the snapping yellow of the fire that blasts a nugget of wood against the wire screen every couple of seconds. On the mantel above, a half-dozen trophies with figures of athletes stuck to their tops—a female tennis player tossing up a serve, a golfer paused at the crest of his follow-through, a hockey player with his stick on the ice, ready for a pass. Photos of women's softball teams on the wall, McConnell's Auto Stops stenciled over their chests and McConnell himself standing behind the back row, his hands on the tallest players' shoulders and a gaseous smile on his lips. And all around these, portraits of his children in professional soft focus that I can't look at directly. A glimpse of tortoise-shell frames. Braces, white blonde braids.

"Maybe this wasn't right," I say, turning back to McConnell with considerable effort.

"No, no. It *was* right. I'm *glad* you're here." He takes a step toward the chair nearest him and rests a hand on its back but makes no further motion to sit. "Now you said you had some questions. Ask away, Mr. Crane."

"Well, maybe now isn't—there's no need really."

"No *need?* Wrong!" He makes a game show buzzer sound in his throat. "I think there *is* a need."

Standing there above me in the deathly heat of the living room of what would have once been described by bell-bottomed real estate agents as an "executive home," fixed by the size of his bones and his rage, it strikes me how *married* McConnell looks. Neither happily nor unhappily, henpecked nor contented. Simply married in the sense of a man who could not possibly be anything else, one who assumed the obligations and privileges of matrimony as they came to him without imagining how anything could be otherwise. Though there may well be none of what would generally qualify as love in his heart, he would undoubtedly be considered a good husband by all.

"Alright, O.K." I struggle, seeing as he is prepared to wait forever for me to speak. "For example, I was wondering how well you knew your daughter's friend, Ashley Flynn. I mean, were you aware of the kind of friendship they had, the things they did?"

"They were *girls*. Kids who hung out with each other. Now if you're asking me if I ever sat down with Krystal and Ashley and had a long heart-to-heart with them about the nature of the universe, no. Maybe I should've. Maybe I should've told them to watch out for perverted teachers who want to take them for drives. But I never did. Why did I need to? This was a good town. They were good kids." He pauses, bends a little at the knees allowing more light to fall across me where I sit. "Are you saying they *weren't* good kids?"

"Of course not. I'm not saying anything. I guess all I'm asking is if you were aware of any reason they had which might—if you knew of any problems either of them may have had."

"Problems?"

His face, which must normally have appeared as a generous platter of ruddy skin and heavy-lidded eyes, has gone from red to the same dusty grey as the clouds outside the window behind him.

"Just the usual things," I say. "Did they have any difficulties at school? Any attempts at running away from home? You know what I mean?"

"No I *don't*, frankly. What would they have to run away

from? I can't speak for the Flynn girl—for *Ashley*—but my Krystal had a good home right here. A home her daddy worked hard for every day of that girl's life."

He pauses now, and in the same moment a robin thuds into the sliding glass door behind him, falls to the patio and makes its way under the gas barbecue where it flaps its wings uselessly against a garden gnome. But McConnell doesn't turn, appears not to have heard a thing.

"Let me tell you something about my daughter, Mr. Crane," he continues, voice lowered. "My wife and I were blessed with four children, Krystal was our youngest. We raised her in this house. She watched TV in this room, talked to her friends on the phone sitting in the chair you're sitting in right now. If we ever had a question, we prayed to God for guidance and He provided it."

He rises now and casts a shadow over me once more.

"Problems? The only problem she ever had was Thom Tripp. And the only person I can blame is myself. Because I knew there was something wrong about the way the three of them got together every week, a grown man and two girls. What did he call it? *The Literary Club.* No way, I never liked the sound of that, and I told Krystal so. Told her I didn't like her spending so much time with that weirdo, coming around to the garage sometimes in that Swede car of his for a wash or a fill-up, looking out through the windshield with a dead man's face. But oh no, she told me it was fine, nothing to worry about. It's *creative.* So I let her go, and that was my mistake. But I'm not a man who makes the same mistake twice, Mr. Crane."

I'm surprised by the sudden force of a single, choking cough, and have to lean forward to swallow back the resulting acidic lump gathered in my throat. Definitely time to go. But my legs are tingling stumps and I've sunk too low in the chair to lift myself out. My mouth is still working though, throwing out things before I can recognize what they are.

"What are you saying, Mr. McConnell? It sounds like—"

"A threat? Well, that's for lawyers like you to decide, isn't it?"

His body stiffens now, a towering statue that swells with his next clenched words.

"But let me tell you exactly what I *am* saying. No matter what you do in that courtroom, your client is going to hell. God knows he's taken my little girl from me, taken her away from her place in our house. No sir, I promise you that man is damned to hell."

He takes in a shuddering breath, though not from fighting back tears, but from the discipline required in restraining himself from taking two steps across the deep pile of the room's carpet and pounding a fist into my face.

"I'm sorry, Mr. McConnell," I find myself saying, "but I think I should leave now."

I lift the notepad from my lap and try to stick it back into my case but everything is spiraling away and I end up dropping both notepad and pen on the floor.

"No, no, *no*. Don't go just yet," McConnell says. "You came here to ask your questions, and I want you to ask them. We have nothing to hide in this house. Unlike yours."

"Is Mrs. McConnell available?"

I don't know why I ask this. Maybe to have him go summon her so I can make a dash for the door.

"Available? No, I'm afraid she's on medication from her doctor that doesn't allow her to answer questions from sick lawyers. See, Mr. Crane—" he takes a step forward and then back again, as though without the aid of the chair he clings to he would lose his balance entirely "—this house has been visited by evil. And while I don't know why, I *do* know who the deliveryman is."

He licks his lips clear of bubbled spit, lifts his free hand and waggles a thick index finger at my face.

"I give you my solemn word. If you manage to get Tripp off, I'll kill him myself."

He releases his grip on the chair so that he can now hold both hands out before him, two fists clenched a perfect, bloodless white. But what he says next is a whisper through the airless heat.

"Hear me now? I'll snap his neck, cut him wide open and stick his dirty heart down his throat. Understand?"

From over his shoulder the robin flaps into the air and throws itself over the neighbor's fence.

"I understand," I say and manage to rise, gulping hard to keep down the hot churnings of my stomach. I also manage to stick the pad and paper in my bag and take a step toward the front hallway without passing out. Moving fast, but McConnell easily catches up behind me and speaks at what sounds like inches from my ear.

"That's a sin, I know, to kill. But I'm only human. And God would forgive a man for bringing an end to evil, don't you think?"

I make it down the impossible length of the tiled front hallway to the door and pull it open. But before I'm out he puts his hand on my shoulder and the strength of his grip causes the muscles there to seize in startled pain. Around us the house uttering a thousand crunches and squeaks, shifting to accommodate McConnell's movement.

"You want to know something?" he says. "You must be a very sick man yourself, to do what you're doing."

Something in his lowered voice and desperate grip makes me certain that his wife is listening. Has been listening all along. Sitting at the top of the stairs in her housecoat, the tranquilizers deadening her ears just enough to prevent them from catching her husband's whisper.

"You don't know me," I say, releasing myself and stepping unsteadily out onto the straw welcome mat.

"No, I don't. But Christ does," he says before gently closing the door. "Christ knows you very well, Mr. Crane."

Sixteen

The papers on my desk are reproducing. The case law briefs mating with the witness statements, the cross-examination binder having it off with the Post-It notes. Every time I return from the bathroom or a sandwich run there's a new litter of bewildered 8½ × 11s blinking up at me. Nothing I can do about it but turn my eyes from their hungry faces, venture out into daylight once more for another interview. Today's visit offers about as much promise as the one with McConnell: my own client, Thom Tripp.

Outside, the morning's rain has picked up from a despondent drizzle to a straight and windless assault, heavy drops of cold gathering speed over miles of sky and exploding on my shoulders, pant legs, the crown of my head. I make a mental addition to my shopping list to go along with the thermal undies: heavy-duty umbrella. Too late for this morning though, and by the time I splash up the front steps to the Murdoch Prison for Men I'm totally soaked, the rain finding its way into places where rain is usually forbidden such as the inside of my shirt, my shoes and the crack of my ass. As I approach the reception desk and see the same mischievous guard as before grinning at me I'm uncomfortably aware of my buttocks squishing and slipping against each other like mating seals.

"Good morn', Mr. Crane. A wet one, isn't it?"

"Wet? You could say wet."

"Here to see Mr. Tripp?"

"Would there be another reason?"

"No, no." He pretends to consider, bringing a thoughtful finger to his razor-burned chin. "I suppose there wouldn't be, no."

I'm taken again to Interview Room No. 1, and again the leprechaun tells me to make myself comfortable. It isn't easy, given that I'm once more forced to wait for what I suspect is an intentionally long time, shivering in a drenched suit better designed for striking a nicely cut shape before judges or ordering drinks at mahogany bars than keeping moisture away from the skin. By the time Tripp is produced the room's institutional coolness has buried itself deep in the bones and I have to swivel my jaw loose before speaking.

"I'm sorry I haven't come to see you sooner, Mr. Tripp— *Thomas*—but I've really been diving into things and I just haven't had a second."

He doesn't respond, but sits down in the chair across the table from me without having to be coaxed.

"How have you been? Are you being treated satisfactorily?" I ask, testing to see if his verbal skills are on-line.

"I'm fed. I walk around an empty gymnasium forty-five minutes a day. I have two-year-old magazines brought to where I sleep. I'd say I'm treated very well."

"Well, that's good. Do you have any other concerns then, anything at all, before we continue?"

He says nothing, but pushes his breath through a slight opening in his lips that whistles out in either resignation or boredom. His eyelids lower a notch at the same time, and I decide to plunge ahead before I lose him altogether.

"I wanted to go through some things with you now, Thomas, some fairly specific things relating to the Crown's evidence. I should tell you right off that so far it all looks quite encouraging. They've got no eyewitnesses, aside from some teachers who saw you and the girls walking to your car after school sometimes, and we're not denying that anyway, are we? But there are still some circumstantial bits and pieces that I'd like to be able to explain away. For instance, the muddy pants in your laundry hamper and the mud on your shoes. Is there any way that could have happened aside from walking through the woods at Lake St. Christopher?"

Tripp drops his elbows on the table and slides them forward as though to form a pillow on which to settle for a nap. But he doesn't go that far, and instead his head hangs unsteadily over his outstretched arms.

"They were dirty so I put them in the laundry," he says.

"Of course. But can you think of a way they might have *gotten* dirty?"

"I took them off to get into bed, saw they were covered in mud, and threw them in the hamper. That's the first time I noticed."

"Fine, fine. You don't remember how the mud got there. The next thing I need to ask you about though are the pictures you kept in your bedroom."

"Pictures?"

"The catalog pages of female models. Teenagers. On your wall. Remember?"

"Uh-hmm."

"Could you explain them for me?"

"I liked them there."

"Why's that?"

Tripp's nose wrinkles itself up nearly half an inch as though in preparation for a sneeze or in a show of repugnance for having picked up a sudden bad smell. But I can't smell anything except the sourness of my wet wool suit, and in the end Tripp doesn't sneeze either, his nostrils descending once more to pull in a long, shaking breath.

"They just *stayed* there."

"Stayed for you to look at?"

"They couldn't go anywhere, could they?"

His head moves another inch closer to the table.

"Mr. Tripp, please. What I'm asking for here are specific responses to pieces of evidence that the Crown intends to advance. Understand? So if they say you had pictures of girls modeling underwear on your bedroom wall for *bad* reasons, we want to say they were there for *normal*, or at least, *not so bad* reasons. Now, may I make a suggestion here? Maybe you had those pictures because you lost your daughter in a custody fight with your ex-wife a few years ago, and you missed Melissa so much you put images of other little girls up there to ease your pain. How about that?"

"Melissa?"

"Your daughter. Were you thinking of her when you ripped those pages out of the catalog?"

"No. I don't know. I wasn't thinking. Just that if I put them there, they would *stay*. Because where could they go?"

Take a deep breath, plow on.

"One more question we need to cover, and this is probably the most important. It's about the bloodstains in the backseat of your car. The police found a few spots on the upholstery, and they've sent traces of them off to the lab along with some blonde and dark hair found there as well to see if any of them match. Now, even if they do, all that it shows is that one or both of them were in the back of your car, and that they lost some blood there at some point. It's not conclusive, but you can see how that wouldn't be so good.

So let me ask you: do you remember how those bloodstains got there?"

His head is turned away to where it drifted in the middle of my explanation, less from distraction than real puzzlement. The normally tight crease of his mouth is opened up and he chews at his lips with yellowed canines. I give him time. Perhaps these are signs of a struggle toward considered thought, and I'd be a fool to interrupt.

"You didn't mention the shirt," he says finally, keeping his head turned away.

"What shirt?"

"Didn't they find it?"

"Find what? The shirt? I'm not aware of any shirt."

"It's just funny they didn't . . . they had a search warrant . . ."

"Mr. Tripp, what *shirt* are you referring to?"

"*My* shirt. The one in the freezer. If they'd just asked I would've shown them, but they never asked. 'Thom, is there anything else here you could show us?' If they'd said that, I would've taken them to the garage out back, opened up the freezer and handed it to them. But they never did."

He laughs gently in disbelief. The kind of laugh one hears in coffee shops and post office lineups from people telling stories of foolish politicians or incompetent bosses. It's the most normal sound I've heard from him yet.

"So your shirt's in the freezer, and the police didn't find it in their search. O.K. But why did you put your shirt in the freezer in the first place?"

"Because it had *blood* all over it!"

With this Tripp lets out a roar, pulls his arms off the table and brings them down upon it again. Big-time laughter, muscular and fierce as a shouted threat. The tears that now trickle down his cheeks the sufferings of a perverse humor, not signs of whatever else he suffers from.

"Thomas, listen to me now. Whose blood was it?"

"It wasn't *mine*."

"No? Then whose?"

He comes in close, leans across the table far enough that I can smell his yeasty breath.

"Krystal's. It was Krystal's blood," he says. "Do you want to know how it got there?"

"First things first. Where's the shirt now?"

"It's funny, actually."

"Thomas, tell me exactly where the shirt is. I'm serious. Right now."

I check my watch.

"Locked inside the freezer, down in the garage out behind the building. They must have thought it belonged to the neighbors or something."

"Where's the key?"

"Which key?"

"To the freezer."

"Inside the flour jar in the cupboard. But the apartment's locked, and I don't know where *that* key is."

"Not to worry. But listen carefully now: I advise you, *strongly* advise you, Thomas, to keep quiet about this, alright?"

His eyes endure a spasm of repeated blinks and his lips fold together and disappear into his mouth but he says nothing more. I have no choice but to take this as confirmation of his word.

I get up and knock on the door, concentrate on keeping my breath even. But the guard takes longer than he should, and before I get out of there I hear Tripp's voice over my shoulder. Words I have to turn and have him twice repeat before I catch them.

"Melissa is my daughter's name," he says.

As I leave I glance back and see him being brought to his feet by the two men who will return him to his cell, his head shaking in wonder and a trembling smile of pride on his lips.

Late that night I go for a walk by Tripp's apartment. The convenience store below is dark, which I expected, the hours of business stuck on its door stating that it closes at eleven. The apartment above is dark as well. In fact the only light the building emits comes from the reflective band of yellow police tape that crosses the doorway to the staircase up to Tripp's. No car, homecoming drunk or nocturnal dog walker has passed by since I've been here, which must be something close to half an hour.

I head up the lane that runs between the convenience store and the house next to it, to where the garage is. Sticking my face up to its window I find the freezer, a lunar glow reflecting off its white enamel surface.

From there I pass through the side lane once more and around to the door up to Tripp's, ripping the police line off and sticking it into the pocket of my overcoat. Then I set to work on the lock. Although I've never done this sort of thing before, I've had the benefit of defending enough car thieves, b&e artists and other unofficial locksmiths that I've acquired a pretty good idea of the techniques through osmosis. And as it turns out, this one isn't much of a challenge anyway. An old handle lock with a gaping keyhole that, after sticking my nosehair tweezers in and fiddling around for a couple minutes, clicks open without any trouble. Then up the stairs to Tripp's door, tweezers again at the ready, but there's no need. The fools left it open, and with a quick turn of my gloved hand I'm in.

Tripp was right about the key: buried in a mason jar of enriched-white above the stove. But I don't leave yet. Move around the corner and into the living room, lit only by the orange fog that seeps through the window from the street-light outside. Everything neat and tidy, teacherly even: the bookshelves organized according to binding (one wall of hardcovers, the next coffee table books buttressing stacks of alphabetized paperbacks), the 14″ TV topped by old greeting cards ("Lordy! Lordy! Look Who's Forty!"), the beige furni-ture arranged in a careful square on the perimeter of the matching beige rug. I'm expecting pictures of the daughter everywhere but there's no sign of her. The room little more than a low-budget stage set of a room, a bachelor pad before the bachelor has moved in.

But the bedroom's a different story. The police have left the catalog pages on the wall, every inch plastered with the crinkled gloss of giggling, pointing, hand-holding girls. On the bed, a fresh pile of clippings and stacks of *YM* and *Seventeen*. Waving arms about for balance on roller blades, applying cucumber slices to closed eyes, kissing a clear-skinned boy as parents peep out at them approvingly through living room curtains. The discarded covers: "Love Quiz: Is He Ever Going To Treat You Right?" set on the pillow next to "No More Bad Hair Days!" From every corner comes the same sour odor that Tripp breathed at me across the interview room table, the hot gust of his insides. Some-where behind me the electric baseboard heater ticks and rages.

I hold my breath and back out, pull the door shut behind me, breathe again. Down the stairs, I pull out the police line I'd ripped off on the way in. Tack it back to the door frame using the back of a hardcover *Criminal Code* I'd brought along for a hammer, then around again to the garage.

More lock luck there, or at least further evidence of the local constabulary's stupidity, for while the main door for the admission of cars is locked, the side door for the admission of humans isn't even properly closed, let alone bolted shut. Once in I pause for my eyes to gather enough light so I can shuffle over to the freezer. Trying to stick the fussy little key into its fussy little lock in the semi-darkness results in a pounding chest pain so great it can only be the final precursor to a full-blown coronary. Then, with my hand shaking in widening loops, the key suddenly slides in buttery smooth as though toying with me from the beginning, and the garage's silence is broken by the crypt-like squeak of the freezer's lid as I heave it open. For a moment my eyes are blinded from the light of the internal bulb reflecting off the crusted ice within. Then I see it, lying in a bundle next to a stack of frozen T-bones and tub of rainbow sherbet: a blue-striped button-down with a dozen dime-size stains over the arm and shoulder. I was expecting something more explicitly horrible, splashes of gory crimson on perfect white cotton or a clear plastic bag clotted by telltale pools and smudges. But it's just a shirt with spots on it.

I pull it out and tuck it inside my coat. Then I'm out the door, down the lane and back in front of Tripp's building, half expecting the street to be clogged with police cruisers, curious neighbors and snuffling search dogs. But there's not a soul but me. One arm across my chest holding Tripp's shirt in place, I walk back to The Empire Hotel with long strides, wondering whether anyone who looked my way would see a man who'd just done something wrong, or one whose head was lowered only to shield his eyes from the rain.

S e v e n t e e n

Someone slips a note under my door. Standing in the middle of the honeymoon suite, my body still dripping from the shower and in it comes, a flash of white traveling across the floor. The shadow of another's hand playing across the light from the other side, the brief, awkward flight of the paper—all a too-easy betrayal of walls, locks and doors.

After waiting for the sound of the messenger's footsteps to recede back down the stairs I squint over the note's childish print, made less readable by the almost dried-out purple marker used in its execution:

> Dear B. Crane, "Honey. Suite":
> Brian Flynn on phone. Says "Sorry didn't call back sooner."
> Says "Can meet today." He lives at 212 Grange.
> He says "10:30 a.m. would be good."
> THE MANAGEMENT.

Brian Flynn. Ashley's father, with whom I spoke briefly at the same time I contacted McConnell, telling him how I'd like to get together at his leisure to ask a few questions. He said he'd get back to me later. And now he wants to meet this very morning. All *The Murdoch Phoenix* had to say about him was that he was a single father, laid off from the nickel mine several years back. He seemed to actively avoid the media throughout the investigation, regularly failing to

attend press conferences during the search and, later, choosing to leave the histrionics to McConnell. So why does he
want to talk to me now? Had McConnell convinced him that
this would be a good opportunity to vent on the next best
thing to the bad guy himself? Or was it another trap, the big
man standing before the window over at Flynn's right now,
poring over a leatherbound Bible, cooking up new hexes for
round two? No matter what the plan is, I'm obliged to go. All
for the potential benefit of my boy Thommy T.

But before I reach the door I notice something I'd
already forgotten: Tripp's bloodied shirt on the floor where
it was dropped the night before. The sight of it lying there
next to my own dropped shirts, pants and cotton miscellany
causes me to stop, my eyes pondering its shape as though a
complex piece of sculpture. But it's not. In fact there's
nothing to it at all. A polyester–cotton blend nearly a decade
past the fashion even if cleaned and pressed, but in its
present condition nothing more than a stained and crumpled
rag. If I just look at it there beside my own shirts, as a shirt
among shirts, the distinction between them blurs and fades.

So what message could this particular shirt carry all on
its own? That I'm now obstructing justice, that's clear. Clear,
but unknown to any but myself. And as for Tripp? So little
blood, really. Would it have meant all that much when the
police discovered it, as they surely would have when some
bright spark finally got it in his head to find out who owned
the freezer and crowbar the thing open? It wouldn't mean
the end of the game, but it would've been an unhelpful turn
of events, to employ an understatement. Tripp would be
forced to testify in order to explain the blood away, and even
if we could devise something good on that count, God knows
what further self-incriminations might escape his mouth on

cross-examination. That's the real issue, or at least as real as any other.

I pick the shirt up, stick it in the plastic bag it came in along with the wrappers from yesterday's lunch and skip downstairs, out onto the street. Pop open the trunk of the Lincoln and toss it in.

Here's a distinction drawn after extended time spent in the company of liars, pushers and thieves: What's far more amazing than how easily one can come to do wrongful things is the ease with which one can then go on to forget about them.

Brian Flynn lives in the kind of house that is only nominally a house, there being no other word in English usage to describe such a structure ("shack" or "shed" not being quite right either). It's the sort of lopsided affair one sees in towns like this, their occurrence tending to increase for every mile north one travels: square-faced facade with a door in the center and two small windows on either side encased in plastic to help keep out a greater portion of the winter's cold, a sparsely shingled roof supported by walls of equal parts wood and tar. A forgotten place, or a place that should have been forgotten long ago, being originally constructed as a short-term residence for contracted laborers with the view that, when the contracts expired, it would be abandoned and eventually razed. But here it is. Forty years past its due, a wavering plume of woodsmoke rising from its tin chimney and a mailbox stenciled THE FLYNNS at the gate.

I park directly out front, consider for a moment keeping the engine running in case McConnell awaits inside and I need to make a swift retreat, but decide against it. Flynn lives at the end of a street made up of "homes" like his own, many with motorcycles and despondent beer guts topped by vacant faces squinting out from the front stoop. In such neighborhoods, leaving a rented Lincoln Continental on the street with the engine running may be unwise. So instead I pocket the keys, knock twice on the door's splintered surface and ready myself for an immediate attack. But when the door is scraped open it's not by a towering threat but by a small man with shaggy black hair and a shapeless beard beginning to yield to outcroppings of grey.

"Mr. Crane?" he asks, his eyes closed as though unused to even the dull light of a day such as this.

"Thank you for returning my call, Mr. Flynn."

"Wasn't going to at first, but then I thought, 'Why not? It's not like you're Mr. Busy these days,'" he says, throws a dry laugh out into the street. "So I guess you might as well come in."

He steps back and I squeeze in through the narrow space afforded by the front door which the frame's leaning angle opens only partway. Inside the house is cramped, dark (the sun unable to penetrate the rain-streaked plastic over the windows), bookless, but warm. There's also a smell of burnt coffee, canned tomato soup and cigarettes which, taken together, isn't as unpleasant as the individual components suggest.

"I have to tell you, I was a little concerned about coming over here today," I say, standing on the bubbled square of linoleum that counts for the full extent of the front hall. "I thought that Mr. McConnell may have been here with you."

"Lloyd? Never spoken to the man in my life," Flynn states flatly, now standing in the middle of the living room in a plaid shirt and Montreal Canadiens pajama bottoms.

"Never?"

"Well, no, not never. Called here a couple times last year when Ashley and Krystal were hanging out a lot, saying he didn't think it was a good idea for my girl to be spending so much time with his. When I asked him why he thought so he'd just say, 'C'mon now, Brian,' over and over, like I should know without his saying. And he was right, I guess. I did know."

"I don't understand."

"Because he's got money and I don't."

Flynn's arms twitch at his sides like snakes held by their ends.

"But I thought none of that would've mattered after the girls went missing," he continues, "so I left a couple of messages with him at the time. He never called back. Still, you've got to give the man the benefit of the doubt, right? Considering all he's been through."

"Benefit of the doubt. Quite right."

I take off my coat and hang it over my arm. Flynn doesn't move. For a moment it seems this may be it, the interview's over, he's frozen to his spot on the threadbare shag forever. But when he responds to what I say next it's with a disarming gentleness.

"Mr. Flynn, may I say at the outset how sorry I am about your daughter."

"Oh yeah? Well, thanks for saying so. It's funny, but not many people have. They *look* at you alright, sometimes with sad faces and other times just curious. But usually they don't say anything. They've probably done all their talking to Lloyd, and they figure there's not much point in giving their sympathies twice."

He takes the coat from my arm as he speaks and places it over the end of the room's fake leather couch with black hockey tape over the holes where the stuffing has begun to escape. When he's finished speaking he lowers himself into a brown La-Z-Boy with a foldout leg rest. To his right, a side table equipped with a giant ashtray with Pope John Paul II's face painted in its basin and the remote control to the TV, an old set with a cabinet made of molded plastic shaped like a baroque wood carving. He signals for me to sit on the couch, and I do.

"Not much, is it?" he asks, and while I know he means the extent of his worldly possessions, I shake my head and pretend not to follow. "My humble home. Ain't much. But it's amazing how you get by. No job for six years now. The breathing's not so good these days." He bangs his chest by way of illustration, and in fact it *doesn't* sound so good, a rattle inside him like an empty can kicked down an alley. "God knows what sort of nastiness got in the lungs all that time underground, but they're sure as hell not good for much anymore. Then again, I don't know if I've missed much. Don't get a speck of mail but whatever the government sends me. But like I said, it's amazing how you get by."

Flynn smiles absently, reaches into his shirt pocket, pulls out a cigarette and lights it without looking at his hands.

"Must have been hard. Bringing up a child all on your own," I say, realizing I've left my bag with my notepad in it by the door, but I stay where I am.

"Well, she wasn't a child long. And she was never a problem. Never, not from day one. I can't say I was much of a father. I'm not taking any credit for myself, no sir. She was just a sweet kid somehow all on her own."

He exhales a shaft of smoke from the hole in his mouth where his two front teeth used to be. Again without looking, digs his hand back into his shirt pocket and extends the pack to me. Under normal circumstances I'm not a smoker (not for health concerns, but a mortal fear of yellowing teeth and the acceleration of wrinkles) but I take one from Flynn now along with his lighter and give him a nod in thanks.

"You know how fathers always say their daughter's just the spitting image of their mothers?" he asks me. "Well, with Ashley, it really was the truth. The very spitting image. Would you like to see for yourself?"

"Why not?"

With this Flynn lunges out of his chair, leaves the room for a moment and returns with a white binder with *Your Wedding* scripted in flaky gold on the cover.

"I stuck all the wedding photos in the closet and put pictures of Ashley in instead," he explains, giving me a look that suggests certain things are too messy and happened too long ago to be worth going into the details. Then he opens the album up near the middle and shows me a picture of his daughter wearing a pink tutu, dark hair tied in a single braid, arms held up in a circle around her head. It was taken in this room, in the place where Flynn now sits, the only difference being that behind the girl stands a stubby artificial Christmas tree sparsely entangled in tinsel.

"That's Ashley," he says, pushing the picture closer so that I have to stick my cigarette between my lips and move to the other end of the couch to take half the album on my knee.

"She's eleven there. Always wanted to be a ballet dancer. Never knew where she got the idea, but from as soon as she could talk that's all she wanted. Well, what could I do? There was no classes for that sort of thing up here, and even if there was I couldn't have afforded—well, there *weren't* any ballet classes. But I got her that tutu there anyway, secondhand.

And my God, didn't she wear that thing every minute she could! Come home from school and on it went. And on she'd go, spinning and kicking around the place 'til dinner and then up round and round again 'til bed. Had to move all the furniture over against the walls to give her room! I thought my neck was going to snap off from the angle I had to watch the TV at. Not that I minded. No. Of course I didn't mind at all."

He turns now to the album's back page and puts his finger on the face of a woman in her early twenties with small but clever eyes and a slightly fierce smile broadening her mouth.

"That's her mom," he says.

"I see what you mean. Very similar indeed. But I must say, there's definitely some of your genes in Ashley as well, Mr. Flynn."

"Really?" He pulls the album back to his own knee and takes a close look. "Which part?"

"The eyes," I half lie, for though both the girl's and her father's eyes were blue, hers were liquid circles and his twinkly slits. "I believe she had your eyes."

"You think?" He sits back, pleased. "Maybe she did, y'know? Maybe she did take something from the old man."

For a time neither of us speaks, just smoke, and after I stub my cigarette out on the Pope's forehead Flynn sticks the pack out at me and again I pull one out. It occurs to me that perhaps I should take the lead here, direct him to some area of inquiry that may be of use. But the truth is I've forgotten what these areas are.

"The police came to talk to me soon after the girls disappeared," Flynn starts again, "and at first I thought they were just being supportive or something, giving me plenty of

'We're very sorry' and 'We're just coming by to get the details straight here, Brian.' Then I realized they thought I might have been the one. That they were coming around so much and asking questions because they wanted to see if I'd slip up. And why not? Strange guy, unemployed, lives alone, nobody seems to know him. Isn't that the sort of person who does these kinds of things?"

He takes an aggressive pull from his cigarette and looks up at me.

"Isn't that why you're here?" he exhales. "To see if you can pin it on me so you can save your guy?"

"I would if I could. But the police had nothing on you, and so far neither do I."

"And you're just here to see if you could dig something up. Well, I guess that's what you're paid for, right? I guess Tripp deserves his rights and all that. And you're the man who's been given the job, so it's no fault of yours. Let me tell you something."

In one fluid movement he scrunches his current butt out and lights another, sticks his free hand into the wiry scrub of his beard.

"I used to work in a mine outside of town until management figured we'd dug too deep, it was too expensive to go deeper when you could just dig another hole someplace else, so they closed us down. Was out of work nearly two years. And then the men at another mine up the road a couple hours went on strike—saying it wasn't safe and they were trying to get the owner to do something before somebody got killed. But when a bunch of their management guys came to town advertising for temporary workers, I went. And I knew what it meant. I was a strike breaker, a scab, whatever. All those men on the picket line had their own kids and bank loans and the rest. They needed to work. And me and the others that went up there, we just walked through their pickets to do their work for them, and nobody laughing but the owner."

He runs his tongue over lips so dry they've lost their color, pulls on his nose between forefinger and thumb.

"But you know what the bugger of it all is, Mr. Crane? I'd do it again. Because I had my own little girl, my own bills to pay. I had my *family* to take care of, y'see? And while I knew that what I was doing was taking money from those men and bringing that mine closer to shutting down once and for all—while I knew all that, none of it meant a thing. Because it was a job, and I had to take it. Just like you. You've got your job, and nobody's going to like you for doing it—*I* don't like you for doing it—but you've got to. Besides, there's nothing you or the judge or McConnell or Tripp can do about it. Or me. Nobody can bring her back."

Flynn sits back in his chair now and looks about him as though there were others in the room who until now he'd been ignoring. Finding it's still only the two of us, he rests his eyes on his mud-caked shoes and moves them back and forth, confirming that the feet within belong to him.

"I'm sorry, I've been going on so much I haven't let you ask a single thing," he says after a time.

"Not to worry." Take another puff. "Well, let's see. I guess I'm mostly wondering about alternative explanations."

"Oh yeah?"

"For example, do you think it's at all possible that Ashley ran away from home? Took off someplace with Krystal and the two of them just haven't called home yet?"

Flynn's shoulders fall away from his neck. "You mean, do I think she's alive?"

"Someplace else."

"No, sir, I don't."

"You sound fairly certain."

"That's because I am."

"You mean, you don't believe Ashley to be the type to run away from home? As far as you're aware, she was happy?"

"I'm not saying she was happy. I'm not saying she wasn't. I'm telling you, I know she's dead."

"Mr. Flynn—may I call you Brian? I'm not trying to tell you about your own life, but it couldn't have been easy bringing a teenaged girl up all on your own. Maybe there was boy trouble. Maybe she went off to have a little adventure and got carried away. Nobody could blame you for that. I'm just asking if you would admit that it's possible."

He twists what's left of his cigarette into the ashtray and sits forward.

"I'm going to tell you something now that you can take as fact. With me and Ashley, all we had is each other. That's it. If she were alive today, I'd know about it by now. She wouldn't leave me here alone unless it wasn't her choice."

With this Flynn jerks back and circles his hands over his hips, feeling the pockets for the lighter. Eyes returned to his shoes.

"I'm sorry, Mr. Flynn. But would you mind if I used your bathroom?"

"Left at the end of the hall," he says without looking up.

I move around him past a narrow kitchenette to a stunted hallway of four open doors: linen closet, bathroom, Flynn's shadowed bedroom and, directly across from it, a tidy off-white square containing a single bed. Ashley's room. I step inside and the first thing I notice is the smell, somehow entirely distinct from the rest of the house despite the open door. Fabric softener, one of those sporty, unisex colognes, and somewhere beneath them the faint traces of gym sock. But nothing out of place now, the navy-striped comforter smoothed carefully over the bed. I glance across the hall into Flynn's room—peaked ranges of laundry, an unglued Pamela Anderson poster folding over itself on the wall beside the bed, the vague corona of sunlight at the edges of tightly drawn curtains—and recognize that it wasn't Ashley who kept her room this way but her father. After she'd gone. Somehow it's obvious that this is where he's spent a number of his subsequent afternoons, picking up the randomly dropped clothes and folding them back into the drawers, washing the sheets and vacuuming the carpet as though in anticipation of an exacting guest. On the walls, the boy TV stars she'd likely grown out of but hadn't got around to taking down, a single framed watercolor of a twirling ballerina on a solid blue background, dancing in space, in sky. The top of the dresser dense with photographs slid into clear plastic sleeves. Postcards—Niagara Falls, Maple Leaf Gardens, the Peterborough Lift Locks—wedged around an oval vanity mirror. All of it as it was before but now pondered over, dusted and straightened. The kind of room you peek into on guided tours of historic homes, fixed and untouchable on the other side of a red velvet rope.

Move closer to the dresser, my nose probing through the valleys of photos. Ashley glum in her Confirmation dress, taking a vicious whack at a leaping field hockey ball, standing beside her father on a beach of stones the size of dinosaur eggs. None of her mother. I guess her to be the sender of the postcards although I don't check to see.

Then my fingers find a single loose photograph tilted against the bottom of the mirror, pick it up to hold close before my eyes. Ashley and Krystal standing side by side in white lace dresses with blue ribbons. Standing in front of a leaf-dappled forest, hands held. Their faces not quite grim but kept willfully straight like actresses posing for a period portrait.

It's the only thing I've touched but somehow I can't put it back. Instead I'm sliding it into the inside pocket of my jacket, stepping out of the room and remembering to leave the door open as I'd found it. Leaning into the bathroom to flush the toilet, lowering then raising my fly before returning to the living room and landing on the sofa with a relieved sigh.

"Better?" Flynn asks, a new cigarette worked into an orange rage.

"Much."

He holds the pack out to me again and I take two, slip them into my breast pocket. "For later," I say.

"No problem. Here, take a couple more. You never know."

"Thank you." I throw them in with the others. "I was just wondering, Brian, about how you felt with regard to Ashley's participation in Tripp's after-school group?"

"She was crazy about it. Krystal too, the both of them. Making up little plays together in Ashley's room there but never letting me see. You know girls. Everything's a big secret." Sucks the cigarette in his fingers down to the filter and keeps going so that for a second I'm convinced he's about to swallow what's left. "Why do you ask?" he says instead, the butt a dried bean between his lips.

"Just that Mr. McConnell felt that the girls' being in that club was somehow not such a good idea."

"It wasn't any school club that did them harm, Mr. Crane."

He waves the air in front of him with the back of his hand.

"Just one more thing," I say. "Why did you decide to call me back? It's one thing to understand what my job is, but it's another to allow me into your home. You must hate me."

"Oh!" He laughs once, then coughs. "There are *things* in this world I hate, Mr. Crane. Things I'll definitely hate forever. But people? Not really."

Thinking he's finished I slide down the couch to collect my coat, but he stands sluggishly and laughs once more before speaking.

"As for why I bothered to call you back, I'm not sure. No sir, I'm not sure at all." He shakes his head, then looks up at me directly, an irregular pulse at the corners of his mouth. "I suppose it's because, other than the police, and the TV and newspaper people at the beginning, you're the only one who's called."

I thank him for his time and the cigarettes, leave him standing in the crooked door of his house that is a house only for lack of a better name. Rooted there with arms now lifeless at his sides and on his face the faraway look of the unconsoled.

Eighteen

I can't work. Not like I used to, exploding minor inconsistencies in the police notes into fatal flaws, automatically discerning the irrelevant flotsam from the nuggets of pure gold among the facts. I've been slowing down. Time I should have spent organizing the mass of Crown evidence has instead been invested in taking longer and longer night walks around town with fallen leaves scuttling behind me on the cracked streets. Staring out the tall window of the honeymoon suite at the locals lurching about or killing time in the cool drizzle that threatens to extinguish their cigarettes. Or, more often than anything else, gazing up at the pictures of Krystal and Ashley, their eyes staring back at me in what I've come to take as some kind of impossible effort toward communication. Trying to say something to the one guy in town who is the least interested in having them say anything at all; unless under circumstances of their being alive and well, returning on the Greyhound from touring with whatever band it's important for kids to tour with these days or a failed attempt at finding waitressing jobs on the west coast.

And there are other concerns. While I know the last thing mild paranoia and bad work habits need is the continued use of a drug known for its side effects of mild paranoia and bad work habits, I can't stop myself from setting new personal records for daily coke intake. I've already gone through more than half the thermos that was supposed to last until Christmas and it's not even Halloween yet. Even though I live on my own in the city and rarely seek the company of others, somehow up here the isolation is more concentrated, as though something imposed from the outside. The alternative relief of rye-and-gingers and barstool companionship in one of the local taverns has been ruled out. The Lord Byron has given me the creeps since my first and only visit, and the couple other places I've walked by at night just seem too sad to be entered.

But it's all worse the longer I go without a line. Step over to the bedside table and cut a couple fat ones. There. No excuses *now*.

Pull the chair in close, straighten the nearest police report before me and stare down hard at the words. First one, then the other, string them together. Remember *reading*, Barth? Maybe it would be easier if there weren't such a distracting contrast between the black print and white page. I push the lamp to the far edge of the desk. Darker now, but no clearer, the paragraphs blotching together in the middle, glistening blobs spreading out to steal whole chunks from sentences. Touch one and my finger comes back slick with red grease.

Fucking nosebleed. Dripping out fast over the pages and now on my shirt. All at once I'm pushing the chair back, wiping hands across my lips and smearing them over the back of my pants. It comes with the territory: the exploding vessels, the burned-out septum. But this is an especially bad one. A geyser of thin stickiness spilling liquid copper down the back of my throat.

In the bathroom slapping at the toilet roll, whole yards spinning off onto the floor, scrambling it into a loose ball and pushing it against my face. Wad after wad thrown into the sink and the whole time I'm ignoring the voice in my head—*apply pressure*—because I'm not exactly sure what it means. But after a time just mopping seems to do the trick, or slows it down anyway, and I roll up a couple tight cigarillos of paper and cork them in each nostril where they're soon glued in place.

Back to work, Barth old boy.

But it's still no good. After five minutes I stand again and walk to the window to look out over the empty intersection below. It's late, though not that late, last call at the bars only half an hour ago (an occasion marked by a collection of howls and slurred threats echoing down the street). There's nothing to look at now but the absurd changing of the traffic light, directing movement that doesn't exist. Press my forehead against the cool glass. Exhale. Leave stains.

Then I see something.

A glimpse of movement across the street, two figures stepping into the circle of streetlight. Girls in drab cotton dresses, once white with fancy lace at the seams but now stained ivory, the lace in need of restitching. Around each of their waists a tattered blue ribbon tied in a partly loosened knot. Standing in front of the old Bank of Commerce, a cold-faced limestone vault with Corinthian pillars out front half-dissolved from acid rain. Eyes raised to where I stand at the window. One light-haired and the other dark, the light one snug in her dress and the dark one shrunken inside hers.

"Hey!"

I knock on the window harder than I need to, rattling the loose glass in its frame, but they don't move.

"HEY! *HEY!*"

They give no sign that they hear me aside from both of

their arms rotating at the shoulders in a steady, almost mechanical movement. Except these girls are real. White skin shining out from beneath and through their hair, the caps of their knees distinctly visible just under the hems of their dresses. They've got to be freezing their asses off, no jackets on a night like this, as dry an evening as Murdoch's seen in the past two weeks but probably the coldest yet, the air having taken a final turn towards winter. Serves them goddamn right if their hands fall off.

"Who are you?" I shout through the glass, breath curling back into my face.

Then the answer arrives on its own: a couple of the doughnut shop girls trying to mess with me. Went out and blew twenty bucks on a couple thrift-shop dresses, waited in the dark until I came to the window so they could do this little Ash and Krys memorial freak-show in my honor. Apparently the crank calls weren't entertainment enough.

So now I'm pulling open the bedroom door, pounding down the stairs without thinking to grab my coat. When I'm out the front door my first plan is to run straight at them but I don't, not right away, just squint across the street to where they stand. From here I can better see their too-white faces, thick with pasty foundation, eyes blotted out with mascara. It's the Goth look. Big with certain girls of that age, all Anne Rice novels and fishnet stockings. Punk witches cooking up spells for the bad guy's lawyer.

"I know who you are, you know!" I call across at them. "I can get your numbers. One call, and believe me, you're both in deep shit."

They keep waving. Cast my eyes over them again and notice they wear no shoes. The tiny pink crescent moons of their toenails standing out like polished stones.

"You're doing a very stupid thing here, ladies." I step out into the street. "There are *charges* for this."

Something aside from makeup shrouds the details of their faces, an angle of light that effects a veil of shadow. I keep my eyes on them and step forward. Their mouths enlarging as I approach, borders marked by gummy lipstick.

"You think this is funny? *I* don't think it's fucking funny. I think you're some very sad hick bitches is what I think."

Take a step across the yellow line at the street's midpoint and follow it with another. Close enough to see their mouths open. Strings of spit caught between their lips. Close enough to hear—

HHRPROOOONNKK!!!

A pickup truck barreling through the intersection directly to my left, weaving into the wrong lane without slowing, its huge front grille widening like the mouth of a deep-water fish. No headlights on, just a green glow from the dashboard illuminating a blankfaced, ball-capped driver with Abe Lincoln sideburns. There's time to catch all of this, to understand that in the next second it will meet the same place where I stand, but not time to move.

Eyes closed, but I can still see the peeling stick-on racing stripe and jagged rust holes around the truck's wheels as it blows past my face. Knocks me down with the suction of air it creates in its wake, the back of my head smacking neatly against the pavement on the way down. A white flash across my eyes followed by blue pinprick static. A million strings of pain spun out from rear molars, sinuses, top of the spine.

By the time I get back to my feet the truck is lurching around the courthouse corner at the far end of the street, giving me a double blast on its horn as it goes.

"Homicidal inbred!" I shout into the empty street. Then I see that the street *is* empty.

The black-eyed girls in ragged dresses and bare feet are gone.

Nineteen

I dream of water.

Not the sparkling, pale blue kind, but frigid, black, suffocating. The plots are varied: swimming in an indoor pool with glass French doors all around looking out on a lush garden; lying in a tub with the hot water rising slowly to my chin; taking a drink from a crystal glass. Comforting, even tedious dreams that bring me down to the edge of a sleep where nothing is remembered. But then everything changes. My muscles cramp and I sink in the pool's deep end, the lush garden outside the window now a seething body of vines crashing through to wrap themselves around arms and legs. Close my eyes in the bath and a hand comes down on my head, presses me under until the scalding water is taken in. The crystal glass breaking in my grip and shards of it flowing into my mouth, slicing their way down to my lungs.

Wake with the covers kicked down to a damp roll at the end of the bed. So tired I feel sick. And just as I manage to convince myself that it was only a dream and that I better put my head back down so that I can grab a couple hours before dawn—the phone. Down at the front desk. Echoing up the stairs and under the door.

Pull the pillow up around my ears and let it go until sleep returns. And when it does the dreams again, different and the same every time.

*

I should rip them down. Pull the already yellowing pages off the walls and turn this room back to what it was instead of the obscene shrine it's become. I'm going to, no question about it. I've got enough to worry about without glancing up every fifteen seconds to make sure they're still there.

And they always are. Still there, but are they *still?* It's that photographic trick, the one where the eyes in a picture follow you wherever you go. At the desk. Stepping out naked and dripping from the shower. Lifting myself up onto bare elbows in the morning. Every moment I'm dead in their sights.

Smiles that change. An adjusted angle caused by the head turned to the left instead of the right will do it, the double-take play of low-wattage bulbs. It's nothing more than shifting perspectives but there it is, a fraction of movement carried out behind my back. Giving me an insinuating look not entirely masked by ample cheeks, oversize adult teeth and eyes a little pinched in the trained constriction of a posed smile. And then the mask disappears again. It never *was* a mask. It's the assembled features of a face and nothing more, two faces, flat and benign, free of opinion or interest. Still. But with eyes that are somehow always busy. Devouring the dust hanging in the light from the window, pulling in the tangled bedsheets, gathering up the pens, pencils and paper-clips and claiming all of it as theirs.

Somebody brings clean sheets every third morning and leaves them outside the door in a pile. It appears that I'm expected to change the bed myself. And maybe I will sometime. But so far I'm just pulling the sheets inside and throwing them on top of the ones before, so that now a stack of white cotton folds stands crooked as a drunk against the wall. Definitely whiter than what I'm sleeping on at the moment though, the covers thrown back to reveal rolls of pinched grey blotched by stains that may or may not be my own.

I get up from the desk to pull the covers back into place, more to hide what's underneath than from any real effort at tidiness. But I don't even get this job done before my attention is again drawn away. Something heavy stuck between the comforter patterned with hunters firing orange-tongued rifles up at passing ducks and the pink polyester blanket beneath. *A History of Northern Ontario Towns* by Alistair Dundurn. The book I took out from the library, the one Pittle recommended.

Carry it over to the window and set myself on the ledge. The old kind of recycled paper flecked with brown fibre, almost every page randomly punctuated by gummy spots the color of hot dog relish. The whole thing typewritten, gaping breaks between the lines and notched paragraphs. A home-made job ("Published by A. Dundurn Press, 1982"), there's even some handwritten corrections visible in places above the text. The dedication: "For My Fallen Colleagues of the Royal Highland Riflemen, 2nd Division."

I turn to the table of contents and run my fingers down the list of towns. Blind River. Sturgeon Falls. Thessalon. Capreol. New Liskeard. Then Chapter Five: Murdoch.

> Before its settlement less than a hundred and fifty years ago, the area where the town of Murdoch now sits at the gateway to the great Northern Ontario wilderness was nothing but untouched Canadian Shield: 300,000 square miles of naked Precambrian rock, forest and deep, crystal lakes. Natural gifts that had yet to be exploited to their full potential by the Algonkian tribes who for previous centuries were largely oblivious to the

vast riches they lived, hunted and fished on. It took the
arrival of the first civilized white settlers to the region
at the end of the Eighteenth Century—mostly United
Empire Loyalists, hearty farming and merchant stock
from Great Britain seeking adventure and a better
life—before the land was finally recognized not merely
as barren bush but as a glorious opportunity . . .

And God save the Queen. Pittle wasn't kidding when he
described Dundurn's work as amateur. White Man came,
White Man saw, White Man sold it all off cheap. The same
story that could apply to virtually any Canadian town.

Scan down through the rest of the Economic Origins
section and start again at Social Character.

. . . It has been argued by some that the true tenets of
the Victorian Age were more fully embraced in the
young Canadian nation than within even the United
Kingdom itself. There is little question, however, that
the whole of Ontario society at the turn of the century
was caught in heated debate over the moral future of
the province, and that the greater part of this debate
was primarily concerned with the public sale and
consumption of liquor. Through the 1890s, prohibition-
ist organizations such as the Sons of Temperance, the
Independent Order of Good Templars and the Women's
Christian Temperance Union had over 40,000 registered members! And in an 1894 Ontario-wide plebiscite,
400,000 of the Age of Majority voted 65% in favor of
prohibition. Within Murdoch County, that figure rose
dramatically to eighty-nine percent.

Among other things, this result clearly indicates
the worthy foundations of Murdoch's moral history.

Mostly devout Orangemen, Murdoch's fathers boasted one of the largest lodge memberships north of the County of York. Intent on preserving their Protestant ideals in the savage New Country, all of the men's organizations of the town—Odd Fellows, Knights of Pythias, the Orange Order and the Masons—closed their membership to those explicitly involved in the liquor business. However, it should be noted that drink was permitted for its use in formal toasts made during meetings. Because of the established traditions unique to each of these orders, such toasts tended to be numerous . . .

I skip ahead again to what Pittle must have wanted me to find in the first place: Appendix: Murdoch's Lady in the Lake. Dundurn's tone is just as serious with this material though, treating it with the same sober consideration as Murdoch's honored contributions to both world wars, the suffering during the Depression and the Queen Mum's ribbon-cutting visit at the new, "state-of-the-art" high school in the early 60s. At moments the writing even slides into obvious sentiment, an effort to capture the dramatic details with a flourish of language.

. . . A woman wearing nothing but the rags set upon her but a considerable beauty shining out from beneath her long, bedraggled hair . . . two transfixing daughters, each carrying something of their mother in the sometimes hardened, sometimes playful set of their faces . . . Many took the view that she rarely spoke because she didn't understand the language, others that she simply chose not to speak at all . . . descending with a chilling scream . . . now said that her spirit can still be seen roaming the woods next to Lake St. Christopher, seeking to take the hand of others' children ... the lonely cold of an unblessed, watery grave ...

No mention of the daytime skinny-dips or the male visitors she may have entertained. Nothing about the state-sanctioned hysterectomy or the townsmen who flushed her out onto the ice. But there is a brief telling of her escape from Bishop's Hospital, the "mysterious" and "accidental" drowning, her voice calling out to any who might have heard on the shore, to her daughters, to "the wicked, war-torn world." Then there's a double-spaced gap separating all of the preceding from a rather strange summation:

> ... They say there's a fraction of truth in every story, no matter how hard it may be to believe. In this, the Lady of Murdoch is likely no different. But how much truth there can be in a tale of a vengeful spirit returned from the dead to lay claim upon the living is a matter of faith more than fact. One way or the other, Murdoch's history has been shaped as much by this one unnamed stranger as by influential merchants, the passing fortunes of industry and the decisions of elected officials. What remains of her is the memory of a life, which is nothing less than history itself. We will never know who we are if we fail to remember what has come before—both the victories and the disgraces. All the public pride of glory and the private shame of ghosts.
>
> It has been said that we only fear that which we do not know. Yet perhaps what we fear most is not the possibility of the unknown, but all of the horrors that we know to be true.

The chapter ends here, with this insertion of amateur metaphysics to go along with the amateur history. Still, there's something in this section of Dundurn's writing that feels different from the rest. The brief emergence of a voice. Intent, fervent. Something personal.

I close the book and push myself up from the window's ledge, looking again at the confusion of sheets on the bed. For a moment I actually wonder if a couple had silently entered the room to use the honeymoon suite for its proper purposes behind my back, leaving everything twisted and warm, a vague sweetness in the air. And me reading history in the background.

There's nothing to do but go to bed myself now. Empty my pockets out onto the flaky varnished surface of the dresser. The sound the coins make like an ancient machine clattering to its final stop.

I place Dundurn's book there on top of the change and spiraled tufts of lint, but something in the angle of the spine flips the back cover open a second after I pull my hand away. There, glued to the inside of the last page, a small yellow envelope holding the Due Date card.

Pull it out with my thumb and lay it flat, run my finger under the stamped dates and handwritten names. Last borrowed only six months ago. The signature the same as the one beside the X at the bottom of my Form of Retainer. My client. Thomas R. Tripp.

I confess it's something of a personal lawyer joke that my worst mark at law school was in Professional Ethics. Would never have taken it at all if it hadn't been mandatory, which could be said for most of my colleagues as well. But at least they went to the trouble of faking it, offering up the "right" answer for every hypothetical put to them by the forty-five-grand-a-year Justice Ministry schmuck hauled in to teach it. From what little I can recall, the entire course could be broken down into a handful of fundamental rules one had to repeat a dozen times out loud in order to pass:

Don't take *all* the money held in trust for someone else.

Take a good long look before accepting sex from clients in exchange for fees.

Try not to lie, but if you feel you must, try first to say nothing at all.

And this: if a young lawyer ever feels he's losing control of a case—however slightly—he should seek the advice of a senior member of the bar before things are allowed to go any further.

That would be me.

So it is that the next morning I call Graham with the intention of talking to him one-on-one, but he's not in. And when he calls back I can tell immediately it's from the boardroom, over the speaker-phone, and that Bert's there too, the clicking of his lighter and bubbly throat clearings giving him away.

"So, Bartholomew, how goes it? Everything in order and geared up, I trust?" Graham sings, using the same voice he uses on his most humorless clients.

"Pretty much. I mean, there's nothing in the disclosure materials that we didn't know already. And although the DNA results aren't back yet, no matter what they say I think we still look good."

"Of *course* you look good. Always did, always will. Now, what about Sir Thomas Tripp of The Village of Murdoch. Is he being reasonably cooperative?"

"Cooperative wouldn't be quite the word, no. He's not

entirely stable, actually, although he'd fall well short of insanity on a psychiatric assessment. But he does claim to hear voices."

"What kind of voices?" Bert joins in from what sounds like the furthest corner of the room.

"It's not clear. A woman, I think he said. Or a group of women, talking together all at once."

"Sounds like the definition of hell to me," Bert coughs.

"Is he going to be *alright*?"

"I shouldn't have to call him to testify, if that's what you mean."

"That's *exactly* what I mean. Very good. Any other preliminary matters?"

"I wouldn't call them *matters*, but yes, there're some things I wanted to—some vaguely troubling things I thought I'd air out. Nothing to cause concern, but I felt that bringing them to light at this point might be a good idea."

"Bartholomew, what *are* you *on* about? Have you fallen in love or something awful like that? If so, I know Bert and I can offer nothing but our strongest discouragements."

"It's not love. It's little things. Coincidences. Funny stuff."

"Intriguing," Graham says, sounding not at all intrigued. "Do go on."

"Well, for example, there's this stripper who was working in the bar downstairs who's been calling the hotel almost every night, waking me up. I know it's her because I answered once and it was her voice."

"And what did she want? Your lap for a private dance, perhaps?"

"No, Graham. Crank call sort of shit. But there was

something about—it's like she wasn't just kidding around. You know what I mean?"

"No," Graham says at precisely the same moment Bert says, "Yeah."

"And she's not the only thing. There's some people in town trying to get under my skin. To distract me."

"And how is that done?"

"The other night there were two girls standing across the street from my bedroom wearing these old cotton dresses. Waving up at my window. And it's getting pretty bloody cold up here."

"I'm sure it was just your fan club, Bartholomew, bidding you out onto the balcony for a speech or blessing."

"Don't fuck around, Graham. It's like they were trying to freak me out."

"Now, now, *now*," Graham soothes. "There's no need to be *freaked out*. We're here and we're listening."

"And so far we haven't heard shit," Bert cuts in, collapsing into a chair that screeches in protest as it accepts his weight. "So some kids do a little routine on you. Small towns are like that, they don't like outsiders. Especially outsiders doing the job you're doing. My advice is acquire some balls and get on with it."

"Thank you for that, Bert. As usual your comments have been very thoughtful."

"Piss off."

Nobody says anything for a while, and I consider hanging up, walking straight down to The Lord Byron and injecting two or three rye-and-gingers into my system before calling back with the excuse that we must have been cut off. Then Graham's voice returns.

"Well now, gentlemen. Shall we move on?"

"Wait. There's another thing. Kind of funny."

"We like funny."

"I've been around to the lake a couple times where Tripp is accused—where whatever happened happened. Anyway, I bumped into an old lady, a Mrs. Arthurs who lives on the water who told me this story about an escaped mental patient after the war who was living in the woods, trying to get some of the local kids to go with her, kidnap them I guess, and—"

"What war?" Bert interrupts.

"WW II."

"That was over fifty years ago!"

"I know."

"So what's she got to do with Tripp?"

"Nothing, I'm sure. See, she kept trying to kidnap the kids in town because they'd taken her own kids away from her after they put her in the hospital. But before she could, all the men in town hunted her down and she ended up falling through the ice on the lake. They *forced* her out there. More or less executed her without a trial or reporting what happened or anything."

"The point, Bartholomew?" Graham laughs impatiently.

"The point is that Mrs. Arthurs is a witness."

"A witness to *what?*" Bert closes in on the receiver again. "To *nothing*, that's what. Nothing *you* have to give a shit about. Your client is Tripp, not a bunch of fucking geriatric vigilante woodsmen."

"I know. I know that," I say, finally hearing my own voice, how reedy and young it must sound at the other end. "I'm sorry. I'm just tired, that's all."

"Well then, could we now lower the curtain on Count

Barth's Monster Horror Theater for a moment and turn our minds to the matter of *relevance?* For God's sake boy, if you took every campfire tale this seriously I'm surprised they didn't throw *you* in the madhouse long ago. Now can we *please* proceed, but with the colorful local mythology edited out?"

There's the creak of a reclining chair followed by Bert's laugh that manages, always, to underscore a humiliation.

I manage to turn to my notes and muddle through a point-by-point summary of Goodwin's disclosure and the other items I've arranged under the heading EVIDENTIARY MATTERS, leaving out Tripp's bloody button-down, its removal from his freezer and deposit in the trunk of the Lincoln.

"Well, everything sounds in order. Doesn't it, Bert?"

Nothing.

"If that's all, Bartholomew, perhaps we can relieve Mr. Tripp now of the burden of our time and have you check in again, maybe next week, say, with a further update before—"

"There's something else."

I hear my voice scratched up another half octave.

"Oh?"

"I've been thinking that I may take you up on your earlier offer."

"Offer?"

"I may need some help."

Bert snorts.

"Now, Bartholomew, I'm aware you're probably feeling nervous. That's perfectly understandable! My God, I was a *wreck* on my first murder. There's so much more to be *mindful* of. But Bert and I have absolutely every confidence—"

"It's fucking open and shut!" Bert shouts, his mouth now wrapped fully around the receiver. "Open and fucking shut!"

"It's not the facts, Bert. It's the whole thing, keeping it all together, you know? I know I'm not being very clear."

"No, no, no," Graham chirps, but his heart's not in it. "We know *exactly* what you're talking about, Bartholomew. It's only that we know your apprehensions to be perfectly common. No defence lawyer, not a single one known to *history* is unfamiliar with what you're experiencing. The eve of trial, the facts disclosed and assembled, strategies considered, your client's directions clear as they'll ever be, and *still* there's a butterfly in the bowels keeping you up at night. All perfectly common."

"Yes. I guess that's true."

Again there is a period with no sound traveling down the line, and it goes on long enough to make it clear that there will be no help from Lyle, Gederov & Associate. Maybe it's the publicity the case is getting in Toronto, a public outcry against the leniency the courts have shown to perpetrators of violence against children and we're not going to take it anymore, etc., etc. Or maybe they've just decided to let me handle this on my own no matter what comes up for the benefit of enriching my legal education. Whatever it is, the result is clear as the silence that separates us over the conference line.

"What's going on with you, Barth?" This is Bert, his voice not quite level but not bristling with his usual rage, either. "Are you trying to say something you haven't told us yet? Do you have a *real* problem up there or not?"

Good question. And what I end up saying surprises me, the words escaping my mouth before I have a chance to haul them back in.

"I'm scared," I say.

There's a long pause free even of clicked lighter, creaking chair or blown smoke. And when a response finally comes, it comes from Bert.

"It's your fucking job to be scared," he says with what might be taken for the restraint one hears in words of confession or kindness.

Twenty

There's an orange line down the middle of the Georgian Lakes High School parking lot that separates the pickup trucks from the rest of the cars. A sign at the entrance clearly tells you which way to go: TRUCKS to the left and PARKING to the right. It can't be a space concern, as the lot stretches far beyond where the vehicles end, all the way to a low wire fence that divides the cracked pavement from the cemetery beyond. Maybe it's a kind of mechanical social club, the trucks preferring the exclusive company of their own kind and the cars just having to get along with each other in the automotive melting pot. And they're all here: the peppy Japanese sidled up to the overfed Americans and, standing alone among them, the silent Germans, conserving their energy. To the left, the pickups sit solemnly together, backs to the crowd. Bumpers and rear windows pasted with their founding principles: "Register My Firearms? No Fucking Way!" and "Ass, Gas or Grass—Nobody Rides for Free." But whatever the rationale for the rule I obey it along with everyone else and park the Lincoln at the end of the line of cars, an overbearing guest that everyone pretends not to notice.

It's a long walk to the half-dozen steel doors at the brick backside of the school's main building, past the whittled benches of the smoking area and the cluster of yellow portables, each slightly lopsided on shifting cement blocks.

Beyond them, the playing field goalposts raise their arms to the sky as though praying for rescue. The shouts and whistles of athletic practice. A flutter of papery carbon drifting down from the incinerator's smokestack.

This is all as I expected, but once inside I'm suddenly disoriented. I thought I'd feel grown-up, an oversize man high above the gaggle of children, the hallway drinking fountains passing at my knees, head ducked under doorways. But instead everything feels enlarged, stark and looming under the fluorescent lights. Especially all the dark-eyed kids standing at their lockers on either side of me, staring out at passersby like penitentiary inmates. Many boys and some of the platform-shoed girls as tall as me, some taller. They say nothing as I go by, but there's still a confusion of noise: resumed conversations and scoffing laughter over my shoulder, a muffle of late-80s AC/DC played too loud over the P.A. between classes. Yet all of them notice me, their faces set to show how unimpressed they are that an unidentified adult is passing through their school.

Or not just any adult. Bartholomew Crane. Mr. Tripp's lawyer, the guy whose picture was in last week's *Phoenix*. Maybe it's not adolescent rudeness that makes them stare; maybe they know who I am. And who else would I be? Nobody around here wears shoes like this or a shiny satin tie of handpainted orchids. Even the gawky grade nines have figured it out, young enough to point at my face without concern that I may have seen them do it. And aren't those the doughnut shop girls standing up ahead, there in the corner next to the trophy case? It's hard to tell, their individual faces too close together, heads held in an even circle that blurs one set of features with another's. I probably couldn't recognize them anyway, having not gotten a good look the first time. But I decide it must be them. And though I can't hear anything above the electric guitar solo now shattering down on us all from the ceiling speakers, I know they're talking about me.

I turn the corner furthest from where they stand and slide along the wall. Push aside a couple of guys in Dungeons & Dragons T-shirts on my way into the principal's office. But when I look back through the window the doughnut shop girls are gone, washed away in the rough stream of passing kids.

"Can I help you?" the secretary behind the counter is asking me, maybe for the third time.

"I have an appointment with Principal Warren."

"Oh yes."

It's not until after the secretary has flicked a switch on the panel beside her and spoken—"Mr. Crane here to see you"—that I realize she never asked for my name.

"Would you like to take a seat?" she asks me, and I would, but before I can make a move Principal Warren is shuffling out at me from her office, her legs constrained by a long wool skirt coiled tight around her hips.

"Mr. Crane," she says with a trace of exasperation, as though she'd been looking for me all over the place.

"Thank you for agreeing to meet with me," I say, extending my hand. But instead of shaking it she slides her fingers across my palm as though wiping something off her own hand onto mine.

"My office?"

"Fine."

I follow the moving pillar of her skirt into a small cement room decorated by yellowed certificates set in crooked frames. On her desk a family photograph posed before a gas fireplace—wife nested in an armchair and behind her two boys in braces with a chunky husband gathering them up by the shoulders—that somehow looks as though it was generated by a computer. Principal Warren herself is now standing above me next to her desk, looking down at me with the same expression as in the family photo: impatient, suspicious, but also vaguely distressed, as though she'd eaten something too spicy at lunch.

"The Board's lawyer tells me I'm not compelled to answer your questions," she says with a voice that comes out in the discrete blasts of machine-gun fire. *Rat-a-tat-tat-tat.* "But I want to be fair."

"I understand."

"Because it's important to make clear that this whole thing—well, it's pretty much torn this school apart."

"I can appreciate that."

"But we've made every effort to ease the pain. Unprecedented counseling resources have been made available. I have done all I can do, given the circumstances. And yet I also have to tell you that I'm aware—on an unofficial level—that there are certain individuals—certain *parties*—that have taken the view that I'm partially to blame for what happened. And this *concerns* me, as you can appreciate. From a legal as well as the more obvious personal perspective."

"Blame you? How?"

"That I failed to remove Mr. Tripp from his duties prior to the event. That I could have prevented things."

She blinks once, slow as a drawn curtain between scenes, and when she goes on it's in a more openly agitated tone.

"Which is a claim that I regard—it's *ridiculous.* I mean, it's well and good in hindsight to say somebody should have kept him away from—but *prior* to the fact, you know, it's very difficult—there're proper procedures. There're policies. You can't just fire teachers because you notice certain person-ality—certain oddities."

She stops now, breathless, still standing inches from my knees. What I took to be suspicion now a barely restrained desperation on her face. And it's this look that makes it clear: she thinks she's in trouble. She might not get that 2.4 percent raise as per the collective agreement which also allows for certain exceptions in cases of extreme incompetence. So she agreed to talk to me because if she gets called as a witness in the trial she wants to show how nobody could have known in advance that Tripp was a killer. And maybe that's not her only worry. It's a small town. Parents are upset. The Board has promised to look into things. There've been whisperings of negligence, suspension, civil actions. She's talking to me to save herself.

"Well now," she starts again, "how can I be of assistance to you then, Mr. Crane?"

"A little history would be nice. Specifically, I'm wonder-ing how you would characterize Thom's behavior prior to the girls' disappearance. Why don't we start there."

"His behavior." She releases a tremulous sigh. "Well, we *had* noticed some changes, to be honest. But you have to appreciate that Mr. Tripp had an impeccable teaching rec-ord. Committed to his students, a jovial presence in the staff lounge, even popular with the parents. And never stingy on his availability for extracurriculars. So I feel it was entirely understandable that for the first while I was prepared to give him some time to sort things out."

"Sort what things out?"

"His personal life. An area I knew little about, I must confess, so I can't really be expected—"

"What evidence was there that he'd changed?"

"Oh—how do I put this? I suppose you could say he was *distracted*. Some students made note of it. It's all in his file. I did have some student teachers sit in on his class to take notes—to observe his performance from a casual perspective—but beyond that, my hands were tied. I mean, as you may be aware, there are quite stringent union regulations which protect—"

"So you sent in your spies. And what did they find?"

"I wouldn't characterize them as *spies*."

"Beg your pardon. Please go on."

Principal Warren sighs again, looks about her as though she'd just noticed the walls slowly closing in around her. Then she looks down and sees that she's still standing. But instead of moving around to her chair she settles on the edge of the desk, perches a fold of thigh onto the wood surface but keeps her toes on the floor, the tendons in her ankles straining to prevent a sliding collapse to the floor.

"Well, what they observed was what I would categorize as an *inattentiveness*," she continues, a finger rising to flick back a strand of hair that isn't there. "Staring out the classroom window for minutes at a time while students engaged in unruly conduct right in front of him. Spitball fights, standing on the desks, leaving the room without permission and the like."

"And you still didn't do anything about him?"

"Mr. Crane, teachers who lose control of their students are *hardly* unusual."

"Were there any other problems? I mean, was he otherwise able to carry out his obligations?"

"Of course. And you'll find no documentation to the contrary."

"What about the Literary Club? You weren't concerned that an emotionally disturbed man was spending so much time with two young female students?"

"There were no formal grounds for concern. In fact it seemed an encouraging aspect of his job performance at the time. Krystal and Ashley seemed to get so much out of it, and the Board was very supportive. Granted almost every one of Mr. Tripp's applications for budgetary supplements."

"What did he need money for?"

"Not him. Little things that the girls needed. Makeup, props, costumes. That sort of stuff."

"Can you tell me why a Literary Club would need costumes?"

"Performances, I suppose. I'm not sure anybody really asked. But I can tell you—in fact I'd like to *emphasize*—that budgetary procedures were not my personal area of responsibility."

"No, of course not."

Principal Warren slides a few inches along the edge of the desk to assist the flow of blood to her legs. Crosses her arms.

"Well, I do hope I've been of some assistance," she says. "Although, in dealing with such a tragedy, it's likely inappropriate to conceive of it as people taking sides."

"Actually, it's likely the only way to conceive of it."

She gives me a look like a hound that's just picked up a strange and troubling scent.

"Perhaps—you know, it may—oh," she says, abandons the thought. The arms uncross, reach down to the desk's surface to support her now obviously painful position.

"I was wondering if I might meet briefly with one of your

teachers here," I say. "Miss Betts. I understand she used to be a friend of Thom's."

"Well, you're of course free to make your own inquiries. But I can't assure—let me check her schedule." She says it *shed-yool*. Reaches behind and lifts a huge blue binder to her lap all without moving from her place on the desk. "Well, she's running a practice at the moment. You're free to wait until her next spare, which will likely—"

"So she'll be outside then?"

"Miss Betts is the field hockey coach. And field hockey is generally not considered an indoor sport, Mr. Crane."

With this she smiles, hard and fast. Throws herself up to her feet, extends her hand over my shoulder to show me the door which is no more than eighteen inches from the back of my head.

"I may give you a call," I say on my way out.

"I would always welcome an opportunity to clarify my position," she says brightly as she closes the door behind me.

There's a cold drizzle settling over the flapping ponytails and stocky calves of the Georgian Lakes girls' field hockey team as I skirt along the sidelines toward midfield. The players appear not to notice me though, screaming for passes and uncalled penalties, their faces pale as chicken skin. At the foot of the bleachers stands Miss Betts, polished whistle between her teeth, her body wrapped in puffy layers of nylon windbreaker over cotton sweat suit. Behind her sit the half-dozen substitute players, silent, rubbing their forearms for warmth.

"Miss Betts?" I ask when I'm only a couple feet from where she stands but she doesn't look my way. Then her voice, a chesty bark echoing out over everything else.

"NOTHING FANCY! *C'MON* TRACEY! NOTHING FANCY!"

I turn to watch now as well, and there's the girl who must be Tracey with her stick held loose along her waist like an infantry rifle pointed directly our way.

"Excuse me. Miss Betts? My name's Bartholomew Crane," I try again, my eyes now following a heroic rush toward the goal by a girl with bruised kneecaps that ends in a vicious slash to her ankles and a sprawling skid fifteen feet across the mud.

"GET UP NOW, ZOE! SHAKE IT OFF!" Miss Betts shouts to the fallen girl, but refuses to call a penalty. I'm about to suggest that the foul was so clear you'd have to be blind not to see it when she says in a normal speaking voice but still without turning her head, "Thom's lawyer?"

"That's right. I was wondering if I could ask you about him."

"You can try. HUSTLE!"

"O.K. What happened that made him start to act strange in the time leading up to Ashley and Krystal's disappearance?"

"Nothing really. Just the total destruction of his life. One of those divorces with so many lawyers involved it probably left both of them broke. But Thom was never worried about the money. It was Melissa that he wanted. To keep his daughter. So when the judge awarded him joint custody I tried to tell him, 'Hey, you did alright there, guy,' but he wouldn't say anything. Just get this dark mask around his eyes like the Lone Ranger or something. And then he really fucked up. TASHA! WOULD YOU DO ME A FAVOR AND GET UP OFF YOUR ASS?"

She keeps the whistle clenched in her mouth, the little

ball inside rattling with her words as though caught halfway down her own throat.

"Fucked up how?"

"Started trying to see Melissa when he wasn't supposed to. The idiot. Courts do not take kindly to fathers mooning around their daughter's schoolyard on days when they don't have visiting privileges. Everybody gets very upset. And so I try to tell him that, and he just gets that Lone Ranger face again. I DO *NOT* LIKE BALL HOGS! Told me how one time he went to Melissa's school and walked in the front doors to try to pick her up or talk to her before her mother got there, or something like that, but the vice-principal sees him coming and calls the cops. Because everybody knows about this guy, right? So the cops come and write him up some ticket saying he's in violation of the custody order and leave him there outside the school grounds and tell him to leave the girl alone. And then it starts to *rain*. I swear to God. Thom Tripp was not the kind of guy to make stuff like that up. Just pissing down on him. But he doesn't move, staring up at all the windows of the school to find Melissa's face and sure enough he does. She's right up there on the second floor looking down at him along with everybody else in the place—they'd heard the sirens, eh—and that's her dad, just standing there. This drowned rat of a man waving up to his scared little girl."

Now Zoe is running over toward us, one of her bruised knees dripping a neat line of blood into her sock. "Rock out there," she pants. "Got scraped up."

"SUB!"

One of the girls from the bleachers behind us trots stiffly out, giving Zoe a swift whack on the behind with her stick as she goes.

"I heard that he later tried to take Melissa away," I say,

the words turned to a billowing mist against the side of Miss Betts's face. "That's why the court finally denied him access. Why the wife moved away."

"I heard that too. But Thom wasn't saying much by then. To anybody. I mean, I still cared about the guy, right—he was in need of some serious help—but what can you do? I say hello to him and all he can do is give me this 'Do I know you?' look. DIG! DIG! DIG! After a while, looking out for a guy like that starts to get a little tiring."

There's the crack of lumber as one of the bigger girls gets away a good shot that's stopped dead by the goalie's ribcage.

"NICE SAVE! NICE SAVE!"

"What about the Literary Club, all the time Thom was spending with the girls? Did anyone think that was unusual?"

"Absolutely. The way he was all hush-hush about it, like he was running a goddamn cult instead of a discussion group or whatever it was. Even rigged up a little curtain he threw over the window of his classroom door on Thursdays after school so nobody could look in. Definitely weird. But those girls, they just loved it. Pretty much dropped everything they used to be into except for that club of theirs, which wasn't a club at all really, just the three of them. All top secret. And that's probably what they liked about it. Girls that age love to keep their secrets."

"So you really don't know what they might have been doing in there?"

"Like I told you, I don't have a clue. Nobody did. And Thom wasn't telling."

Within seconds the drizzle turns to rain that may be the coldest yet, the play before us now obscured by a shifting wall of grey. But it isn't stopping them. I can still hear the crack of sticks meeting each other, the strained cries working to hack the ball to the opposing end.

"Would you agree to be a witness if I need you?" I raise my voice another notch to be heard through the patter of rain on Miss Betts's nylon shoulders. "To testify as to Thom's character? I know you two were friends, and he could use your help."

"You know what?" she replies after a time. "I really hope you're a good lawyer. Because that's the only kind of help Thom Tripp needs now. And as for me being a witness for him? After what he did? Let me tell you this: Ashley used to be on this team. I used to be her coach. She was a good kid. She had a spark. Krystal too. There's nobody around here that doesn't miss the both of them like hell."

For the first time Miss Betts turns her head away from the field to look at me, her broad face glazed in moisture.

"I'd rather be the first to throw the goddamn switch than help that bastard one inch," she says, then turns away from me again and blows her whistle. Three sharp blasts through the freezing rain that call her players in.

Even with all the lights off behind me the grey of the laptop's screen is giving me a headache. One of those dull, not-going-anywhere numbers that leads you to seriously consider knocking your skull against the nearest door frame. Turn off the computer and watch the last traces of color flee into the corners. The room swelling in the darkness.

I'm feeling around for a pen, making a list I can't see. There on the legal pad before me in oversize handwriting so that I might make sense of it in the morning. A descending column of invisible names. "Don't just deny. Blame it on somebody else." Another fundamental Grahamism, but it was a rule I knew already.

McConnell

Flynn

The dads. Always a good bet. McConnell almost too happy with the way things are turning out, too quick with an angry, vengeful word for the press. And those threats. If I can get all that in we might be in business. Flynn a poor second, but was so certain his daughter was dead he didn't even want to consider the possibility that it could be otherwise. Maybe parents have their instincts. But they're also the most likely to do their own children harm, statistically speaking. A patriarch who can't control his anger. A lonely, disposable depressive. Snapshots any jury could recognize from miles off.

Laird J.

Any kid who keeps a detailed scrapbook on two female classmates who end up going missing has got to be considered suspicious. And if I could dig up some evidence of an interest in Satanic heavy metal or an obsession with horror movies, we could be onto something.

Runaways

They're not dead at all. Or might not be. The lake's not that big, but the wide world certainly is for girls who had something to run from. Krystal's house couldn't have been a barrel of laughs, and Ashley was surely smart enough to figure out that a job somewhere on her own offered better prospects than sticking around with her going-nowhere old man. And best of all: still no bodies.

Unidentified third party

Get one of the profilers from the R.C.M.P. to shock the courtroom with the number of violent psychotics currently at large on the continent. Just the suggestion of a stranger-passing-through-town scenario might be enough. People know the warped psychologies of serial killers better than their own these days. Or they've at least seen *The Silence of the Lambs*.

T.'s assistant

Even if the lake disposal scenario sticks, it's still a hell of a job for the teacher to have pulled off all on his own. If I can fish a name out of him we could sell his friend and plead our way down to something reasonable. Sometimes five years can feel like you've gotten away with it.

I close my eyes and roll my head back on my neck, grind a satisfying pop from the cartilage. Time for bed, if I can find it. But for a time I stay at the desk and face the wall, not sure if my eyes are closed or whether the dark is all that I can see.

The Lady

I write this without seeing it on the page but feel its shape in the slow "L," the coiled "y" of my hand. Then I fold the paper into the smallest square I can squeeze between my fingers and flip it back over my shoulder. Wait to hear the sound of it meet the floor but there's nothing but my own breathing and the touch of rain against the glass.

Twenty-One

The next morning delivers blue sky, clear light and even a swirl of warmth in the air, and with these invitations Ontario Street is the busiest I've seen it. This is to say that at any given moment half a dozen squinting mouth-breathers could be observed scuffling along, wiping at their noses and waiting for the light to change. I head up toward the courthouse, nodding at those I pass. Nobody responds but I pretend not to notice, chin held up to the sun. Why not? Things—the whole confused lot of them—may not be as bad as they seem. And after all, even if they are, they bear no direct personal consequences. It's not *me* who sits languishing in a prison cell awaiting his fate. No, sir. I'm out here on the sunny street, overcoat unbuttoned, fresh oxygen and Colombia's finest replenishing my blood.

When I reach the top of the street I make a left and soon find myself standing at the library's front door. Ten after nine and it's still locked. Consider turning around but knock instead, and in a moment the door is opened by little Doug Pittle, his eyes blinking up at me in amusement.

"Been here eighteen years and that's the first time anyone's knocked to be let in before nine."

"It's ten after, as a matter of fact."

"Ten *after*, then. It's still the first time anyone's ever knocked on this door. Period."

We walk down the hall to his desk and from its edge pick

up a paperback *The Catcher in the Rye* in the advanced stages of decay.

"The library's most popular selection," he explains, cutting off a strip of duct tape and wrapping it around the book's spine as I hold it for him. "There's a long-standing rumor at the high school that it contains an explicit sex scene. They'd be so much better off going with D.H. Lawrence. Or even *Wuthering Heights*."

"Don't you subscribe to *Sports Illustrated?* Surely the swimsuit issue would be in the highest demand."

"It would be. But the town council banned it after it was discovered that photocopies from it were being distributed at the school. *Black and white* photocopies."

"Desperate times require desperate measures."

When he's finished snipping off the excess tape I put the book back down and look out the narrow window next to the desk. Two men in leather hockey jackets smoke outside the courthouse doors across the way, waiting to be tried or questioned or ordered to relinquish their drivers' licences. When finished, they flick their butts like flyfishermen, send two orange flares arcing under a sky now flattened by cloud.

"So, was your earlier research here fruitful, Mr. Crane?" Pittle asks, taking an X-Acto blade to a cardboard box on the floor containing what appears to be the new installment of the *Encyclopedia Britannica*.

"Call me Barth. And it was very fruitful, yes. But I have a question this time around."

"Oh?"

"Of a more historical nature, I suppose."

"I see."

He stops lifting the volumes out of their box and looks up at me in that unflinching, scientific way of his.

"The other day I bumped into a Mrs. Arthurs, out there on Lake St. Christopher. Nice lady, though given to quite fantastic stories. The one she told me involved a certain Lady in the Lake, attempted child abductions, and her fall through the ice to her death. I'm summarizing here to save you from the macabre details. What I'm wondering is if any of this rings a bell with you."

"Of course it does," he says now, stands, his eyes never straying from mine. "Everyone who lives around here knows *that* one."

"So it's a lie?"

"Wouldn't say that. More like Murdoch's Loch Ness Monster, but without the benefits to the tourist trade. In fact, there's a number of people up here who blame The Lady's bad vibes for the lake's lack of investment. The thinking is that nobody wants to put money into a place known to be inhabited by a spirit intent on possessing other people's children. And there's a certain logic to that, I guess."

"And what do you think?"

Pittle slides a hand into a pocket of his corduroys, combs the other through the front tuft of his hair.

"I think Helen Arthurs is a valued relic and entertaining in her way," he says, taking his time, "but quite likely deep in the late stages of senility. I think the woman behind The Lady in the Lake was real but has been dead for a long time and these days is just something high school kids use to scare themselves with at Halloween. It's become a tradition for guys to take their girls up there to tell them their version of the tale, smoke a couple joints, drink booze stolen from their fathers' liquor cabinets and try to get laid."

I step away from the window to lean my back against a standing bookshelf holding the whole of the Reference section: a copy of the Toronto phone book, a taped-together *Oxford English Dictionary*, a color atlas of the world and the *Guinness Book of World Records.* All of it shaking slightly from a brand new tic that pulls my shoulder blades together with a sudden violence every few minutes.

"So you don't believe there's anything to it?"

"Believe? That's different. You've been up there yourself, haven't you?"

"To investigate the circumstances—"

"Then you know what it's like. What do you believe?"

I answer with a sequence of cleared throat and unhinged mouth.

"O.K Tough question," Pittle finally laughs. "And not fair. I don't think I could answer it myself."

He pulls both his hands from pocket and head to scratch his beard with a sudden vigor, takes a moment to smooth the longer whiskers away from his lips. "So what was your question?"

"I guess you've already answered it, more or less."

Pittle returns to lifting the box's contents onto the floor. In his miniature arms each book appears to be the size of the stone tablets Moses carried down the mountain.

"You mind if I ask a question of my own?" he asks with his back turned.

"Go ahead."

"I'm having trouble seeing what Mrs. Arthurs's story has got to do with your client."

The shoulder blades pull together and the *Guinness Book* thumps over onto its side on the shelf.

"Tripp? It's got nothing to do with him. How could it? I was just wondering how nuts the old lady actually was."

"*Which* old lady?"

"Mrs. Arthurs."

"So you were wondering if she—Mrs. Arthurs—could be of assistance to the defence's case?"

"No. Of course not. No, no." I work up four mechanical shots of laughter. "It's of cultural interest only."

"I see."

Pittle's head remains set to the work before him, the muscles in his shoulders pushing tight cords against the inside of his cable-knit sweater. Outside the window, a clutter of sparrows emerge from the remaining leaves of a giant maple, startled by some invisible threat. I push my back away from the bookshelf to stand before Pittle's desk.

"Listen, Doug," I say, keeping my throat as loose as possible in order to deliver a just-a-guy voice. "I don't want you to think that I—"

"I don't."

Pittle stands now and turns to me, his teeth sugar cubes buried in facial hair. "Lawyers, reporters. Librarians, too," he says. "Questions are our business."

For a time both of us stand there with eyes cast at different corners of the room. Through some crack in a doorframe or windowpane comes the faint smell of woodsmoke.

"Well, thanks, Doug," I say finally. "But I suppose I should be getting back to the real world now."

"Sure," he shrugs. "Any time."

But before I move I do an odd thing. Raise my hand to wave at him as though he were standing at some distance away. A stupid, inexplicable gesture, but Pittle doesn't acknowledge it. It takes a conscious effort to bring my arm down again. To prevent any further strangeness I keep both hands busy by sending them to my throat where they straighten my tie all the way down the hall and out into the broad world of light.

Seeing as I'm in the neighborhood I decide to drop in on Tripp on my way back, justify my *per diem* with a social call on the guy who's paying the bills. Short and sweet, a hang-in-there-big-fella pep talk—this is what I have in mind. But then the interview room door opens and it's clear that even this modest plan was overly ambitious. My client's face an enlarging moon, bloodless, puff-jowled.

"You look well, Thom," I lie as he lands in the chair across the table from me, his hands absently hooked to the opposite edges.

"I wouldn't know. They don't let me look in any mirrors."

"That's cruel and unusual punishment for anyone to endure. Want me to smuggle one in for you?"

"I've gotten used to it, actually," he says, moving his head around on his neck in a slow orbit of mechanical crunches and squeaks. "A little while longer and I'll have forgotten who I am altogether."

"Well, you just give me the word if you need anything else, O.K?"

"Anything. Right."

I've been in here thirty seconds and it feels too long. Like sitting next to the drunk who's decided to talk to you and you alone on a poorly ventilated subway car. And there's something that comes off Tripp's skin—moist, feverish, a wet sheepdog sweat—that shrinks the space around him.

"Just thought I'd check in on you. See how things were

going," I say, tensing my knees for a quick lift up and out of here. "But if there's nothing else, I might as well get back and—"

"Have you been up there?"

Awake. My client sounds awake.

"Where's that, Thom?"

"The lake. Where else?"

"Well, yes. I have been up there. As a matter of fact."

"They always wanted to know about it."

"The girls—"

"How it was so deep that it never got warm, not really, even at the end of summer. About throwing a penny from shore and trying to find it among the rocks, the only thing shining up through all the silt. And the swimming contests— last one from the raft to the beach did all the dinner dishes. Oh *Lord!* They'd make me tell them so many stories I didn't have any more to tell."

Tripp shakes his head as though it was connected to the rest of him by a loose, insufficient spring.

"It's a hell of a lake, alright," I say. "Quite lovely."

"They *were* lovely," he exclaims, the neck straightening with a liquid click. "And *curious.* Curious kittens. Told them so many things that by the end I didn't know what was true. Or what they'd made up themselves. It got so that the things they said may as well have come out of my own mouth."

And then he actually does open his mouth, a brief choirboy oval that may have been an illustration of his point or an expression of surprise.

"Water that *never* got warm," he continues when his lips are brought together again. "And dark enough that you couldn't see your own feet below you with your eyes wide open. Make you wonder what was down there. Told them what *I* thought, but didn't they have their own ideas!"

Tripp laughs formally in the way of a politician attempting warmth in an election interview.

"All this makes me wonder about something, Thom."

"Hmm?"

"The Literary Club. What went on during those meetings?"

"Read books," he says abruptly, pushing back from the table and placing both hands on his stomach, jaw thrown about in a cud-chewing circle. "Then we'd talk about them. That was the idea. I think at first some of the other teachers didn't think it would work, that young people today don't *read books*. And they were right. They mostly don't. Never had any more of them who wanted to come other than Ashley and Krystal. And a boy—"

"Laird."

"—for a time, but he quit, which makes perfect sense seeing as boys read books even less than girls."

"So that's it? Things were the same even after Laird—after the boy was gone?"

"For a time, yes."

He wipes his hands down the front of his prison overalls as though trying to remove something sticky from the palms or swipe away a layer of crumbs under his chin. Takes his time and I watch him. There's something in this motion—deliberate, self-conscious, a little ashamed—that makes him appear at once much older and younger than he is. He could be a child worried about getting in trouble for making a mess at the dinner table. An ancient bachelor noticing a mysterious crust on his hands and wondering what it could be, how long it had been there, or if anyone had noticed. But when he speaks again it's with a measured calm, his face raised to me, both youth and age gone from his face once more.

"One of the things I tried to teach my students is that narrative—what happens to us, the things we do to others— that the whole thing is organic. Of course it was a waste of breath most of the time. But those girls, they understood right away."

"What do you mean by organic, exactly?"

"Always changing yet always connected," he says, throws his hands a few inches into the air and spreads his fingers wide. "Always alive."

"So once you'd taught that lesson to the girls, what else did you do?"

"Let them grow."

"Let who grow?"

"The stories."

Tripp pulls himself close to the table, composes his face into a mask of teacherly consideration. The face he would have once used in making submissions to a school administrative board.

"We shifted the mandate, I suppose you could say. From a reading group to something more creative. After that, there really were no more lessons to teach."

"Is that why it became so private? I spoke to your field hockey friend, Miss Betts. She told me of your practice of lowering a blind down over your classroom windows during meetings."

"Environment is important," he shrugs.

For the first time during any contact I've had with Tripp I stand up, pace the perimeter of the room. It feels like I may be getting somewhere. Although it's totally unclear where that somewhere might be at least he's talking, and I'm hoping a little personal height advantage might help direct him where I'd like him to go.

"Did you keep a copy of the materials—of the fictional works the three of you wrote?"

"We didn't really work with texts. Too confining, and it took too long. The pen can never keep up with the mind." He raises his eyebrows. "Did someone famous say that or did I just make it up?"

"I'd put my money on you, Thom."

Position myself a few feet behind him, my shoes sandy clicks on the tiled floor.

"Tell me one of the stories the girls made up."

"There was only one. Or many all joined together."

"So give me a little sample."

" 'Fair is foul, and foul is fair.' "

"That's nice, but it's not entirely original."

Tripp doesn't try to turn his head to face me. The result is a slight echo in the small room, a fraction of doubling and delay. Four voices speaking at once from behind each of the walls.

"Your principal at the school, Mrs. Warren. I spoke to her too. We were both curious about your budget for the club."

"You've been a busy bee."

"Why would you need money for costumes, Thom?"

"Not me," he says, holds out his arms and draws them back with his words. "For Krystal and Ashley."

"So it was a play?"

"A story. I've told you that."

"And how did it end?"

"You'd have to ask them."

"But I can't."

"So you say."

The back of his head still as a mannequin's. The skin of his neck a waxy grid of wrinkles, the hair glued into each of the pores.

"Sounds like you all became very close," I say.

"As much as any family can be close. Which is how much, Mr. Crane? I have no doubt you've done your research into these things. How close can a father be to a daughter in a time—in a world where everything changes so easily?"

"They weren't your daughters."

"No, they weren't. They weren't indeed." He makes a sound that could be either a sob or a scoffing laugh. "It is a comfort when your lawyer has all the facts straight."

"But he doesn't. Not yet. Which leads me to my next question." I take in a tight breath. "There's a book I found at the library here in town. A history—"

Tripp suddenly spins around in his chair and faces me, a fluid turn involving the upper half of his body that cuts my voice off in my throat.

"You hear her too, don't you?"

"I'm sorry?"

"You heard me. Just as well as you can hear her."

"*Who*, Thom?"

"The Lady. She speaks to you too, doesn't she?"

"No, she doesn't. And I thought we discussed this matter earlier. An insanity plea is something we can consider, if you'd like, but at this juncture I feel our position is relatively secure. So there's no need for these displays—these desperate measures, O.K.? Just save it in case we need it for later."

What I thought might have been progress now collapsing

into the black of Tripp's eyes. He's gone again and it's time for me to go too. Six sharp raps at the door to make sure somebody hears and comes quick. Because the truth is the better I know my client the more he puts me off. And it's not the fear he creates in me but what I see of it in him that does it.

"'When shall we three meet again?'" he says when the guard comes to let me out, and although I could answer the line with the one that comes after there's no way I'm going to play along.

Outside the air smells like rain again, sour as burned peat. I half jog back down Ontario Street and manage to jump through the front doors of The Empire just as the first drops splash off my shoulders.

"Ah! Now that's a piece of good timin'!" the front desk clerk calls out from the dark as my foot hits the bottom step of the stairs. "Message for you."

He bends down to find the note but I'm ready for him, closing my eyes to avoid the sight of his thin-skinned head. When I open them again an arm's stuck out with a quivering slip of three-lined paper in its hand.

"Mr. Goodwin from the Crown's office. Says you ought to call as soon as you can. Sounds kind of excited."

I bound up to the honeymoon suite and dial Goodwin's office without taking off my coat.

"Crown Attorney's Office. Peter Goodwin speaking."

"Goodwin. It's Barth Crane."

"Ah. Hello, Barth."

"So?"

"Beg pardon?"

"You have some news?"

"Oh yes. Certainly do. There's new materials to be added to the Crown's previous disclosure."

"New materials?"

"I advise you to come round and have a look yourself because—"

"What is it?"

"It may not be appropriate over the—"

"Tell me what you've got, Goodwin."

"Perhaps—"

"*Now*, if you don't mind."

There's a pause as the big man at the other end takes a labored breath of savored pleasure.

"The DNA results are in. The blonde hair in the Volvo, Krystal's hairbrush and the backseat bloodstains," he says, taking another full breath to deliver the next two words.

"They match."

PART THREE

PART THREE

Twenty-Two

I think of the single photograph in my space in the city. How its details are more distinct here than if held directly to my eyes, the faces assuming a life they've been denied in their time spent behind the frame's glass. The smiles turning to laughter in the moment after the shutter closes, my mother's high and breathless, my father's a regular series of quarter notes, the same rattling string plucked on a stand-up bass. What caused them to laugh this way, to fall into each other's arms, dizzy from its release? It's the recognition of their own foolishness, the spectacle they're making—married adults made giddy by posing for a vacation snapshot—this is the fun part. Otherwise serious people whose company could still wipe all seriousness away, a shared joke passing wordlessly between them.

Slide my hand over the papered walls of the honeymoon suite and work my way back. My mother first, the chances always better with her. But the effort only yields the same jittery super-8 clips, over and over: sitting behind the wheel of a station wagon, turning to face me while she talked and me wishing she'd just keep her eyes on the road; raising a glass of white wine to her lips with one hand while lowering dirty plates into the dishwasher with the other after the dinner party guests had finally left; lifting the lid of a mother-of-pearl jewelry box to pull out a pair of earrings while inspecting her wrinkles in the bureau mirror. What else? Her mouth. Thin, but generous with kisses.

Wait for more pictures to appear on the screen of my closed lids. But nothing ever comes, and eventually the houselights are raised and the usher arrives to tell me there won't be a show tonight so I might as well go home.

At least with my father I've got the facts. All the handed-down accounts and loving testimonials from various peripheral Cranes, the caretakers for the remaining years of pre-adult purgatory that followed my parents' death. With them, I was brought up on sighed repetitions of how great my father was and how kind, examples of the infinite extent of his patience, and always, in hushed wonder, a word about his renowned devotion to his wife. Always, too, a hand placed on my cheek. The same cheek, the very same *face* as my father, it was said. So much your father's son!

For all the years I spent at boarding school I refused to look at myself in mirrors. Wore my hair in a crewcut so I never needed to find where to part it. When I was old enough to shave I did so in the dark, feeling for the missed patches with my fingertips. Through these habits I came to forget my own face. I wanted enough time to pass so that when I looked again I would see neither father nor mother, and only myself. They were gone now, and what little they'd left me with was slipping away. And if I couldn't know enough to make them whole, I would know nothing at all.

When I looked again in the mirror I saw all the same things I thought I'd forgotten except now less distinct, anonymous, a face made up of used parts.

The next time I looked I was a man.

Twenty-Three

As soon as Goodwin told me that the blonde hair and bloodstains found in the back of Tripp's Volvo had matched I hung up on him. Not a very professional response, I suppose, but sometimes an inclination for spontaneity can get the better of me. This is regrettable for a number of reasons, not the least of which is that now I'm not certain what the test results actually are.

Later I call Goodwin's office back but his secretary tells me he's out for the rest of the day so I make an appointment for the next morning. And when the morning comes I'm out early. A little too early as it turns out, as I have to wait outside the courthouse doors in the rain for half an hour before they're opened. This is still preferable to any extra time spent alone in my room surrounded by the Incredible Grinning Wallpaper, yet to be removed for reasons unclear even to myself. Every time I reach out to hitch a finger under the corner of one of the pages my arm freezes before it gets there and only a double-barreled whack from the thermos permits the full use of my limbs again. I'd rather stand in the rain.

When the doors are finally opened I settle myself in Goodwin's office and wait for his arrival. By the time he shifts his gut around the corner of his desk I've thoroughly drenched the chair I sit in, drops of water plinking onto the waxed tiles underneath.

"You need a towel?" Goodwin gusts, a regretful grin visible beneath overhanging cheeks.

"That won't be necessary. I prefer evaporation."

"I'm not one to tell another man his business, but you really should get your hands on an umbrella."

"I'll take it under advisement."

Goodwin shrugs, extends his thick arms out over the stacked papers on his desk, finding what he was looking for and lifting it back in front of him. All of this is done with such deliberate movements one can feel the man's concentration, his struggle to animate a body which, if left to its own devices, would choose inertia and continued enlargement over action and purpose.

"This is the full text of the DNA test results," he says, patting the file's cover with his palm. "My secretary is assembling your copy right now."

"That's fine. In the meantime, however, could you give me an idea of precisely what the results *are*?"

Goodwin gives me a look that suggests that maybe if I'd stayed on the line for five more minutes I would have known the results yesterday, but it's more a look of amusement than anger. It's not right. I'd rather he simply not like me than find me funny.

"Well, as I indicated yesterday, there's a match."

"Between what?"

"Krystal's hairbrush sample, the backseat hair and the blood."

"Only Krystal?"

"That's right. As far as the *blood* goes. But there's also a match between the dark hair found in the backseat and the sample taken from Ashley's brush. Now, if you require an adjournment in order to review these conclusions, I'd be prepared to consent—"

"There will be no need for an adjournment. And what conclusions could possibly follow from any of this? Or I should say, what conclusions do *you* think may follow?"

Leans back in his chair, his gut rising up over the desk's edge like a whale's rounded back breaking the surface to take in air.

"Well, I think the blood and the hair that matches it both come from Krystal McConnell. That's clear. And I think this fact further indicates that she was in Tripp's car—likely on several occasions—and that on at least one of those occasions she was bleeding."

"Bleeding *when?*"

"The test doesn't determine that."

"Exactly. So she could have left those drops there anytime. And we're talking about *drops*, nothing more."

"I don't see—"

"*I* don't see what you think you have here, Pete. Hair and a few red stains."

"Well, on a balance of probabilities, I think we can show—"

"*Fuck* 'on a balance of probabilities'! Unless there's been some radical new development in the search for McConnell and Flynn's bodies, they're still missing, right? And that's all you know for sure. You know the two girls left their hair in their teacher's car, but nobody's denying he drove them home after class sometimes, so there's nothing interesting about that. And the blood? Not the volume you'd expect from mortal wounds, is it? And from only one of them. Seems you've got more explaining to do with this evidence than me. Or am I missing something?"

"There are witnesses that will testify to seeing Tripp and the girls together in the car at various times. Maybe you're forgetting that."

"No, I'm *not*. I'm *not* forgetting that. I'm merely disregarding it because it's irrelevant."

"I don't think it's irrelevant. I think this is evidence that connects the girls and their blood to Tripp and his car. It's a connection I believe the jury will make as well."

"Juries will make connections between anything if you ask them nicely. But they can just as easily be told to pay no attention to any of it. And don't forget I get to go last."

He sighs sharply, the sound of airbrakes released by an idling tractor trailer. Something about it makes me want to pull a clump of his curling, nose hairs out with my bare fingers.

"Mr. Goodwin," I say instead. "I'll share with you what my mentor, Graham Lyle, often told me whenever I'd try to see more in the facts than was actually there. He'd tell me, 'Bartholomew, it's a fatal mistake for counsel to allow wishful thinking to stand in the way of logic.'"

The folds of Goodwin's shirt dive beneath the desk and his head 3-Ds forward, the redness in the cheeks now raised to the level of his hairline.

"Don't *patronize* me, Mr. Crane. Alright? That's all I ask. You can play the cocky bastard as much as you like. I don't care. But *don't* tell me how to do my job."

I'll say this: these words are delivered convincingly.

"Fair enough," I flutter my eyes closed. "I agree to refrain from any further impositions of professional advice. You have my word."

"Thank you. Now perhaps we could return to any outstanding matters regarding the supplementary disclosure. Do you have any questions I can help you with?"

The flash of anger is already gone, the color fading from hanging jowls. No question about it: this guy has some impressive skills in the emotional self-control department. Not surprising really, considering the man's endured a lifetime of being too quickly dismissed. Maybe he's trained himself to use this to his own advantage—wait for his opponents to stop taking him seriously, and then roll over them. More likely he's just developed a couple of tricks in order to preserve his dignity. And who could blame him for that?

"I'd like to know about your witness list, as a matter of fact," I say through a surprisingly urgent throat clearing. "Who's going when?"

"Well, I expect to begin with Bill Butcher, the O.P.P.'s Chief Investigating Officer on the case. He'll do a review of the essential Crown evidence."

"Right. Who's next?"

"My psychological expert, who'll provide background on the current leading theories on the motivations behind child abduction, that kind of thing."

"But nobody's even done a psych evaluation on Tripp yet."

"That's true. We're interested only in mapping out certain general background factors—"

"But he can't say anything directly *about* him, right?"

"No. Not directly, no."

"Sure, sure. And then?"

"The teachers. They'll talk about Tripp's apparent breakdown following losing custody of his daughter, giving the girls rides, his relationship with them in the Literary Club."

"Whatever."

"O.K. Next it's Mr. McConnell—"

"McConnell? Why? What could he possibly say?"

"Nothing as to the facts, I admit. But I think he deserves an opportunity to address the court. He wants that opportunity."

"I'm sure he does. But I might as well tell you now that I will object like hell to his being permitted that opportunity."

"Fine. Whatever the outcome of that, I've next planned for some of Butcher's assisting officers, then our DNA expert to interpret the results, and that's about it. I'll of course give you notice of any further additions."

Goodwin's secretary steps in behind me with a bound copy of the DNA report held out before her.

"Thanks, Corinne. That one's for Mr. Crane."

She extends the document out in front of her the full length of her arm as though it's a vicious animal that's been temporarily tranquilized, drops it into my lap and clicks out of the room.

"Murders make her nervous," Goodwin explains.

I stick the report into my case and rise to leave, my damp suit clinging to ribs and thighs in gravity-defying wrinkles.

"Barth, can I tell you something? And I don't mean anything by it beyond professional courtesy."

"Sure."

"You don't look so good."

"No? Well, I'll make a point of being more *attractive* for our next meeting."

"I didn't mean—"

"Truth is, I haven't been sleeping all that much lately. Burning the midnight oil."

"Of course. It's a pretty stressful time, I know."

"Maybe for you, pal. You *should* be stressed. But believe me, I'm fine."

I turn then, my clothing making an audible squishing sound with every step. Try to keep my back straight as I go but I can't really feel it anymore, and it would make no difference now anyway. It's too late. And the worst of it is that of all the fellow sufferers in this world it was the fat man who'd felt sympathy for me.

Twenty-Four

Jury selection is a tricky business under the best of circumstances, but up here the process poses a special challenge. The field of candidates clucking and tooth-picking in the hallway outside Courtroom 109 compose an unsightly logjam of humanity, their faces set by experiences and gene pools I'd prefer not even to consider. Uniformly hirsute, vinyl hockey jackets stained by a sticky, mysterious goo, noses and lips threatening to fall off from the abuses of grain alcohol and tobacco. Their loose-skinned expressions communicating less impatience than a pained confusion.

"No need to bring in the local intelligentsia, Pete," I say to Goodwin as I settle at the counsel table next to him.

"You're the one who wanted people from the surrounding area and not from town. I've only accommodated your request."

"And for that you have my appreciation. I just had no idea so many distinguished members of society would have selected the woods north of Murdoch as the place to work on their memoirs."

It's true that the field for jury selection was partly my own doing. We'd considered a change-of-venue motion early on to bring the trial down to be heard in Toronto, but Bert argued persuasively against it on the basis that in highly publicized trials of this kind, no town in the whole province could put forward a dozen people who weren't familiar with the reported facts. In fact, it was decided that requesting the Crown to gather a jury to be selected from the northern half of the district would render people with the greatest chance of not having a clue about anything in the outside world. In any other place, Tripp would have already been unanimously villainized as the demonic child snatcher. But up here, where creepiness of all but the most severe kind is largely put up with, the defence stands a reasonably good chance of pulling twelve blank slates from out of the trees.

"Well, what say we bring them on, Mr. Goodwin?"

Goodwin waves his forefinger at the court clerk who sits in front of the bench with eyes already half closed. Having been interrupted from his clerkish dreams, he shuffles off to bring in the man designated to oversee the proceedings.

But it's not a man. It's Justice Naomi Goldfarb. This is very good news. Well known to be patient with the defence and strict with the Crown and, perhaps best of all, famously antagonistic toward all in the constabulary. Consistently over-looked for appointment to the Court of Appeal due, it is said, to her outspoken criticism of the Old Boys' Club which still runs the show in Upper Canadian halls of justice. I feel for her. The poor woman's been assigned this nasty business, necessitating a long stay away from her comfy Forest Hill digs where I've drunk deep from the wine cellar at her annual garden party held for invited members of the criminal bar, my own invitation issued solely by virtue of my place of employ. I've appeared before her on a couple of minor matters in the past though, so she'd likely be aware that this is my first murder. Another blessing. Now I can play the defence *naif* who needs his hand occasionally held in order to get him through the complicated unpleasantries.

"Good morning, gentlemen," Goldfarb sighs as she

mounts the steps to the judge's chair, arranging the layers of
her robes over the armrests. She has a rib-rattling voice and
a sarcastic look permanently draped over her face which,
when seated, can barely be seen over the edge of the desk
from where Goodwin and I sit in our places below.

"Good morning, Your Honor," I chirp in before Goodwin has a chance.

"Ah, the joys of jury selection! Mr. Crane, do you expect
to exercise your right to twenty peremptory challenges of the
jurors to be arrayed before you this morning? I ask only
because it would be really nice if we could select our twelve
before the end of the day, don't you think?"

I stand and give her what I hope to be my most accom-
modating Crane smile.

"While I *reserve* the right to challenge some of those I will
make inquiries of today Your Honor, having viewed the
candidates in the hall outside on my way in this morning, I
have every expectation that the *defence* won't be holding up
the proceedings, at any rate."

"Very good, Mr. Crane. I applaud your optimism. Mr.
Goodwin, please have the sheriff usher in the first of our
lucky contestants."

And so it begins. By lunch we've got eight suitably
unbiased neanderthals under our belt, and by mid-afternoon
the full twelve plus four on reserve have been duly questioned
and given full approval by yours truly. Four retired mine
workers, a marina owner, two self-described "lumberjacks," a
manager of a Christmas tree farm and four bearded mumblers who, reading between the lines, are American draft
dodgers who've been in self-imposed exile so long they
haven't yet been made aware of the twenty-year-old pardon
allowing them the full freedoms of the civilized world. All of

them but the marina owner are men, and all, when asked if they had any knowledge of the accused, answered either "No" or "Who?"

They'd do just fine.

"We're ready for opening submissions a week from today, gentlemen?" Goldfarb winks as she gathers herself up from where she sits, visibly anxious to get in another few hours of city time before the coming Mondays-to-Fridays she'll be required to be stationed in the boonies. Again, playing Goodwin's physical disabilities to full advantage, I leap to my feet to offer my response first.

"Absolutely, Your Honor. And looking forward to it too."

"Well, that makes one of us, Mr. Crane."

I haven't called on Tripp yet to inform him of the hair and blood DNA results. The problem is that it's so easy to forget about him. Or, more to the point, it's easy to *pretend* to have forgotten about him. But it can be delayed no longer.

After Tripp is deposited with me in Interview Room No. 1 we manage to exchange some niceties—hellos, a bloody shame about all this rain, even a joke about prison food— and I wonder if today, now that it's coming down to the wire, he's prepared to offer me some help.

"I'll come right to it, Thomas," I start, then tell him about the DNA findings and outline their potentially grim connotations. For a time he appears to consider my words with an appropriate sobriety, places his hands together on the table. Then a mournful downturn hooks itself to his lips once more. Eyes straying away to the dream-in-progress projected onto the enameled wall.

"They had such *nice* hair," he inhales delicately, as though savoring the memory of its smell. "But they'd laugh

when I told them they should tie it up with a bow maybe, that
they'd look even prettier that way. Just laugh at me when I
told them that's how all the girls used to wear it, years ago."

"That's amusing, Thom. But let's stick with the program
a minute here, O.K.? First of all, is there anything we can say
to explain how that blood got there? I mean, if you think the
truth will sound bad, is there anything else?"

"If the truth sounds bad?"

"Don't you see how this looks? It's pretty obvious to me,
and it'll be pretty obvious to the jury as well if we can't
provide some way of answering the Crown's spin on it."

Tripp winces, reshapes his mouth into a polite smile.

"Not sure I—"

"Do you think I'm stupid? The longer you play dumb,
the bigger the shit we're both going to find ourselves in. And
your pile will be far bigger than mine, I promise."

I'm shouting now, louder than I intended, but Tripp
only sits back in his chair and watches me with detached
interest.

"How did you cut Krystal, Thomas?"

"*I* didn't do *that.*"

"No? Then how did it happen?"

"By accident."

"*Whose* accident?"

"Krystal's!" he shouts now himself. "Horsing around with
some of the boys out by smokers' corner after school and got
in the middle of some wrestling match or other and scraped
her knee. One of the other teachers brought her in and was
going to call her father but I said I'd take care of it. Because
I knew the trouble she'd be in if Lloyd found out that she'd
been *smoking* with a bunch of *boys* instead of being inside at

choir practice where she was supposed to be. She just hated going to choir practice! 'Only *Christians* go to choir,' she'd say, and stick out her tongue—like this!"

Tripp now sticks his own tongue out and laughs from the back of his throat. I can't help but notice that its surface is coated in a glistening layer of lime-green film, and that he displays it for an unnecessarily long time before pulling it back in.

"So I took her in the car to the clinic," he continues, "and they put four stitches in her knee. When they were done I dropped her off near her house. I noticed the blood on my shirt the next morning. And in the car, little dots in the backseat. I didn't mind, though. They were just stains. And they were Krystal's."

"When did this happen?"

"April Fool's Day. Isn't that amusing?"

I study Tripp's face for evidence of a lie but it's an impossible task. Even in my few years of practice I've had to deal with some remarkably accomplished liars, some you *know* are so good you will have made yourself promise to never believe a single word that comes out of their mouths. The next thing you know you find yourself thinking that maybe on *this* point, this *one* issue, they're speaking the truth. But they're not. And this is the art of all great liars: making you believe the single fiction that among all the others is most important for them to have you believe. Tripp may well be a great liar himself, or he may only be the fucked-up dullard that he appears. All I know is that I've never met anyone— client, witness or otherwise—who provided so few clues.

"Thanks, Thom. I'll come by again next week to see you before the big day," I say, but he looks at me as though he doesn't know what day I'm talking about or why it would be big.

"Bartholomew, this is Houston. Come *in*, Bartholomew."

Graham's voice on the speakerphone.

"Roger, Houston. This is Bartholomew."

"So good to hear your *voice*, old man! Just wondering how our star is doing up there in the land of the midnight sun. Oh, and I *heard* who was assigned to your case. Dear Naomi. Lyle, Gederov and the entire Toronto underworld owe her so much. Three cheers for Justice Goldfarb! *Hip-hip-hooray! Hip-hip—*"

"Graham, I was sleeping," I lie. "Can we do this another time?"

"Of *course* we can. You need your beauty rest, I know. Only wondering when you were planning on getting back down to the city for a little strategic pow-wow with us old guys. The festivities start tomorrow for you and I think before things move too far along in the Crown's case it might be nice to have a three-way brainstorm. Make everybody feel better. What say thee?"

"I wasn't planning on it, actually."

"No?" He smacks his lips as though working on a hard candy at the back of his mouth. "You think that's wise?"

"I think it's better that I stay put up here, that's all."

"I applaud your commitment, but perhaps a meeting of the minds would only make things a little clearer for us *and* for you before things really get rolling. And you could eat some real food. My God, you must be *dying*! Do they even have a Thai take-out up there? Or a *steak house* for the love of—"

"I'm fine. I'm not hungry." Easy now, Barth. He's listening for cracks. "And you know what? There's really no need for me to come back down to the city. I'm ready to rock up here. Everything's cool."

For a moment I can almost hear Graham's thoughts gaging whether I'm bullshitting or not, if he was prepared to insist at this point, how all this would pass with Bert. But when he speaks next it's warm and teasing.

"Cool and *ready to rock*, eh? Well, can I at least make a request that you let us know how you're doing every once in a while? The last thing we want is the wheels falling off our boy's little wagon."

"I'll stay in touch. I just need to get some sleep now, that's all."

"Well, you do that, my good man," Graham says rather doubtfully. "You get some sleep. And you stay in touch too, or I'll have to come up there myself and give you a good thrashing. Understood?"

"Yes, Pa."

Then Graham's gone and there's nothing but the room again. And me. Me and the room.

It's the eve of trial and I'm walking the streets of town wishing for morning, for a cigarette, for a little company. Three things I normally have no interest in. Surely this is an initial sign of middle age, the sudden desire to dispose of old habits and take on some healthier new ones. Because it's all going, isn't it, little by little? Not only am I not getting any younger (easy enough to accept given its impossibility), but I'm *getting older*. My body calcifying, mysterious pains flashing through internal organs, muscles aching without just cause. Basic mechanics sliding out of my control and nothing but the brain left to count as my own. Which wouldn't be so bad if it too hadn't become doddery, endlessly gabbing away to itself but always failing to arrive at conclusions. It's not even *interested* in conclusions anymore. All it wants is to avoid the big questions and gnaw at a harmless puzzle every once in a while. Still, overall I must consider myself among the lucky. At least I'm not worried about my weight.

In fact, now that I think of it, if anything I'm aware of how light I feel. The weight of a forgotten name. A party balloon blown full of nothing. If I couldn't look down and know that my feet were still tied into my shoes I wouldn't be surprised if I just lifted off the ground once and for all, drifted up past the buzzing streetlights and slumped hydro wires into the supposedly infinite night sky. And the thing is I wouldn't really mind, not too much, although I'm not crazy about the dark and have every reason to believe it would be cold up there.

The offstage yowl of a backyard cat fight. A car washes past in the street, brake lights glaring. Nobody looks my way.

After a while I stop at the playground at the side of St. Mary's Elementary, plant myself into one of the canvas swings. Hold my legs out straight and creak back and forth through solid air.

I'm thinking: this is where kids play. Watched by parents standing on the other side of the fence or from their idling minivans, believing that if they could just manage to be around their children enough of the time they might afford them some protection. But how can you protect them from something you can't see? What defences can be drawn against the anonymous monster that lives three doors down the hall, delivers your mail, gives you a smile on the way to the bus stop, lies next to you in bed?

I'm thinking: maybe this was Tripp's daughter's school.

Maybe he even pushed her on this same swing once, or stood below her as she clambered over the bars of the jungle gym to make sure he'd be there if she fell. Maybe this was the same place where he stood outside in the rain, looking up at her face in the classroom window. Thinking of how much he loved her, how desperately he missed her and the injustice of being denied her company. But who knows? Maybe he was thinking to hell with all the goddamn lawyers and cunning ex-wives and court orders that say you can't come within two hundred yards of your own child. Maybe he was already working on alternative plans. How he would take her away and nobody would ever see either of them again. How maybe he'd do something bad to somebody else if it all didn't work out. Or then again it could be that he was just another awkward father who didn't quite know how to love.

Nobody really thought it was the English teacher anyway until he was arrested. He looked normal enough. So why are we always surprised when normal-looking people do terrible things? Almost all of my clients have been the sort about whom it is said that they look and talk just like you or me. Because they *are* you and me. And this is the only really startling thing about the evil of the world: not that so much of it exists, but that nobody ever expects it.

Later that night I dream of being asleep in my bed in the honeymoon suite. I know it's a dream even as it's happening. Everything as it actually is but with some of the details slightly altered: the distance between my feet and the windows the length of a bowling alley, the desk looming with stacked paper on the verge of collapse, the moon hanging like a paper plate over the town but casting no light into the room. Yet when I look up at the ceiling I know where I am. The feeling the same as looking at your own reflection in a mirror: *I know I am here; I know I am there.*

There's the room's coolness that keeps me from sleep even with the covers pulled around my ears. The newsprint on the walls that in the dark gives the appearance of a *papier-mâché* cave. A nearly human sculpture that is my clothes thrown over the back of a chair, a squirrel digging through the eavestrough outside the window.

Then a new sound. So distant at first it could just be another layer I've added onto the others but slowly coming forward, distinct. The brush of something soft against wood, the squeak and snap of the floor taking on new weight. Outside the bedroom door, moving down the hallway. Closer.

Now I wish the dream was boring again, that I could go back to being an insomniac in an imagined room. But this wishing doesn't stop the sound from filling out, unmistakable footsteps landing slow but heavy through the walls. I turn my head—the rustle of hair over the pillow loud enough for the whole hotel to hear—and keep my eyes on the door. Just enough space to slip a note under but it gapes wider even as I watch it. A hand could fit through now. An entire arm, reaching up to the doorknob to let itself in.

But when there's something to see it's not a hand or an arm but bare feet. The skin pale orange in the antique light.

Then I do just as I would likely do in real life: close my eyes and hope it goes away. But it doesn't. It's too real. It is real.

That's why I'm pulling back the sheets, sitting up on the edge of the mattress with eyes locked on the bottom of the door. The feet disappeared from view now; I'm up too high and the angle's changed. But the sound is clearer. A living thing that knows I'm here, waits for me to stand and go to the door.

And then I'm standing and going to the door. My own steps far louder over the floor than whatever waits for me in the hallway although I'm barefoot as well, frozen bones that can no longer feel where the air stops and floor starts.

Hold my ear flat against the wood. My breath a tuneless whistle up through my throat, tight as a straw.

And another's from the other side. A low, sickening rattle.

So cold.

The liquid clack of tongue. Words so unclear they don't even sound as words do but I'm still certain what they are.

Watch as my arm drifts away from my side. The fingers snapping back the bolt, pulling the door open wide and closing my eyes against the staggering wash of frigid air. At once acrid and sweet, bushels of cotton candy thrown onto a fire.

And a woman.

Standing in the middle of the hallway wearing nothing but a moldering hospital gown with holes rotted through to the body beneath. Her face bloated, broken open, envelopes of skin hanging across the dull ivory of her skull. Water still dripping off the long strings of her hair and down her stomach, her knees, collecting in a greasy pool around her feet. Stepping forward to take me in.

Hold me.

Raises her arms and her body enlarges to fill the door frame. Then her mouth. A space the size of my fist, and wider. The size of my head. A mouth stretched to break into laughter or a scream that beads my face with the bitter moisture from her lungs.

Close my eyes and wish it away. But again it's not my wishing that does anything, but a voice. Here in this room where I'm asleep, calling myself out from inside the mirror, from what you know can't really be there but is there nevertheless.

Twenty-Five

Both the quiet of Murdoch's streets and the more or less steady rain that's fallen upon them over the preceding weeks are interrupted on the morning of the first day of trial. As soon as I turn outside the doors of The Empire to walk up to the courthouse I can see the clog of vans with satellite dishes rigged up on their roofs parked out front as well as an orange tarpaulin shelter that's been erected on the lawn to protect the TV reporters' hair from the wind. Two of them out there already, one man and one woman standing next to the war memorial that lists the bronze names of the local dead. Both applying hairspray, daubing at blackheads with makeup-smeared cotton pads and snapping orders at clipboard-holding assistants. Still, now that I'm up here I can see that only a couple of stations have decided to make the trip. Maybe the Lost Girls story has been losing momentum in the editorial boardrooms where such things are decided. Or maybe it's been replaced with some other garish tale, one better able to deliver compelling visuals, violent details, and isn't so inconveniently far from downtown.

Even though I'm wearing my barrister's robes and swinging a heavy leather document bag at the end of my arm, neither of the primping reporters seems to notice my arrival. And that's fine with me. I've been instructed by Bert that the best approach in this case is to lay as low as possible. "Don't give the fuckers anything," were his exact words. "They'll only

turn whatever you say around and make it worse for us." His
"us" left me with the distinct impression that he meant "me
and Graham." Nevertheless, it was probably good advice no
matter whom it was meant to serve, and as I bound up the
front courthouse steps and push open the main oak doors
I'm fully prepared to "No comment" my way through the
throng of hacks and photographers waiting in the marble
mezzanine for their first glimpse of Bartholomew Christian
Crane, the young turk they've come all the way up here to
see if he's got what it takes.

But there's nobody there. Just a couple of robed lawyers
laughing to themselves, their clients following uncertainly
behind them, and a janitor buffing the floor with one of
those machines with spinning cotton mop heads that hover
silently back and forth. But no reporters gathering in for the
serum. In fact the only ones who look my way as I walk down
the hall to Courtroom 109 are the whiskey-faced regulars
sitting on the benches, eyes bleary with hangover, wondering
if I was to be the one to try and put them away for longer
than the last time.

Inside, the courtroom gallery is half full: Mr. and Mrs.
McConnell straight-backed in the front row immediately
behind Goodwin's table; Brian Flynn on his own in the back
at the furthest point from the McConnells he could find;
Doug Pittle with a notepad teetering on his crossed legs;
Laird Johanssen grinning over at me proudly as though he'd
just released a prodigious fart; a half-dozen members of the
press, three crime reporters I recognize from the Toronto
dailies who, as is their habit, sit, one behind the other,
making too much noise.

With a "Good morning" to Goodwin I take my place at
the defence table and arrange the contents of my document

bag around me like a fortress. Then we all wait. And when the clerk's voice finally booms, "All rise!" enough time has passed in silent tension that I can feel the entire courtroom jolt back to full consciousness and stand on legs weakened by being crossed too long. All watch the judge come in and take her position in her high-backed chair, and by the time she grumbles a "You may be seated," maybe ten seconds after being told to stand, it's as though we couldn't have held ourselves up a moment longer, as all our asses crunch simultaneously back down on padded chair and wooden bench.

Then from a side door Tripp is brought in, shuffling over to his seat next to mine, his ankles polyester sticks in iron shackles. Once Tripp is seated the bailiff removes them and hooks them to a metal clasp on his belt to be put on again at Tripp's exit.

"How are you doing, Thomas?" I whisper over to him, and he manages to turn, part lips coated white with unrinsed toothpaste and whisper, "Yes." Yes to what? I'm not about to ask.

The jury is then ushered in from a door on the opposite side and the twelve of them, more bewildered by the feel of their clean-shaven faces and laundered clothes than the unfamiliar surroundings, take their places in the box. Some look Tripp's way, squinting him into focus, but most keep their eyes on the bench. From her elevated seat Goldfarb scans the room, peering over our heads as though trying to find her husband at a cocktail party. Finally she turns to the jury, closes her eyes in the gathering of strength, then opens them at the same moment as she opens her mouth.

"Members of the jury, today is the first day of the trial for which you will serve as jurors for as long as this proceeding requires. Before you hear any of the Crown's witnesses and, if they elect to call any, the defence's witnesses, you will first hear opening submissions from both counsel. I must instruct you that the things they will say today are *not* statements of proven fact. What you will hear today is just *argument*, theories of what did or did not happen in relation to the accused. So just sit back, keep an open mind and try to pay attention. O.K.? Now, without further ado, Mr. Goodwin, are you prepared to deliver opening submissions for the Crown?"

"I am, Your Honor."

"Then we're all ears."

Goodwin lifts himself out of his chair, places his fingertips on the table's edge to feel where it is in case he needs it. Nods once to the bench then turns to face the jury, taking a few seconds to look directly into each of the twelve sets of eyes that goggle back at him.

"We live in a society of advanced technology. Of TVs with two hundred channels, computers that can speak to each other, even genetic cloning. And I can tell you, every scientific and technological resource available to humankind was employed in the search for Ashley Flynn and Krystal McConnell. But it *still* wasn't enough. At first the police classified them as 'Missing.' Then 'Disappeared.' And finally, after enough evidence was collected, they were led to conclude that the girls had been murdered. But, as my friend for the defence will no doubt repeatedly remind you, their bodies have not been found.

"You may well ask yourselves, 'How can two people just go *missing* in today's day and age?' And it would be a perfectly reasonable question. But I can tell you, Krystal and Ashley are *not* exceptional cases. Despite the breakthroughs of the scientific age people still disappear. All the time. In Canada, for example, sixty thousand children are reported missing each year. In the United States, it's twenty-three hundred *every day.* Of course the majority of these people eventually come home, but not all of them. In fact, chances are greater than one in thirty that a year later that child will still be missing. Think about it. One minute they're here, and the next they're gone.

"And when they go, too often it's at the hands of a murderer. But even this isn't uncommon. Would you imagine that in our sparsely populated country there are, on average, over 700 homicides a year? And that's nothing compared to the States, where they manage to get that number up to well over forty times that. And here's a couple other things you might not have imagined: ninety percent of murderers are male, and the number one motive given for why these people decided to take the life of another is 'love.' *Love.* Members of the jury, I needn't tell you that there's something *wrong* about that. What happened to Krystal McConnell and Ashley Flynn was terribly wrong. And while it's too late to save them now, it's not too late to do something for them. We can't change the world through what we do here in this courtroom, we can't make those numbers smaller. But we *can* do one right thing, make one right decision. And that is to find Thomas Tripp guilty of first-degree murder.

"But don't just take my word for it. There's going to be plenty of evidence to support the Crown's claim that these girls were brought to their ends by the man who sits at the table next to me. To show that what happened was this: on Thursday, May the twelfth, Ashley and Krystal went to Tripp's classroom after school as usual to attend a meeting of the Literary Club, of which they were the only members and Tripp their sole supervisor. At the closing of their meeting, he offered to drive them both home in his car, and they accepted. But this wasn't unusual; he drove them home after school quite a lot, actually—him up front and the girls in the back. In fact, they sat in the backseat so much they both left strands of their hair on the upholstery.

"So it is on this Thursday in early spring that Tripp decided not to drive the girls home, but take them out to Lake St. Christopher. The end of the road. Gets out the driver's side, opens the back door where the girls sit wondering what they're doing out there when their parents would be worrying about them and their dinners getting cold. Then Tripp grabs them. There's a struggle. One of the results of this struggle is that Krystal is cut, dripping blood on the backseat. How do we know this? Because she was blonde and Ashley was dark-haired. Because both blonde and dark hair was found in the backseat, and both were sent for DNA testing along with the bloodstains. Because the blonde hair and bloodstains *matched*.

"And now Tripp is dragging the girls off into the woods down toward the lake. But with their attempts to fight him off and all the spring meltwater flowing down the hill—well, you can imagine that it would be quite a muddy business. So muddy, in fact, that the pants and shoes Tripp wore that day were later found caked with it. But despite the girls' struggles and the slippery path he finally manages to get them down to the water's edge where he—well—what *did* he do? Only the accused who sits there before you knows for sure. But Lake St. Christopher is wide and one of the deepest bodies of water in the region. Deep enough to never have something put down in it come back up again, even with all the technology in the world.

"We've come to the end of the story and we're still left

with the question that any right-thinking person must ask. *Why?* Members of the jury, nobody can know for sure what goes on in the mind of a killer, but the answer may just lie in those numbers I mentioned earlier. Maybe he did it out of love. Not the love you feel for your husband or wife or kids or friends. But a perversion of love that's been twisted by a very sick mind. Think about this: Tripp kept pictures of girls cut out from catalogs pasted to the wall in his bedroom. Girls the same age as his victims. Girls modeling underwear.

"Members of the jury, that's our story of what happened and why. Over the course of this trial you will see and hear evidence to substantiate this story. But even more important than the evidence is making a difference. It's giving some peace to the dead *and* to the missing."

Goodwin collapses back into his chair and takes half a dozen noisy gasps for air. I have to hand it to him: he made it through the whole of his opening submissions without physical disaster. But it's still early yet. And now it's my turn.

"Mr. Crane?" The bench nods, and with a humble thank you, I rise.

"Those are undoubtedly some very disturbing statistics Mr. Goodwin cited for you all just now," I start, trying to keep things slow, half drawled. "I make my living in this business, and I can tell you that I'm *still* shocked whenever I hear them. Shocked, yes, but I have no doubt that they're true. Because we live in a terrible world. That's quite a thing to say, isn't it? But we *know* it's true. You can hardly turn on the local news these days without hearing about children gone missing—most often girls, isn't it?—and even though the police and the volunteer search parties are doing everything they can, you know if it's made it on TV it can't be good.

"No, you won't find me agreeing with Mr. Goodwin very

much over the days and weeks to come, but I certainly agree with him that it's a terrible world with enough terrible things in it to give anyone a million lifetimes worth of nightmares. I have those nightmares myself. In fact, I've been having more than my fair share since I started working on this case. And not because I have any misgivings about defending my client, Mr. Thomas Tripp. No. It's because two young girls have been lost and so far they haven't been found. But all we can do, friends—all *anyone* can do—is be good citizens, be vigilant, and do our jobs well.

"And as for our jobs, let's summarize what we've heard so far from the Crown. Mr. Goodwin wants us all to think that this trial is really about assigning blame to someone for something bad that we suspect has happened. Sounds O.K., right? But there are some serious problems here. First, a criminal trial is *not* about assigning blame but testing the sufficiency of the Crown's evidence. I know that doesn't sound as good, but that's our job here nevertheless. Second, while we all *suspect* something horrible has happened to Krystal McConnell and Ashley Flynn, we don't have any idea *what* actually happened. In fact, we don't know if those girls are dead or alive or somewhere in between. We know they're not *here*, but couldn't they just as easily have run away? Hitched a ride somewhere and months from now there'll be a voice on the phone asking for money or a ticket home. I'm not saying this is necessarily so in this case, and the defence is not relying on this hypothesis in any event. All I'm asking is that you keep this possibility in mind, ladies and gentlemen. Remember that we're all here concerning ourselves with murders that may not have occurred at all.

"But let's do the Crown a favor for the moment and take a closer look at their take on things. Mr. Goodwin told you about muddy pants and bloodstains, but—*hoo boy!*—there sure were a lot of holes in his tale, weren't there? Members of the jury, convictions of those accused of first-degree murder cannot be based on suspicions alone. And in this case, this is all the Crown has. Well, maybe not *all.* They've got some circumstantial curiosities and crossed fingers—but not a single piece of direct evidence relating Thom Tripp to the disappearance of Krystal and Ashley.

"Now I want to make it clear to the court that I use the girls' first names because, after the extensive work and research I've put into the preparation of this case, it *feels* like I know them. I've even met their fathers and conducted friendly interviews with them both, and as you can appreciate, such interviews are unusual indications of shared interests between parties in our respective positions. And I think it's because there *are* shared interests here. An interest in mourning the disappearance of two children from the community. An interest in having the Crown present its evidence before an impartial jury. And, most essentially, an interest in seeing justice done.

"*Seeing justice done.* Now that's a phrase we hear a lot, isn't it? But what does it really mean? We might *think* it means punishing someone for doing something as horrible as we *suspect* happened to Krystal and Ashley. It's tempting to let our search for justice slip into a hunger for vengeance. But you *must* resist this temptation. Because seeing justice done isn't about having somebody who doesn't have the right look about them put away because we've got a hunch that they've been up to no good. No. It's about determining the guilt or innocence of this *one* man in this *one* case on the *one* set of evidence tabled at the end of the day. It's a hard job. Nobody's denying it. But for the next while, it's your job. And so it is with respect I ask you, members of the jury, not to merely see that something's done to somebody. See that justice is done."

I sit. Not bad. Ripped a few pages from the Graham Lyle Opening Submissions Handbook, but enough of my own thrown in to be proud of. Visible nods of agreement from the jury, and even the press keep their mouths and laptops shut in the gallery behind me. Justice Goldfarb herself offers an audible sniff of congratulations before starting in with her instructions to the jury about not talking to a soul with regard to what you heard today or will come to hear over the course of the trial, etc., etc.

I should be pleased, but instead I feel the bubble and pitch of rising nausea. Everything inside made tight. I try to shake it by looking over at my client for whom I've just done a more than adequate job, but the sight of Tripp's drooping face just makes it worse.

An unwelcome feeling. But one so strong and unrelenting that for the time I have to wait before it passes I can't help but think there must be something in it.

Twenty-Six

Someone entering the hotel and climbing the stairs toward my room. I don't hear this although I'm still certain, like knowing you're being watched while sitting alone in your room. And now it occurs to me that maybe I've been alone in the upper floors of The Empire Hotel too long altogether. I've come to know all of its yawnings and groans to the point that there is now an unsettled intimacy between us. This is why I feel the footsteps on the stairs before I hear them, deliberate and hollow. Sharp knuckles through the wood.

I don't ask who's there, don't look around for something heavy or sharp just in case. Instead I go to the door without thinking and pull back the bolt.

"Hey, Mr. Crane."

Eyes open to a soggy Laird Johanssen, the three-quarter length sleeves of his Meatloaf T-shirt dripping Murdoch rain down to his fingertips. It's the *Bat Out of Hell* album cover with a demon biker blasting out of his grave riding a flaming Harley.

"Laird," I sigh, and realize that I'd been holding my breath. "How did you know this was my room?"

"Guy downstairs," he says, shaking back the jellied cables of his hair. "Told him I was your associate."

I stand back to let him in and immediately Laird's presence in the room feels absurd. Nobody else has been in here the whole time of my stay and now that I have a visitor it's the doughnut shop kid with the glasses permanently stalled at the pimply precipice of his nose. I walk back to the desk and sit down but for a moment Laird remains fixed just inside the door. Looks around at the pages of *The Murdoch Phoenix* on the walls, his head slipping into a slow nod.

"Ve-ry *in*-teresting," he says in a German-psychiatrist voice.

"Well it's a pleasure to see you again too, Laird, but what can I do for you?"

He looks at me directly, the shiver gone.

"Actually it's more like what I can do for you."

He moves over to the bed and sits on the edge of the mattress that barks loudly at having to bear his sudden weight. Then he pulls his arms out of the straps of his backpack and zips it open, a vicious grin playing over his lips.

"Forgot to give you something the other day," he says, and pulls out a pink folder, waves it in front of his face as though fanning himself.

"What is it?"

"What do you think?"

The grin, now less vicious than merely lopsided, stitched onto his mouth as though by some botched surgical procedure.

"I can't guess, Laird."

"I liberated it after word got out at school that Ashley and Krystal had gone missing. It was only a matter of time before Principal Warren would come down with the pliers to break open their lockers and hand everything over to the pigs. So I beat her to it, and managed to preserve this little beauty."

He waves the folder again, and I resist the urge to jump up from my chair, snatch it from his hands and smack him across the face with it.

"How'd you get into their lockers without breaking them open yourself?" I ask instead.

"Well, *one* way was to know their combinations." He says "combinations" in four distinct syllables as though speaking to a child.

"They told you?"

"Fuck no, man. I just *knew*."

"And you took whatever it is you have there for yourself."

"That would be the picture."

His mouth gaping at me in what flips between mirth and the masking of chronic pain. But then I think: that's what being a teenager *is*, isn't it? Trying to have a good old giggle while seriously wondering if things might be better if you were dead, or maybe made someone else dead. Youth as a carousel of mirth and pain, over and over and all at once. Usually you only see it for what it is after you've graduated into the shady protections of adulthood and can look back with the wish to do it all over again, except this time in the name of vengeance. But Laird seems to understand all this even as he lives it. Maybe this kid is a little too smart for Murdoch, too gifted for the gifted program. Or maybe he's only exactly as he appears: a weird little fucker who's decided to translate his unpopularity and useless froth of hormones into the kind of superiority found only in the true voyeur. One not content with merely sniffing the air after his subject has walked past, but one who pretends he can manipulate what he watches by watching in just the right way. Laird wants to believe there's been a role for him in all of this, in the lives of Krystal and Ashley and all the other hot girls. And now he wants to believe he has a role for me too.

"You're a smart guy, aren't you, Laird?"

"I didn't bring my report card along with me, but yes. I'd say so."

"You sure seem to know a lot about Krystal and Ashley, anyway."

"Work, work, work."

"Did you know *everything* about them?"

"Not everything."

"What color were their eyes?"

"Blue. Both."

"How much did they weigh?"

"Light. Whatever. I don't know."

He stops waving the file. The grin sags.

"Why did you ask me that?"

"No reason."

"Hey, man, you're not—"

"No, no, I'm not anything. Relax."

But now Laird looks anything but relaxed. Arms stiff at his sides, a look on his face as though he requires immediate use of the facilities.

"C'mon, let's see what you've brought me," I say, pitching up for a jovial tone. What I don't want is him running out of here without letting me see his little prize. "Hey now, let's have a peek," I laugh, and now Laird laughs too, or at least allows the unfortunate grin to return to his face, and hands the folder over to me. Inside there's a single sheet of paper that I pull close so that everything else but its text is blocked out of what I can see.

Rules of the Literary Club
No boys allowed (except for Dad).
No story can be stopped until it's finished.
No real names. No real families.
Everything is make believe.

The words carefully handwritten in blue ink, each sentence resting on dead-straight, invisible lines. Below them, one next to the other, two lipstick kisses for signatures. Perfect red, every wrinkle left marked on the page. The paper held close enough that I can read their lips. The color of their skin surrounding open mouths like maps of two distinct lakes.

"Whose dad are they talking about?" I say after looking at the thing for what is probably a full minute.

"Doesn't say, does it?" Laird shrugs. "But if I had to venture a guess, I'd say 'Dad' is Tripp."

"Why?"

"He was the only other member of the club, remember? And I don't think they thought of *me* as Dad, do you?" He looks at me, licks his lips. "If you're wondering why they thought of him that way—it's a mystery to me, man."

"So you've had this the whole time. After the police search for the bodies and Tripp was arrested and everything?"

"Suppose so."

"And now you're giving it to me?"

"To make the file complete."

I push my back against my chair, scrape its legs a few inches across the floor closer to where Laird sits.

"Why did you keep the rules separate from the rest of the stuff—the rest of the file?"

"Date of acquisition. The rules came later, so I put it in a different place." Laird raises his chin and speaks next in what I take to be his idea of an English accent. "I confess that my current office organization system leaves something to be desired."

"Do you realize how potentially important these documents are, Laird? That you might be in some serious trouble if it were found that you've been concealing evidence?"

"What do you mean?"

"It means that everything you've given me is not just part of some goofy joke. It means that these rules and the girls' file—that it all has potential bearing on a *murder* trial. See where I'm going here?"

"If it's so important, why haven't you handed it over to the police yourself?"

"Maybe I will. Right now I'm trying to analyze whether it may be fruitful to Tripp's case or not."

"How would it help?"

"Well, let's think about alternative scenarios here. Let's think about Tripp *not* being the murderer, but somebody else entirely. Somebody who had an interest in them. An unhealthy, or some would say perverse—"

"Hey, I just collect things, man."

"Like people."

"*No.* Only the stuff about them. I'm not—I mean, don't try and—"

"Is there anybody who can prove where you were the day the girls disappeared?"

Laird's jaw falls open to expose a yellow, undulating tongue.

"I just came up here to help you out," he says, shoulders lifting up to meet his ears as though to block them from hearing anything else.

"No you didn't. You came up here to give me evidence."

"That's not—"

"The first package you gave me at the doughnut shop wasn't enough so you figured you might as well give everything up so that maybe I'd put it all together. Isn't that it? You've been playing a game. Waiting until the police and me

and all the other idiots finally got up to speed on the sick kid
in the smart-ass program?"

"No *way*."

He says this in the unmistakable timbre of boyish protest.
The screeching demand that the goal never crossed the line,
the incriminating thing in his pocket wasn't his, his friend
gave it to him, it was all just a joke.

"Why them, Laird? Why Ashley and Krystal? They
wouldn't let you into their little club and it pissed you off?
Or did you just want to expand your souvenir collection?
Actually have some real girls instead of the gum off the
bottom of their shoes?"

"I didn't *do* anything!"

"Let's start at the beginning: you borrowed the keys to
your parents' car and met them after the Literary Club
meeting that Thursday, asked if they could use a ride home.
Then what did you do? Offered them a couple of Diet Cokes
with a little extra slipped in, something you stole from your
mother's medicine cabinet that she takes on her bad days
and before you knew it they were sawing logs in the backseat.
Then off to the lake, where you had some fun and then—
what?—did you have to use a boat, or did you just swim their
bodies out there one at a time?"

"This is *bullshit*!"

The sight of Laird Johanssen's face streaming with panicked tears is something I could have lived without but there
it is anyway. Spittled lips turned to dancing elastic bands. A
string of clear snot swinging down to his chin.

"I'm fucking outta here, man!" he coughs, but doesn't
move.

"You can tell me. I'm a lawyer."

"Tell you what?"

"Whatever it is that you know. Whatever you did."

"You wanna know something? This—" he says and stops, looks down at his upturned hands as though he expected something to be held there. "I'm gone."

And now he actually does rise from his place on the bed and it moans after him as he sticks his arms through the straps of his backpack. Throws the door open and steps out into the hall.

"I can help you, Laird."

"Never heard *that* one before," I hear him say under his breath without turning, his head hanging from his neck like a dead weight.

Once Laird's gone I watch the door for a while as though waiting for a face to appear in the pattern of cracks beneath two oval knots I've come to think of as eyes. Listen to the echo of Doc Martens galloping down the stairs. After it recedes the furnace switches on and a damp breeze sweeps into the room. The floorboards crackle with the change of temperature, the glass squeaks in its frame. The sounds of the hotel closing upon itself, satisfied that once more there's nobody but its solitary guest occupying its rooms.

After a time I reread the paper Laird left with me. The Rules of the Literary Club. Hadn't Tripp said they'd had active imaginations? It appears he was no slouch in that department himself. I read it over and over, lingering over the lipstick kisses, the capitalized "Dad." Read it for so long the words eventually fall away from their meanings and I take them in only as abstract markings, the liquid loops of what I immediately recognized as Ashley's handwriting. The paper is high quality, likely taken from Tripp's own desk for the purposes of ceremony and posterity. Marbled ivory—this would be its name in the stationery store. And below the written text the waxy blossoms of their lips: Krystal's round and pressed hard, Ashley's a narrow graze. The same crimson flourish, the lipstick passed between them. Maybe I'm sure of which is which from how closely I've studied their faces on the wall. Maybe I'm just sure.

How can you be sentimental over the lives of those you've never known? But I know how it happens. Working with Bert and Graham on homicides where the contents of a dead man's pockets are spilled out over a table to be studied for explanations, hints of poor character, complicity in foul dealings. Everything has sinister potential when thought of as evidence. But then after a while you start to get tired and forget about putting a case together and suddenly the same banal scraps become haunted. Look: there's a matchbook from The Fox and Furrow located in an Oshawa strip mall, a fortune pulled from a Chinese cookie ("You are only steps away from learning the truth you have been seeking"), an alligator-skin wallet with a snapshot of redheaded kids buried among the credit cards, a receipt for forty-seven dollars worth of long-stemmed roses meant for the dead man's wife, his secretary, an unknown beloved. Put it together and it means nothing. It means everything.

It means that Laird is coming forward. He wants to show and tell. He may even be circling around the idea of confessing, a process I've seen before that can take a little time. I tell myself that this is what I'm waiting for. Put a little pressure on and he'll come out with his hands up and we can all go home. I'll be patient. I'll make a clever plan.

I tell myself all of these things. Then I slip the paper in with the rest of the dead girls' file and do nothing at all.

Twenty-Seven

A Saturday morning and I'm lying awake with eyes set upon the door when, for the second time, a note is sent fluttering in beneath it. Watch as its corner comes to stick in one of the grooves between the floorboards and its fold swings open to reveal what from this distance appears only as ballpoint hieroglyphics.

> Dear B. Crane, "Honey. Suite".
> Mrs. Arthurs, "widow" of Duncan Arthurs, called up—
> "I'd like to meet with the lawyer." Says be at Royal
> George Tea Shop
> at 2 p.m.
> THE MANAGEMENT

I take up my position before the window overlooking the corner of Ontario and Victoria. Outside, a young mother with darting, bulbous eyes pulls a shopping cart with one arm and grips the hand of a bawling kid with the other. It's impossible to tell from this distance (and perhaps from any distance) if it's a boy or a girl. The mother stops at the red light, glances down at the child as though unfamiliar with it and only passingly curious about the source of its apparent torment, and continues on when the light changes. When both have nearly passed from sight the thing attached to its mother's hand swings its head to look directly up at me,

sneers in an adult expression of hateful contempt, and
resumes its tortured screeching.

How much worse could coffee with old Mrs. Arthurs be?

The Royal George Tea Shop is one of those pathetic Hail
Britannia places one still finds in certain small Ontario towns.
Cramped cafés distinguished by portraits of the young Chuck
and Di on every tray, apron and mug, framed prints of the
Queen hanging from all available vantages of paneled wall,
and Union Jacks providing the only color to offset the grey
faces of the patrons and smoke-stained lace on every table. A
small chalkboard lists the daily specials in a shaky hand
(sausage rolls, eggs and beans, salisbury steak). Upon opening
the front door I'm greeted by turned blank faces interrupted
from the slurping intake of tea the color of sidewalk puddles,
along with the clamor from a string of bells tacked to the
door to alert all near-deaf ears to any new presence.

"Mr. Crane!" Mrs. Arthurs calls out from a table at the
back, waving her knobbly hand and shaking the roll of loose
skin under her arm in welcome. The dead faces mutter and
cluck in recognition.

"Hello, Mrs. Arthurs. How are you?" I settle myself into
the small chair jammed between the table and the wall
behind it.

"Fine. And you?"

"Satisfactory. Just wondering why it was you decided to
call me. And more to the point, how you knew _where_ to call."

"Ah," the old woman shakes her head. "People know
things round here, don't you know."

"I see."

"And as for the _why_, I just felt I hadn't told you all I
could have at our first meeting."

"No?"

"No."

She opens her eyes wide and sips from her cup, holding it in both of her gnarled hands. When the waitress comes round I order coffee and tell myself that as soon as I've chugged it down, I'm out of here.

"Well then?"

"I didn't tell you about how The Lady has visited me herself," she says.

Her voice lowered to a whisper now but the words are nimble and clear. The chalky circles of rouge on her cheeks warmed by the rush of real color.

"Mr. Crane, you'll think me a madwoman for saying this, no doubt, but I know that The Lady is real, and that she's a demon. A *demon*, truly. And while I don't know for a fact that she had a hand in taking those little girls who are your concern, I know it just the same."

"Mrs. Arthurs, those girls aren't *my* concern—"

"Let me tell you a story. It won't take a second."

The coffee arrives and as I stick my forefinger through the china handle I'm glad to feel that it's only lukewarm.

"When my husband returned from the war he was young—we were *both* young then—and we set about starting a family. Not long after that—in the same spring The Lady fell through the ice, you'll remember—I found that I was with child. Well I was *overjoyed*, of course. Duncan had a good job at the quarry at the time, and while it surely doesn't look it today, that wee place on the lake was more than comfortable enough for us both and a couple kids to boot. And so it was that, nine months later as the Lord intended it, our baby Elizabeth was born."

Mrs. Arthurs lifts her cup again and buries her nose

inside it, emerging a moment later with a watery sigh. Beneath the hoods over her eyes a clear syrup gathers at the rim.

"Well, you can imagine our pleasure, Mr. Crane. Our first-born, and the most beautiful thing either of us'd ever seen. Now I know *every* mother says that about her own, but I tell you sure as anything she was a special one. We had our baby. We had a home. All we needed to get along fine. Or so we thought."

Now it's my turn at my own cup, and in a single gulp I down the contents and place my hands at the table's edge. The old woman straightens herself, dries her eyes with a quick swipe from the back of her moth-holed cardigan, and goes on with increased volume and pace.

"Elizabeth was only a year old when she started to have her troubles. When I'd get up in the middle of the night to look in on her sometimes she'd be lying on her back so *still* I'd put my head down to her just to check. And I'd discover that I couldn't hear her sweet little breaths. So I'd pick her out of there and start crying like a mad thing and in Duncan would charge, shouting, 'What's wrong? What's wrong?' and then Elizabeth would just wake up on her own and start crying a good bit herself, taking all the air she'd been missing for God knows how long into her lungs in a great gust. Well, this went on and on. Me coming in, finding my baby not breathing—not *alive*—and then her just coming back on her own. When it got to be that this was happening one out of every three nights we put her in the truck to see the specialist down at the Hospital for Sick Children there in Toronto. Well, didn't he look her over and stick her under every machine they had and take enough samples of the poor dear's blood to fill a fridge. And they didn't find a thing. It was a *mystery* to them. 'Science has its limits,' was what the doctor said, and could do nothing for us but shake his head. So we took her home. And it started all over again, every other night now. I took to sleeping in a chair right beside her. But I'd always fall asleep myself and wake up all of a sudden to pick her up and bring her back again. And it was then that it struck me. Like a curtain being raised, I swear to God! I knew it was The Lady who was doing this to us. Coming into our house and trying to take my little girl from me, take the breath right out of her. *Please* don't give me that look, Mr. Crane, for what I'm saying is the truth. A mother knows some things."

She sucks her lips into her mouth and the wrinkles in her cheeks disappear, the skin pulled tight over the bones. For a moment she's a worried young mother again, confessing shameful fears. But when she releases her lips to continue the widowed decades return along with her cracked voice.

"I could *feel* her in the house. Feel her without seeing her, understand? But in my dreams I could see her alright. Standing at the nursery window, looking in over my sleeping girl with a smile of pure wickedness on her face! Then she'd lift open the window and lean into the crib with the lake's water dripping off her foul hospital gown, her body green and rotten beneath. Standing there soaking my little girl's sheets and—my God! And when I'd wake I'd go to my baby and scream like a banshee until she came back. But every time The Lady came Elizabeth was brought closer to where she couldn't come back, that witch having gotten more out of her than I could put back in. Took to shouting out over the lake at her, begging her to leave us alone. Duncan thought I'd gone right round the bend, of course, but he'd just pull me back inside, shushing me, telling me all would turn out well. But it didn't. For The Lady never slept and I had to, and one night I gave her a moment too long alone with my girl. I knew before I picked her up that it was so. And all the pleading to heaven would do no good, for evil had taken her for its own and it was over."

Now the tears fall, but not many and not for long. With a single sniff her eyes dry again and I wonder how many times this woman has cried over the years replaying these events. How many lost thoughts had been cleared by that single, disciplined sniff?

The waitress, whose skin is thin as newsprint over her cheekbones, stands above our table and gives me a count-to-three look of eternal judgment.

"More?" she croaks, and I accept, half expecting her to pour the coffee over my head instead of in my cup. I return my eyes to Mrs. Arthurs's face, pretty by comparison, where "pretty" has been stretched to its most charitable limits. The difference is that she's *alive*. Frightening herself silly, breathless, despairing—but alive.

"I'm very sorry, Mrs. Arthurs," I say, pushing my cup to the side of the table. "And I know I don't know much about it, but couldn't there very well be a rational explanation for what happened to your daughter? Crib death, for example. They're still not sure what causes it, and they probably didn't know about it at all back then. But it's a documented condition today."

"Don't you think I've read up about that very thing since? But it's not what took my Elizabeth. I *know* it isn't."

"But you never saw The Lady yourself. Maybe it's something you came up with, you know, to explain something that you couldn't personally accept. You understand what I'm saying?"

"That I was crazy."

"That you were upset."

"She was real, Mr. Crane. She still is."

"For you, maybe."

"For anyone who knows the story."

Around us, the dead faces stare at our table in the fixed and shameless manner of the very old. The quiet of the room disturbed only by the pop of fat from the deep fryer behind the counter, a tape of marching band standards playing over the cheap speakers.

"When you lose a child you start to believe in things you never even thought of before," she says, jaw held stiff. "You come to see how death is never an accident, because there's always something out there that wants to take your little ones away. Turn your back for a moment, lose their hand on a crowded street, fall asleep when you should be awake—and they're gone. That's why a mother's always got to watch."

I push my chair back the two inches allowed it and start to pull my legs out from under the table, but the old woman throws out her hand and places it over mine.

"It was The Lady who took my Elizabeth, Mr. Crane, sure as I'm sitting here now. As it was The Lady who took your girls."

"They're *not* my girls."

When I pull out my wallet to pay the bill she waves me away.

"No, no. I'll get this. It's the least I can do for a young man who's taken the time to listen to an old woman's story."

But she's still got my hand. I make an effort to draw it back but whether I don't try hard enough or whether the arthritic globes of her fingers have more strength than I would've guessed, it doesn't move. Her face floats closer across the table. Wire hairs caught in the straw light of the lamp screwed into the paneling between us.

"A funny thing, your name," she says.

"Bartholomew. Yes. Not many of them around anymore."

"Your family name, I mean."

"Crane? Really? I would've thought—"

"Used to be Cranes had a cottage round the bend past my place, though be hard to see it nowadays. With the weeds and all the rest." She puckers her cracked lips and for a frightening second I expect her to come a few inches further and give me a kiss. "Relations, maybe?" she asks instead.

"Don't think so. You see my family didn't—my parents died a long time ago."

"Ah, then."

Her face rueful, looming.

"Well," I announce too loudly, pull my hand free with a single tug. The table rattling against the wall. "My thanks for the coffee."

I have to balance the table on my knees to move out from behind it, and as I stand in the narrow aisle the grey faces rise from their cups and egg-smeared plates and stay on me, watch me sidestep through them to the door. Mrs. Arthurs watches too. Chin lowered against her chest as though someone had switched her power off. But without turning around I feel her eyes on my back, holding me in place, drawing the energy out of my limbs so that I end up knocking the goddamn bells off the door as I kick my way out.

Twenty-Eight

The Murdoch District Medical Clinic is a single-level construction across from the sign declaring the town limits, the sign bearing what appear to be bullet holes shot through the "O" and the trough of the "M" in MURDOCH. The building's front doors open up into what was once a mobile home, the wards nothing more than two school portables with one of their walls cut out of the pea-green aluminum siding so they could be riveted to each flank of the main building. Aside from an ambulance that sits in the lot and a painted sign directing OUTPATIENTS one way and EMERGENCIES the other, there's nothing about it from the outside that would suggest it was a hospital. But once inside I'm met by the complicated smell of disinfectant, stewed vegetables, burnt coffee and, carried on the air just above these, the vapors of human waste which unmistakably designate places of the sick.

"I'd like to speak to the Emergency Room physician on duty on April the first of this year, please," I ask the woman sitting behind the RECEPTION sign which hangs lopsided from a thread pierced into the ceiling tiles.

"Was that during day hours?"

"Yes."

"Well, that would be Dr. MacDougall. It's always Dr. MacDougall during day hours."

"So he'd be there now?"

"Is it day hours?"

"I suppose it is."

"Then he'd be there."

I'm directed down the hallway on the right to where the "Emergency Room" is located: four folding chairs arranged around a TV broadcasting an American soap opera, a nurse behind a narrow metal desk and, muttering to himself as he crosses the hall between the two examination rooms, Dr. MacDougall. As I approach I try to hear exactly what he's saying but the words are lost somewhere in his dense Scottish brogue and the carrot-cake beard which has colonized the whole of his chin, neck and cheeks.

"Dr. MacDougall, can I speak to you for a moment?" I ask as he rushes by the position I've taken up directly between his destinations. In the one room sits a kid with angry welts blooming around his mouth, and in the other a pregnant woman lying back on an examination table and chewing gum with an unnatural ferocity.

"Sign up with the nurse first, *then* you get a look over," he responds before stepping around me into the pregnant woman's room and closing the door behind him. I have no choice but to hold my place and wait for him to come out again, and when he does I put my hands on my waist and stick out my elbows to block his way.

"It's about Thomas Tripp and Krystal McConnell."

He stops in front of me and raises his bloodshot eyes. The whiff of hangover rising up from an open collar.

"Who *are* you?"

"Barth Crane. Thom Tripp's lawyer."

"Ah."

"I was wondering if you saw Krystal McConnell before her disappearance, stitched up her knee—"

"Now lad, don't you think we should be speaking about this in private?"

"If you could spare a moment."

"Ach, I've got nothing *but* moments to spare, Mr. Crane."

He steps around me once more, scribbles out a prescription for the kid with the welts and ushers him out while waving me in.

"Nuts," he sighs as I pull the door closed.

"Sorry?"

"Allergic to nuts. I keep telling him to stay away from the devils but he can't resist. They'll be the death of him one day, though."

"That's rough."

"Not so rough. I see a good deal of rough in here, by God, but a wee fellow who passes out every time he sticks his finger in the peanut butter jar is not so rough at all."

MacDougall stands and opens the small window above the counter cluttered with boxes of surgical gloves, tongue depressors, adhesive bandages and jumbo tubes of lubricating jelly.

"Mind if I smoke?" he asks, already digging his hand into the breast pocket of his lab coat and pulling out a pack.

"Not at all. Although I would've thought that hospital policy wouldn't—"

"To *hell* with hospital policy, Mr. Crane," he snaps, lighting his cigarette and slumping back down into his chair.

"Fair enough. You're the doctor. Which leads me to my question: did you treat Krystal McConnell for a scraped knee on the first of April of this year?"

"Are you planning on calling me as a witness?"

"Depends on your answer."

"What if it's 'yes'?"

"Then my answer would be 'yes' too."

"Bloody hell!"

The doctor takes a long haul on his cigarette, managing to burn the thing down to half its original length.

"Did Tripp bring her in?"

"He did."

"You put four stitches in her knee?"

"Indeed. She said she was pushed around by some of the older boys at school. Flirting."

"Of course. Thank you. That's all I really need at this time, doctor. You can expect a subpoena sometime in the next couple of weeks."

"Sure, sure."

He keeps his eyes on me as I rise with what I assume to be his upper lip rolled thoughtfully beneath his whiskers.

"I was just wondering if your Tripp told you the funny part," he says, stubbing his cigarette out in the stainless steel bedpan he pulls out of a cupboard next to him.

"All he told me is that Krystal got hurt at school, that he drove her in here to get stitches and then took her home. Where's the funny part in that?"

"Well now, it's not surprising he left that out of his story. But didn't he tell the nurse who was doing the paperwork that *he* was her father."

"What?"

"Filled out the form just that way. 'Patient delivered by father, Lloyd McConnell.' But I saw him standing there myself and I knew damn well it was Thom Tripp. My own son's been in the fellow's class, y'see. Lucky for him that particular nurse was new up from Toronto and couldn't have told the difference between Tripp and The Lord High Mayor, but when she told me later how strange that girl's father was behaving, all sweaty and worked up, nobody knew what she was talking about. I mean, why would he even *try* pretending he was McConnell? What's the point in trying to fool anyone about that?"

"Were the authorities contacted? The police I mean, or the high school?"

"Why would I do that?"

"Because Tripp might have been considered, I don't know, dangerous. Impersonating a young girl's father—"

"Now look here. While in hindsight what Tripp told our nurse that day makes a little more sense, at the time there was no way to know he was *dangerous*. We get some very strange people in here. Some have become strange over time, others were strange to begin with. If I was to call the cops every time one of them walked through our doors I'd be on the phone all day."

"Well, thanks again, doctor. You've given me something to think about."

"Like whether you're going to want to call a witness to tell a funny story like that?"

"Among other things."

I pull open the door.

"Sure you won't join me?" he asks, shaking the cigarette pack once more and sticking one in the middle of his beard, but I shake my head no and let the door close behind me, walk out past two new faces sitting in the waiting room. A man holding his wife's pale hand as she rocks back and forth in pain but with eyes fixed on the TV. A greasy spoon waitress using two kinds of paper towel to sop up a puddle of spilled coffee. One absorbs, the other disintegrates. At this, the husband turns to look up at me with both helplessness and accusation, uncertain as to who to blame for his wife's suffering, for cheap paper towels that always let you down. My face must offer no answers, for in the next moment his eyes return to the screen. "It's the quicker picker upper!" the TV chirps as I push through the Emergency Room doors and out into the stabbing rain.

Twenty-Nine

Night.

Sleep comes riddled with dreams whose hectic events and grisly climaxes leave me sitting up on one elbow, eyes blinking at the door to check that the chain lock still sits in its groove. Try to remember the details but they're gone, leaving only the panicked impression of being unable to move, to escape. But soon the body demands that I try again, and I lower my head to the pillow hoping that this time I'll be left alone until morning.

But it's still night when I next wake. A shattering sound outside the door. The phone.

So I'm pulling on pants, socks, shoes, buttoning up a shirt. Dipping two fingers deep into the thermos and making barnyard sounds with my snout. Slam the door behind me but the sound is buried in the next ringing that rains down from the floors above as much as from below. Only when it finishes do I allow myself to breathe again, a smacking gulp, and with it a flood of circulation in my ears like poured sand.

It won't let me move. Feet gripped to their places by invisible fingers reaching up through the floor. Staring down to where the peeler's room would have been in my dream, to the far end of the hall that, even as I watch, pulls away into the shadows left by an unreplaced overhead bulb.

Lower my eyes so that I won't see whatever it is I can

almost make out walking forward from the dark and throw myself forward, hands waving first for balance and then to swing me around the banister and down the stairs. A blind dance that goes on long enough for the phone to twice repeat its alarm. Each ring slightly closer to the last as though it knows that I'm here beside it now, a hand unconsciously clenched to my chest to calm the sudden pain there.

Then I wait. Maybe it'll stop without me having to do a thing and then I can like pull the cord from the wall or leave a nasty note for the concierge and go back to bed. But it rings three more times to remind me that none of this will happen, that it won't stop until I answer. So I do.

From out of the watery static comes the peeler's voice, trembling but insistent. Heard not so much from a place at the other end of the line but from upstairs, from within my own ear.

"*You like the show the other night?*"

"Fantastic. I love these customer service follow-up calls too. But can I tell you something? Your timing stinks."

"*I know you.*"

"Congratulations. But why are you going to all this—"

"*I know what you like.*"

I hang up carefully, place both hands over the receiver as though their weight alone might prevent it from ringing again. In my ears the chatter of accelerated blood. A single set of headlights flash past on the street outside, through the grime that coats the narrow windows on each side of the door. But no more ringing. Not even the rumbling of muzak bass lines coming through the wall from the Lord Byron Cocktail Lounge. No way I can go back to my room in a hotel so quiet.

Besides, now that I'm down here maybe a drink would

do me good. Maybe two. The depressants clashing with the stimulants and having it out once and for all. What I need is ice bobbing in golden syrup, a rock glass slippery with cold sweat. The delicate spray of ginger fizz.

Through the leather door to the Lord Byron and straight over to the bar, making a point of keeping my eyes from the rest of the room. Place both hands flat on the varnished wood, raise my chin to the barman who scuffs over with his gut leading the way, a square of curling black hair peeping out through the space of a missed button on his shirt.

"Slow tonight," I say.

"Empty as City Hall on a Friday afternoon."

I nod. We nod together, the barman once and me a half-dozen.

"You're the lawyer, aren't you?"

"That would be me."

"No wonder you need a drink."

"Double rye-and-ginger, if you don't mind."

His eyes linger on me for a second, his belly pointed accusingly in my direction, but eventually he turns to pull a forty of Canadian Club from the lit-up bar display and pours me a biggie.

Now I can turn. The room isn't entirely empty but it's close, only a single guy in a fluorescent orange raincoat in the front row and a table of three polyester button-downs at the back, speaking in the too-loud tones of employee complaint. Salesmen probably. Compiling all the bullshit they have to put up with from head office, how these roadtrips north are useless, getting new orders up here like trying to suck blood from a stone. It's a bar occupied by those serious about their purpose, here to *drink*, no messing around. None of us have ordered beer.

The stage is empty and the d.j. leans against the outside of his booth smoking and making a great show of tapping the ashes onto the carpet even though four tin ashtrays sit within arm's reach of where he stands. But he's got to get back to work in a second (the Stones's "Paint it Black" coming to its closing repetitions), so he grinds what's left of the cigarette out on the tabletop next to him and steps back into the booth, pulls the mike too close to his mouth.

"Alright, gentlemen, it's *showtime* again here at The Lord Byron and this time up, something a *little bit* special. Please give a big Murdoch welcome for Lori and Michelle!"

But nobody welcomes the two women who hammer up the steps to the stage in white leather heels and teddies with blue satin ties around their middles. No applause when the d.j. lowers the needle and tinny sugar-pop crackles out over the room. "Lollipop," the novelty tune with the girl harmonies and the *POP!* in the middle. The drinkers take no notice. Don't consider the advanced age of the two dancers who are now linking their elbows together and spinning each other around in a show of exuberant youth. Aren't looking at the cheeks of smeared rouge, dyed hair pulled back into girlish pig-tails, falsely blonde and falsely brunette.

> *Lollipop, lollipop*
> *Ooo, lolli, lolli, lolli*

They toddle to the edge of the stage and pick up props, two oversize, rainbow-swirled lollipops, and pretend to take swiping licks at them. It's meant to be funny, a campy bit of strip club humor. But nobody laughs or applauds. All of us fully occupied by the grave business of drinking.

Halfway through their act I step off the stool and escape to the bathroom, pull the vial out of my pocket and spill out half its contents over the porcelain back of the toilet. Not a fair fight anymore, what with this stacking the deck in the stimulants' favor. Tap out another line for the hell of it and one more to hear the fat lady sing.

By the time I make it back to the bar and circle my finger in the air for another round the lollipops have been ditched and the music changed to The Beatles' "Michelle" in apparent honor of the stripper of the same name, though it's impossible to tell which one she is. The satin ties have been dropped to the stage and a sleeping bag hauled out, both of them rolling around on its quilted puffiness, undressing each other while making sulky faces at the room. It's a slumber party routine, forty-year-olds playing naughty teenagers. Because I'm the only one who watches them directly they settle their eyes on me as they pull each other's straps off their shoulders and let the material shimmy down their chests.

After a time I'm distracted by the sound of crunching bones that seems to fill the room. Coming from me. Rear molars grinding each other down to powdery stumps. Turn my head away from the stage and tell myself to *breathe normally*, look straight ahead through the raised levels of liquor bottles and into the tinted mirror behind them. The dancers are still visible from this angle. In fact there's nothing else but them, glowing slightly in the reflected darkness.

But now something's different. Instead of women sloshing together on the stage the mirror shows two girls, the hair natural and cheeks flushed with real blood, their bodies a smooth assembly of muscle and skin. Close my eyes, wipe the smear of sweat from around my mouth, throw back what remains of my drink. Open again and they're still there. Lean and vivid, smiling back at me between the Day-Glo liqueurs and straw-colored scotches. Turn to the stage and it's stretch marks and raised veins. In the mirror two girls: one light, one dark.

Michelle
my belle

The phone behind the bar starts to ring. Once, but loud enough to entirely block out the music, the call of "Let's *see* it!" from one of the button-down salesmen and the gasp I release at its splintering bell.

In a single motion the barman picks it up and turns with the receiver held out to me.

"For you."

"Me?"

"You'd be the one, pal."

"Male or female?"

"Definitely female."

"Take a message."

I knock the bar stool over in a clattering spin as I step off but I don't stop to pick it up. Keep my head down, yet I'm still aware of some of the customers turning to watch me, a silent swiveling of heads like robots in a department store window display. It's too dark to be moving this fast and before I make it to where I think the side door might be I slam a knee into a table near the stage and send a geyser of beer onto its surface, green in the gelled light. One arm held in front of me like a linebacker running with the ball. An open palm to push through the door, the spilled-beer-owner's chest, whatever unseen thing might get in my way. Then my hip crunching into the handle of the fire door and I'm out.

The rain has recently stopped, water gurgling down the storm drains under the curb. There's the blinking of a failing streetlight bulb. An old metal ice-cream sign creaking on its hinge outside a vacant storefront window. All the feeling numbed from the outside in, moving to freeze the muscles around my heart once and for all.

I'm way too old to be this high.

Tat, tat, tat.

Knuckles on glass, behind and above.

Turn back to face the hotel, eyes crawling up the stained brick. There, beneath the leering gargoyle faces of Murdoch's founding fathers. Standing in the backlit window of the honeymoon suite with the taped-up photos and printed newspaper columns visible on the walls behind them. The girls in the cotton dresses with eyes poured full of shadow. Waving down at me.

I run.

Leather soles skidding over wet pavement, mouth gaping in a scream that, if released at all, doesn't reach my own ears. Floating above myself at the height of the street's rooftops. A well-tailored madman running from nothing.

By the time I reach the courthouse corner the pain in my lungs doubles me over, spitting for air. A sound in my head like the beating of wings. Somewhere in the wind the carnival smell of spoiled meat.

When I stand straight again I force myself to turn and look back to the window, knuckle the burning sweat from my eyes. Focus on the outline of The Empire Hotel, on the one square of yellow above the rain-blackened street.

Still there, eyes set upon me.

It can't be so at this distance, two full blocks away, but I'm certain I can see the splintering cracks of powdered skin around their mouths, teeth bared through wax lips. Pulling open to throw out a laugh. To speak.

But this for just a second. For in the time it takes me to draw my next breath the overhead light is flicked off and the honeymoon suite is dark once more.

Thirty

The rest of the night is spent walking the streets waiting for dawn to arrive. I'm aware of the cold but don't feel it, recognize the rain for what it is but not for its soaking through my pant legs to stiffen my knees. By the time the first light crests over the eastern rooftops I'm empty of everything but the idea of pillow and mattress and sheets. And somehow I make it back to The Empire, up the stairs, through the door to splay myself across the bed, all outside of memory.

But I'm denied half the sleep I need by the ringing of the bedside phone sometime in the morning. Cold plastic banged against my ear.

"Sorry if I got you up," the voice at the other end says in response to my grunt of acknowledgment. "Wondering if you had any lunch plans."

"Who?"

"It's Doug."

"Oh? What time is it?"

"Twenty to twelve."

"Twenty," I cough, and the sound of it is painfully amplified in my own ear. "Twelve."

"Calling about your visit the other day. Your mention of Mrs. Arthurs and her story about the—her recollections with regard to the lake. Remember? We were discussing—"

"Yes. *Doug.* Yes."

"It's just that I've done a little footwork of my own. Prepared some things—"

"Prepared. Good."

"—and I thought we might get together over lunch to go through the results. Do you like wings?"

I can't think what he means, and for a moment I summon the image of a closet full of hanging white angel costumes wrapped in clear plastic with feathery attachments smelling of mothballs.

"Wings?"

"Spicy," he says, pauses. "*Chicken* wings."

"Oh. Delicious. Sounds good."

He gives me directions to Offside's, a sports bar located in a strip mall on the highway north of town, and although I take them down as carefully as I'm able it's not until he hangs up that I finally recognize who it was who called.

Today's Friday, the trial adjourned until the following Monday in order for Justice Goldfarb to "consider submissions made on preliminary matters" but more likely to afford her the time to make her standing eight o'clock dinner reservation at Scaramouche. The end result either way is a day off. And instead of doing something sensible like some real work I'm out of bed and slipping into dry clothes, sliding into the Lincoln and pushing it out of town.

But it's not far. Just beyond the Dairy Queen (CLOS D 4 THE SE SON) and the high fence around the sewage treatment plant. A sign in the window urges me to CHECK OUT OUR PATIO!, so I do, peeking over a wobbly trellis enclosing a dozen overturned tables and posters of the Budweiser bikini girls stapled to the fence. A stack of empties giving off the smell of stale bread and piss.

I step back and walk around to the front door. A

sun-yellowed menu the size of a broadsheet newspaper taped
to the inside of the glass with headings like Gut Busters,
Meaty Madness and Hall of Fame Fries. Inside there's something immediately recognizable about the place, in the carpet
crumbled with peanut shells and ash, the humidity of spilled
draft, the aquatic flickering of television light. The same
feeling you get in golf club bars, airport lounges, magazine
stores with X-rated back rooms, cramped diners with chain-
smoking cooks. Men's rooms.

There may also be women present in these places, of
course. Perhaps even a good number laughing in the middle
of the room beneath a warm dome of menthol smoke. There
may even be a woman in charge of the whole show, one with
obvious vices and arms thick as tenderloin who'd sooner kick
your ass out the back door than look at you. But it makes no
difference. A *sports bar*. And although I have no interest in
sports or the opinions contained within the bloated heads
hanging above their beers or the battered food that leaves
corrosive stains in its waxed-paper baskets, I know that this
place was built for me.

Listen to the fret-house babble of color commentators,
the jabbering marketplace of sports: plus/minus average, shot
percentage, career-high penalty minutes, PGA, RBI, NFL,
ERA, NBA, total yards rushed, shots on goal, 140 yards to the
pin, wind against. No greater philosophical beliefs than the
bold slogans for electrolyte drinks, half-ton trucks and cross-
trainers: Drink it Down, Like a Rock, Just Do it. A place
where accusations hurt no one and there can be no blame
because if your team won they won and if they lost the ref
was fucking blind.

Pittle raises a hand and waves at me from his table, his

figure especially dwarfed under the giant screen TV that is now showing two gleaming black men pummeling each other in a ring at Caesar's Palace.

"I hope this isn't taking up too much of your time," Pittle says as I take the seat across from him.

"Not at all. Besides, everybody's got to eat sometimes."

"That's true." Pittle looks at me, twists the hair on his chin between busy fingers. "It's just that I wanted to share some things that may be of interest to you."

"To my case, you mean."

"No. To you."

I could fight this distinction but shrug instead, sit back in invitation for him to continue.

"There's good news and there's bad news."

"Oh yeah? Give me the bad news."

"There's only one document in the entire county archives that makes any reference to Mrs. Arthurs's Lady in the Lake."

"The good news?"

"It's a handwritten manuscript written by none other than Alistair Dundurn."

"So it's the same thing as the book I already have, right? *A History of Northern Ontario Towns*. I don't see how that's helpful."

"No, it's different. And I never said it would be *helpful*."

"So what is it then?"

"This."

He disappears beneath the table and for a not-quite-awake moment I expect a hand puppet to appear in his place, a red-nosed ceramic face that tells dirty jokes in a squeaky voice. But then Pittle returns and brings with him a bundle of wrinkled papers bound in a leather satchel. Places the package down in front of him on the table and lays his hands on top.

"This," I say, "is paper."

"A manuscript. Dundurn's. Except more like Dundurn's own memoirs. Very interesting stuff. A later work than his history, probably written at the same time as he was going a bit wonky. Which either makes it more honest or completely unreliable."

Pittle wriggles back in his chair and grips the ends of the armrests, his head tottering on his neck. At that point the waitress arrives ("Have youse decided what youse want?") and Pittle orders a pint of Ex and twenty Suicide Wings. Then she turns doubtfully to me and I ask for the same.

"You sure you like it hot?" she almost sneers, and I wonder why she didn't ask Pittle the same thing.

"Hot as you can make them," I tell her with forced relish, and she curls her upper lip towards her nose in a troubling expression I take to mean *Oh yeah, pal? We'll see about that.*

"So," I say after the waitress has left. "What's so interesting about our friend Mr. Dundurn's life?"

"Not much, I expect," Pittle raises his eyebrows. "Aside from the fact that he was there on the night Mrs. Arthurs described to you. The night The Lady went through the ice."

Above our heads a commentator's voice on the giant screen interrupts to announce "We've just learned that he's suffered a severe concussion, ladies and gentlemen. Johnson *will* be scratched for at least the first two games with Chicago." The voice is excited, even cheerful, slowing only to emphasize *concussion* and then instantly picking up again.

"How do you know he was there?" I ask.

"Well, he doesn't actually come out and *say* it of course. But he slips in enough hints to make it clear."

Pittle clicks open the satchel and pulls a single sheet out from the manuscript pile before him, holds it close to his face and reads through its trembling creases.

"'The men watched her fall through, and not a soul among us said a word. For they *knew* what they had done. And while there was a darkness settling upon their hearts, there was also the relief that the town was once more safe from physical or moral threat.' Did you notice the slipup in there? 'Not a soul among *us* said a word'? Dundurn's manuscript is entirely handwritten, but the 'us' stands on the page uncorrected. I think this shows that the entire work is nothing less than a personal recounting of the event. A confession, really."

The waitress returns with our beers and slides them before us, watery suds spilling over the sides and rushing into a moat around the base of the glass. Without a word both of us pick them up and glug down the first third in sudden thirst. Then, a moment later, first Pittle and then I fill the air with belches passed through clenched lips, a sound like the release of radiator steam. Neither of us excuses ourself before speaking again.

"So he knew her," I say.

"Everybody knew her. But he might've been the only one who found out what her story was. Or some of the pieces, anyway."

"And?"

"She was Polish. Not a great thing to be in Europe during the early 40s. Dundurn doesn't say how he found even this out because she had no passport or documentation of any kind. But I suspect he went out and visited her where she was camping in the woods near the lake. To interview her."

"Maybe for other reasons too."

"What do you mean?"

"Mrs. Arthurs told me that some of the men in town would go out there to spend a little time with her. Before the wives found out."

"I see."

Everywhere I turn to look at something other than Pittle's face my eyes meet only televisions. Hanging on chains in the corners, pulldown screens taking up entire walls, three smaller units nesting in the boxes above the bar originally designed as wine racks. Each one showing a different athletic spectacle: a body sculpting show hosted by a man whose skin is so oiled and packed with sinew he looks like a sausage fried to the point of bursting; a stock car race where cameras set on the dashboards showed just how tedious driving around an oval track two hundred times must be; a highlights tape of downhill skiing accidents featuring one neck-snapping accident after another.

"O.K., so one way or another, Dundurn was researching The Lady," I say, taking another gulp of beer. "What did he get?"

Pittle lifts his hands and they hover over the papers like two metal detectors searching the sand for buried change. Inside his beard, something quivers.

"Not much, in the end," he says. "Her English was almost nonexistent, and I don't think she was much of a talker anyway. What we do know is that she arrived here in the summer of 1945 as a DP, but without official papers, as I've said, which suggests she'd managed to—"

"DP?"

"'Displaced person.' The government's term for all people left homeless by the war. A refugee. Somebody that made it out."

"But how'd she get here?"

"Who knows? She'd probably been on the road in Canada for a while, camping out, staying away from the larger cities and towns where they'd be more likely to ask questions. As for how she got out of Europe? We have to be talking about a very resourceful woman here. Keep in mind that Poland was the first place to undergo Nazi 'Germanizing.' The Nuremberg anti-Jewish laws served as the model for similar regulations aimed against the Polish people generally. Basically this meant complete loss of rights, nationhood, name. Children between six and sixteen were forcibly taken away from their families to be brought up as Germans, a policy which entailed their being sent to institutions to be 're-educated' in order to erase their language, culture, history along with everything else. And they were the lucky ones. The others, the 'undesirable elements,' were sent to the camps."

"All this is in Dundurn's papers?"

"Mostly the transcripts to Nuremberg Trial No. 8, actually. I did some research of my own."

Pittle's face exhibits no pride in this, his voice offering only the evenness of professional clarification. Above me, the same commentator states the word "concussion" for a second time.

"What made her 'undesirable' then?"

"She was a single mother, which suggests in itself that her husband either fought in the Polish military or was one of the first ones sent to the camps. Maybe he worked in the

government, was an academic or a writer—one of the ones
they took care of right away. There could have been secondary concerns as well: after the Jews and the Gypsies came
Communists, the mentally ill, pregnant women, homosexuals.
She may have been one or all of them. But my bet is she
wasn't thinking of herself at the time. She had to get out of
there in order to save her daughters no matter who she was—
they would have been just the right age to be taken away. Not
an easy thing, but she pulled it off. It would've made a great
story, but she certainly didn't tell it to Dundurn. As far as we
know she didn't tell it to anyone."

"And so she ended up here."

"One of the camp barracks at Auschwitz was called
Kanada. It was where all their food, clothes, gold, jewelry and
other confiscated goods were kept. It was real, but in another
sense it was totally imaginary. Somehow the name had meaning for all of them. A safe, protected place. I didn't know
that. Did you?"

"No, I didn't," I say, throwing a finger up to rub at the
bridge of my nose as though bitten by some invisible flying
thing.

Then the waitress arrives with two baskets of slippery-
looking wings, each liberally glazed with a fluorescent red
ointment. "Suicides," she announces as she sets them down
and drops two rollups of cutlery into the puddles around our
now empty beers. Pittle orders two more.

"They look good," I lie, staring into the piled limbs in
front of me. Pittle says nothing in return, his small hands
already clenched before his mouth, grappling with his food.

"Well now," I push on, pulling a wing of my own out of
the carnage. "She got out, made it over. What I'm wondering

is why she wasn't given official refugee status when she got here."

"Maybe she didn't ask for it. Maybe she was too used to running. And even if she had asked, her acceptance wouldn't have been a foregone conclusion. Canada's immigration and refugee policies in 1945 were not what you'd call liberal, particularly given that a world war had just come to an end. We were way behind the other Allied nations in accepting DPs, and in the end it took a couple of years for the government to really open the doors. So she must have figured she'd be better off going up north and trying to melt into some backwater on her own."

"And you think that's why they took the girls away from her? Because she didn't have the right papers?"

"Could've been. But more likely because she was different. Non-communicative, husbandless. And from what you've told me there were also rumors that she had been providing certain—that she was 'morally questionable,' according to the language of the day. Based on this, they probably also assumed she was nuts, or called her that in order to do what they wanted with her. Either way they locked her up, shipped off the kids and forgot all about it. That is, until she broke out from the hospital and started inviting the local kids for a walk in the woods. The rest is history, as they say."

Pittle places his hand on the cover page of Dundurn's journal then quickly pulls it back, leaving an oily stain of chicken fat and tabasco in its place.

"Dammit," he mumbles, mouth full.

"She escaped the war and made it to freedom only to be hunted down right here in happy old Murdoch."

"It's funny, isn't it, in a terrible sort of way."

"Funny," I say, feeling the broken ice lapping up to the knees, the chest. Arms held out to the puffing faces on the shore. "Terrible."

For a time neither of us says anything while Pittle eats and I pretend to eat. These things really *are* hot, yet utterly tasteless except for the painful burning they leave on the end of my tongue. I glance over towards the bar and find the waitress standing there looking back at us, and although it's too dark to make out her face I imagine a cruel, satisfied smile playing over her lips.

"O.K. Doug. Let's go back a second," I say once I've given up on lunch for good. "Even if I go along with your interpretation that Dundurn was there at the lake when it happened, how does that help me with Mrs. Arthurs's theory that The Lady has come back to claim Flynn and McConnell? Not that that's possible. But as a matter of argument—"

"As a matter of *argument*, of course." He lowers his wing and clears his throat. "Well, Dundurn goes on to detail certain instances where The Lady was said to have reappeared in the years following her death. Sightings up near the lake. Walking through the trees at night in her hospital clothes. Rising up out of the lake at dusk, or a scream echoing out over the water in the middle of the night. What's most interesting perhaps are the reports made by children. Cottagers' kids running in crying to their mothers saying that a mean, green old lady had approached them, asking them to take her hand and go for a little swim. Crazy stuff like that. Dundurn figures that these stories even played a part in the region's failure to make it as a viable tourist destination. People got the creeps bad enough that they decided to spend the extra money to buy places fifty miles to the south. You can take that argument or leave it. But what's important is that Mrs. Arthurs isn't alone in her opinion. It's just that she may be the last person alive to express it."

I nod once and finish my beer. Lay my napkin over the food in front of me like a white sheet.

"Why didn't you tell me about Tripp, Doug?"

"Sorry?"

"The last name on the sign-out card of that Dundurn book I took from the library was his."

"That's interesting."

"Yes, it is. And given that the circulation desk of the Murdoch Library is not exactly a busy place, you would have known about it. And then you recommend the same book to me."

Pittle smiles once, a carnivorous flash, then pulls it back into the bush.

"I didn't know what he was looking into specifically at the time," he says. "I mean, it's just a book of local history, right? The guy can read. But after he was arrested and the rest—I had some ideas of my own."

"So then you handed it over to me."

"You were interested. So was Tripp. And I thought if you saw his name in there it might mean something to you."

Now Pittle slurps at his beer, lifts a muscular wing to his mouth. "So?" he asks, takes a bite.

"So what?"

"What do you think he was doing with Dundurn's book?"

"Listen, Doug, I'm not sure I can—"

"Off the record."

"Legally speaking, 'off the record' doesn't mean a thing."

"I give you my word then."

It's moments like this they drill into you at law school. How never to betray your client's confidence even with your closest friends, colleagues or loved ones, and Pittle not even qualifying as any of the above. And yet I want to tell him something. Part of me thinks I might make the unclear clear through putting it into words. Part of me just wants to say it to someone else.

"Tripp ran an after-school club with Ashley and Krystal where they would read books and talk about them, do creative writing exercises and other stuff like that," I start, and Pittle stops eating for the first time.

"I'd heard something about that."

"Well, that's how it all began, anyway. But I have reason to believe it went further. That they started to dramatize events. Put on plays of their own making. That was one of the rules, as a matter of fact. Nothing could be real."

"And you think this is of importance to the defence?"

"Probably not. But it might be important, nevertheless."

For a while we keep our eyes lowered to the table, let the static of sports statistics fill our ears. Then Pittle shakes his head as though he'd just stepped through cobwebs.

"The imagination can be a very dangerous thing," he says.

"How's that?"

"When you stop seeing it only as hypothetical and take the step into making it real. Think about it. This is really what we mean when we talk about someone having an evil mind. Charlie Manson, Oppenheimer, Hitler, Dahmer, whoever. People who let themselves go too far into their heads."

"C'mon, Doug. There's an entire body of science—the hangover of traumatic childhoods, chemical imbalances, whatever. There're many other ways of explaining—"

"I'm a librarian," he interrupts. "A part-time reporter. I prefer my world to be the world of facts. At the same time I know the control it takes to keep it that way. Sometimes I wish I could be something different. But I have to resist those kind of thoughts. Remind myself that so long as I stay with the facts, I'm safe."

"Safe from what?"

"What I might be if I let myself."

At the bottom of our baskets the waitress has thrown in a wet nap that each of us now struggles to rip open. Inside, the sharp lemon of jet travel hygiene. I smear it over the bottom half of my face as Pittle, so aggressive with his food a moment ago, now makes delicate stabs at his lips and pushes his basket to the side of the table. A male voice from the TV above us panting, "I just went out there to kick some butt and that's exactly what I did."

Then Pittle starts again, this time jumping forward in his chair, hands diving and poking up through his papers. "I can't believe I didn't even show you."

"Show what?"

"Dundurn's picture."

"What difference does it make what he looks like?"

"Not him." He pulls a square of paper away from a paperclip, holds it a foot away from my eyes. "Her."

I hold out my hand and he drops it into my palm. Too small to convey an entire person really, a white-fringed square the size of a commemorative stamp. Black-and-white, but more yellowy brass than anything else. And coated with a fog that at first obscures the subject: a woman in a buttoned cardigan (a little too tight at the shoulders) framed from the waist up. Hair tied and pinned into a disordered nest the color of carbon dust. A long, weary neck, riddled with vertical bulges that could be muscle or tendon or vein. And a face of the kind of beauty that somehow resists the simplicity of such a term, a beauty against the beautiful. A face like a historical map, rough marks indicating shifting boundaries, the outside bordered by hypothetical coastlines. Not aged but suggestive of vast expanses of endured time. The face of Europe pushing through an out-of-focus lens.

"So?"

"So."

So she was real. Real in the manner of the unreal. Someone you could base a story on, as soon a romance as a tale of vengeful horror. A once-living woman, but more than this? Nothing but a flayed, insistent slip of history.

"Hard to believe this woman is the Lake St. Christopher monster," I say after a while.

"She's not. Or only a part of her is."

"And which part is that?"

"What we've had to make up. The worst parts we could imagine." I throw my head around the room for a last tour of the televisions. Pull my wallet from a back pocket but Pittle holds up his hands. I thank him for the beers, say we should do it again sometime soon. Raise myself as he assembles his notes and photocopies into a pile and pushes them across the table at me. But I shake my head, eyes held above the words on the paper.

"Don't think I'll need that, thanks."

Pittle frowns briefly, launches back into his chair. "How's the trial going?" he asks as I put on my coat to leave.

Struggle for a moment to think what it is I'm being asked.

"It's only just started," I say.

Outside, the clouds have broken up into islands of ice caught in a grey stream. The air cold enough to tighten skin against nose, chin and forehead. Make my way over to where the

Lincoln's parked with the unsure steps of a Legion Hall drunk, an old man crumpled under the burdens of solitude and war stories.

I keep both hands buried in coat pockets. The right plays its fingers over a slip of glossy paper. No larger than a pack of matches but it fills my hand, warms through the layers of fabric to the skin. A picture of a woman, a face stolen from an unfinished history.

Thirty-One

Everyone loves a crime scene.

This is where I'm parked, looking out the Lincoln's passenger window at Murdoch's most recent historical site. It must be that I love a crime scene as much as the next guy, or at least as much as the guys and their guests who came out here last night and built a fire on the other side of the police tape using an empty beer case for kindling. Around it the evidence of secondary entertainments: strewn beer bottles and a mickey of Captain Morgan, a forgotten hash pipe and a condom (unused) left wrinkled in the dirt like a shed snake skin. The Murdoch Tourist Board is clearly missing an opportunity here. They should be commissioning a statue. There should be guided tours.

I'm here for a tour myself. A search for a derelict cottage which, if Mrs. Arthurs is to be believed, lies somewhere down the trail on the undeveloped side of the lake. Pop a couple of Extra Strength Tylenols to combat the headache that threatens to claw through my forehead. Blast the car's heater and let it blow over hands and face until the skin feels like it's about to curl back from the bone. Ready.

I follow the trail past Mrs. Arthurs's, keeping my eyes straight ahead in case she happened to be fussing around her woodpile again. Beyond her property the path narrows and reduces my progress to a hunched stumble, an arch of cedar branches scrabbling across my back. Twice my head connects with wet bark and twice a *fuck* exits my mouth to echo out into the dripping forest. A bloodstain appears on my pants (dropped from my hand, cut trying to push aside a tentacle of spiky sumach) but I'm not yet wondering why the hell I'm out here or what I hope to find. I just keep going.

How is it that if one walks far enough in the woods one eventually comes across the rusted frame of an abandoned car? There's never an obvious indication of how it got there, no nearby road, level field or habitation. In fact the fin-tailed sedan I see now, fifty feet off the trail and obscured among the high ferns, is so tightly encircled by a half-dozen glacial boulders there seems no way it could have gotten there unless dropped from above. Stripped of all rubber, leather and glass, its rims buried in the soft earth, the hood gaping open. For a time I stare at its drooping front grille and its headlight sockets stare back at me, bewildered, watery with moss.

Further along, further in. On either side grass-riddled rock pushes up through the earth like hairy moles. My nose four feet above the root-veined earth sniffing its damp, vegetative perfumes. Keep looking to one side and the other but aside from occasional garbage and a couple outhouse-size sheds with unclear functions there's no sign of the man-made.

Then I see something. It's only because half the leaves have fallen and I happen to be looking in the right direction that I notice it at all given its near invisibility forty feet down from the trail. The forest hides it, claiming it for its own, the mounded sod of the once-cleared lot now taken over by the looping vines and saplings straining up over others to take a greater share of the light. Inside this wild growth, a long abandoned cottage.

I crunch through the weave of mature branches that

block my way off the trail and walk around the building's exterior. It's not unlike the other cottages on the farside of the lake: same sturdy rectangle with a framed window at the front looking down to the water, a door opening up onto a narrow deck that sags into a frown, and at the back, three windows for each of the bedrooms. What's different is twenty-odd years of neglect evidenced in the warped roof, missing shingles and windows shattered by bored canoeists or the impact of birds who saw the glass as a reflected piece of sky. Under the mildewed eaves, plate-size holes where the rac-coons have broken through, and two watery bundles of grey paper, one tattered and loose, the other the current home of a thousand sleeping yellowjackets. All of this crumbling rot in only a couple decades of expired winters and summers. And in a couple decades more it would completely lose its definition as a place where people once ate and slept. That's how conservative Mother Nature is, the fussy old dear. Always turning everything back into itself, taking all the neatly assembled elements apart and making it all green and brown chaos again.

Step up onto the front deck and the wood moans in soggy complaint under my feet. The front window cracked in a zigzag from the top left corner to the bottom right, but it's otherwise intact and keeps the wind that comes up off the water from carrying its moisture inside. It also protects the spiders from the elements, who have established layers of web thick enough to create a gauzy haze between inside and out. But if I cup my hands around my eyes there's still sufficient light to distinguish interior details, wan outlines standing out from the dusting of shade.

What's surprising is how much stuff is still here. A couch with leaping deers over its upholstery, a pine dining table standing on three legs, a wagon wheel coffee table sheltering Scrabble and Monopoly games, even a Ouija board with the alphabet, numbers zero through nine and YES and NO in the corners. Most remarkable are the bookshelves occupying every available inch of wall space. There's a shattered bottle of Crown Royal against the far wall and empty soup tins littering the entire living room floor, but by the look of it the books have been left not only unharmed but untouched.

I pull away from the glass and try the front door which swings open after a couple of scrapes across the uneven floor. The room trembles as I walk in, unused to the moving presence of weight. I wipe my feet on an old *Globe and Mail* taken from the pile someone had made in a corner of the kitchen and used for kindling. Although there's plenty of garbage all over the place, for the most part it's been left as a place where living people had once arranged things how they liked them. Stepping inside this order feels like an infringement. The disruption of a vulnerable balance.

But I don't leave yet. Instead, I gravitate toward the opposite shelf and randomly thumb through some of the books. Penciled notes in all the margins now in varying states of dissolve depending on their exposure to the air and moisture and the type of cover that bound them. After a time I stop trying to read at all and pull my thumb across the edge of the pages, the old paper sending a breezy caress across my face. Let the tips of my fingers play over the dusty lead of the print, feel for the indentations the words have left in the paper's surface and close my eyes. Imagine how meaning might exist in the touch, like the shape of a familiar face, like braille.

When I open my eyes I slide the book in my hands back in the precise slot I took it from, straighten the room so that

it appears with the same even face as before. The room's
trembling and the wind's free movement through the open
door have brought an odd animation to the space. A can
rolls and clinks across the floor. A flock of leaves blows in
from the deck. From somewhere within the walls the release
of an aggrieved sigh.

I'm startled by the noise my shoes make in the sudden
lunge to get out before the door is blown shut. Grab the
handle and plow it back against the wall, my heart popping
out a syncopated drum solo high in my chest.

The rain coming down harder now, but it's not the rain
that quickens my step back up to the trail. It's the feeling that
I've disturbed something that was meant to be left alone, like
one of those ancient Egyptian crypts that were carefully
hidden underground at the end of a complicated maze but
that people eventually discovered and busted open anyway
just for the hell of it. On my return I pass Mrs. Arthurs's
place as the trail curves back toward the road but I don't slow
down. I can't stop from turning to look as my stride turns
into an awkward jog. And though the trees obscure my view
and the afternoon's light has almost completely yielded to
the sudden dusk I'm sure I see the old woman's face in the
window with a single kerosene lamp flickering on the table
behind her, staring back at me with the palms of her hands
held white against the glass.

Thirty-Two

Why do people who do certain things for a living all look the same? Is it the looks that determine the job, or does the job conform the looks? I'm thinking about tax lawyers (nearly always bespectacled, narrow-shouldered, easily startled), undertakers and bureaucrats (both loose-skinned and hound-faced, the muscles responsible for smiling withered from lack of exercise), but mostly police detectives, the most aesthetically homogeneous profession of them all. I'm looking at Bill Butcher, Chief Investigating Officer for Murdoch Region, the man in charge of marshaling the police's evidence and the Crown's lead witness. Sitting up in the stand, responding to Goodwin's questions. A man who could be nothing other than a cop.

"We found the brown pants about a third of the way down inside the laundry hamper in the hall," Bill Butcher is saying, his voice disciplined into deep consistency. No emphasis, no cracks, all business. That's what he's working for up there, that's what he likes to hear. A moderately intelligent man who enjoys power and the appearance of responsibility, but who enjoys even more a starchy lunch followed by deep-fried dough and coffee. A man who's seen enough to know that life is a rough ride and that people are as often desperate and mean as not, but who in the end is more vain than philosophical, the signs of his flagging youth (breasts growing out over a widening gut, liver spots, a firing range score that is the source of jokes back at headquarters) keeping him up at night far longer than the violence and cruelty that plagues a fallen world.

"There was no indication that there had been an attempt to hide them," he's saying. "The muddy shoes were next to the door alongside a pair of slippers and rubber boots."

I make notes. At least my hand makes notes, twitching across the page, but I'm unaware of the words it authors. When I raise my eyes from where they've been resting the clerk, the cop and the judge all look my way.

"Mr. Crane?" Justice Goldfarb's voice.

"Yes, Your Honor?"

"Are you with us?"

"Yes. Sorry. With you now. My apologies to the court."

"It's your *turn*, Mr. Crane."

"Of course. Begging the court's indulgence. Just collecting my notes."

It's the afternoon of the second day of the cop's testimony. How much longer was I expecting him to go on? I haven't even started and I'm fucking up.

"Detective Butcher, I'd like to begin with your search of the place where Mr. Tripp allegedly parked at Lake St. Christopher on the day in question," I hear myself saying, watch Butcher's head go down to his own notes and his mouth emit an answer. It appears that I'm doing something.

Maybe it's in the eyes. In cops it dulls their brightness, turns them into dark buttons. School and hospital administrators tend to have eyes like these, but with lower lids. The eyes of people whose jobs involve processing paper without vested interest in their content.

"So would you say that you've had less experience

investigating homicide cases than the majority of your colleagues in Toronto?"

Time has passed since the crime scene questions, and the counsel's lectern where I stand is thick with paper on which I've recorded answers and prepared new questions, but I can't recall how I've brought us here.

"I can tell you I've dealt with some cases up here that detectives down in the city wouldn't know *what* to do with," the cop is saying. From behind me, a man's throat releases a vulgar laugh.

What did the peeler's voice on the phone say? *I know what you like.*

"Objection!" Goodwin is calling from his chair.

Objection? Objection to what?

"Fine, fine. I'll rephrase the question, Your Honor," I say, and then go on and say something else.

The cop's eyes are unchanging, but he lowers them to his notes less and less. He must be holding up well. Looking down at the notes is a classic indication of flailing, an effort to buy some time. This guy looks like he's got all the time in the world.

So cold.

"You found mud on the pants and shoes—but let's make this clear—no *blood* on anything but the car's backseat?"

The nerdy kid, Laird Johanssen. *I keep a file on all the hot girls.* Isn't that what he'd said?

"*I'm* not trying to draw any conclusions from the underwear photos, Mr. Crane. That's the jury's job, as I understand it."

Coming in through the nursery window, taking the breath from a baby's lungs.

"Come *on* now, Detective. Would *you* describe the accused as a man with the physical strength to do what the Crown wants the jury to believe he did?"

"Could you repeat the question?"

Christ knows you very well, Mr. Crane.

"You're a father, aren't you Detective Butcher? Couldn't you understand another man missing his little girl so much he would reach for whatever reminders, whatever small comforts he could find?"

"No, sir. But I can't speak for anyone but myself."

The Lady never slept and I had to.

"I think I've already answered that, Mr. Crane."

"No further questions, Your Honor."

An inch of Scotch tape at the top and bottom is all it takes to hold her there. I've found a square of uncovered wallpaper in the "V" of sandy light above the bedside lamp and it fits perfectly. A piece of crinkled gloss standing out from the melt of typeset columns, an island of up-close definition in a sea of letters and dots.

I guess at what her name was. I think of naming her myself. Stand close, hands against the wall for balance. Eyes searching, pushing in.

I commit the lines of her face to memory.

Thirty-Three

Bishop's Hospital lies at the end of a gravel side road off the main highway heading north. Only a small wooden sign marks the place to turn. This would be odd for a regular hospital, where people rush in the middle of the night to have babies delivered, limbs set in plaster or hearts pounded back to life. Insufficient for a place requiring a sign official-looking and prominent enough to be caught in the panicked swing of headlights. But not so odd for an asylum, halfway house, old-age home, or whatever combination this place is. Just a sun-faded square of plywood stuck on a knobbly pole knocked into the soft soil of the ditch.

I make the turn and bump along the "S"-shaped entry-way, dripping boughs bent low enough to scrape across the Lincoln's windshield before lifting away to expose the hospital at the end. The building is a converted brick house, better suited to its present purposes than the dwelling place of the single family for whom it must have been originally built. Out front is a wide circle for cars to park with a long-abandoned flower bed in its center, and everywhere else the underbrush has been allowed to creep up against the walls to cover most of the first-floor windows. In fact every effort appears to have been made (or *not* made) to let the place fall into an advanced state of overgrowth and disrepair. The easier then to be hidden and, with luck, forgotten.

I approach the single reception desk tucked into the

curve of the staircase where a nurse sits with head lowered over papers. Behind her hangs a full-size portrait of a twenty-something Queen Elizabeth sitting on her throne, her youth weighed down by scepter, crown and robes. I'm expecting crosses or a religious mural somewhere, somebody haloed or bleeding, but aside from Her Majesty there's nothing but bare walls.

Clear my throat to pull the nurse's attention away from what turns out to be not papers but the romance novel she's buried her head in. When she raises her eyes to mine she exposes a face much older that I would have expected, a complicated map of wrinkles and clouded eyes.

"Welcome to Bishop's. I'm Nurse Fergus. What can I do for you?" she says in an accent even more abrupt than Mrs. Arthurs's, the tone flat and lean. A born and bred local.

"Satisfy curiosities," I say.

I tell her that I'm Thom Tripp's lawyer and that I'm researching the origins of a curious episode in the local history, namely The Lady in the Lake. I'd like to look over the medical records, see if she had a name and what happened to the two girls that were taken from her. When I finish, Nurse Fergus looks up at me with her two-dimensional face, pug-nosed and frowning as a Pekingese.

"I wouldn't say 'curious' myself," she begins. "I wouldn't say 'episode' neither. Now I can't claim I remember her myself—I started here in '54, and by that time she was gone. But even then you couldn't speak of The Lady without someone around here giving you a look."

"Would there still be a medical record available on her?"

"Under what name? She never told anyone, which makes sticking her file into the alphabetical order a tricky business, as you can imagine."

"But might there be an Unknown Persons section to the files where she may be?"

"Possibly. We could take a look and see. But I'm not so sure just *anybody* can come along and look at another person's file. And I told your friend Thom Tripp the very same thing."

Nurse Fergus opens her eyes wide and shows a knowing playfulness in the blood-vesseled whites.

"Tripp came here to look at her file?"

"Told him that there's procedures for access to hospital records. Or you have to at least prove that you're a relative."

"Why? Did he say why?"

"I didn't ask, to tell you the truth. But even if I had, I'm sure I wouldn't have gotten very far. Your friend is not the most talkative man to walk the earth."

"He's not my friend."

Nurse Fergus lowers her eyes, shrugs.

"Can I see the file, nevertheless?" I ask, sensing she may wave me away if I don't press on.

"I've told you. There are procedures. Unless you're a relative?"

"I'm no relation. But I *am* a lawyer, and I can assure you that this is all entirely proper."

"That so?"

"Absolutely."

Nurse Fergus does something with her mouth that could either be an early symptom of Parkinson's or an effort at a girlish smile.

"First satisfy *my* curiosity," she says. "What's this got to do with what you're up here for? Are you following your friend, or was he following someone else?"

"Neither. It's nothing," I say, and go for a smile myself. "It's just an interest."

"An interest."

"They say everybody should have a hobby."

"Well you've picked a bloody strange one, I must say."

And she's right, of course. I'm losing my grip on the trial of the season and all I can do is waste my time looking up a dead old girl with a bad reputation. Because I can't go back to the honeymoon suite to do something useful. Can't push the image of her face from my mind, the husk and song of her imagined voice. Because all I can do is let Nurse Fergus grip my wrist and take me down the main hall to the Records Room where she pulls open a bottom drawer densely packed with worn files.

"More Unknowns here than you'd guess," she says. But it's only a few minutes before she sticks a thin, oil-stained folder under my nose with a croak of satisfaction. "She'd be this one."

An exposed water pipe gurgles uncomfortably above my head. Both of us wait for it to subside and in this time I notice how close we stand to each other, pushed together by filing cabinets, hanging bulbs, damp boxes stacked on the floor. The air an invisible steam of mildew, pine cleanser and sweat.

"Shall we have a look?" Nurse Fergus takes a half step closer to my side, crosses her arms together under rolls of cardigan, turtleneck and breast.

"A peek?"

"A peeky-boo."

Only two pages. A standard admission form with "Nameless" printed in the space allotted for patient identification, and under TENTATIVE DIAGNOSIS the words "Unable to mother." The second page is a two-paragraph handwritten report outlining her escape from hospital. Apparently she'd used the old knotted-together-sheets-to-make-a-rope routine, tied the one end to the bedpost and threw the other out the third-floor window, breaking through the glass with her bare arm. Then down she went into the snow, scrambling into the woods in nothing but her gown and slippers. At the end, the underlined sentence: "Red Ward recommended for patient upon return."

"Not much in the way of detail," Nurse Fergus comments as she reads with her chin on my forearm.

"What about her children? There's nothing in here about them, or where they ended up. And nothing about her hysterectomy."

"How would you know about that?"

"Town gossip."

"You must have been speaking to some of the old folks around here if you've heard *that* kind of gossip."

"Nurse Fergus, I *always* seek the company of old folks wherever I go."

I wonder for a second if this last bit would be taken as offence. But apparently not, for she only grins wider and sucks at her dentures in satisfaction.

"Back then, you didn't have to explain things as much," she says. "Today of course you can hardly strap one of the rough ones into their bed without having to have a lawyer come round to sign some form or other. But when I first came here everything was run the way the doctors wanted it. Truth is, by the time you ended up in a place like this, chances were nobody else wanted much to do with you anyway. So they used to do hysterectomies without the patient's consent, and all sorts of other things—some far worse, really—without much paper to show for it. And as for taking a mother's children from her, well, you'd just get the justice of the peace up in the town to sign an order and you could ship them out to the main Toronto orphanage without another word. From there, God knows where they'd end up."

I return the file to the approximate place she pulled it from and rise, the silk violets on my necktie brushing across her knuckles as I go.

"Thank you for your help. I didn't imagine I'd find very much—"

She takes me by the elbow with a bony firmness.

"Are your curiosities satisfied *now*?"

Pull my arm away. A girlish giggle at my back as I half-run down the hall.

When I get back to town there's still time to visit Tripp before they shut the cellblock down but I call instead. Then I'm left on hold long enough that sleep, curling and warm, begins to settle around me where I sit. But before it has its way with me I hear the receiver being lifted at the other end and the wet, halting sucks of my client's breath. There is no greeting, and for a time I imagine him at a bare table in one of the fluorescent rooms of the Murdoch Prison for Men, the phone held to his ear from almost forgotten habit. It's clear that if nobody else spoke—neither me nor the guard standing behind him nor whoever whispered to him privately in his head—he would stay this way forever.

"Thom? You there?"

"Who's this?"

"It's Barth, Thom. How're things?"

"Do they let me have visitors?"

"Who would you like to have visit?"

"Tuesday's the day. Visitors come on Tuesdays. To see the others."

"You're allowed visitors too. Who would you like—"

"Can I have pictures?"

"Can you—what kind of pictures? Because it all depends."

"You know, I'd actually prefer them to the real thing. To be frank."

"Well, with pictures it all depends on the *subject*, Thom, so if you—"

"You know the subject. It's been the same subject for some time—"

"—hey, hey, O.K., can we just get back—"

"—unless somebody changed it without letting me know."

Tripp coughs, sending something hard flying around inside him, and resumes his powerful breathing that sounds down the line as the crashing tide of the sea.

"Thom, just listen for a second. I want to ask you something, alright? About the case."

The tide draws back up his nose.

"Our story is that the bloodstains in the back of the car came from Krystal's scraped knee," I say. "That it happened on a different day from her disappearance, right?"

"Our story."

"So how did the blood get on your *shirt*, Thom? Isn't that strange?"

"Are you asking me to explain what—"

"Yes, I am. Asking you to explain how the blood got on your shirt if she was sitting in the backseat with a cut on her knee."

"They come and go on Tuesdays. But *pictures*. Pictures are different."

"Thom, please, don't change the subject when I—"

"It all depends on the subject though, doesn't it?"

"That's right. You're goddamn right about that. And right now the subject is trying to save your fucking ass, Thom. So for Christ's sake could you just—"

"Now isn't *that* an odd thing! An English teacher who'd rather have pictures than books!"

Tripp makes a sputtering suppression of laughter, a flapping of lips so close to the mouthpiece that it distorts into an imitation of flatulence. But that's thankfully all. The laughter doesn't escape, and soon the respiratory tide returns, proof that the unstoppable oxygen machine that is my client is alive and well.

"I apologize for my outburst. But I have some questions, Thom, and I would like it—I would be so *pleased* if you could help me out with some of them."

Nothing from the other end. But I can sense him listening.

"For example, I was talking to a former colleague of yours the other day. Miss Betts. She told me about the trouble you had with your divorce, being denied custody of your daughter. Now, all of that may be something we might think about using, or worse, it might be something the prosecution might want to use. But I'd like you to tell me what happened there anyway, so that I can answer—"

"A face like her mother's," he says, so softly I barely hear it.

"Is that who you saw up in the window of Melissa's school the day you tried to visit her and the police kept you away? Was it your wife's face that you saw?"

"No. Melissa was crying. My wife never cried." He turns his head away. "All her teachers standing behind her trying to say teacher things and pull her away but she wouldn't let them. Because she was my little girl and she wanted to see her daddy."

I have to strain to hear the last of his words, each of them fading after the other as though the phone was being slowly pulled away from his mouth.

"Did you try to take Melissa away, Thom? Is that why they wouldn't let you see her anymore?"

"There's that word again. Take, take, take. But I ask you: how can a father *take* his own daughter?"

"So you're saying that you *did* then. Or tried to. As far as the law is concerned."

"I thought being a father was supposed to be the most natural thing in the world," he laughs now. "I couldn't tell you *as far as the law is concerned.* But that's where you come in, isn't it?"

"I suppose it is, Thom, yes."

I imagine him there in his prison overalls, his boyish skin in need of a shave, a trace of dinner still in evidence somewhere on his fingers or chin. And now that the talking is over he's allowed his face to loosen again, his features returned to their usual setting of gummy distraction. Not that he's mad, exactly. It's that he's decided that wherever he goes in his head is better for him than any of the currently available offerings of the waking world.

"Listen, I'll let you go now, Thom," I say. "I'll visit soon."

The receiver is halfway to its cradle when the mechanics of Thomas Tripp's body are interrupted by a request from its brain.

"Bring pictures," he says.

Thirty-Four

"It is my opinion that Thomas Tripp's profile is consistent with that of a reactive psychotic."

This is Goodwin's expert shrink, perched high in the witness box, eyes held open in the falsely earnest, disinterested way common to those of his profession. This one, however, is even worse than most: all clipped beard, fleshy lips, designer glasses that look like some kind of ancient navigational device. Whenever he finishes speaking he turns first to the bench, then to Goodwin and finally to me, giving each of us the same blinking second-and-a-half of gooey innocence as if to say *You see, I have no personal interest in this. I'm merely offering my professional opinion.* But what all of us know—even Goodwin deep down—is that this guy's a prostitute. A $400-an-hour witness fee hustler who would declare his own mother a reactive psychotic under oath if a lawyer hired him to.

"Could you please explain for the court, in general terms, what a reactive psychotic is?" Goodwin is asking, turning to the jury with a pained look. He knows as well as I do they're not so good with words greater than two syllables.

"Well, the term describes an individual who, as a consequence of suffering a certain trauma—an *emotional* trauma—responds in an extreme way. The brain defends itself by shutting down some of its elementary faculties or dissolves previously held behavioral boundaries, such that the result is a psychotic state which may be either short-lived or prolonged."

He gives us the punctuating look again: one, two, three. *Just trying to help*, his fussy beard and glasses say. *I just happen to know all about this stuff. I'm an expert.*

"I think it's important to emphasize that I'm just dealing here with a case profile," he's saying now—what the hell's his name? Ganzer? Panzer? "Mr. Tripp has never been a patient of mine, so I can't speak to any extensive personal knowledge of his history. But I feel, based on the information in the file provided to me by the Crown, that I am able to make some tentative conclusions."

"That's fine. But just to get all of this straight, are you saying that it is your view—your *tentative* view—that Thomas Tripp is insane?"

Nice one, Pete. Serve the good doctor a high beachball just to make sure he can smash it back.

"*No*, not at all. No, no. In fact I'd like to make it very clear that psychotic behavior or the presence of a psychotic condition does not necessarily mean that the subject is insane. Indeed, it is my understanding that being *legally* insane has nothing to do with being psychotic, neurotic or otherwise, but concerns the subject's ability to understand the difference between rightful and wrongful actions."

At this point, I rise. Slowly though, pushing back my chair and lifting myself up with hands planted on the desk in front of me.

"I *object*, Your Honor. The doctor may be an expert able to provide descriptions of certain psychological illnesses for the general education of the jury, but he is surely not an expert for the purposes of articulating the legal definition of insanity. And even if he *were*, this is not an issue in the current proceedings. Nor will it be."

I slouch back down again, keeping my eye on the doctor. And he returns my stare without change in what I now see as his decidedly pubic face.

"Quite right, Mr. Crane. Doctor, I would ask that you limit your comments to the area of your particular expertise," Goldfarb tells him, but her heart's not in it.

"Of course. I *apologize*, Your Honor," Dr. Pubic minces.

Then Goodwin's back up there, guiding his man through the file, the sorry history of Tripp's life. A bright student through university and teacher's college, an early marriage to his high school sweetheart, the slow climb up the departmental seniority ladder, the birth of a daughter. Fully functional *domestic support systems* is how the doctor puts it. Then it all starts to fall apart. The marriage first, followed by much unsuccessful counseling, the loss of his only child. Isolates himself from whatever friends still bothered with him. The only thing he could apparently still focus on was the Literary Club, with meetings held once a week and a total membership of two.

"But *many* of us have to go through stresses of this kind in life, doctor, and not *all* of us are psychotics," Goodwin is saying, looking once more to the jury whose very faces seem to prove him wrong. "So what's the difference, in your view, between a reactive psychotic and any other person who's undergone emotional trauma?"

"Actually there're a few differences," the doctor chirps. "Generally speaking, there are three categories of psychological activity: normal, neurotic and psychotic. Arguably there is also a fourth—insanity—but I guess we'll leave that aside for the moment." Another look in my direction at this, his eyes milky circles. "Now, neurotic behavior involves any number of symptoms, including anxiety states, hysteria, obsessional neuroses, and others. The distinction between these and a true psychotic is that a neurosis embodies what may be called a mental conflict, but the basic character of reality remains, whereas in the psychotic the very structure of reality itself is altered. Put another way, the real and the unreal are so confused that eventually they become one and the same. Now, in Mr. Tripp's particular terms, I think we can draw certain broad characteristics of . . ."

He goes on to make sweeping, objectionable swipes at my boy Tripp, the sort of prejudicial psychobabble that should have me leaping to my feet every five seconds, but I remain seated and silent. The truth is, all this talk has me considering my own troubled profile. What would the doctor—*any* doctor—make of an admitted seer of visions, subject of phantom visitations well beyond the mere bed-shaking, key-hiding, footstep-on-the-stairs variety? As the doctor's lips smack away at painting my client out as Norman Bates, I wonder whether I myself may have graduated from harmless neurotic to a more advanced stage. The water certainly tastes bad up here but is likely still well below government-recommended levels for mercury and lead, and I haven't eaten anything since my arrival except for factory-made sandwiches enriched with enough preservatives to keep them fresh deep into the twenty-first century, so it can't be poisoning. It also seems I don't qualify as a reactive psychotic, given that I haven't reacted to *anything* in the past twenty years. So what is it, then?

I make a mental note to eat more fruit.

"Although Mr. Tripp made no detailed statements of any kind to the police following his arrest," Goodwin is saying now, eyes cast downward at the prepared questions he's plowing his way through, "he did, however, at one or two points during initial questioning, state that he had nothing to say, and even if he did, he couldn't remember. My question to you, Doctor, is this: Can memory also be affected in situations of trauma?"

"Absolutely," says the hairy mouth. "Again, I can't speak directly to Mr. Tripp's condition, but there are documented cases where extreme stress has given rise to nothing more or less than clinical amnesia. That is, an entire section of the individual's life is not merely repressed but, in effect, wiped out entirely."

"Is this lost memory recoverable?"

"Potentially."

"So if Mr. Tripp were to testify that he can't remember any events of Thursday, May the twelfth, for example, we wouldn't be able to tell if it's a case of amnesia or whether he's just—"

"Objection!"

I'm up. I've let too much slide between the fat man and Dr. Pubic already, but now they're about to go right off the map.

"The doctor is in no position to hypothesize on testimony that hasn't and may never be heard. Your Honor, I really think the Crown has now reached the absolute limit on advancing any probative evidence from this witness."

"That's fine. I'm done anyway," Goodwin grins before dropping into his chair.

"Mr. Crane, perhaps this would be a good time for our afternoon break," Goldfarb sighs, rubbing her eye with the heel of her hand. "Back here in ten, people."

I'm the first one out. Make my way to the bathroom and

lock myself in the stall furthest from the door. Time for some clarity assistance. And here it comes, lumped out over the back of my hand, individual grains tumbling off the pile and onto my pants, the toilet seat, the floor. In my haste to get some of it in I break one of my own fundamental rules of cocaine etiquette: I *snort*. An industrial nasal suck that echoes off the tiled walls and aluminum partitions. And another. Then, most shameful of all, I allow an involuntary *Oh yeah* to croak past my lips before I pull back the bolt and step out to the sinks.

Crank the taps until the water rushes hot and loud. When I think I can actually hear my skin start to pucker I lift my head and peer into the mirror's fog with a startled breath.

Movement behind me within the billowing grey. Something over my right shoulder that definitely wasn't there before. A disembodied head floating closer, its face enlarging to reveal a lick of damp hair across the brow, eyes screwed deep in their sockets.

"McConnell."

I may say this, I may not. My heart beating in painful hiccups.

Why him? Probably heard me in the stall too, which explains the crude smirk held stiff on his face. And now I can't stop myself from sniffling. Wiping too. The back of my hands, the palms. Both wrists glazed in clear snot.

"Don't look so good there, hot shot," he says.

"I'm fine, thank you." The water splashing up, spotting through my shirt in warm bites.

"So. The client's a child murderer and the lawyer's a junkie. Nice."

"There's a big difference—" I begin, but the distinction's lost in a fainting flush of adrenaline. I shut off the water with a screech of the tap, my face a lump of dripping dough in the mirror before me. Turn to find that McConnell now stands closer than I thought. That even if I move now I'll have to step around him to get out.

"Don't go just yet, Mr. Crane. We have a few minutes before you have to be back in there to tell your dirty lies."

"Lies?"

"Like how you had such a nice and friendly interview with me before the trial as if I was your best buddy or something. Made it sound like we were both on the same side, which as you know couldn't be further from the truth."

"Are you on anybody's side in this besides your own?"

"What are you saying?"

"Brian Flynn told me that you've never spoken to him about his own loss. That you wouldn't even return his calls. I would've thought the two of you had a lot in common. But apparently you didn't see it that way. Must have thought your daughter was better than his, I guess. Then again, you always made it clear that you never liked Ashley. You wouldn't deny any of that now, would you?"

I have no idea where this comes from. Gulping for air, cocaine tears trickling over my cheeks that I can only hope McConnell mistakes for sweat. All I want is to get the hell out of here and I'm provoking the man who stands between me and the door. Fucking lawyers. They never give up.

"She wasn't the right sort for Krystal," McConnell is saying. "And so what? It wasn't her fault her father's a bum."

"He's on disability," I offer foolishly. "His lungs."

"A man has to work."

"Maybe a man feels like he has to do other things too, sometimes."

"What do you mean?"

I ignore the question, fall back to let my ass rest against the slippery edge of the sink. "Sounds to me like your daughter had good reason to run away from home."

"You say another thing like that and I'll rip your god-damn throat out."

"That's a threat."

"No, sir. It's the truth."

I push myself away from the sink with both hands as though launching a boat into rough water. Legs poured full of gelatin. Heading for the space between McConnell and the stalls next to him where there might be enough room to get by without touching.

"You think you don't feel so good now?" he hisses, reading my mind. "Believe me. This is nothing compared to the fire you're going to burn in when you're dead and buried, hot shot."

I'm directly in front of him now, eyes level with his stubbled, heaving Adam's apple. It's clear that if there was room to pass around him a moment ago it's gone now. He's going to have to move. Or drop dead. Or explode into a fluttering cloud of ash.

"I would think that you should be worried about hell yourself," I tell him, my face weaving a foot-and-a-half below his chin, "seeing how you know that you never loved your daughter properly when she was alive, and now that she's dead you're—"

But I'm not allowed to finish. It's McConnell's palms slammed into my chest that prevent me. Lifting me an inch off the floor until my back crunches into the aluminum of the paper towel dispenser. Part of me—a flailing hand or elbow—connects with the silver button on the hand dryer, and now there's a distant jet engine drone along with the

whirring of pressurized blood in my ears. And something
else. A looping incantation pushing through everything,
plaintive and thin.

"How *dare* you? How *dare* you? How *dare* you?"

I say nothing in response. I don't resist. Eyes on the four
of our shoes assembled together like awkward dance partners.
Then McConnell pulls his hands away and I slump in the
effort to support the whole of my weight on my own again.
When I finally look up it's to see his face twisted in what
appear to be equal parts grief and puzzlement. But arms
slack at his sides, no words left in him. Take the chance and
slide to the door, blindly push my way into the cool air of the
hall.

I manage to lurch back to the courtroom and sit at the
defence table with eyes on the clock, refusing to look back
into the gallery. Willing the sweat beading up on my forehead
to stay where it is. But when Goldfarb calls me to my feet
again it falls over my face anyway, salt drops trickling into
eyes and open mouth.

"Now, Doctor," I start, clearing my throat with a loud
percolation of loose stuff. "I'll make this brief because, with
all due respect, a cross-examination of a witness who has been
unable to offer any evidence is a waste of the court's time.
Nevertheless, for the sake of *clarity*, let me hit a couple of
points. You have never met, let alone spoken to or examined
my client. Is that right?"

"That's correct."

"So all you're dealing with are mere possibilities—conditions that may or may not be applicable to Mr. Tripp?"

"I was asked to provide background on some established
profiles."

"*Profiles*, yes, but you don't know Mr. Tripp any better

than you know me, or Justice Goldfarb, or him." I stab a finger in the direction of one of the jury's lumberjacks. "Do you, Doctor?"

"There's a difference between knowing and the consideration of one's behavioral traits and tendencies."

"There is? Could you explain that for me?"

"Well, simply put, psychology is the science of personality, whereas knowing someone is something, well, deeper."

"Deeper. You mean 'deep' like the *truth*? To know someone is to know something of the truth about them?"

"I suppose, in a manner of—"

"And science, as you've said, isn't about the truth *per se*. It's about traits and tendencies. It's about categorizing, yes? Psychosis, neurosis. Sane, insane. It's about fitting people into slots. Isn't that right?"

"If by that you mean diagnosis, then yes, that's a primary clinical function."

"But it's *not* a primary clinical function to *know* a person though, is it? Because, in the end, science can't tell us why a man does what he does or why he doesn't, why he forgets or why he remembers, can it?"

"I would suppose not with the precision you're suggesting, no."

I wipe my face with the arm of my jacket and take two jagged breaths through the broken glass in my chest. My head separating from my neck, rising up into the white globes of the ceiling lights.

"So let me ask you. What good are your psychiatric speculations to this court, Doctor—a court charged with the job of determining innocence or guilt—if those speculations can say nothing about *why*?"

"I don't understand the question."

"How's this then? How can you, a *psychiatric expert*, say anything about my client when *knowing* him isn't your business?"

Approving coughs from the gallery. A telltale smirk at the borders of Goldfarb's lips. Goodwin harrumphs. But then, for the first time all afternoon, the expression on the doctor's face changes. The mouth puckers, the furry chin juts out, and the eyes—goddamn it if the eyes don't *twinkle*.

"From what I can tell, I'm very glad I don't know your client, Mr. Crane," he says. "But then again, as you've said, knowing him isn't my job. So I suppose it must be yours."

Thirty-Five

Outside the window the night swirls and disperses like ink poured into water. "The days are getting shorter," I hear the locals state the obvious to each other on street corners as I pass, their eyes held up to the sky. But for me, the more accurate observation would be "The night is coming sooner." And when it comes it stays longer, keeping me from sleep, from the fleeting distractions of work. I wish for night-lights. The pink plastic ones with the ten-watt bulbs. Maybe if I could stick a few of those around I could push the worst of the shadows back from all the corners.

Brush my teeth again. Never used to in the city, but up here I've really taken to it. I've found I can kill a whole seven minutes with a single meticulous scrubbing. What's important is to really get into "those hard-to-reach places" the packaging warns of. Such small pleasures also allow for a check to see how I'm scoring on the ghoulo-meter. Every time I look in the mirror now it's like time-lapse photography, my face aging at the rate of one year for every passing day. Worse, these false years are not treating me with any kindness whatsoever, introducing colors to my skin better suited to the stuff collected in bus terminal ashtrays. A little surprised I can still see myself in mirrors at all anymore the way I've come to live like a vampire: don't eat regular food, awake most of the night, fingernails the yellowed sharpness of talons. And feeling a little monstrous too, in the pained, baffled way of the walking dead. Although I'm not. Not yet dead. There's still a heart (a clenched fist that sucker punches surrounding organs from time to time). And still a soul. Or whatever weightless thing it is that lifts away on its own occasionally to look down at me as I try to work at my desk. Pauses before something jerks it back like a balloon whose string has almost passed beyond the tallest grasp. And whenever this happens I always think, plainly and briefly and in italics: *I want to be alive.* Not *I'm too young to die* or *Life is good* or even *Happy to be here.* Just hangs there for a second like the product slogan flashed at the end of a commercial. *I want to be alive.* And then a wave of foolishness—it's a rather obvious thing to construct as a *sentence,* after all—along with a swift brush of fear, like hair pulled across your cheek.

Well, boo-hoo for me. When all this is over I'll treat myself to a week somewhere warm followed by the psychotherapy all my ex-friends pointedly recommended before writing me off. If that doesn't work I'll attend at the first church or suburban rec room that reports a weeping statue of the Blessed Virgin, light a candle and leave a large donation. Later I will be reformed. But what I need now is a couple hours of headfuck-free work time. So I take my seat again, rub hands together to bring feeling to the fingertips. Pull my head back to whatever lies at the top of the To Do pile.

Laird Johanssen's file. Didn't I throw it out? I should've. I should now. But instead I pull it open and finger through what's inside. A full-size brown envelope with SOUVENIRS printed over it in marker, that bulges sharply in places with whatever is kept within. Turn it over and spill the contents out onto the desk.

The first thing I see is two locks of hair, one dark and

one light, each bound together by a small elastic band. The shameless fellow must have begged their stylists for a sample from whatever had been swept into a pile under the salon chair after they'd left. As this image plays itself out I find that I've lifted the hair to my own nose, one lock at a time, breathing in the faint scent of the different conditioners— one lemon, one vanilla—that still cling to the brittle strands.

There's a pellet of yellow chewing gum with a molar print dried into its smoothness like a fossil. A cheap silver-plated bracelet with "Happy 13th Birthday, Ashley! Love, Dad" engraved on the inside. A pair of sunglasses missing one of its arms with green lenses shaped like the eyes of a cat. A cassette of Nirvana's *Nevermind*, a wrinkled loop of tape pulled out and twisted into a waxy nest. A photograph of Krystal standing in front of her open locker and a pull-out Leonardo di Caprio poster taped to the inside of the metal door behind her. A startled smile on her face, both hands stuck in the top shelf wrestling with a stack of textbooks, her head swiveled to meet the camera's flash. There's something in the dry fatigue at the edges of the eyes that suggests that although she's been surprised to hear her name and turn to find her picture being taken, she recognizes in the same instant that it's only Laird. She was hoping for one of the cute guys, Josh or Steve or Matt, or at least one of the yearbook photo-editor geeks. Not pizza-faced Laird, always taking little pieces of you away for himself.

There's also a scattering of papers, some clipped together and others on their own, leathery from repeated foldings. The first sheaf neater than the others, a handwritten essay with "THE REAL TRAGEDY OF ROMEO AND JULIET, By Ashley Flynn" printed in red pen across the top of the first page. I flip to the end and read the final sentence: "In many

ways, Shakespeare's play is tragic because it puts the selfish
interests of families in conflict against pure love, so that, in
the end, neither are ultimately allowed to triumph." Beneath
this, Tripp's written comments ("As usual, an excellent
appreciation of Shakespeare's moral polarities") and, in the
bottom corner, a boldly encircled A+. Another is a page of
newsprint ripped from the school paper, *Perspectives*. The
bottom half taken up with a poem by Krystal McConnell
under the headline "1st Prize Winner: Literature" and
entitled "What's Inside of Me." Again I skip to the last lines:

> *All the things on the outside are just a big show*
> *So what's really inside of me? You'll never know.*

Two photocopies of the girls' entries in Laird's yearbook
from the previous spring. The messages cursory, impersonal,
obligatory. The first in Ashley's hand:

> Hey L. J.:
> Well, it's been a great year (class trip to Stratford, the
> Cougars winning the Cup) and it's been nice having
> you around. Maybe we'll see ya in the summer.
>   Ashley F.

The "Maybe we'll see ya" a telling use of the corporate
"we," its purpose to remind someone like Laird of where he
belonged. But the message also graced him by the promise
of "maybe" an accidental meeting with someone important
this summer. Who knows, they might even say hello to him
as they passed.

Krystal even more dismissive, through a devastating,
adult politeness:

Laird,
Good luck with whatever!
Krystal McConnell

But Laird didn't care that they wanted nothing to do with him. They didn't need to know him to be worthy subjects for capture, worship and preservation. If hot girls were more accessible they would be less important to a kid like Laird Johanssen anyway. Maybe what makes the Lairds of this world love beauty from a great distance is the very impossibility of that love ever being returned.

So which was I? The adorer or the adored? The truth is I can't remember. And there's nothing to help me: no yearbooks stuck at the bottom of closets, photo albums, letters and notes collected in a shoe box. Somehow I emerged from youth without any evidence of my having been there. All of it made to disappear, just as Ashley and Krystal were.

Dead or alive something happened to them, and now all that's left is Laird's collected bits and pieces, a wrinkled envelope marked SOUVENIRS. Their handwriting speaks in my ear as I read it. The hair glints as though the dull light of the desk lamp is instead the brilliant luster of an afternoon sun. The bracelet warmed by an imagined wrist, its delicate pulses of blood.

Here and then not here.

Disappeared.

Taken from the world but not understandably, without motive or reason or story. To disappear is to be denied an ending to yourself, the one gift that death can give.

That night I turn on the TV and it fizzes and cracks to life. A bad picture tube that flattens heads and loses its vertical hold any time a voice is raised. I get through a real-life cop show featuring a German shepherd separating a fleeing crack dealer from his left arm, the last half of *Jerry Springer* (the topic: "You're My Sister and You're Sleeping with My Son!"), shots of expensive beachfront homes turned to sparkly piles of chrome and glass by a hurricane in Florida. All of it reduced to a comic routine, even the violence and domestic tragedy and the power of Nature all going for the laughs. The flat heads weep, resist arrest, slap each other across the face without consequence.

I turn it off to waggle a plastic spoon into the thermos. only to have it slip out of my fingers when the phone rings.

"Barth Crane here."

"Oh my. You're in! I hate to sound like your mother but I *must* say it: *Why* don't you ever call?"

"Nothing to report, Graham."

"Surely there's *something.*"

"Just been doing some research." I turn to The Lady's photo on the wall behind me. "Pulling things together."

"Very good. No *problems,* then? The locals stop their little shows? *Les danseuses exotiques* curtail their prank calls? No more old women falling through ice or attempts to *freak you out?*"

"This is my case, Graham. Do I call you up just to be a sarcastic bitch when you're working on a trial?"

"I wasn't talking about the trial, old man."

What if Graham could see me now? The walls plastered in curling newsprint. Most of Tripp's file still unopened on the desk. A written account of Mrs. Arthurs's story of The Lady glowing out from the laptop's screen.

"Really, Graham. When I called that time I think I was drunk, for Christ's sake. Everything's peachy now, if you'd just stop smothering me."

I turn on the TV again, mute the volume on the remote. It's the funny home video show, a family winning $10,000 for footage of its father being swarmed by bees and falling off a stepladder while trying to screw a basketball net over the garage.

"Smothering? I'm so *sorry*. We don't want to *smother* our boy, do we? Back to it then. And you just ring if anything develops. We're following things in the papers down here, and you look *good*. Although, may I suggest a haircut?"

"Haircut. Right."

"Night-night."

I pick up the spoon again, dip deep. Tape the curling corners of newspaper down with another round of Scotch tape. Hold her picture in my hand, and instead of dreams stay with the hair transplant specialists, cellulite creams and psychic hot lines until dawn.

Thirty-Six

Another walk through the drizzle up Ontario Street, another five minutes spent promising that today, finally, I'll take my lunch break to buy a goddamn umbrella. I'm tired of spending my daytime hours sitting in the high-ceilinged space of the largest courtroom in Murdoch with drips of water finding their way down the back of my neck, over the nubby length of my spine. And why does it have to rain so much at this time of year anyway? It's not like anything's *growing* up here. Take a look around: everything's *dying*, the streets littered in brown and yellow layers of wet death—

"Mr. Crane!"

It's one of the TV reporters, the woman. Attractive on-air (sharp mouth and self-consciously hard-boiled voice) but up close the professional requirement of excessive makeup becomes gruesomely apparent.

"I understand that Krystal's father, Lloyd McConnell, plans to take the stand today," she says, pulling a cameraman along behind her on a microphone cable. "What will be your strategy on cross-examination?"

"Did you actually think I'd answer that question?"

"Well, do you have *any* comment? About anything?"

"I think not."

I continue on, feeling a greater dampening through the shoulders of my suit than usual due to this delay on the courthouse steps. But before I make it all the way up she tries again.

"Mr. Crane! How do you respond to Mr. McConnell's claim that anyone who would defend a man like Thomas Tripp is a hell-bound degenerate himself?"

Turn to face her and wipe a line of half-formed icicles from my chin.

"Hell-bound degenerate," I say aloud to myself. Consider the term for a moment and resist a smile before heading inside.

The morning begins with Goodwin rising to call Lloyd McConnell to the stand. The next second I'm up myself to object.

"Yes, Mr. Crane? And why would that be?"

"Perhaps the court would be best served if the substance of my objections were not heard with the jury present."

"Perhaps that's so. Better safe than sorry, right? O.K., members of the jury. I know you've only just sat down, but would you mind filing back to the jury room for a time while we sort this matter out? I advise taking the opportunity for a second round of coffee and doughnuts. And Mr. McConnell, could you step out into the hall as well for a moment? Maybe you'd like some additional refreshments yourself. It may be a long morning."

When the jury has shuffled out and the bailiff closed the door behind them, Justice Goldfarb looks down at me with her more or less permanent expression of wry suspicion.

"I think I know, but let me ask anyway: What's your problem, Barth?"

"It's the matter of relevance, Your Honor. I have no problem with Mr. McConnell venting whatever frustrations he's understandably dealing with at the moment. But this courtroom is not the right venue for such therapy. I would respectfully remind the court that what we're up to here is Mr. Tripp's trial, and unless Mr. McConnell can offer any evidence to assist in its determination, I submit that he has no place in this procedure."

I turn to check on Tripp, but his head is turned away at an odd angle as though his ears are picking up some faint radio signal he's attempting to fine-tune.

"Mr. Goodwin?"

"Your Honor, Mr. McConnell's testimony serves a very particular purpose, and that is to meet the suggestions made by defence counsel in his opening submissions that Krystal and Ashley may be nothing more than runaways. I submit that what Lloyd McConnell has to say about Krystal will address the credibility of such a suggestion."

Justice Goldfarb stabs a finger into her mouth, pulls something out from her rear molars, flicks it to the floor, and replaces her hands in front of her in a single motion.

"Mr. Crane?"

"First, I made it clear in my opening submissions that the defence was not basing its case on the runaway theory, but merely asking the jury to keep it in mind as a possibility. Mr. McConnell's testimony is therefore not necessary. There is tremendous potential for injury to be done to proper procedure here, Your Honor. I'd ask you to consider that."

This last bit clearly a threat that if she allows McConnell to go up there's automatic grounds for appeal, and we both know it. But Naomi Goldfarb, I'd forgotten, doesn't respond well to threats.

"*Thank* you, Mr. Crane. Any suggestions, Mr. Goodwin?"

"Well, I would remind my friend that he is free to to any particular piece of evidence that advances from the object testimony. And perhaps he can take some comfort from the fact that the prosecution seeks only to show that Krystal McConnell was not the sort of young woman to run away from home without leaving a sign. The defence raised the question of the victim's character, not me, and I'm only trying to meet that question by the only means available."

Goodwin sits, pleased as punch, and for a second the entire room is held in breathless suspense, wondering if the moment has come for the legs under his chair to finally collapse.

"How's that sound to you, Mr. Crane?"

"Not so great, Your Honor. But I see where all this is going and I would simply ask the court that if it decides to permit Mr. McConnell to testify despite my objections, I be permitted a broad scope for my cross-examination."

"Broad scope?"

"He means 'go for the jugular,' Your Honor."

"I resent that remark—"

"*Easy* now, boys. I understand what you're asking for, Mr. Crane, and I'll keep it in mind. Because it's my ruling that if Mr. McConnell wishes to testify, he can, as I'm sure that Crown counsel has advised the witness of the rough ride cross-examination can often be. So, let's bring the jury and Mr. McConnell back in and get on with the show."

When the jury's back in their box McConnell is called once more, and up he comes, the floor creaking under the awkward bulk of his weight which this morning has been wrapped within a navy blue suit cut a little too short in the arms. From the waist up he's managed to affect the body language of obligation—rounded shoulders, chin raised, eyes pulled wide. But as he takes the steps up into the stand his lower half gives him away. An aggression betrayed by A-frame thighs, inflexible knees, his shoes grinding into the carpet as though extinguishing someone else's dropped cigarette. When the Bible is produced he lays his hand on its cover and raises the other with a rehearsed solemnity, and I imagine him standing before his mirror in the master bedroom at home, training for this moment while his wife wipes her eyes raw and pops her pills in the en suite bathroom next to him. Having stated his "I do" that echoes off the plaster walls longer than one would think possible he takes his seat, chest heaving inside his shirt like a wild animal smuggled in and now demanding release.

"Mr. McConnell, I'm aware that this is tremendously difficult for you—" Goodwin shakes his head, realigns the puffy necklace of flesh above his collar "—but could you help us here today by describing for the court what kind of girl your daughter Krystal was?"

And it begins. Home, hearth, family, church. The blueprint of the perfect nuclear family unrolled and explained in excruciating detail. He's got it all figured out, the plodding narration to a rec room slide show committed to memory. And although not a word of it has any probative value whatsoever, I let it pass without a peep. On and on it goes, bravely, without tears, the words occasionally trembling with emotion before being gathered up to a proud baritone once more: "I remember on one picnic up at Killarney Provincial Park, Krystal got this bee sting and didn't her cheeks swell up like two grapefruits." "Quite an author she was, always sticking her beautiful poems up on the fridge door. Would you like to hear one?" "She was always honest with us. We built our *house* on honesty."

My turn comes after lunch. Start with some meandering

niceties, let the jury's cafeteria sandwiches and brownies settle in their guts, then get to where I want to go.

"Mr. McConnell, you've made a special point of telling the court about the honesty in your house, particularly as between yourself and your daughter, isn't that right?"

"Yes, that's right."

"What I mean is that it was very important to you, to your family. Not telling lies."

"It was important. But isn't it important in every—"

"You're the breadwinner of your house, right?"

"My wife doesn't work, if that's what you mean."

"And you're a religious man?"

"I attend church. I believe in God."

"In rules?"

"God's rules."

At this McConnell looks over at Goodwin, hoping for a signal. But Goodwin is buried in his notes, trying to guess where I'm going, and McConnell is left alone to fold the skin of his forehead into ruddy pink waves.

"And as head of the household, liars are something you would have trouble tolerating, right?"

"I'd have some trouble. But with Krystal, there was never—"

"With Krystal there was never need to punish her, was there? You've told us how, with your other children, you'd sometimes have to lay down the law; but not with Krystal, isn't that so?"

"That's correct."

"But if you *did*, you *would* have, wouldn't you?"

McConnell's shoulders have crept up to meet at his chin.

"Mr. McConnell, do you understand the question?"

"Yes."

"Yes what?"

"Yes, I wouldn't have treated Krystal any different."

"You'd punish her then?"

"I'd do *something*, but—"

"You'd do something. I see. Well, what if I told you that I have a witness who will testify that Krystal *was* in fact lying to you. Would you have done *something* if you had known that?"

"It would depend."

"How about if she was smoking cigarettes with boys outside the school yard. Do you allow your children to smoke, Mr. McConnell?"

"How do you know she smoked?"

"I'll prove it later. But let's just hypothesize for the moment. Would you do *something* to your daughter if she was lying to you, if the lie involved her smoking and flirting with older boys she knew you didn't approve of when she should have been attending choir practice?"

"If it's true."

"Let's assume it is."

"I think sometimes a father has to do certain things. For discipline."

"Discipline. Punish. You'd do *something*, correct?"

"If I had—"

"Would you say that you have a temper, Mr. McConnell?"

"I'm a businessman. Sometimes you've got to show people that they can't get away with trying—that you don't appreciate being taken for granted."

"Is that why you pushed me around and threatened my bodily safety in the men's lavatory of this very courthouse two days ago?"

"What? All I—"

"*Objection!*"

"Mr. Crane!"

Everybody's up. Goldfarb shaking her head and Goodwin throwing his arms about him as though the words he wants to use are dancing in the air around him.

"Are you initiating new proceedings against the Crown's witness here, Mr. Crane?" Goldfarb scowls. But there's a brightness in her eyes that shows she's enjoying this just a little.

"I'm not trying to make criminal accusations here, Your Honor. I'm merely trying to advance to the jury a particular quality of the witness's relationship with his daughter. I mention events of the other day for that purpose alone."

"What does it *matter*?" Goodwin finally splutters.

"If it's not true, your witness can deny it," I say, turning to him with an innocent shrug.

Goldfarb looks at us both, then pushes her chair back with a metallic pop.

"Ask the question again, Mr. Crane. But cautiously."

"Thank you, Your Honor."

I place my fingertips on the table in front of me and turn back to face McConnell in the stand.

"Did you or did you not, sir, lay your hands forcefully upon my person in the bathroom down the hall of this courthouse two days ago?"

McConnell opens his mouth with a crack of his jaw, looks up into the ceiling lights before answering.

"Yes. But we were discussing—"

"Yes you pushed me, and yes you threatened me?"

"I was upset."

"And how much do you weigh, sir?"

"What?"

"Just curious. How much, give or take a few pounds?"

"Two-thirty."

"A big man. And strong I bet, too. You try to stay in shape?"

"I'm fairly active. For my age. What does—"

"And what would you say my client's weight is?"

"I wouldn't know."

"Guess."

"One-fifty. One-sixty."

"Little guy."

"Not big."

"No, but *you* are."

"What the hell are you getting at? I mean, it sounds—"

"Let me tell you *precisely* what I'm getting at." I hold an open palm above my head. "I'm telling you that you, sir—a self-described disciplinarian with admitted tendencies toward violence—had the same if not greater opportunity and motive to murder your own daughter and Ashley Flynn as the prosecution has so far shown against Thom Tripp."

"You filthy bastard! How *dare*—"

"In good shape, got eighty pounds on my guy—"

"*Objection!*"

"—more than enough power to carry those two girls under those big arms—"

"—how *dare*—"

"—felt you had to do *something*—"

"*Objection!* Your Honor, *please*, this transgresses—"

"God *damn* you!"

"ORDER! ORDER PLEASE, IF YOU DON'T MIND!"

Goldfarb is banging her gavel. A welcome sound. As Graham is so fond of saying, "It's not a real trial until the court has used its little hammer. *Bang, bang!*"

"Mr. Crane, could you let me in on where these questions are going?" Goldfarb asks once McConnell and Goodwin have exhausted themselves.

"Your Honor, Mr. McConnell has taken the stand with the understanding that he would be vigorously cross-examined. And that this cross-examination would be permitted broad scope."

"Fine. But broad scope doesn't involve bald accusation."

"And I'm not accusing anyone. I'm merely trying to illustrate the absurdity of the accusations against my client by demonstrating the ease with which a case—slim, but no slimmer than the one faced by Thom Tripp—could be made against Mr. McConnell. I'm showing that it's crazy to support the charge that this 150-pound teacher—" I place a hand on Tripp's shoulder "—murdered two of his students because he was found to have worn muddy pants. I apologize if my questions did anything more than achieve this aim, Your Honor."

"Fair enough, Mr. Crane. Now, do you—"

Goodwin's up, waving a finger in the air as though tracing the flight pattern of a fly.

"Your Honor! You're going to *accept* that explanation? I think counsel for the defence deserves to be reprimanded and limited in any further—"

"Sit down, Mr. Goodwin. I think Mr. Crane's explanation was perfectly satisfactory. I advise members of the jury to keep these remarks in mind, as a matter of fact. And as for you, Mr. McConnell, I sincerely hope you will accept the defence's apology."

McConnell growls like an old dog who's heard the postman coming up the path.

"Good. Now, Mr. Crane, any further questions?"

"No, Your Honor."

"Well, people, whaddya say we break for the day?"

Nice. Couldn't have gone better, actually. I managed to malign McConnell's father-knows-best character as well as deliver argument before the jury that went on to be met with the endorsement of the court. Very nice, indeed.

But as I collect my papers together I glance back to the far corner of the courtroom gallery and find Brian Flynn sitting there staring back at me. And in his eyes a look of disappointment so great I can only turn from it, throw my things in my bag, and walk out with eyes held to the floor in a burning flush of shame.

Thirty-Seven

That night I dream I'm standing on the shore of Lake St. Christopher, bare feet glowing through the green water. Behind me, up the slope of high weeds, the abandoned cottage at the far end of the lake set in solid shadow, its front window sending back a wavering version of the moon, blue, half sliced. Watching the pencil-size ripples lap in against my ankles. The kiss of rock and water.

And watch the ripples turn to waves. Splashing higher up my legs. Somewhere out over the dark water the fizz of held air released, beading up to the surface.

I try to turn but there's no feeling in my feet, invisible now under a cloud of silt. It takes both hands lifting up at the knees to pull myself out, slip up onto the stone-embedded beach.

Behind me, something stands. Breathes.

Then I'm pulling the weeds out of the ground to hold myself up, tossing dew-slick clumps over my back as I kick up the hill. An idea that if I make it inside the cottage I'll be safe. But whatever follows from the water has now made it onto the shore, wet skin slapping over mud. Air clacking down into liquid lungs.

The steps up to the deck iced with moss and at the top my feet splay out from under me, knees slamming down hard onto the wood. I throw out my hand to break my fall and fingers are stabbed with splinters as they graze across the door.

Scramble to my feet again, kick myself forward. The door moves but doesn't open, jammed in its frame. The creak of another's weight behind me on the bottom step.

Pitch against the door again but only half my weight's behind it this time, there's no room or dry footing to start from. Stand there frozen, no sound but its rattling breath against my back.

The mouth opens. A hand on my shoulder, turning me around.

When I wake I call Goodwin's office expecting to leave a message on his machine but instead there's a shallow wind blown into the receiver as he picks up, gathering the strength to announce himself.

"Goodwin."

"Hello, Pete. It's Barth."

"I'm glad you called. Wanted to congratulate you on a fine performance this afternoon. Really first-rate provocation."

"It's a specialty."

"No doubt. What can I do for you?"

"I'd like to schedule a meeting. Nothing too terribly urgent. But maybe sooner would be better than later."

"I must say this doesn't sound like you, Barth. Everything's either earth-shattering or it doesn't matter at all with you. Am I right? Which is it?"

"More on the earth-shattering side, I guess."

"How about now, then?"

"Tonight?"

"You're up, I'm up. And I wasn't planning on going out dancing."

"Fine. I'll be there in twenty minutes."

Great. I've called a meeting with the prosecution and I

don't even know why. Not *exactly* why. But I can't possibly tell Goodwin I really called because the night was billowing up outside my windows again and I can't make the room bright enough even with all the lights on.

So as I slip my still-damp overcoat on over still-damp shoulders I think of something I can say to Goodwin that will actually make sense. Around me Ontario Street has been transformed into a swaying kaleidoscope of colored light. Christmas decorations hanging off the lampposts, winking bulbs nestled amidst molting pine boughs and tinsel. Above, wavering across the intersection, eight sneering reindeer haul a sled with a drunken Santa at the helm, his one arm severed at the shoulder and swinging accusingly at me as I pass. *Ho-ho-hokum.* The only town in the world that can make Christmas junk look worse than it normally does.

And none of this doing my concentration any favors, either. By the time I buzz in at the courthouse side door and make my way to Goodwin's office I still have no idea what I'm doing here. But it feels safe in the empty hallways, so I tell myself to come up with something fast if only to avoid a quick return to the honeymoon suite.

"Barth? I can hear you out there. Come in, I've got something for you," Goodwin calls out from behind the door. I push it open to find him standing before his desk, arms held behind his back.

"I couldn't help noticing that your exposure to the precipitation we've been having hasn't improved since our last meeting, so yesterday I went out and got you this."

Goodwin lets his arms swing out in front of him. In his right hand he holds a black umbrella with a duck's head for a handle.

"I just couldn't see a fellow officer of the court shivering like a hungry dog all day, every day. Someone had to do something."

He extends the tip out to me and I take it.

"This is well above and beyond the call of duty, Pete. But thank you very much."

Goodwin nods, shoos the glaze of surprise off my face with a wave of his hand. "'Twas nothing at all," he says, and shifts his way around to take his seat behind the desk. "Now that protection from the elements has been taken care of, what is it you wanted to talk about?"

"Well, I suppose I'll just come right out with it, Pete," I say, unconsciously polishing the top of the duck's head with my palm. "We can bring this whole thing to an end, you and I, if we choose. If bringing it to an end would ultimately be consistent with the principles of justice. You know that, don't you?"

Goodwin screws his eyebrows up at the base of his meaty forehead. "Not sure I follow."

"It's just that we're well past halfway through the Crown's evidence at this point, and unless you've got something devastating lined up, all your best shots have been made. And it's not enough. I don't want to sound *judgmental* or anything, but let's face it. There's a whole whack of reasonable doubt out there still and I haven't even started the defence's case yet. Given these circumstances, I felt obliged to suggest to you the possibility of withdrawing."

"Withdrawing?"

"Dropping the charges. It would be wrong to go on. Let's pack it in and we can all have a drink and go home."

I'm trying at a friendly smile, but the muscles necessary to keep it raised erupt in periodic tremors that loosen my skin into pliant rubber. In the silence that follows I imagine how

Goodwin must see me, try to gage how charmless a sight I must make. A soggy, grey-faced addict pleading for an easy way out.

"Before I respond to your suggestion," Goodwin starts gravely, "I want to ask you first if you're alright. I'm serious, Barth. You really look *ill*."

"Don't worry about me. Why are you so concerned about *me*? I could stay with this thing all the way to the end. I could drag it on for months. But what's the point? We both know it'll end in an acquittal, and I'm just trying to save us all from time uselessly spent. That's all."

"I understand. It's only that I can't help thinking—and I apologize if I'm way off here—I can't help thinking that maybe you're raising this issue at this point because you're hesitant about advancing the case for the defence."

Goodwin's fingers drum over the distended dome of his stomach.

"No, *no*. Can't say you're right about that. Maybe I haven't made my position sufficiently *clear* here, Pete. I'm trying to save my time, my client's money, the resources of the court and your own reputation by asking you to consider a withdrawal. See? *I'm* fine. This isn't *about* me. I'm concerned about *you*, about your *position* in this. Now, if there's an ace up your sleeve you'd better tell me about it now because otherwise there's no case. Wouldn't you agree?"

"There's no ace, Barth. There's only what you already know. And it's not a lot, I admit. But there's *something* here. Two young people are dead—two people have been *murdered*—remember? If I back out now, I couldn't live with myself. Know what I mean?"

I hold my mouth shut, will the facial tremors into submission, look to him to continue.

"Maybe you're right. Hey, you probably *are* right. At the

end of the day, we don't have enough. But on the other hand, I don't think it's unethical for the Crown to press on. Think about it. There's still the car bloodstains and hair, remember? What are we going to do about that?"

"File it under Nice Try, that's what. Because we've got a witness, Dr. MacDougall from the medical clinic, who will testify that Krystal scraped her knee out smoking with the boys in the school yard and that Tripp brought her in for stitches. And as for the hair, well, it's no secret that Tripp would drive both of the girls home after their Literary Club meetings, and that it was their habit to sit together in the back."

With this Goodwin unclasps his hands and sits forward, a bloodshot puzzlement replacing the sympathy in his eyes.

"So you weren't kidding in there today?"

"Shocking, isn't it? In fact, she was so scared of how angry the old man would be if he found out she went to Tripp instead, and he covered for her. None of this helps the inferences you would have the jury draw from the DNA findings, does it?"

"No. I don't think it does."

"So I'm really just thinking of your own ass here, Pete. Given that the ultimate outcome of our business here is obvious. So why don't we close the book on this one, before it becomes embarrassing. What do you say to that?"

"They were *girls*, Barth," he says. "Look."

He tosses two 8 × 10s of Ashley and Krystal over the desk at me and they surf across the other papers into my hands.

"Point being?"

"Just look."

So I do. And it's their faces again, the same ones I've stared at for what is now probably an accumulation of several waking days.

Look at you look at me.

This is what weeks spent alone in a room full of pictures will teach you. That in time, every image turns into a kind of reflection. There, in the watery surface of the photographic finish. That's me. The face of the watcher caught watching himself.

All along, these pictures have been looking out from morning newspapers, TV screens, police bulletin boards and from above 1-800 numbers on milk cartons to see the same thing they saw every day when they were alive. Always there out of the corner of their eyes as they cracked a popsicle in half over the rim of the corner store garbage can or walked through town holding each other's arms with heads thrown back in sugar-high laughter. Always the faces of men, lips held even and cheeks sucked tight in the hope it might make them invisible. Watching the girls and wishing for them, for the return of their youth, for sunglasses. Believing they are too old and obviously normal to be suspected of bad thoughts or of doing harm only with their eyes, but never entirely believing any of this either.

"So?" I break away, toss them back into Goodwin's lap.

"He killed those girls, Barth. And not for money or revenge or something you might think defensible given the context. He killed them because in his mind they were nothing more than those photos there. Because it's not murder if all you kill is an idea."

"There's not anything—"

"I'm probably not as good a lawyer as you," he interrupts. "But don't make arguments with me that you don't really believe. I'm good enough at this business to tell the difference."

I allow him a second for this.

"I'm not asking you to withdraw because of what you think I believe," I eventually try again. "I'm asking you to withdraw because you're going to lose."

"And I can't do it, Barth. It's because I believe Tripp is a murderer. And I don't want to piss you off but I think you believe that too, and that's part of why you want to get out of here so badly. But I don't want to question your motives. I just have to question my own. And I can't withdraw the charges against your client without, well, *dishonoring* the memory of those girls. I know that sounds icky or something to you, but it's how I feel. My reputation can go down the river, but I can't turn back now. I'm sorry."

Goodwin lowers his chin so that it seamlessly joins his neck and he rocks a little in his chair, its squeaking the only sound in the room.

"I guess I never really imagined you'd do it. But I had to try. This living out of a suitcase thing can drive a man to desperation, you know?"

I try at a laugh, but Goodwin says nothing, just raises his head high enough to look at me with liquid pity in his eyes once more.

"Thanks again for the umbrella," I say, and leave him alone in his office, too small for a man of his size.

Thirty-Eight

The first day with my new umbrella and it snows. A swirl of flakes that linger in the air as though in conversation before melting the instant they meet the earth. The sort of snow that often occurs at this time of year, a sign that winter is the true state for this country and that, in case anyone was wondering, it's on the way. It's pretty though, and preferable to the rain that instead of washing Murdoch clean has floated mud, candy wrappers and dog shit out from their hiding places and onto the open sidewalks and streets. I take the umbrella anyway for the walk up to the courthouse and clip its metal tip over the concrete with every step, the snow hanging off my eyelashes or turning to teary droplets as it lands on my cheeks.

As I reach the top of the incline I look up and across William Street to see the courthouse lawn more agitated with cameramen and clipboard holders than usual. As one of them notices my approach a scrum forms to block my way, microphones sticking out from the tight collection of bodies like antennae twitching for any sign of life.

"Barth! Hey, Barth! What do you have to say in response to McConnell's comments of yesterday?" The TV woman's voice, barking out above the grumbled inquiries of the others.

"I don't believe we've been introduced."

"Alison Gregg, CBJT-TV Toronto. But you can call me

Ali," she says, and the men keep quiet, sensing she's got a better chance of getting somewhere.

"Good morning, Ali. Now, I must admit I haven't read the papers this morning. Nor have I watched any television of late, so I really don't know what you're talking about."

"After court yesterday McConnell came out here to tell us he was considering legal action against you for suggesting that he was as likely to have committed the murders as Tripp, and that you lied in your opening submissions when you said that you'd had a cooperative interview with him before the trial. He called you a *liar*, Barth. Any response?"

No. That's what I should say. *No comment today, ladies and gentlemen. Now if you'd kindly step aside.* This is how Bert would have me handle such a situation, how I know it should be handled myself. After all, there really isn't anything to respond to: the lawsuit threat was spurious, the rest of it nothing more than McConnell's usual stage-stealing rant. But something in the sight of the reporters' faces, hungry and expectant, moves in me a desire to speak. No, that's not quite it either. It's not them at all, I can hardly even see their faces amidst all the equipment and huddled parkas. It's coming from me. Words seething up to find their way to the outside. And when they reach the air each of them hangs there alone for a second before drifting away into the charcoal sky.

"You've got the wrong guy," I say. "I don't answer questions, I ask them. Raise doubts. Responses are for those who have an *interest* in the proceedings, not defence lawyers."

"C'mon, Barth. Doesn't it bother you to hear this stuff? Comments that damage your professional reputation?"

"It seems you're still a little confused, Ali. My professional reputation is not based on being *nice*. Moral indifference is my talent. And right now Mr. Tripp is paying my bills."

She pauses for a moment, surprised to be getting somewhere. Although it's probably too late already I know I should make a run for it now. But instead I remain fixed at the center of their tight circle, run my tongue over chapped lips, ready to surprise myself with more.

"You sound like a mercenary," she says finally.

"No, like an actor. Because all of this is theater. That's why you're here, isn't it?"

"We're here to report what's happening. People have a right to know."

"People have the right to be occasionally horrified. What your audience loves most is to shake their heads, tell each other how the world is going to hell, pass on all the rumored details of the worst crimes of the day before finally declaring they can't listen to another word about it, it's all too awful, why does the news always have to be *bad* news? Then they compare notes about the game last night—when are they going to trade that Swedish bum on defence?—or did you see the inspirational story on *Oprah* about the kid with the rare disease that left him looking like an eighty-year-old dwarf, and won't a donor please come forward so we can suck out their bone marrow for a one-in-a-million chance for a cure? It's all harmless gossip. There'll be trivia game questions. Ten points if you remember either of the names of the two dead girls up in northern Ontario a couple years back, and a bonus of twenty if you get them both. So maybe the public has a right to know, Ali. Or maybe all *this*—" I swing my arm around to take in the semicircle of furry microphones and black-eyed cameras "—is nothing but slightly shameful family entertainment."

I take a step forward but nobody moves to let me pass. The TV woman pulls a strand of hair from her mouth, clears her throat.

"One more thing," she says. "If Tripp didn't do it, what do you think happened to those girls?"

The sky above dimpled with snow, flakes of a size that make a flat thump upon impact with shoulders and boots. We're statues gathering drifts on extended limbs, faces hidden to all those who stand outside the circle.

"You know something?" I start, pull myself back. "I'm really very tired now, Ali, and the day hasn't even started yet. So if you could all please step aside, I've got to get back to work."

And they do step aside. Microphones retracted, notebooks drawn against chests, mouths held shut. I move through them and hear only my own footsteps and the rattle of runny noses. But as I scuff up the slick courthouse steps I can't help but look back. Air taken in, warmed and released in irregular cycles, rising above them like white smoke lifting from dying embers.

"Excuse me! Barth! Can I just clarify something?"

It's Ali Gregg's voice again, its practiced toughness gone and replaced by the higher pitch of confusion.

"Are you trying to tell us that you think Tripp did it? That you believe your own client is guilty?"

I should say something to that, I know. Tell them of course not, not at all, I never meant to suggest anything of the kind, where'd you get that idea? But instead I slip inside and let the heavy door close behind me, pretending not to hear.

Thirty-Nine

That evening I return to The Empire Hotel with rivulets of meltwater from the morning's snow trickling over my shoes. Black shoes now brown from the mud I had to plug through to go from the courthouse back door, behind the library and down a backyard lane to avoid the pack of reporters waiting for me out front. There's now $250 in ruined Italian leather on my feet but it's well worth not having to look again into the hollow faces of the press, openmouthed and circling in like a pack of wild things that feed upon the flesh of the living along with the dead.

But of course it's already too late. My morning's candid performance may have stunned them all for a second, but they must have soon collected themselves to beam back the image of counsel for the defence in the Important Murder Trial of the Week having what appears to be some kind of low-grade nervous breakdown on the front steps of the court. Not terribly momentous as *news*, perhaps, but undoubtedly close to the top of the something-you-just-don't-see-every-day list. So when I finally duck into the hotel's front door I'm not surprised to immediately hear the concierge's voice come out at me from the murk of the lobby.

"It's a lucky thing I caught you there, Mr. Crane, 'cos I've got a wad of messages from your lawyer friends down in Toronto as thick as my thumb!"

I wait for my eyes to adjust so that I can scuff over and

take the messages from his hand. A wad as thick as two thumbs, by the feel of it.

"Thank you. Another thing. I was just wondering, does that young woman who dances in the Lord Byron—the one with the longish blonde hair—is she still a guest here?"

"You mean the *young* young one?"

"Yes."

"Well, she weren't *ever* a guest here."

There's a pause, and I'm thankful that the darkness prevents me from seeing the concierge's puzzled face or the terrible map of veins etched into the top of his head.

"Only danced the one night. Came in here saying she'd never done it before and wanted to give it a shot. Must not have liked it much."

"I see. Well, thanks anyway."

"A damn shame, though," I hear him say as I make my way to the top of the stairs. "We don't get 'em that young or pretty up here every day. No sir, we have to live with whatever hand-me-downs we can get, so to speak."

All of the messages have come from either Graham or Bert and all are marked URGENT. I can hear Graham holding the concierge's hand through the message-taking ("Can you please make sure that Bartholomew gets this, *and* that he understands it's urgent. Now, can I help you with the spelling of any of that?") or Bert's more direct approach ("Just get him to fucking call, alright Einstein?"). The offices of Lie, Get 'Em Off & Associate must be having one of those days marbled with tension, office doors continually swinging open and slamming shut, and before it's all over one of the secretaries bursting into tears.

Despite all this, I decide not to call back. It's not a fear of having my employers tear a wide strip off me, nor is it humiliation for having done a profoundly unwise thing. I just don't have the energy to pull the cellular out of my bag, turn it on and punch in the numbers.

Then the bedside phone rings.

In one spasm I pull the cord out of the wall and roll onto my back on the bed. And just when I start to think that the time has finally arrived to figure out the larger significance of recent events and make some serious decisions as to what to do next, sleep comes.

When I wake it's with the suddenness with which one responds to a noise, but the cool air of the room is silent. The night has collected again outside the windows, and the wind that sways the streetlight sends a shiver down from the back of my head, although I'm still fully dressed in my suit on top of the sheets. A quarter past three and there's no good reason to get up now, but I know that sleep won't return for me tonight.

I screw the top off the thermos and have to stick my hand in up to the wrist before my fingers hit powder. Pull up a choking dose and bury myself in it, coming up flush-headed in the instant, gushing heat. Biting down hard on my lip to make sure something can still be felt.

And then I'm tipping the thermos over and spilling a crystal mountain out over the table, going at it without division or counting lines. Somewhere inside my head a door slams shut but I keep pulling it in, blowing the mountain into shape-shifting dunes. Something splashing into what remains on the table, a thousand transparent explosions. Thoughtless, narcotic tears.

Stop only when the blood starts. A blasting flood I don't

attempt to cut off at first, let it stain where it falls. When it finally begins to slow I staunch it by pressing the nostrils together and counting to sixty until they're dried shut.

Then I'm putting on my coat again, stepping out the door and down the hall. Leaving my room, the hotel. I'm aware of this. But it's as though I observe myself from another place. Watch myself creak down the stairs, out the doors and into the Lincoln, starting it up with a roaring pump of gas. Then I'm up the street with a screech from the back tires, driving round the corner and taking the road north out of town.

Out beyond the last of the streetlights, beyond any light at all but the shallow range of halogen white that beams out from the front of the car. Arms so heavy I can barely keep them on the wheel. A sound in my throat I recognize as my own voice. A wordless moan of fear.

Come to the turn for Fireweed Road and I'm slamming on the brakes, taking the corner on the fly, the wheel cranked with the flat of the hand, and make it like I've done it a dozen times. Arms extended before me, steering in jerky corrections. Swerving onto the cusp of a cottage lawn then wrenching the wheel back to swing the car through the soft gravel at the side of the road. Too goddamn fast. Why am I driving so fast?

"Why are you driving so fast?"

In the car with me. A girl's voice coming from the backseat.

"Yeah, what's the big hurry?"

Another. A girl as well but different from the first. Throw my eyes up into the rearview mirror but nothing's visible in the plush gloom.

"Who are you?" I hear myself scratch out from the back of my throat.

"Don't you *know*?"

"Yeah, don't you *know*?"

Giggles. But in this child's sound there's also an edge of something older. A viciousness that cuts through the sound-proofed space between us.

The speedometer needle shaking to the top of the circle, to the limit for travel on paved highways. A number far too high for a curving lakeside road at night.

Then movement in the backseat. A whisper of cotton over leather. The voice I hear next only inches from the back of my neck.

"You seem to know the way, don't you?"

Throw myself forward against the wheel but that doesn't move me any further from its cold breath. An arm resting on the back of my seat, a mouth that sighs through the crack below the headrest. There're waves of odors now too. The candy-sweet lilac of children's play perfume. Bloated fish washed up onto the mud shore.

"Are we going to get to see her, Dad?"

"Will you show us this time?"

"*No!*"

The word comes out of me not as a word at all but a canine whimper.

"Because we know who *you* are."

"Yeah, we know *you*."

Then it's my scream that blocks out everything else. Through the windshield the headlights flash upon oncoming trees, the wheel spins out of my hands, the car slams its side against their trunks but keeps going. Even the screech of folding metal is drowned out by this single, wavering scream.

A pair of frigid hands placed over my eyes.

But in the time it takes another scream to reach my lips there is the crunch of the car's front connecting with something that stops it dead. Then, for what is either a long time or no time at all, there's nothing.

It's still night. The cool air swirls in through the place where the windshield used to be, having already dried the better part of the blood trickling out from the cuts caused by flying glass. A sound in my head like a hornet trapped inside a paper cup and a throbbing behind my ears that expands with every beat of pulse. But I can still see. I can still hear.

As for my legs, I'm not so sure. Twisted around each other so tightly beneath the wheel they won't move on their own. I use my hands to lift one knee up, setting it off to the side as I bend the other in the opposite direction, flinging it out the open door. In a moment, blood rushes back down both legs in a painful tingling and with it the feeling slowly returns.

It's only then that I notice the car is still running. Despite the crushed hood and the steam that swells out from beneath it, the engine sputters on. I could back up out of here and roll home right now. But instead I pull the keys out of the ignition and let it rattle to a stop. And at the same moment as the night's quiet descends upon the wreck, a powerful dizziness floods my head. The space inside the car is suddenly too small, and in an awkward spasm I topple out onto the wet earth.

Mud instantly glued to every inch of me. I'm surprised by its weight, the way it makes lifting each limb a test of endurance. Hands held at the sides of my head, legs wobbly as a glue sniffer's. Stumbling down the path that isn't really a path at all but a zigzagging indentation through the brush. The wind drying the rain, leaves and blood into a second skin.

Please, please, please.

I ask myself to stop, or think I do. For along with the noise in my head there's now the added sound of the lake coming in hard on the shore, driven by a wind that rips over its surface. Stand on the last rock at the furthest point out into the water, slip my shoes off with my heels and kick them in. Ahead of me the night rolled out like endless black carpets.

Don't.

Then I'm in the air. A forward collapse more than a dive. Yet in the time it takes to meet the water I take in the dome of stars over the lake, the glint of distant whitecaps, a whiff of cherry woodsmoke before it all goes.

And cold. A flashing current of electricity that stops the heart for the space of four beats before it resumes, making up for lost time at double speed. Working to move the blood to my arms and legs, now kicking and circling in a heavy breaststroke. A glance back shows that I'm already a hundred feet from shore and heading further out.

It's quiet out here. Just the ruffle of air passing my ears, the pant and spit of my mouth. All of me below the water's purple line except the top half of my head. So small a thing it could dip under without any sound at all.

You're drowning.

An exhausted man just stepped out of a car wreck, fully dressed in clothes now ten times their normal weight. But I don't turn back to give myself a chance. Keep lunging forward, pulling my body out to the deeper place. Drifting lower so that with each breath more water comes in than air.

You're under.

And I am. Kicking my way down deeper to where the water is dense as stone. To where the slime of lake bottom weeds licks my arms. Swaying tentacles that are easily pushed aside at first but in another second have slipped a noose around my neck, tied my hands together in a tight knot.

The panic now. A final choking cough before taking the water in but there is no sound, only a teasing veil of bubbles over my face. The rest of me struggling at the weeds, flipping like a hooked fish, but they only bind me further inside their swaying body.

Then the muscles finally yield and I can do nothing but absently pull at each slick arm, one by one. And one by one they give way, wrenched from where they grow to be collected in my fists. Then I'm pulling my way up, chin first, squeezing my lips shut for one more second, just hold on until I'm out, until—

The air.

Dog-paddling back the way I came, the range of motion allowed my arms and legs now so limited I'm capable only of wriggling forward just below the surface. Watch the dark rocks of the shoreline approaching. Keep my eyes on them in the hope that so long as I can see them they won't go away.

And they don't. I pick the nearest one. Pulling myself onto its flat surface with my knuckles, my fingers still clamped shut around two handfuls of weeds. Lurching to my bare feet, from the rock to the mud shore, into the trees and back up to the road.

When I get there I collapse into the Lincoln and turn

the key. The engine hacks and there's a knocking like someone trapped under the hood, but it starts.

Go. Get out of here.

But as I raise my clenched hands to the wheel I see something in the dimness of the car's overhead light that freezes a scream in my throat.

There, gripped tight in my hands, I hold not green weeds pulled from the lake's bottom but a thick clump of human hair, light and dark.

Forty

The Lincoln makes it back into town—it must—because the morning finds me pulled into a ball under the sheets, damp footprints leading from the door to the bed. I don't remember the drive back, climbing the stairs, pulling off clothes. Or the package that sits next to me on the bedside table. A loose roll of pages from the latest *Murdoch Phoenix* with a bundle of hair sticking out at both ends and leaving droplets of water on the varnished wood. I don't remember wrapping it up like that and leaving it there so close, but it all must have happened.

Pull back the sheets and haul myself into the shower, the hot water assaulting shoulders and chest. Bend to scrub the dried mud from my feet and it comes off in black clumps and liquid strings. My back burns.

When I'm done the effort of lifting my legs over the side of the tub sends dark stars popping before my eyes. Water rushes down over my skin to an instant pool on the floor. There's the thought that I should really wipe it up and then in the next second I'm on the floor myself, splayed out like an unmanned puppet under a circulating cloud of steam. In a minute I'll raise my hand to the door handle and crawl out into the cool of the bedroom, wait for the fluttering hitch of my breathing to clear. But for now I just stay where I am, sinking and floating at once.

*

They say madness runs in families. Like cancer, obesity, hair loss or rotten teeth, it's handed down to descendants who have the bad luck to inherit the loony-tunes gene from some straightjacketed uncle or granny banished to the attic in the days when such measures were considered nothing more or less than good manners. I don't know my lineage well enough to say for sure, but I always thought the Cranes were relatively free of crazies swinging off the limbs of the family tree. So where did it come from?

It wouldn't be so bad if all I had was an uncomplicated disease of the body. Something slowly debilitating and pitiable, a dystrophy or sclerosis maybe, something with a high enough sympathy profile that it gives rise to television commercials and annual charity telethons. I could lend my services to the cause as a role model, a man-who-continues-to-function-despite-his-handicap story which would feature yours truly being wheeled into courtrooms to ensure the rights of able-bodied misfits and misunderstood thieves. It would be great exposure for my practice, and besides, I don't have much use for my body anymore anyway. But my *mind*! It seems that I'm losing one of the few things I value in the world, and all because the Crane semen-and-ovum trail can be traced back to some long-forgotten lunatic.

Or maybe it's all just the drugs. Building up, hiding in the brain cells I have little need for anymore such as those responsible for erections or kindness to strangers. Teenage acid, wicked college weed, the purified cocaine of the salaried adult—all finally organized in a unified attack. Not madness, but betrayal from within.

Well then. It's war.

I will lay siege to my enemy! Cut off the supply lines! Call the sentries to the gate!

In this combative spirit I forgo my usual wake-up line and instead light up one of the cigarettes Flynn gave me. It's not nearly the same effect at all, but I'm glad to find that a few good hauls are at least enough to permit me to remain standing and dress in the normal sequence. Still, somewhere between tucking the shirt in and finding my socks I'm stopped by the pictures on the wall.

Ashley Flynn.

Krystal McConnell.

Too real to be strip club schoolgirls. Too easily imagined crossing the street with hair storing up the glittering heat of the sun or yawning in a rain-pelted bus shelter to function as fantasies. It's never been real youth I've desired in my entertainments, but youth played out as a predictable game. This requires low lights. A few drinks. The anonymous company of similar-minded consumers. Without these the people on stage only remain people.

Fatigue, paranoia, some major chemical overindulgence over the last several weeks leading to a full-blown anxiety attack. The more reasonable explanation. God knows I've called upon the pacifying effects of valium on several hundred occasions over the last few years, so it's no surprise that under my current stress I should experience some nervousness. My doctor, therefore, is ultimately to blame for last night. Failing to automatically prescribe me a refill on my last bottle of tranquilizers is, now that I think of it, tantamount to malpractice.

I make a mental note to write him a terse letter of vaguely legal threats when this is all over.

Make a further mental note to get my hands on one of the local physicians and secure an order of calm pills.

Then I finally pull my gaze from the walls, hunch over

to the bedside table and cut myself a line of the powdery white just long enough to get me to lunch.

I decide to take a new route up to the Murdoch Prison for Men, slip off Ontario Street and into the mixture of postwar apartment blocks and low-rent retail located behind it. Three-story buildings with shared balconies, stolen shopping carts parked on the crabgrass yards, and all with names like Champlain Towers, Huron House and The Algonquin set like gravestones over the doors. Between them the soft-core video store and coin laundry with a single old man stooped low to watch his tumbling undershirts, the small appliance repair shop (SPECIALIZING IN VACUUMS), the convenience store with a poster over the whole of its window announcing that it was only five months ago that they issued a $2,400 winning lottery ticket from their machine. On the sidewalk, nobody but the very young and very old: two boys popping BBs off at each other with air rifles half their height, a pair of shrunken ladies walking in silence beneath crumpled fancy hats. I move past them all but none turns to look. None but me lift their head to hear the far-off drums of thunder over the bay.

On the corner at the end of the block the neighborhood's makeup changes with the appearance of a tall-spired but narrow church. Our Lady of Perpetual Help. It must have been more or less where those junipers are now next to the front doors that old Dundurn buried himself in a snowdrift years back. What had Pittle said? *Funny his choosing to impersonate an ice cube outside of a Catholic church, being a diehard Presbyterian all his life.* And he was right. It was kind of funny.

Next door a church-run thrift shop called Petticoat Lane selling donated toys, blankets, romance novels and winter coats. Through the window I can see a couple of mothers inside with strollers parked before them, digging through the piles of kids' T-shirts and sweaters spread out over the tables. Then I think: long underwear. Now that I'm here, I might as well grab some thermals to put an end to my courtroom hypothermia once and for all.

So I'm pushing through the door and heading for the back where a small sign marked MEN hangs from the blade of a broken ceiling fan. They've got everything in here, especially if you've got a thing for pink cotton track pants. Or baby blue socks. Or T-shirts with airbrush paintings of kittens, fields of wildflowers, wolves howling under a full orange moon.

But they also have men's white cotton underwear collected in huge cardboard boxes at the back. And this is where I am, bent over the one stuffed with all the longjohns, looking for pairs my size with the fewest visible stains. They smell clean enough though (they have to wash all this stuff before they sell it, right?) and you can't beat the price: a quarter each or six for a dollar. I've got two pairs in hand and I'm digging deeper when I hear someone come in the front door behind me. A familiar voice, leaden and drowsy.

Without pulling my head fully out of the box I look back. A man emptying the first of two garbage bags out over the front check-out counter. Girls' clothes. Spreading them out for the woman in charge of receiving donations, each T-shirt carefully folded, each pair of jeans flat and stiff as though pressed before being brought in.

"They're not doing *me* any good," the man says, and tries to smile at the woman behind the counter. "Maybe there's someone else who can make some use out of them."

Brian Flynn handing over Ashley's things, all the stripes

and florals and brights collected in the drawers of her well-ordered room. Watch him stroke his hand over each offering as though something in the touch of the material brought a particular recollection back to him.

I can't stay bent over the underwear forever. And seeing as there's apparently no back door, there's nothing else for it but a walk straight down the narrow aisle to the front. It's just going to be a little awkward, that's all. Moments such as these pop up now and then, and probably less for me than others. Less than for all those people with ex-wives and ex-husbands, discarded friends and onenight stands who wait for them around every corner. The trick is to make such moments as brief as possible.

So I'm shaking my arms so that my overcoat falls square over my shoulders, weaving through the heaps of hand-me-downs. Flynn doesn't turn at the sound of my step, continues to pass his hand over each of his donations before finally placing them into the arms of the woman behind the counter who wears a look of barely veiled distress.

I'm almost past him now and it's clear that I'm going to make it out without a word. But then I'm doing precisely what I need not do. Pausing to the side of Flynn's back beside the second garbage bag he has leaned up against the counter. Opening my mouth and saying hello, waiting for the ripple of recognition to pass over his face. Then I'm saying hello again.

"Here for the bargains?" Flynn replies once he's returned his eyes to his hands.

"Just looking around."

"Well, you won't find much in the way of business suits in here."

The woman watches us from her place three feet away, her face now frozen in appalled discomfort.

"I just wanted to say again that I'm sorry, Brian. About everything." I nod at Ashley's folded T-shirts.

"You are? Well, that's *awfully* nice. Thank you *so* much."

"I don't blame you for feeling how you must feel."

"You know something? I don't believe someone like you could possibly feel anything for anyone. You're missing that part of your brain or whatever it is that makes you give a shit."

"Just for the record, I meant what I said."

I lower my head and start for the door. But before I can get by him Flynn's arm shoots out to block my way.

"Why'd you do that to McConnell? You tore that man apart."

"I was trying to make a point. A legal point."

"That he might have done it."

"Well, with all due respect, he might have."

"Why not me then? Right from the very beginning I'm so sure she's never coming home I don't even bother to go on TV with him or offer a reward. You've got to wonder. And hey, look at me now. Getting rid of all her things. Maybe it's evidence. When you think of it, Mr. Crane, I could do you as much good as McConnell. So why not pick on me?"

"Because it wasn't you sitting in the stand."

"That's *it*?"

Try to keep looking at him but it's impossible, my eyes suddenly burning and dry as though held open to a driving wind.

"You'd better get back to your work," Flynn says finally, pulling his arm back. I try to think of something else to say, just a couple of perfect words that must be out there somewhere, but they don't come for me.

Then I'm sliding around behind Flynn's back and

stepping out onto the sidewalk outside. The drumroll of thunder again, sounding closer.

A numbness over the skin beneath my clothes, an itch from the inside out. For although I know I ditched the long underwear I'd found back in the cardboard box they came from, there's still the kind of shameful thrill that comes with all minor, unnoticed thefts.

"Been a while, Mr. Crane," the leprechaun guard behind the desk says to me as soon as I walk in the door. "A good while, indeed."

"Nice of you to say. I've missed you too, Mr . . .?"

"Flaherty."

"A pleasure to see you again, Flaherty."

"Wish I could say the same."

"I assume I'll be put in the same place as usual. You know, the room with the one-way window that allows bored public servants to enjoy the entertainment of confidential conversations? I'll expect Mr. Tripp to be brought to me there shortly."

At this Flaherty rolls his eyes but says nothing. Instead he leads me down the hall and opens the door to Interview Room No. 1 before clipping away to bring me my man.

In the few minutes I'm left on my own I wonder what condition my client will be in this time around. Because I want something from him today: a reasonably conscious, semi-coherent client capable of giving me a straight answer. But judging from the look on Tripp's face as he's brought in, it may be too much to ask.

"Good morning, Thom. How're you holding up in there, old boy?" I start, not expecting an answer, though he surprises me by offering one.

"Not so good."

"No?"

"They don't keep them out."

"Who? Keep what out?"

"The walls," he says. "Not even the walls in here keep the voices out."

He shakes his head as though he hadn't really expected they would. For a time we sit staring blankly at each other, then each of us takes a turn glancing at the bare wall as though taking in the view through a window there.

"Well, I should tell you I've got some good news and some bad news," I force myself on. Tripp's face suggests no preference to hear one or the other first, so I choose for him.

"The good news is that I visited the Murdoch District Medical Clinic and spoke to a Dr. MacDougall who recalled your bringing Krystal in the day she scraped her knee. The bad news is that the registering nurse identified you as her father on the admitting information form."

"Why would she do that?"

"Because you *told* her that's who you were. Everyone in town knows that you're not Lloyd McConnell, and you're telling someone who's creating an official hospital document that you are. Why would you do something like that?"

"You know, they were really very imaginative girls."

"Are you saying that Krystal wanted you to pretend you were her father?"

"Make believe. A good story should *make* you *believe*."

"Like lies."

"What's a lie if you believe it, Mr. Crane?"

"Let me try a theory out on you," I start again. "You told that nurse at the clinic you were Krystal's father because that's how you wanted Krystal to think of you. How you wanted both of them to think of you. Am I right?"

Tripp grimaces for a second as though suffering some kind of intestinal discomfort. Then he collects himself and looks at me hard. Hard enough that I feel like maybe he can actually see me.

"You can be anyone you like, if you allow yourself," he says. "But I've found that it's probably easier if you start out as nobody. What's to stop you from being anything if you're nothing to start with?"

"I don't know, Thom. How about the fact that you *aren't* nobody? That your driver's license has your name and picture on it, that you used to teach English at Georgian Lakes High School and that everyone in this town knows you're Thomas Tripp? How about the fact that you *aren't* Lloyd McConnell, that Krystal's *not* your daughter? That you already have a daughter of your own?"

"I don't have anything."

He throws both of his arms above his head, knuckles cracking, and brings them down again as though in preparation for a piano recital.

"But I'm really glad you're keeping score," he says evenly. "Because that's exactly what I expect of my lawyer. Certainty."

"Sorry to let you down, but I have to tell you that your lawyer's not certain about a damn thing right now."

"You know who *you* are, don't you?"

"Less than I did before."

Tripp cocks his head.

"Yes," he says finally. "I believe we do have similar interests."

"Like The Lady?"

"She's not an *interest*."

"You signed out Alistair Dundurn's history book from the library. And then you went to Bishop's Hospital and tried to look at her medical records. Doesn't that show an interest?"

"They were always asking for more details."

"Ashley and Krystal?"

"They couldn't possibly walk into a mental hospital asking for a dead woman's file, could they? A couple of teenagers?"

"And you were only too happy to oblige, weren't you, Dad?"

He says nothing to this, appears not even to have heard it. Crosses his legs, turns to face the far wall as though lending his attention to another conversation going on there entirely distinct from our own.

"Thom!"

I don't shout it, but the anger turns my voice into a cracked whip. He turns his head back to where I sit but keeps his legs facing away so that he looks like a leisured man in a café twisted around to hear the daily specials recited by the waiter.

"I'm going to try this one more time. Did you or did you not take Krystal and Ashley to the lake on that Thursday?"

"A teacher must always accompany his students on field trips. That's policy."

"But did you *make* them go with you?"

"It was their idea."

"And they were wearing their costumes? The ones you got through the school's budget for the Literary Club?"

"I told you. They insisted on details."

"Why, Thom? *Why* did you take them up there?"

He sighs, but not despairingly. It's not the sound of a man bringing his mind to an awful memory but the everyday sound of mild impatience. The tedium that comes from answering literal questions in literal terms.

"They wanted to see The Lady for themselves. To make sure she was real." He wipes at a narrow band of perspiration shining below his hairline. "And you know something else? I think she wanted to see them too."

"How do you know that?"

Tripp frames me in a condescending stare for a moment, then claps his hands together and treats himself to a burst of resounding laughter.

"Because she *told* me, of course!"

The things that amuse my client. And in the noise of his amusement I feel only the straining competition of two distinct desires. I want to kill him. I want to laugh along with him.

When he finishes both of us sit looking at each other for a time with what might be mistaken for grudging fondness. Then I set my elbows on the table and fill the space between us with an almost intimate whisper.

"Thom, did you kill Krystal McConnell and Ashley Flynn?"

He doesn't breathe. It's as though his usual vast inhalations of oxygen have been stored up for occasions like this. And when he speaks the laughter of a moment before has evaporated entirely.

"You said you didn't need to know that."

"I need to know it now."

"That's funny. I thought part of what I'm paying you for is to remain single-minded. That caring would cost me more. Have your fees just gone up, Mr. Crane?"

"Just tell me the truth."

"'In my experience, such things rarely make a difference.' My lawyer told me that."

"I know you remember what happened, although you probably don't want to. You'd do anything rather than remember. All the voices in your head—they're meant to cover it up, but sometimes they still leave holes for all of it to come through, don't they? So I'm asking you. What did you do to those girls?"

Now Tripp makes a clicking sound in his sinuses and draws in an impossibly long, whistling breath. When he's full his face turns a newborn pink before letting it go, curling over the table. A warm wind carrying the smell of boiled meat.

"They lived for stories."

"Thom, listen, you've already—"

"So one day I told them the story of The Man Who Lost Everything."

"Are you the hero of that one?"

"I'm the villain! The bad husband and father. There's nobody worse."

"So you told them the story of losing your daughter then showed them what a good swimmer you are? Is that it?"

"Losing and taking are two different things."

"So Melissa was *taken* from you. What are Ashley and Krystal then?"

"Maybe you should ask them."

"I can't do that. They're dead."

"But you can still hear them, can't you?"

"We're the only ones here, Thom."

"You can be here and not here at the same time." He points a finger at me across the table, pressing rhythmically at the air until I can feel its flaring stabs in my chest. "Take enough steps away from the living, Mr. Crane, and you'd be surprised what company you keep."

"None of this answers my question, Thom. In fact, you haven't answered *any* of my goddamn questions since I came here. Why? *Why* can't you tell me this one thing without giving me all this bullshit?"

"What if I told you that I don't know?"

"I'd say you're lying."

"Well then, there you have it. You've asked your question and you've got your answer. Feel better? Has your burden been lifted?"

"I think you're the one who should be worried about burdens."

"Oh I'm past that, Mr. Crane. Look at me. I'm a *prisoner*."

"Well, you could be in here a lot longer if you don't help me."

"Freedom doesn't mean anything to me anymore. So what difference could the truth possibly make?"

"It makes a difference." I glance over Tripp's shoulder to the one-way observation window and catch the shadowed moon of my own face. "It makes a difference to me."

Then Tripp does something terrible. Pulls back his lips high enough to crack the skin and bare a line of red, sore-looking gums. My client smiles at me.

"Make believe," he says.

Forty-One

The next day is passed by explanations of DNA identification technology delivered by the goggle-eyed lab rat the Crown has brought up from Toronto. I feel for the poor bastard though, trying to teach a remedial science lesson to the jury who looks back at him as though auditioning for the chorus in *Deliverance: The Musical*. It gives me a chance to doze off for five-second hits of sleep. A tricky business which involves holding your head up with one hand and positioning it so that your closed eyes will be hidden from the bench. This part is essential. Judges are universally intolerant of sleeping lawyers, mostly because their own seating arrangement prevents them from indulging in the same pleasure themselves.

And each time my eyelids spring back open it's with the terrible image of Bert Gederov and Graham Lyle having kittens all over the boardroom floor two hundred miles to the south because I haven't yet returned their calls. The reason is simple: despite my best efforts, I haven't come up with a reasonable explanation for my remarks to the press of the other day. But by the time court is adjourned in the afternoon (the DNA dweeb having just finished his "introductory remarks") I know it can no longer be avoided. If I don't call back tonight they're liable to pop up for a visit themselves, and neither of them would arrive in good spirits. Bert because it would mean a day not spent in court (hating this more than anything else in his broad taxonomy of hates) and Graham because of the hives, watery eyes and swollen glands he suffers from the moment he travels outside Toronto's city limits.

"Well, well. It's a good thing I caught you! Phone here at the desk's been ringing off the hook!" the concierge calls out from the shadows the moment I walk in The Empire's doors.

"I know about that phone."

"Beg pardon?"

"You've got some messages for me?"

"Some? A bundle as thick as my—"

"Thumb?"

"My thumb, yeah. One of the fellas that's been callin' is as foulmouthed a sort as I ever spoke to. A Mr. Buggeroff or Getyerrocksoff or something."

I move forward toward the stairs, keeping my eyes away from the glowing head.

"Here you go," he says, sticking the messages into my waving hand. "And good luck with that Buggeroff character."

"Good afternoon, Lyle, Gederov & Associate. Can I direct your call?"

"Hi, Doris. It's Barth."

"Bartholomew," the receptionist whispers. "They've been on the warpath looking for you. Is your cellular not working?"

"I guess I just haven't turned it on for a while. Are they around?"

"Both in the boardroom right now, actually."

"Good, I guess. Time to meet my makers. Hook me up."

There's a moment of muzak while I'm put on hold ("The Girl from Ipanema") and then the click of the boardroom speakerphone being switched on, the background hum of fluorescent lights and air-conditioning.

"Bartholomew! You're *alive!*" Graham sings at a considerably lower register than usual.

"Nominally. How are you?"

"*Concerned*, frankly. Bert is here with me and I think I can speak for him when I say that *he's* concerned as well. Why have you refused to return our messages? Can we start there, Barth?"

I've never heard Graham quite like this before. Clipped, a viciousness barely concealed by a thin skin of businesslike civility. It's far more unsettling than the raging abuse I've come to expect from Bert.

"I guess it's because I knew what you were calling about," I say.

"And?"

"And I didn't much feel like explaining a public relations mistake when I had a trial to concentrate on."

"*Public relations mistake?* Are you fucking kidding? You stand there and talk straight into the cameras about what it's like to be a mercenary who doesn't give a fuck and you call it a *public relations mistake?* You *blew* it! I told you to keep your mouth shut and then you go and sing like a birdie at the first question they ask. Do you realize how this makes us look? Or are you too fucking stupid?"

This is Bert.

"I recognize that this makes you look bad. But I didn't intend to—"

"Hey, Barth. Can I ask you something? Are you some kind of fucking idiot?"

"Some kind."

"Prick!"

"Gentlemen! *Gentlemen!*"

Graham's on his feet judging from the distant sound of his voice. It's his habit to stand whenever Bert gets rolling, as though in preparation to make a run for the door if things get entirely out of hand.

"Now, Barth. Can we get back to the motive for your comments of the other day? *Why* did you say those things?"

"It just happened. That's a poor excuse, I know, but one minute I'm standing there trying to find a way through them to the door and the next minute all these things are coming out of my mouth."

"Barth, are you having problems?"

"No. Problems? Yeah, I guess I've been having some problems."

Bert lights a cigarette, scoffs and brings up a load of phlegm from his throat in a swift sequence.

"What sort of problems?" Graham continues.

"Nothing specific, really. I mean, Tripp is being totally unhelpful. And then there's other things too, I don't know. I haven't been sleeping much, I guess."

"*Awwww!* Poor baby! Not getting enough sleepy byebyes?" Bert coos, then follows it with a punctuating snort.

"What's most troubling of all," Graham goes on, "is the matter of your confidence in your client. Do you remember that part? When asked directly as to whether you yourself believed in your client's guilt, you walked away. *Walked away!* Infinitely worse than screaming, 'He did it! He did it!' from the rooftops! Bartholomew, really, what in heaven's name were you thinking?"

"I didn't say I thought he was guilty. I didn't say I thought he wasn't."

"Well, why couldn't you have said *something*?"

"Because he's as good a pick as any. I couldn't say I have every confidence in my client's innocence when I don't."

"Why the fuck not? Why not say what you're *supposed* to say, for God's sake! You know what I don't get about all this shit? How come you're the Goody Two-shoes Boy Scout all of a sudden? 'Oh *no*! I couldn't *possibly* tell a lie!' Jesus Christ, Barth, what's happened to you up there?"

The line goes quiet as they wait for me to respond. But I can't say any of the things they want to hear. *Don't worry, it won't happen again. I was just joking around. My comments were taken out of context.* It's too late.

"I'm sorry. I guess I'm just having a bit of a rough time up here. A lot of things have been going on that I'm having trouble putting together, you know? No, you wouldn't know."

"Sure, sure," Graham says uncertainly. "We *understand* the pressures of a trial of this kind. We just need to know if you're telling us you're not able to continue. The truth now. Can you get this job done on your own or do you need to be bailed?"

"Yeah. No problem. I'm going to finish it. I need—it's important that I finish it."

"Are you sure?"

"I'm aces."

"That's the spirit! Now we'd ask you to stay in touch a little more, O.K., Barth? And answer your phone when it rings."

"Sure."

"And Barth?" Bert craning his head back to blow smoke directly into the air above him.

"Yeah?"

"Get some sleep, alright? And if the bogeyman keeps you up in the nighty-nights, give me a call and I'll send my mother up there to hold your hand. She's got nothing better to do these days."

"Thanks, Bert."

"Right then! Good luck with it and *do* stay in touch!"

Graham's false briskness has returned, calling the conversation to a close. I should be relieved. But instead there's a bubble of sudden panic rising in my chest.

"There's something—" I start, but the line's already dead.

Forty-Two

Pulling up outside the Emergency Room doors of the Murdoch District Medical Clinic and Dr. MacDougall there to meet me. Smile on his face like on open fly, smoking with the smug conviction of a man who's been the first to learn that science has been wrong the whole time, that in fact all that nicotine and tar and pesticides has never done the slightest harm to a single soul.

"The boy's been asking for you," he states flatly as I step out of the Lincoln and attempt to pass him on the way inside.

"The nurse called me. That's why I'm here."

"I didn't know you'd made such close friends among the teenaged subculture of our town, Mr. Crane."

"Not sure I know what you mean."

"People have seen you about, haven't they? Hanging out with the kids at the doughnut shop. Mooning round the high school halls. And now wee Laird's using his one phone call on you."

"It's a real mystery, isn't it, Doctor? But obviously the best minds of Murdoch are on the case, so I'm sure you'll have everything figured out soon."

He gives me the slow up-and-down that's meant to communicate suspicion rather than read any signs I might be showing.

"End of the hall," he says after he's taken all of me and the remainder of his cigarette in.

Laird's room no larger than a walk-in closet but at least he has it all to himself: the subterranean clangs within the heating vent that lolls out tongues of gaseous heat, the nylon roses set in a mug on the bedside table, the window screen with a hole at the bottom as though a fist had been plunged neatly through. And the patient himself. A bony extraterrestrial under the single sheet.

"How you doing there, Laird?"

"How's it look?"

"Not too damn good."

"Sounds about right."

There's no sign of physical injury outside of the IV tubes and ECG beeping out the truth of his mortal condition. The room's size forces me to stand closer to him than I'd prefer, however. I could reach down and take the banana-peel skin of his hand in mine without moving forward another step.

"All this has a certain self-inflicted look to it," I say.

"And you'd be correct."

"What's your poison?"

"Acid. Rolled up a sheet of blotter and kind of ate the whole thing," he laughs, shoots a tail of mucus out his nose. "Then I headed out on this major quest but started to trip really fucking bad. And I guess I must have passed out or something, because some guy peeled me off the highway, brought me in here and the next thing I know I'm having my stomach pumped and they've got me hooked up to all these bags and machines and shit."

"Where did you think you were going?"

"Let's keep in mind that I *wasn't* thinking. But I guess I had an idea I was going to make my way out to the lake."

"Why?"

"I wanted to go for a swim."

A thousand needles pushed through the whole of my body. Instant stabs of cold in the overheated room.

"Wrong time of the year for that," I say.

"Tell me about it."

He motions his chin toward the table and I pour some water into the empty plastic cup that sits there but his hands don't rise to take it, so I have to dribble it between his lips myself. Palm behind his head. Teenage boy vapors rising off his skin.

"And once you came around you decided to call me," I say after returning his skull to the wet indentation it's left in the pillow. "Not your mom or any of your friends."

"I've told you before. I don't *have* any friends. And my mother? Please. I'll be lucky if she pays for my cab home."

"What about your father?"

"Missing in action."

Laird closes his eyes for a second and the lids come down purple, thick and shining.

"But still. Why me?"

"I guess I wanted to tell you because I had a feeling— because I know that whatever I say to you is privileged or whatever, right?"

"No. You're not my client. But if there's something you want to tell me about the trial, I assure you that I—"

"I thought about doing things to them too, man."

He looks so small. Not that Laird was ever a big kid. But there was a rangy breadth to the space he filled before that's gone now, his head turned to face me and everything else narrow and still under the covers.

"What kind of things?"

"Sex and shit. And worse."

"Try me."

"Like hurting them."

"And did you?"

"No. But sometimes it feels like whether I was the one or not—that it doesn't make much difference if you thought about doing the same things yourself."

Behind me the intercom is calling out for *Dr. MacDougall, Dr. MacDougall. Please come to Emergency, Dr. MacDougall.* The nurse's actual voice at her desk down the hall as loud as her amplified one.

"That's an interesting philosophical debate you've introduced, Laird," I say, voice lowered. "But I'd still like to know what I'm doing here. You want a shrink, talk to Principal Warren. But I'm a lawyer. I defend people who've *done* things. And you haven't done anything. Unless there's something you're not telling me."

"What I'm not telling you is that I'm scared shitless," the kid says and is immediately silenced by a lengthy spasm of shivers as though to prove the point. "It's like I see them sometimes in these places around town. All of a sudden, just turn my head and *bang* there they are. Laughing their heads off with mouths that could swallow you whole but quiet, quiet."

"You're talking about people who are most likely dead, Laird."

"No shit. Hello! *I'm* the guy in the hospital on account of he thought he was losing his fucking mind."

Laird throws his eyes over to the cup of water on the table once more but I pretend not to notice. His oversize spectacles set like welder's goggles to forehead and cheek.

"What were they wearing?" I'm asking now, wobbling almost directly above him. "The girls. When you saw them."

"That's the other weird thing," he says, bringing his voice

down now along with mine. "It was like these old-fashioned dresses. But ripped up and stained all over, as if it was the only thing they'd been wearing for the past year-and-a-half. Nothing else but—what's *wrong* with you, man?"

"Don't they have any goddamn chairs in here?"

"Have a seat here if you want."

He pats the surface of the bed as though bidding the family dog up for a nap but instead it's me planting myself next to him, legs dangling over the edge like water balloons.

"You O.K.?"

"Fine, fine. Hot," I manage, gesturing a paw toward the heating vent.

"I know, man. I'm buck naked except for one of those hospital thingies that no matter how you tie it your ass is always sticking out, and *I'm* warm in here."

"Did you help Tripp, Laird?" I ask in a rush, the words mingling with the kid's nervous laughter.

"With what, man?"

"Did you do something to them together?"

"You don't seem to understand that what I'm getting at here is that I *could* have. But then intention is half of the criminal act, isn't it, Mr. Crane? Who knows? Maybe I would've said yes if he'd bothered to ask me."

I'd like to move away from him now. Slide forward and return my body to its own command but I'm sinking where I am, half tilted against Laird's skeletal pokes and jabs.

"I'm not saying my client did anything, by the way," I say in place of moving. "I was only speaking hypothetically just now."

"No, you weren't. But don't worry. I won't tell anybody."

There's a moment when I consider denying this, or telling the kid to go fuck himself, or bouncing up off the mattress and out the door without another word. But the moment passes.

"I think you have to do something, man," the kid's saying now, the words clicking out through blocked sinuses.

"Like what?"

"I don't know. But everything's fucked right now and unless somebody steps up I have a bad feeling it's going to stay that way."

"I'd like to help, I really would. But I still don't know what the hell you're talking about."

"Yes, you do, Mr. Crane."

"How can you tell me—"

"Have you given my files over to the police yet?"

"As a matter of fact, I haven't."

"And why's that?"

"I'm still considering my options."

"Bullshit."

Solid footsteps coming down the hall that send creaks through the ceiling tiles, rattle the metal strips that hold the walls in place.

"You're keeping them for the same reason I did," he says.

"And why was that?"

"To make them mine, man. But the thing is that now they're dead it feels like I'm fucking theirs."

Shoes scraping to a stop at the door.

"Ach, well now. Isn't *this* comfy cozy?"

Dr. MacDougall a mile above us in the overhead lights, grinning like an ape.

"I was just leaving."

"Oh no, no. I wouldn't want to disrupt such a *comforting* scene as this."

I'm up now and none too steady, but there must be something on my face that gives MacDougall cause to go easy because he slides back to let me out without another word. And with his retreat there returns a trace of the bitter energy I've come to depend upon over the course of my professional career. The sugared blood of pride bringing me back to life.

"Hey, Laird, you want some advice?" I say as I step out the door.

"Sure, dude."

"Next time you decide to OD, do it right."

Forty-Three

That night I go through the usual contortions, paper ruf-
flings and brow furrowings at my desk in a half-hour show of
work before pushing back the chair and panning my eyes
around the room. The wallpaper of words and faces now so
familiar I can note daily changes in the individual pages: an
air pocket enlarging under Ashley's chin next to the door, a
tear through "Search Area Expanded: Exhausted Police
Admit Desperation" that flaps in the radiator's rising air. The
Lady's face pushing out from the flat light of the bedside
lamp.

At this point it's my habit to fix my sights on the only
other interesting object within view. The thermos. But
tonight it's impossible to look at, sitting beside the bundle of
wet hair that even now drips the water it was pulled from into
a widening puddle around it. What I need to do is fit my
substance to my surroundings. Coke is fine for sharpening
the passing imagery of downtown hustle, but up here it just
makes the grotesque more apparent. What's required is a
good, old-fashioned depressant. What I need is a drink.

Down I go to the old Lord Byron Cocktail Lounge where
it's burlesque night again, the stage lit watery blue although
currently empty, the room occupied by a sparse distribution
of anesthetized onlookers.

"Double rye-and-ginger, please," I tell the bartender as I
settle on a stool at the bar. While he pours I look over at

where I sat on my first visit, a corner dark enough not to see a hand held by another's on the tabletop or a leg touched beneath it.

"Excuse me," I ask when the bartender returns. "I'm just wondering if you have a certain dancer working tonight."

"Yeah, we have a *certain* dancer," he says, and nods behind him at a round woman with hair dyed the color of turnips wearing a cotton housecoat and high heels strapped to swollen feet. "Only got the one tonight."

"Then maybe you can tell me the name of a young woman who was in here a few weeks back. Long hair, just came in that one night. Local girl."

The bartender looks at me, then down at his own hands that lie on either side of my drink. Hands grey from rinse water bleach, the skin riddled with bloodless cracks.

"We don't much deal in names around here," he says. "Girls like that are better off without names, don't you think?"

I give a slight nod of thanks, pick up my glass and take a long gulp. Four stools down from me the only dancer of the evening pushes herself off her seat and pounds over to the stage while a new tape is clicked on, and through the speakers' hiss comes the acoustic guitar opening of "Stairway to Heaven."

"Oh yeah!" someone shouts out from the darkness at the side of the stage as Turniphead heaves herself up the small set of stairs that elevate her onto the stage. "Oh yeah!" to the pointless grin that appears on her face, the hands that stroke over shifting hips as she stalks the stage's perimeter. "Oh yeah!" to the breasts that awaken beneath the housecoat's loose folds, to the flash of dimpled ass afforded by an awkward lift of terry cloth. When the heavy rock second half of the song kicks in, the housecoat drops in a lumpy ring around her feet and the patrol continues, now in glaring, wobbly nakedness.

Clomps to the edge and pulls up a furry white rug, shaking it flat. With some difficulty she bends over at the waist to undo the straps on her high heels, letting each of them fall with a strained grunt. Looks my way for a moment and summons a smile of invitation before lowering herself to her knees on the fake polar bear fluff.

I try to do the courtesy of returning her smile but cannot. Cannot take my eyes from the different parts of her rolling around on the rug and then coming together to be wrapped up inside it. That's when the sadness comes. A sorrow that exceeds the spectacle before me, shot directly into the blood, swift and paralyzing. "Oh yeah!" the call goes out when the fingers go down, a parted flash of inside shown to the drunk and afflicted outside.

"You want another?"

The bartender's voice to my left but I can't turn to respond. Somewhere above me Robert Plant delivers the lines that, if played backwards, say something about Satan leading everybody to hell.

"Hey, pal, you want another of these?"

"No more," I say without turning, holding my hand over the empty glass. When the song ends the audience provides a dozen smacks of applause and rises up to the bar, having decided it might do them good to have another before the next show.

The following morning I go down to give the Lincoln a lookover. It's in as rough shape as I would have expected (the front hood folded in complicated patterns like unfinished origami, the windshield serrated around the edges with glass teeth) but remains unticketed out front of the hotel. It also starts, but with a new sound now warbling up from below the floorboards, a screech of mechanical grief that strikes an identical timbre to that of a Yoko Ono performance from the late 70s. Give the gas a couple of hits to clear the valves and the engine bawls in response as though expressing its concern that I'm behind its wheel once more. Stroke the top of the dashboard to provide it some reassurance and after a time the car lowers its complaint to a weary gurgle.

It's a Sunday morning (the dispiriting clang of church bells to the west, the murmurs and tweets of an externally amplified organ to the east), and despite the sky's burdened clouds, the rain stays where it is for the moment. Roll up Ontario Street and make the turn heading out of town, the wind funneling in through the missing windshield in bites and stabs.

Right onto Fireweed Road and around to its end. Frayed bits of yellow police tape still flapping off a few trunks and the tree that brought the Lincoln to a stop now showing a hacked circle of white flesh, but the place is quiet, returning to itself. While I could just as easily crawl out over the front hood I kick open the driver's side door with my heel and set off on the trail that circles the lake, noting the now familiar landmarks as I pass: Mrs. Arthurs's place, the skeleton of an old sedan tucked among the ferns. It's a long walk, but without the rain less disorienting. The jumble of spruce, birch and black maples on one side and the lake's scudding brown on the other to let you know where you are.

Take my time, stopping along the path to listen for what the forest would sound like if it didn't know I was here. There's the ridiculous desire to hide in the squelch of fallen leaves and wait for metamorphosis into—into what? Something simple. To live the life of a nut hunter, web builder, berry gulper. To wish never to go back. A man in need of a shave but dressed in clothes exclusively designed in Milan, standing on a mud path passing through a threadbare forest. Making wishes.

I move down toward the lake, every step sending bubbles farting up through the deadfall. When I'm near enough to the water that I can hear it I crouch down behind a low chokeberry bush and look through its hairy leaves. See myself as I would actually appear from the stony beach: a man bundled in a soiled overcoat, peering out white-eyed from the bushes. This is what The Lady would have seen had she turned from her daughters bathing in the shallows, her skin puckered from the chill and arms held above her as she wrung out her long hair. She would turn but she wouldn't have to look to know she was being watched. Who was it this time? It never mattered. She'd given up on names a long time ago.

A man with needs, watching from his hiding place. A gentleman this time perhaps, one who could offer her help, shelter, protection for her children. Or perhaps he could offer her nothing at all. Nothing but the single thing he'd come for, in secret, ashamed at how low he'd allowed himself to stoop and the lies he will later have to tell to those he claims to love. But still he'd come.

And she will let him watch. Let him approach too, if he has that kind of courage. And if he appears kindly or strong or well-off she will send her girls back to their place in the woods and let him speak to her in his lowered voice although she won't understand the words. But this won't matter either. She's looking for other signs now, the setting of the frame, the light and play of the face that could signal the possibility of truthfulness. Even here in the New World she has no trust of any but her own daughters and herself—no—she's not sure she could even include herself among the truthful anymore. So she'll go with him even if none of the signs are there, and in fact they almost never are. They came only for her silence and her beauty and for the things she will allow. It's not even their brief attention or corner store gifts that she cares for. It's that after seeing how dark the hearts of men can become she's simply grown too tired to hate them for something so common as this.

I watch her too. Then, when the awareness of the thing exchanged between us finally arrives, I close my eyes and push myself to my feet again, turn and lurch back up toward the path.

The abandoned cottage, obscured the last time, has even in the few intervening days been largely revealed, the cover of vines, leaves and creeping shrub now browned and fallen. Slip down to its front deck where I stand for a moment in the lamenting wind. Everything—the water, the trees, the sky—yielding to a blanketing of winter shadow, a wash of grey you could almost mistake for smoke. It strikes me again that, outside of the dozen or so weeks of overwhelming beauty each year, this country can be ugly as hell.

The front door pushes open as it did before, the floorboards, bookshelves and walls shuddering as I enter as though a chill has set upon them. Maybe I've been recognized. That Crane face, no question about it. The mildewed couch, amputated dining table, wagon wheel coffee table and every book on the shelves seem to lean in a little closer to get a better look.

"It's me," I say, and the silence is like an intimate welcome.

I take a seat on the sofa's thinning cushions, the foam stuffing bulging like yellow custard out of holes in the seams. From here, the lake looms through the cracked front window, the intervening growth of skimpy evergreens unable to entirely block the view. The same view as my parents must have had, sitting here waiting for a thunderstorm to pass or meal to be prepared. A small living room but large enough for the playing of cards, board games or chess. It would have been warm in the summer, of course, although it's frigid today, the collected moisture from the cushion beneath me already creeping through overcoat, pants and boxers, quickly bleeding toward bare bum.

Step over the garbage on the floor and into the galley kitchen. On the counter there's an empty bottle of aspirin, bag of charcoal, a tourist brochure for *Bobby Orr's Birthplace: The Home of Hockey* and a styrofoam box that once contained a Big Mac (how far must it have been transported before being consumed here, in an abandoned lakeside retreat?). There's also, curling and bubbling next to the single sink, a University of Toronto alumni magazine from 1968. My father's. There beside the more contemporary detritus, in probably the same position it was left, never to be put along with the others fastidiously organized on the bottom shelf in the living room.

That's where I go now to patrol the room's book-lined perimeter. There must be over a thousand volumes, some shelved two deep and other rows with slim paperbacks laid over their tops. Why did he bother to bring them all the way up to this place? It couldn't have been an intellectual's dusty pride because there wouldn't have been an audience up here to show them off to. He must have simply wanted them here. Books were my father's society, the extent of his private life outside of his marriage, the occasional departmental wine and cheese, the son growing up episodically before his eyes.

When I come to a leatherbound copy of *The Collected Keats* I pull it out from its slot and press it hard against my chest. The promising, mysterious smell of old book fills my breath and I keep it inside me, the cowhide and dampness and ink lingering within like held smoke. Pull it open to the signed title page: "Prof. Richard Crane, University of Toronto, March 29, 1962." Inside, various lines and stanzas have been encased by brace brackets with phrases like "physical/spiritual unity" and "beauty = supremacy over death" underlined outside them. Pretending to read but really just looking at my father's notes in the margins. The jagged lines of his handwriting, the way the pencil was always kept sharp— is this what he was like? Meticulous, brisk, whittling wood and lead into fine points? The words themselves say nothing, coded references lodged in a professor's brain. Still, I like touching the pages in the same places he must have.

I turn ahead and fall upon "Ode to a Nightingale," the poem I memorized for university. Start to read it off the page but the voice in my ears is not my own but my father's. I can't see him or how he would have sat or stood, don't know whether it was a selection he would use whenever called upon to make a toast or the only lullaby he would have known to put me to sleep. But there's still his voice.

> *Fade far away, dissolve, and quite forget*
> *What thou among the leaves hast never*
> *known*

I try to see the words as my father would have seen them for the first time. Looking not for their meaning but whatever charm came before all of that, the thing that seduced him into a life of language. When the poem is finished I close the book shut and tuck it into the outside pocket of my overcoat. It feels heavy there, tugs at my shoulder. But it's not going back.

Circle the room one more time, taking another look at all the things that now give rise to vague recognition *as things*, the collected pieces that distinguish a room from merely bordered space. But soon enough these too will go, all the particularity of chosen furnishings, comforts and entertainments dissolving, falling apart, leaving this place as nothing more than the kind of 14×12 fakepaneled affair one finds in nearly every pre-fab summer retreat around here. A building in fast decline without annual visitations from its caretakers, amateur nail-knockers and paint-slappers, without the voices to clear the cobwebs from the corners.

Down the short hallway to the bathroom. A chocolate fur growing out from the drain in the tub, a shower curtain with a map of the world printed over it pulled from half its hooks. Turn on the taps at the sink and a froth of rusted orange coughs out, sprays up in a fountain of sulfur. A medicine cabinet that screeches open when I pull the door from its magnetic clip, so full of Wilkinson's disposable blades, lipsticks and scattered band-aids that half of it falls out into the sink. What surprises me is that it's still here, all the intimate tools of hygiene. Wouldn't they send somebody around to collect this stuff after they died? Then again, who would ever volunteer to drive up here just to bag the toiletries? So it was all quite sensibly left behind, and it's all still here. The leftover miscellany of lives pulled from their habits.

My parents' bedroom, containing a soiled box spring
with a black crater in its center. Cheap Bauhaus-copy bedside
tables on either side etched with graffiti.

Tony FUCKED Deb here until she screamed like a
CAT—July 24, 1989.
JIM MORRISON IS ALIVE AND LIVES IN BRAZIL!
Eat the Rich, Then Puke Them Up.
my dick hurts.
I Lov u, Kathy. Do you Luv me 2?

I think of all of these strangers in this room, of Tony and
Deb and Kathy wriggling out of jeans and throwing sweat-
shirts against the wall to look at each other's bronzed bodies
in fluttering, kerosene light. Not caring whose bed this might
have been in the past, or if they did care it only added to the
fun, the idea of screwing in the same place once coldly
occupied by Mr. and Mrs. Joseph Normal of 24 Middle-Aged
Lane. They would make a point of marking their youth with
a show of roughness and appetite. Fill the air with exhalations
of pleasure and congratulation that grow louder in turn,
pushing through the walls and out into the woods because
who else was around to hear? The room sharp with the
curdling of semen and cinnamon perfume.

I'm pulling the drawers open on the dresser left in the
corner. Nothing in the top two except cigarette butts and
rolling collections of mouse turd. But in the bottom drawer
something heavy that rattles to the front when I screech it
open. A hairbrush. Old-fashioned black enamel handle inlaid
with a swirling plastic meant to look like pearl. The bristles
spun together with hair. My mother's.

I don't know this, of course. It's not that I remember the
brush itself or can identify the hair as hers. Just as likely to be

another woman's. Left behind after the decision that they wouldn't be staying in this too-quiet cottage for another night. But when I bring it to my nose and take in the smell of it—woodsmoke and honey—I don't consider the more likely possibilities. Believe the individual strands I roll between my fingers could only be hers.

Time to get out of here.

But on my way through the sitting room towards the door I find myself instead kicking at the legs of the dining table, wrenching them out from their sockets. Then I'm balling up pages from the pile of newspapers and building a cone in the fireplace, setting the wood in a pyramid on top, lighting a match from the pack Flynn left with me and tossing it into the center. Within minutes it builds into a modest blaze, the furniture varnish sending up a black smoke that smells faintly of licorice. Gold shadows thrown over the ceiling.

I set to work pulling more of the furniture apart. Stack the spokes of the wagon wheel, panels from the top of the dining table and the backs of the kitchen chairs, all of it breaking apart easily if I stand on it in the right places. It's not vandalism if it's yours, and who else's would it be now? Maybe all given over to some executor to look after but they'd long since given up, maybe deciding to sit on the property for a couple of decades and hope for a rise in the market that will never come. So it might as well be mine. The final scraps of my inheritance popping and seething in the blackened hearth.

There's no satisfaction in seeing it go aside from the warmth it gives off. In fact it's this burning that makes the entire cottage feel suddenly animated, revived from a long sleep. The floor creaks as it expands against the foundation, shadows moving at the edges of my sight that could be figures embracing against the wall, running in through the door from outside or rising from the sofa after a nap.

Build up the flames until they arch high into the mouth of the flue, then pull a couple of my father's books off the shelves and sit down at the end of the sofa to read. I limit myself to final chapters. Endings pulled apart from the stories they belong to, some tidy and hopeful, others drifting off enigmatically with people staring out of windows over autumn fields or driving away from gravesite visits. Moments vibrating with significance because they're the last thing we're told. Decisions can now be made, morals drawn, characters designated as villains or heroes or mere comic relief. But I keep myself to the endings so that I don't have to judge, so that all I'm left with is the final moment, expansive and mysterious. And on every page my father's coded marginalia. The brace brackets and arrows of his private thoughts, working to pull all the threads together.

Try to keep reading but the light's already fading, the fire big enough to warm a yellow circle before it but no longer bright enough to read by. Check all the pockets, but no. Didn't bring my coke. I've gone all day and until this moment hadn't thought of it, and now that I have I expect at any second to begin the sweating, burn-headed process of becoming chemically upset, but nothing happens. Outside, the dark of early winter evening falls across the glass as a purple curtain.

I dream of my father. Working at his desk with books splayed open on top of each other, holding selected pages to the air. Lifts his head to smile at someone he hadn't realized was there. Walking across the room to where my mother stands against a window stippled with rain. Kisses her once, steps back, raises his hand. Then carefully begins drawing on my mother's mouth with his pen, coloring her red lips blue with ink.

I'm awakened by the cold. The fire now nothing but a circle of papery embers, a single pair of red eyes still glowing out. The room poured full of night. Feel around the floor at my feet for more wood but it's either all been used or is further than I can reach. The air a vapor of wet smoke that would make you choke if it weren't so cold. Sit unmoving in the dark for a time, a ball in my throat I can't swallow away and the dried crust of sleeping tears below my eyes.

It takes three attempts before I finally get to my feet. Everything held stiff like a plastic doll with moveable parts but only if you make them, one at a time.

Must be awake. You can't feel an upturned beer cap screw into the sole of your foot in a dream. You don't bend down to pull it off with a smear of your own blood that you lick from your fingers without thinking, leaving the taste of rust and crunch of sand on your tongue.

Takes half the night to lift my head up straight enough to look out the window, squint down to the scissored line of trees around the body of the lake. No wind and nothing moves. It could be a painting. A flea market oil canvas where all the colors come from some combination of perfect blue and black. I think of how often Nature presents itself as cheap art, nothing more than the paintings over Holiday Inn beds. Sunsets, distant hills, the subtle degrees of night. It could all just be a picture if nothing ever moved.

Then something moves.

The bloom of fear in my chest before anything else, before I blink my eyes dry to make sure. Something standing, pulling up crooked and pale from the lake's edge. Faceless but facing me. A single blanched figure under the starless dome of night.

Rising up from the weeds that grow out of the sediment along the shore and squishing onto the mud, the thin grass that aprons the jutting stones and roots. Up the slope toward my place at the window, legs brushing through the grass, its shape enlarging with every step. Slow as the scream in your throat that could wake you from a dream if it could find its way out.

So cold.

The sound it makes fractures over the lake, through the woods, the walls, so that it comes from all places at once. A woman's voice that could be a half-mile off or whispered in my ear.

When it reaches the top of the slope and pauses in the tall grass that reaches to its waist I shut my eyes hard, think for a moment of escape, of turn and hide. But the order doesn't go out. Nothing works.

The watery slide of bare feet on the deck outside coming to a stop outside the door. Then for a time there's no sound at all.

When I open my eyes I move forward to the window but I can't see around its frame to whatever may be there. Wait for the doorknob to turn, for its hands on my throat, the knowing crack of its laughter. But there's only my own warm air blown blue over the glass.

I'm so cold.

I don't want to. I'd rather wish myself into a dream, into

a hidden thing that watches from the corner. But I know I won't do anything now but float away from the window, cast the shadow of my hand across the wall to open the door.

Please.

Standing there. A young woman with long hair smoothed over bare shoulders, water beading down over the perfect white of her stomach, her arms. Candied freckles across her chest. Hair covering the whole of her face except for lips puffed blue with cold.

Hold me.

And I do.

Pull her icy skin to me, the bones light within her. Breathe in her skin until I'm full. All of it real as pain. Real as touch, the taste of copper and salt tears on my mouth.

When I stand back she raises her hand and lifts the blonde strands away from her face. Ashen, pleading, and something else. Eyes fixed on mine, mouth parted at soft corners. Something like mercy. A face in its shape and features not unlike my own.

Forty-Four

It's only just past eleven according to the illuminated clock outside Steele's Funeral Home by the time I make it back to town and park the Lincoln in its place in front of the hotel. There's nothing left to do but go inside but I can't move toward the door. Bend back my head and look up at the dark windows, the gargoyle heads of the founding fathers, the dripping letters of The Empire's electric sign. Then I walk.

Just like one of the stupefied street mumblers I've watched passing below the honeymoon suite's window, talking to myself loud enough that I can hear but if one were to pass beside me they'd catch only discrete syllables, left to wonder at what the smartly dressed young man in the mud-stained overcoat could be saying to himself. Traffic braking hard as he crosses against the lights, hands rising to his mouth as though he believed a cigarette might be wedged between his fingers but when they got there they were empty, so instead he rubs them over his lips, over the words that pass through them, out and up into the air.

Caroline Rosemary Crane.

I used to love saying her name. Caroline, with the "i" always long, because to make it short left it sounding like *crinoline*, a sweatstained, mothballed Sunday hat pulled from an attic trunk. But Caroline with the "i" long created a sound roughly equivalent to the idea of *girl*. The echo of a song in its three syllables, an age-old lyric not yet faded from memory.

I say her name aloud.

A plastic captain's telescope that showed a tumbling kaleido-scope of painted sand.

A set of watercolors used to paint a fairy landscape on the wall over my bed.

A train set that never worked.

It was summer. Me and Caroline. Limbs loose and achy from swimming, long walks into town to buy some indigestible licorice or sugar crystals that exploded painfully on the tongue, lying out on the dock, whispering meaningful non-sense to each other in the sun that made us drunk. Our skin reaching a brownness that left us perfect, smooth as peanut butter. Freckles across Caroline's nose that, if stared at too long, caused prickles behind the eyes.

Somewhere in the background, so far off that only their voices could reach us were our parents. Two sets of Cranes, Patricia & Stephen and Liddy & Richard, polished and lucky and content. Donning silly aprons (PROFESSORS DO IT ... ACADEMICALLY!) to cook meals for the six of us but making enough for twelve. Grown-up couples that kissed on the lips, threw arms around waists, squeezed bums. Sometime after four the drinks appearing in congratulations for having spent another day in the place they thought about the rest of the year and being able to forget about their children, off playing secret games in the trees. Nobody much bothered that they were first cousins and quite evidently in love.

*

Once or twice I pass someone lifting a garbage can to the curb or opening the side door to let the cat in, but the sidewalks are mine alone. A town of drawn curtains, blue TV light flickering behind them, old sofas and tricycles collected on front porches. The smell of smoking fat and boiled bones. The insulated vibrations of marital argument. All of it falling away, the last leaves the wind pulls from the tree.

We rarely saw each other outside of Christmas, Thanksgiving and those six weeks every summer. The sole explanation for this was that we went to different schools. She had her friends, I had mine. Ground to be lost if we turned our backs on our home turf for a moment. We imagined we belonged to distant, unbridgeable worlds.

It's ridiculous now, of course, given that my parents and Caroline's lived in nearly identical neighborhoods only three subway stops apart in Toronto. Although our place was regarded as "downtown" and theirs "uptown," you'd have a hard time telling them apart just from walking their streets. Houses like the ones I walk by now. Brick cubes containing *families*, mini-societies existing within the boundaries of a three-bedroom, 1½-bath fortress, the walls protecting the valuables within, if not love then at least privacy. That's where I grew up, where Caroline Rosemary Crane grew up: in red brick, no nonsense, single-family-dwelling Ontario. Where the streets are named after British generals and the neighborhoods little more than consistent rows of distinct privacies, families separated from each other by politeness and indifference and the cold.

All around me Murdoch sends its children to bed.

*

It was my idea.

Our parents a little drunk in the luxurious way of those who know that no real harm will come from their drinking, that this is their just reward for being born with the right name at the right time and with enough brains to capitalize on it. Uncle Stephen stumbling around at the barbecue with the tin of lighter fluid held above his head and everyone thinking that surely this time he will light himself into flames, they even say so out loud, laughing. My parents and Aunt Patricia rolling cold gin-and-tonics over their brows, looking out across the water from their fold-out canvas chairs as though a show were about to begin. And it was. In fact the setting of the sun had already begun, lazy and hesitant in the way of August afternoons.

We liked the way our parents were at this time of day but never said so. Instead, what I whispered into Caroline's ear as we let the screen door slam behind us was "They're going to start *necking* soon if we don't get out of here."

A canoe ride before dinner. Permission from our parents like taking candy from a baby after a couple of stiff Gordon's. But of course they couldn't leave it at that, according to the adult tradition of always saying too much. It could never only be *Have fun!* or *Don't be too late, we'll be eating soon!* There had to be *embarrassment*. So as we push ourselves out into the water they're calling after us with their stupid joke of the season that they all find so hilarious.

"Kissin' cuzzins!"

Ringing out from each of them it seems, as though they'd come up with it for the very first time on their own.

"Kissin' cuzzins!"

Big laughs and glasses raised high in salute as we cut into the patterned ripples of the wind.

At first we head toward the island. Our standard adventure is to climb the cliff peeking out from the trees at its center and take in the view. Kiss in the name of marked occasions. Maybe kiss for a while after that for its own sake. But I decide that today's the day for a new destination. The beaver dam at the lake's far end where there are no cottages, no sunhats or beer bellies waving at us from their docks.

Caroline telling me she's going to miss me after the summer ends, that she wishes it never would. Tell her I know what she means. But what I don't tell her is that I already miss her. That days like this are gone even as they happen.

We pull the canoe in at the opening to the beaver's stream, plunge bare feet into the muck. When we reach it I walk out onto the dam (I have to, we've come here for a show of boyish courage after all) and Caroline tells me to get off it (she has to, she's come here to protest shows of boyish courage after all). I tell her the beaver won't mind, he's left this place to build another. She asks me if this is true and I tell her it is, grateful she didn't ask how I could tell. Above us the sun falling in a three-count. A cloud of fireflies emerging from the trees. The desire for a kiss.

I take us back out on the water far enough that the mosquitoes think twice about following. In our wake the water whirlpools then flattens again so that after a second or two you'd never know anything had just passed through it. Caroline so beautiful and I tell her so. Tell her twice and it's the truth.

Knees astride, leaning forward to meet her lips. A kiss that's meant to be different, to communicate solemn, adult intentions. Eyes closed in the living dream of her skin.

She was Caroline. She was the dark-rippled girl ripped

out of a basement bookshelf *National Geographic* and kept between mattress and bed frame. She was that poster of Marilyn Monroe in a sequined evening gown, eyelashes lowering as though a drug were taking effect. She was my Aunt Patricia stepping out of the lake from a late-night skinny-dip, pushing her arms through a bathrobe left in a pile on the pale stones. Not women but a single, shifting composite. Desire as a slide show viewed from too close for all the particulars to be visible at once.

But she was real.

She wanted to be a vet when she got older. She sang solo soprano in her school choir and won silver at the Kiwanis music festival in grade eight. She was so ticklish the mere mention of the word and the waving of spidery fingers before her eyes would bring on a reflex of laughter, then screams for help, then tears. She was clumsy and broke many glasses, grape Kool-Aid left in a pool of Martian blood on the floor. She could swim like an otter, slipping below the surface and breaking through forty feet away, water beading off her skin as though she were coated in an invisible oil. She had secrets—staying up late to watch her parents have sex "like hogs" from their bedroom doorway, discovering the blood of her first period trickling down her legs at a pool party with boys in attendance, cheating on her final math exam with the formulas written at the top of her thighs—and shared them all with me.

But in the canoe that afternoon she wasn't even there. In her place someone silent and yielding, a mannequin with cleverly warmed surfaces. I wished for her stillness and she gave it to me. Yet for the time I hovered and pressed and searched I wouldn't have known her name. I wouldn't have known my own.

When it finally arrives the sound of her fear comes from across the lake. It comes from underground.

Her body plank-stiff but fists pounding against the sides, water lapping in and collecting in a luminous green pool at the bottom. Told her I'd stop. And did, shushing her with promises and hey, heys and sorries. Moved as far back as I could go to let her sit up but instead she did the one thing you're always told never to do in a canoe. She stood up.

When I make it back to the air it takes me a second to realize Caroline isn't beside me. A second more to think of what to do.

Then I'm under. So deep there's no way I'll make it back with only this one held breath but I can tell she's there just below me, her movements a buffeting current against my skin. Grab her arm with eyes closed and start to kick the other way. But she's heavy. Heavier than she should be, as though attached to a sack of wet sand. A dozen sacks of wet sand.

It's then that I feel a tug from below. Pulling Caroline down. I know this, I'm certain it's true, there's no question about it, it might have been nothing. A weed licking about Caroline's ankle that a single pull could have freed her from. A twinge of cramp in my legs. Something alive from below taking her for itself.

Whatever it is it's strong enough to finally pull her from my grasp. That, or I let her go after a swift calculation of time and distance and possibility. Reach for her again but she's gone deeper—I've floated up—and I can't find her hand.

I tell myself not to. That it will be too horrible and do no good and I will never be able to forget. But I do anyway. I look.

Both our eyes open to each other. Mine to glimpse her

bloodless face pull into the dark. Hers to watch the shadow of her cousin kicking up toward the dancing light at the surface.

That fall I started back at school but my friends from the year before could tell right away that something was wrong. High school kids can sniff out emotional disturbance using the same instincts with which hunting animals smell fear in lesser creatures. Within days concern ("Hey, Crane, are you O.K.? You seem weird") had shifted to aggressive curiosity ("What the fuck is *wrong* with you, man?") and then finally hardened into strict isolation. I could clear a cafeteria table as I approached with my tray of synthetic cheeseburger and fries with the effectiveness of a putrefying leper or grinning airport evangelist seeking converts. Hallways widened before me. The walk to the bus stop now free of flirtation, shared cigarettes and rumor. And with this standing outside of things I came to hate them. The good-looking ones with a genetic licence for casual cruelty, the rich ones with lazy eyes already bored by unquestioned privilege, the clever ones with an obsessive pursuit of good grades which left them like the seals at Marineland, performing tricks in order to have dead herrings tossed into their mouths by whistle-blowing keepers. Each one of them deserving it in their particular way.

Not that I've been antisocial as an adult. That wouldn't be practical, given that one must deal with people in order to get things done. I simply decided to despise them all so viciously I wouldn't even let them see it. Like magic. Or science. A simple, terrible equation: If you hate the rest of the world long enough, eventually you can make it disappear. Or make yourself disappear. One or the other.

*

A beagle too new to have been given a name running under
the wheels of an Eaton's delivery truck.

Three goldfish—Snap, Crackle and Pop—that func-
tioned as appetizer, main course and dessert on the new
piranha's first day.

A toad kept in a grass-filled jar that I thought was singing
to me with his mouth wide open until my mother told me I'd
forgotten to put air holes in the lid.

My legs take me to a park bench next to the creek that runs
below the prison. The sky a glaze of gasoline on the slow
water. Slides over the rocks and passes on out of town
through the system of connected rivers and lakes to Georgian
Bay. I listen for voices in it but there's only my own, picked
up and carried on the water in its constant motion to join
itself.

It was early that October when the Murdoch detachment of
the O.P.P. called and said they wanted to ask me some
questions. Nothing too serious, no lawyer necessary, no, no,
but could I come up sometime soon and have a word? Dad
canceled his lecture, I was pulled out of class and both my
parents drove me up early the next morning, so that by noon
I was sitting in front of a desk with a cop behind it, his face
so empty of color that his head appeared as a cheesecloth
sack packed tight with rice. Behind him, half sitting on the
two-drawer filing cabinet against the wall, a younger cop with
a mustache who said less than the older one but whenever he
did speak asked the tougher questions. Any problems with
handling feelings of aggression? sexual appetites? you're a
good swimmer, right? His crossed arms and the noise he

made through his nose after I gave him an answer suggested he believed in a foul-play theory. Believed I was a murderer.

The interview seemed to go on well into the night but by the time they let me go it wasn't yet five o'clock and the sun still blanched houses and trees from its position behind low, seamless clouds. My parents were silent as they led me out to the parking lot, my mother offering an uncertain smile but my father too embarrassed for any show of emotion right there on the tidy grounds of the police station. They remained silent for the first part of the trip home, talking only after night had fallen over everything and the green dashboard light turned them into phantoms in the front seat.

"So, what did they have to say?" my father begins, as though the question had only just occurred to him.

"Nothing. They just wanted to know about Caroline. How it happened."

"And you told them?"

"The canoe tipped. I tried to save her. She drowned. I told them."

"And what now?" my mother asks, turning around to face me. "Is it over now?"

"Yeah, I think so. They don't have anything."

"Any *what*, son?" My father, a little too innocently.

"Evidence," I say.

A brief look passes between them and with this the conversation ends. The car rushes south to join the highways that increase in breadth as the city gets closer, two-lanes to four-lanes to six to eight, my mother and father dim silhouettes in the oncoming headlights. Somewhere in there I fall asleep.

Were there dreams? Did I hear them cry out, or was it

the shriek of metal torn by metal? Was I awake or did I only later imagine the suspended moment of impact, of flight and spiraling darkness?

I'm being lifted up. Careful, orchestrated hands levitating me onto a varnished wood stretcher and strapping my head still to protect me from any further spinal injury. Being asked what my name is and if I could count the number of fingers the paramedic waved before my eyes (four) as they settled me into the back of an ambulance with buffed stainless steel all around. The line of cars stopped in both directions for what seemed several hundred miles. White lights and red lights, not going anywhere.

A tractor trailer carrying electric blankets to the downtown department stores for the Christmas rush, four cars in front of us when it lost one of its eighteen wheels. Just shredded right off its rim, bounced over the cars ahead to finally bring its two-hundred pounds down against the front windshield. Our car spun out of control, was struck from behind, rolled end over end into the grassy median. The chain reaction caused by our flipping across three lanes resulted in a smoking pileup that was pictured in the Toronto papers the next morning but, "miraculously," only my mother and father ended up as fatalities. Their son, outside of a few nasty cuts, was fine, partially because his parents' bodies in the front seat absorbed the better part of the impact. Everyone agreed that it was a tragedy, shook their heads and said no more.

Then the years of boarding school and holidays with legally obligated aunts and uncles (with the exception of Caroline's parents, who I was told "thought it best" if I stayed away). All of them doing what they could at first before finally surrendering, feeling that I could have made their jobs a little easier if I'd only made a bit more of an effort, tried to be somewhat more responsive, instead of the unreadable kid who was a cause of great concern to the headmaster who suspected me of ripping the last pages out of novels in the library. But in the end nobody could say much about it, given the nature of the tragedy the boy had endured. So the aunts and uncles addressed their checks to Upper Canada College at the beginning of each term, looked forward to the day the kid headed off to university (thank God his marks were good) and, aside from the annual charade of good-natured congeniality at Christmas, could be left completely to his own devices once and for all. And the whole time the kid looked forward to the very same thing himself, feeling that once he'd gained his own space he could refine all the mechanisms that would allow him to wipe his hands of himself forever.

On this point, it turned out that hate alone wasn't enough, although it certainly helped in dealing with the world, the right poses to strike. But hate wasn't so good with managing the past. What I had yet to discover was the simple fact that the best way to get around memory is to forget. That forgetting is not the absence of memory but a thing in itself, with its own mass, shape and texture. The process calls for initial encouragement but then a standing back to allow it to run its own course. A weed gone wild in the garden that will bring about the death of all other things around it if left alone long enough.

The more difficult part was to rid the body of memory. The trick is to convince it that it's not really there. Treat it like a stupid machine and let it rust. Dull it with drink and opiates. Never step on a scale. Avoid mirrors.

It worked.

Hadn't thought of it, any of it, for a long time. Almost

two decades of nothing. And now it's come back out of nowhere. Phoning up in the middle of the night, rising from the water, asking to be held.

"Evidence," I say.

A look that passes between them in the front seat, quick and ashamed.

Neither of them ever told me they believed me. I never told them she was pulled.

Sitting next to my father on the arm of his chair and pretending to read the same page he was reading, each word a soldier, each paragraph a battalion following the one ahead of it into war.

Proposing marriage to Caroline under her father's billiards table, the twist-tie from a loaf of bread for an engagement ring.

Carried, asleep, at my mother's neck.

I smell the morning before I see it: bagged leaves, pine sap and coffee. Then the grey light you don't believe at first, pushing color into the shadows. From the block behind me a car refuses to turn over, a screen door whinges open, a child is told to *stop it right now* and begins to cry. Without raising my eyes the morning lifts up from the sidewalk, the dead grass. Every step slow but sure. My body a solid, living thing in the growing light.

Forty-Five

After court the next evening I drive out to the lake once more. Haven't slept in over twenty-four hours and the full extent of the day's menu has consisted of something the plastic label called a burrito thrown into a convenience store microwave, but I'm neither tired nor hungry. And it's not just another cocaine distraction either. It's those last vapors of burning consciousness that come just prior to final collapse. I'm aware of this as much as I'm aware of the briars reaching and tugging at me across the path, geese honking south overhead, the smoke from Mrs. Arthurs's fire.

I sidestep down the slope past her woodpile, around to the front and raise my hand to knock but there's no need, the old woman already swinging the door open with a nearly toothless show of tonsil and gum.

"Saw you comin'," she says, chuckling, as though this fact alone spoke for some ingenious accomplishment. "Been around here quite a bit of late, haven't you, Mr. Crane?"

"Just stretching the legs."

"Well, well."

She waits, but I have no words for her, so she fills the space herself.

"You want some coffee? There's some just made."

"That would be great."

"Get yourself in out of the cold then and have a seat."

The choice of seating is limited though, given that there

are only two in the entire room and one (an overstuffed recliner shawled in a threadbare Hudson's Bay blanket) is obviously Mrs. Arthurs's roost. Sling my overcoat over a wobbly side table (a Queen Elizabeth II glass paperweight atop a sun-yellowed notepad from the Banff Springs Hotel) and take my seat, a pine kitchen chair apparently designed for dwarfs with extremely good posture.

"Milk? Sugar?" the old woman calls out from around the corner where there's the rattle of cups and saucers being lowered from the top shelf.

"Whatever's going."

When Mrs. Arthurs returns she carries a tray bearing two fancy bone china cups (both murky with drops of cream) and a plate of assorted store bought biscuits.

"Nice of you to drop by. Don't get many visitors anymore," she says, placing the tray down upon a footstool and falling into her chair. "Don't get *any* visitors anymore, to be honest."

"Well I'm not exactly just visiting, Mrs. Arthurs. I've come to ask you a favor, as a matter of fact."

"I can't imagine what I could help *you* with, Mr. Crane."

"It involves the case I'm working on. A rather unusual request, actually."

Lifts her cup and makes a sound like a vacuum being dunked into a pail of water.

"Is this about what I was telling you before?" she asks when she pulls the cup away from her lips.

"No. Not directly, anyway. What I'm here to ask you is to assist me in a matter of evidence."

"Cookie?"

"Thank you, no."

The old woman crunches on a slab of shortbread.

"What I've come here to tell you is that I am currently in possession of something that may be incriminating to my own client in this case," I say. "I'd rather not tell you how I came about it, if it's all the same to you."

A moth hammers against the kitchen window behind me, beats exhausted wings over the glass loud enough that I feel my voice rising to shut it out.

"I'm asking you to present this evidence to the Crown as though you've discovered it yourself."

"To lie, you mean," she says, sliding the back of her hand over her mouth.

"I suppose. In a manner, yes. To lie."

"What sort of evidence would you be talking about?"

I dig into the outside pocket of my overcoat and pull out the newspaper-wrapped hair, place it on the tray next to my cup and give her a moment to look it over.

"Hair," I say.

"I can see that."

"I have reason to believe that it's the hair of Krystal McConnell and Ashley Flynn. If its DNA matches the hair found in the back of Tripp's car, it proves that they're dead, and that they died in this lake."

"Doesn't prove he did it."

"No. But it sure doesn't help him."

"And you want me to take this into town and say I found it somewhere?"

"Washed up on your beach."

"So your man will be blamed."

"So the interests of justice may be advanced. Perhaps we could think of it in those terms."

"Perhaps we could."

The old woman considers the round package without

distaste, lips pursed. Then she raises her eyes, looks at me as though I too were some kind of inanimate forensic exhibit.

"Why not give it to them yourself?"

"Technically speaking, from the point of view of a lawyer's ethical duty, that would be the right thing to do in situations of this kind. Hand the evidence over to the police and withdraw from the case. But I can't do that."

"And why's that?"

"Because even with this—" I cast my eyes over to the hair "—there isn't enough evidence to convict him. So if I withdraw, all it would mean is that some other lawyer would be brought in to finish the trial and Tripp would walk. That's why I have to stay with him."

"But if this hair of yours isn't enough to get your man, why have me give it to the police at all?"

"It might help me talk to him. Get through. It might be enough for him to see that it's over."

I keep my eyes on her jaw, its mechanical circles and clacks still working the biscuity paste around her mouth.

"But you know that I think The Lady did it," she says after swallowing.

"I'm not saying she didn't, exactly. But even you said you thought Tripp probably had a hand in it one way or another."

"And that's what you believe?"

"I'm not sure I believe anything."

"Sounds to me like you do. Otherwise you wouldn't be here, would you?"

I say nothing to this, and instead take a slurping gulp of coffee so hot it instantly burns. Mrs. Arthurs watches me and rocks in her chair for a moment, its spring hee-hawing beneath her.

"So why me?" she asks finally. "There's plenty of others around here who'd like a turn at your man."

"That's true. But I suppose I feel that you and I share something, Mrs. Arthurs."

"Oh?"

"We both know The Lady is real."

"How's that, then?"

"Just like you. I lost someone too."

The rocking stops.

"That girl," she says. "The one that drowned."

The saucer lifting on its own to meet my cup with a crack of hollow bone.

"How do you know about that?"

"I *live* on this lake, Mr. Crane. And twenty years isn't so long ago when you get to be my age."

Clear my throat to recover from the prickling rush of surprise. Surprise at the fact that this one wrinkled widow, this believer in a dead woman rising from frozen waters, this most senior of citizens who lives outside of census takers, daily newspapers and group aerobic classes, this accidental hermit may be the only person on the planet who knows who I am.

"Had a feeling it was you," she says, bringing a self-congratulating index finger to the tip of her nose. "That I'd seen you before. Although you'd only have been a wee fellow at the time. And they called you something else then."

"Richard."

"Same as your father."

"Richard Sr. and Ricky Jr. It was thought of as very cute at the time. Then all the aunties and uncles got together to suggest it might be a good idea for me to change it. After what happened."

The old woman considers me long enough that I can feel the space my body occupies shrinking before her.

"The thinking was it might help save me from being hounded by the press as I got older," I hear myself saying. "But the fact is the press was never really interested anyway. 'Girl Drowns While on Holiday'—it happens every week up here in the summers. But now I think I know why they really did it."

"And why's that then?"

"To help me forget."

"Forgive me now, Mr. Crane. But you'd think a son should never have to feel ashamed to carry his own father's name."

"He's not what I'm ashamed of, Mrs. Arthurs."

She pulls herself soundlessly forward in her chair, the fading light from the kitchen window seeping through her hair pale as ash. Strokes a hand down the length of her neck and pulls the skin tight from her chin. For a moment her face becomes a hollow mask. Deep in their sockets, eyes belonging to a stranger behind it.

"They said you might have been the one," she says, bland and even. "That you drowned the girl yourself."

"And what do you think?"

"I'm asking you."

The moth at the window again but softer now. For what might be a minute or two there's nothing but its last feathery swats against the glass, flipping like dealt cards on the sill.

"Her name was Caroline," I say, eyes fixed on a silver cobweb sprayed into the corner above her head. "I think you would have to say we were in love. Or as much as kids can be in love. Kissin' cuzzins. But that day out in the canoe I tried to go further and I scared her."

"An accident then."

"An accident. But accidents have causes."

The old woman's hands lock together into a sleeping spider on her lap.

"I tried to save her," I go on as though asked to. "Went down to pull her up but she was too heavy. Or I wasn't strong enough. Or something. And I remember it was *cold*, just a couple of strokes down from where the sun touched the surface. So cold it got harder than water, like solid rock."

All of Mrs. Arthurs enlarging now, pressed-in eyes brought closer to mine. Below them her fingers awaken to scuttle forward to the ends of her knees.

"I guess I must have panicked," I'm saying, the words delicate and moist as popped bubbles. "Didn't think I had enough air to make it back up. That if I held onto her any longer she might take me down with her. But now I'm not so sure. Maybe I didn't even try. Not really. Maybe I just gave up."

"Now—"

"I *looked back*. There was definitely enough time for that. If I was really about to drown would I have taken the second or two or three or however long it took to stop and open my eyes? No. But that's exactly why I did it. I looked because I *knew* there was enough time."

"You were too young to remember all that. People forget the worst things, don't they, over time. Or make other things up in their place."

"But I remember now. Caroline reaching her hands up to me close enough that I could feel them brush across the bottom of my feet. And her scream that let the water in. Knew I could have saved her even then and all I did was watch her go."

"There's no—"

"I could have."

"Really no need for—"

"I could have saved her."

Holy Jesus then I'm in her arms. A blubber-faced child wiping my nose on her cardiganed shoulder that smells of bacon and almonds and bedpan. Everything inside me exploding off its hinges. A turning screw that rips up through organs and bone. For a moment. Then I'm pushing away, fingertips digging at my eyes, assembling myself with a pair of bruising gasps. If one were standing behind me it might have appeared only as an incoherent lunge forward that fell well short of an embrace. Nothing more than a momentary loss of balance on my part, legs fallen asleep from sitting too long on the edge of a too-small chair.

"God, I'm sorry."

"Nothing to be sorry about."

"I'm afraid you're wrong about that."

Mrs. Arthurs not even considering something to say. I make an attempt—anything will do to throw a human sound into the room's shattered space—but there're no words left. Instead both of us turn our eyes to the dripping hair on the table. Watch it as though expecting it to move, and in the flickering light of the fire it almost does.

"Well, well, well," she says after a long while before another while passes in silence. Then, just as I'm convinced she's about to announce there's no way, she'll have nothing to do with dead little girls' hair, it would be wrong to pretend something that wasn't true before a court of law, she has no choice but to have me reported, she accepts.

"Just hand it over to the police in town, you say?"

"That's right. They'll take it from there."

"Fine then, Mr. Crane. Though I won't do it as a favor to you. I'll do it as a favor to the wee ones. For we couldn't leave the poor things' hair just sitting there, could we?"

"No, I don't think we could."

She nods, and I down the still-scalding coffee in two gulps. When I place the cup back in its saucer on the table I notice that a small pool of green water has formed there from the slow but unstoppable drip that comes off the hair sticking out one end of the package.

I rise, unsteady as a marionette. But when I throw on my coat it's noticeably lighter on my shoulders. "Incredibly sleepy all of a sudden," I say, startled by an instant yawn.

"Know the feeling. First sign of old age."

Rattle at the door handle before the latch pulls back and it swings open. Long enough for Mrs. Arthurs to get up herself and place a dry hand against my cheek, knuckles the size of chestnuts rolled across sharp stubble.

"Did you see her, then? The Lady? Did you see her for yourself?"

"I've seen her."

"I knew you would. As soon as I laid eyes on you I knew you'd be one to understand."

Turn to face her but the pale outdoor light has washed her away, an X-ray exposing vague bones within a membrane of skin.

"I'm very sorry about your daughter, Mrs. Arthurs," I say and collect her briefly at the shoulders. Careful, hesitant, the way you would lift a crystal bowl up into your arms. And she gives herself over to my grasp, empties her lungs in a surrendering sigh.

"Well, bye now, then," I say when there's nothing left of her.

"Good-bye, Richard," she says.

I'm stepping back up toward the trail. But before I make it the old woman calls after me.

"You know, I never believed you did it, what they said you might have done. I got an eye for these things, and I always thought you weren't the kind."

She means well by this, I know. But I keep walking, head down, without turning back.

Forty-Six

Helen Arthurs, widow of Duncan Arthurs, did exactly as she agreed she would do. The day after our meeting Goodwin called to tell me that significant new evidence had been discovered washed up on the shore of Lake St. Christopher by a permanent resident with "considerable credibility within the community" and would I consent to its being sent to Toronto for high-priority DNA testing or would a motion before Justice Goldfarb be required? With some obligatory grumbling, my consent was granted. The trial was adjourned, the jury advised to speak to no one regarding the substance of the case for the duration of their time away from court, etc., etc. Then we waited. Snow fell, melted, fell again, melted, and on the third falling stayed on the ground with a look of serious intentions about it. I spend the better part of my time lying in the honeymoon suite's bed reading back issues of *Elle* and *Vanity Fair* borrowed from the Murdoch Public Library and gingerly drinking myself to sleep. In the mornings I write down what I remember of my dreams from the night before. In time I start to see all the characters as messengers.

On the fourth day I decide to go for a drive. North, past the side road to the lake, Bishop's Hospital, the last McConnell Auto Stop. The air bracing and loud as the sea in my ears, crashing in through the missing front windshield.

Driving up into the wilder place where there are no longer any signs promising the arrival of another town so many miles down the road. Nothing but the narrow pavement cutting through the trees, skirting bog, working out a short-term lease with everything around it.

Stop for a lunch of tortilla chips and coffee at a gas station with a startling collection of international porn for sale alongside the cigarettes and spark plugs. Head north again. The sun not so much lowering as fading away entirely.

Then I see it. Something up ahead in the road.

I slow well before I reach it and pull over onto the narrow gravel shoulder. A deer. Its hips knocked from their sockets, legs impossibly splayed out from each other. A spattering of blood followed by a smudged trail tracing its effort to pull itself off the road. But still alive: side rising and falling, tongue flicking out of its mouth, eyes looking up at me.

For a moment I take stock of the animal's injuries, estimate where I would be on a map, how far from someplace large enough that it might have a vet. Decide the injuries are too severe, the someplace too far. Then I drag the deer over to the side of the road where I sit down beside it and lift its head to rest on my lap.

Three cars pass in the time it takes afternoon to become dusk, dusk to become night. Two blow past without a blink of brake lights but a monkey-faced woman in a 4×4 slows, glances over at the young man in a dress shirt with the sleeves rolled up, rocking back and forth with a deer's head in his lap. Then, without stopping, drives on.

Listen to it breathing in spasms that bounce my hand into the air from where it strokes the length of its neck. Lies still again, and I count the time in my head before its next breath.

One Mississippi, two Mississippi, three Mississippi, four—

The foaming mouth clicks open wider and pulls another half-cup of life into its lungs.

One Mississippi, two Mississippi, three Mississippi, four Mississippi, five—

How long do we stay together? How long have I stroked its side, making a sound—*shwee-sha*—that I only now remember my own mother making to calm me into sleep? Can't guess. Can't guess the time it is now, how long the animal requires to die. But when it does, I know it. Something lifts away from its skin and passes through me before dispersing into the darkness.

When I finally get up my legs refuse to obey for a time, sandwiched between the deer's weight and the piercing surface of the gravel shoulder. Then I step into the ditch, grab hold of its hind legs and pull. Even though I've got the leverage of the decline on my side it's harder than I would have expected. Not only the animal's weight but the flexibility of its ligaments and joints resists movement, absorbing every effort to haul it down. But after a time I strike upon the method that works best: short, concentrated jerks in the same direction. Taking it two inches at a time results in slow progress through the high grass to where the drooping ferns and willows stand higher yet. After a while I turn to look into the forest and over the ground that glows blue from the patches of snow that survived the day's sun. Another thirty feet or so to be out of view from the road. Grab hold of its legs again, two breaths and a pull that sends a numbing heat up my back. One. Two. *Three.*

Start digging with my fingernails, the pads beneath my thumbs. After a time I discover that the job goes quicker using a flat stone as a shovel, sending the soil up into a growing pile. Will myself to make the hole deeper, broader, eventually rolling into it myself to improve the angle and gage its size. When the earth begins to yield to the limestone beneath it I scrabble out on my knees and push the animal into its grave.

When I'm finished there's a bulging mound left, but I can imagine returning next spring, next week, and not noticing that anything had ever been buried here. The sun coming up weak through the starved branches. Think of words to say but none come and I'm thankful for this, closing my eyes instead and conjuring wordless thoughts for myself, the dead animal and anything else I can think of. A random sequence of face and moment and voice that comes to form a single memory in my mind, a kind of godless prayer.

Later that morning a fax arrives with the DNA results. Two hair extractions from Mrs. Arthurs's package matched with those found in the backseat of Thom Tripp's Volvo, one of them in turn matching drops of Krystal McConnell's blood found on the same. There was also an unexpected aspect to the lab's findings. A third hair type bearing an unknown DNA identity found among the other two. Different from the others even by sight: long, straight and blonde.

"Isn't that rather odd?" Goodwin asked me as he handed over a copy of the lab's written report. I told him I was as surprised as anyone.

Marching up the broad steps to the Murdoch Prison for Men, its blunt facade now almost dignified with a front lawn rolling out before it white with cleansing snow. The failed rosebushes on each side of the door buried along with everything else except for a few pruned branches reaching up, grey and gnarled. It's always the same with prisons. Right there at the gates of some forgotten place of grief and desperation a bored janitor or local do-gooder gets it into his head to plant something beautiful and it never grows.

Once inside I'm almost pleased to see that it's the leprechaun guard behind the desk again, grinning out at me with small teeth held together by wads of tartar the color of caramel.

"Mr. Crane! Looks like you've been out and about," he says, motioning his chin down to the torn, mud-caked bottom of my overcoat.

"Just the unavoidable filth to be found everywhere in your fair town, Flaherty."

"Perhaps if your car had a windshield you could keep yourself a bit more tidy. Have a bit of trouble, did ye?"

"A fender bender."

"Quite so! Quite so!" he nods, allowing himself an appreciative smirk. "Here to see your man?"

"If he has to be mine, then yes."

Without further command Flaherty takes me down the hall to Interview Room No. 1 to await the always unpredictable entrance of Thomas Tripp. Off goes my overcoat and the suit jacket follows a couple seconds later but I'm still dripping sweat down my sides, darkening through the white cotton of my shirt. Now that winter has come they've got it way too hot in here. By the time Tripp arrives I've got my tie loosened halfway down my chest and sleeves rolled up to the elbows. Seems to be feeling it himself, puffing his cheeks out in an effort to catch his breath (did they just yank him out from his morning workout?) and blowing tiny pearls of saliva out his mouth.

"Thom, I regret to say that I'm the bearer of bad tidings

this morning," I try for a fatalistic laugh but the empty echo it leaves in the room tells me to give it up. "As you know, a sample of hair was found at the edge of Lake St. Christopher a few days ago and it's just come back from DNA testing in Toronto. Two match with Krystal and Ashley, and there's a third nobody's sure about. The point is, this means the girls are buried in that lake, that's where they died, and they didn't do it all on their own. This completes the story the Crown's been telling. So much so, I'm afraid we have to reconsider our position in this trial. We need to take a *serious* look at this, you know, and maybe face up to something we'd hoped we wouldn't have to face."

Tripp's not avoiding my eyes as he usually does, but he doesn't seem to be listening to what I'm saying, either. Instead he takes me in with a politely restrained amusement, as though I've left a dried dollop of shaving cream under my nose. When he gets around to responding it's with a teacherly superiority, an adult talking to a child about stealing another's pencil crayons.

"She's been talking to you too, hasn't she?"

"Could you be somewhat more—"

"Because she knows who *you* are alright."

"Mr. Tripp, please keep in mind that *you're* the one accused of double murder. I would ask you to further keep in mind that I haven't been accused of a thing."

"You don't have to be accused of anything to hear them. But you already know that, don't you? And who could accuse you anyway? You're the lawyer!"

Laughter. A hearty cocktail-party bellow, his rheumy eyes glistening from the force of it.

"Well thanks, Thom," I say when he's throat-cleared his way back to silence. "But I'm not much interested in your expert opinion on psychotic behavior in others. You are right about one thing, though: I'm the lawyer, and you're the client. Can we stick with that for a moment without the yucks, please?"

A knowing trick of a smile at the frothy edges of Tripp's lips that makes me want to give the side of his head a full swing with the back of my hand.

"Now, I'm going to give you the benefit of my legal advice. That's part of my job," I start again, keeping my voice low as possible. "I know when a hand has been forced. And in light of this new evidence, it is my obligation to advise you that the best course of action for you to take at this point—the *only* course of action—is to plead guilty."

"To say that I—"

"It will have a positive implication on your sentence, maybe get you into a counseling program a little sooner. It's expedient, Thom, but it's also wise."

"Say I killed them?"

"Strategically it's the only option, and frankly—and I say this on a personal level—you'd be doing yourself a favor."

Tripp considers this, or at least appears to consider it, his hand raised to support his chin.

"It's going to require you to confess," I go on. "But you don't have to think of it in those terms if you don't want to. All you have to do is stand up and say a few words. Admit to each of the elements of the offence in more or less specific terms."

"What should I say?"

"That you took them to the lake after school, walked down to the water with them, did what you did."

"What did I do?"

"Do you really not remember?"

"Sometimes. Certain things."

"Like what?"

"Their faces," he says. "How they smiled and everything would change. The way they could make you believe for a second that nothing could possibly be wrong with anything anywhere."

"That's fine, Thom. That's *nice*. But what I'm asking is, now that we've come this far, don't you remember anything of what happened at the lake that day?"

"Sometimes I'm sure I remember. Other times I'm sure I must be wrong."

"That's how it is, is it?"

"You think I did it."

"Jesus, Thom! *Yes*, I think you did it! Everyone in this town thinks you did it. You're the only one who's not so sure. I'm sorry you don't remember, maybe some day it'll all come back to you, but for Christ's sake it's time for you to admit it. And know what else? I think you *want* to. I think you know that either you take a good look at what you did right now or you're going to be alone with the voices in your head forever."

With the last dozen of these words the most unfortunate thing occurs. My voice breaks. Dry sinuses suddenly melting into a stream of children's glue. But whether out of good manners or the hearing of voices, Thom Tripp appears not to notice.

"I didn't do it alone," he says after I've wiped the heel of my hand across the tops of my cheeks.

"Give me a name then."

Pulls his chin up and shows me something new in his eyes. The fear that's been there all along but hidden by dreams, the distraction of riddles played upon himself.

"It was The Lady."

'You saw her?"

"She told me things."

"Like what?"

"Like she has them now. And that's why they'll never be found."

"That's not good enough, Thom."

"What do you want then?"

"For you to tell me that you killed Ashley Flynn and Krystal McConnell. Because you did and you know it, even if you thought some dead lady was giving you directions from the Great Fucking Beyond."

Cocks his head to the side and in a second the glimpse of fear drains away from his face. Half nods as though the most clever little joke has just been delivered to his ear.

"What'd you do?" he says.

"There's no me *in* this. Do I have to explain again that this—"

"Who did you hurt?" His breath blown cold across the hot room. "Tell me her name."

For a moment I see myself sitting here in the instant chill of Interview Room No. 1 and feel certain that this is how I will stay forever. Thinking her name and willing it to my lips but nothing ever coming out. That this is how it ends, me and Tripp caught in each other's stares, perspiring and shadowless. We're to be roommates together in the eternity of names.

But as it turns out it doesn't end this way at all. Instead I'm a rubber band shot across the room, tumbling up into the air with all my limbs loose and grasping and quick. Then the more specific details begin to arrive: I'm throwing myself over the table at Tripp. Grabbing him by the collar of his prison overalls, his hair, the hanging lobes of his ears, wrenching him out of his chair to the floor. He doesn't have a chance. Didn't even see it coming. But then again, neither did I. Had no idea I was about to sit on my client's chest, set my knees on his shoulders and start swinging down on him with both fists. The sound of contact surprisingly hollow and dull, like checking to see if a coconut is ripe yet, and not at all the bright crack I'd learned to expect from the movies. I wouldn't know otherwise. Until this moment I've never hit anyone in my life.

Part of me expecting one of the guards to burst in and throw me off him at any second, but either they've left their post to fetch coffee or are too busy enjoying the show themselves. Whatever the reason I get in a few direct thuds on both sides of Tripp's head before he starts blubbering for me to stop, blood spilling out from his nose and over my hands, almost orange in the institutional light of guttering fluorescent tubes. Only then does the thought occur to me that maybe this isn't an entirely wise idea, physically assaulting my own client in this way. Knocking the living shit out of him as a matter of fact. And I'm supposed to be the guy's lawyer. There are still professional obligations to consider, basic expectations of conduct, Oaths of the Bar to be honored. But it appears I don't care about that anymore.

Tell me, tell me, tell me, tell me, I'm panting into his face, his collar still bound in my fists.

"Stop!"

"Tell me the truth."

"Why do you care?"

"Because I fucking do, that's why." I loosen my grip. The tickle of air pulsing up his windpipe beneath my hands. "Because I've heard them too."

"So you know."

"I know you have to give their story an ending, Thom. Because keeping it to yourself is going to kill you. It's already killing a lot of others. The McConnells, Brian Flynn, the people in town who loved them. And you're the only one who can let them go."

"What about you?"

"Me too, probably," I say, the air between us thickening into a liquid fog. "It's killing me too."

His breath enters and exits in tin-whistle squeaks, and it's some time before I realize his chest is still supporting the full load of my weight. Without letting go of his collar I get to my feet, bend over close enough that I can smell the sharp lemon-lime of prison soap on the skin at his neck. Then I'm dragging him forward across the tiled floor, his head lowered into his overalls as though tucked within a body bag yet to be fully zippered closed at the top. When I reach the opposite wall I lean him up against it, palms pressed against his collarbone in order to hold him steady.

"It was the Literary Club, wasn't it, Thom? That's where you got the idea to go to the lake. For the girls to wear their dresses with the blue ribbons. For the three of you to have your last performance."

Tripp looks down at his hands that lie limp on the floor, each of his fingers painted with a coating of his own blood.

"'By the pricking of my thumbs, Something wicked this way comes.'"

"The three witches. Was that it? You and the girls going off to the lake to cook up a spell?"

"Not *me*. The three of *them*."

"So they knew about The Lady as well?"

"I told them the story but they'd heard it before. Weren't

even scared. But then they wanted to know all the little details, and when I didn't have anything more to tell they started making things up on their own. That The Lady'd risen up out of the lake and was coming after them. That she was going to take them both down to the bottom with her. To 'ease her pain through living death,' as Krystal liked to put it. Got so that all three of us were living in a ghost story and stayed so long it started feeling as real as anything else."

Tripp manages to raise a hand to wipe the pink speckle of spit from his chin. "They wanted to see her for themselves," he says. "And you know something? I think they finally did."

Then he tells me how he did it, his words cool and plain and slow. Telling how it was the girls' idea to stand out in the water and crouch down to look under with their eyes open to see if The Lady would show herself to them. Up to the waist himself, his shoes planted in the loose mud, Krystal on one side and Ashley on the other. Bringing them close against his ribs when they came up for air and telling them they were his, that they'd always be his, that all he wanted was for them to stay with him forever. Asked him when they would get to hear the ghost's voice too. Right now, he told them. All they had to do was listen in the right way. How if they really wanted to see The Lady they'd have to walk out a little deeper, hold their breath and go all the way under, look as far out into the dark as they could.

And what did they do? I ask him.

They did exactly as I told them, he says.

Then tells of how he kept them under, one hand on top of each head. Not as difficult as it might sound if you keep both arms stiff at your sides, elbows locked. A process requiring patience more than anything else, really. Eyes held out over the pallid scales of the lake's surface. Their screams, if there were any, failing to reach his ears.

And their stillness afterwards. The way they floated next to him for a while, face up, light as fabric, eyes wide as dolls'. How he stayed with them and they with him and for all this time no thought but this passed through his mind.

Oh yes, he answers my murmured interruption. A certain amount of hair pulling was definitely involved.

But with the coming darkness he was reminded that he had to move and without considering the grim logistics involved he simply pushed them out into the water. He was surprised to see how far they went on their own, their white dresses moving about them like wings, hair lingering on the surface even as the rest of them went under until it too was finally pulled down and was gone. Even at the time he was aware of how none of this—their struggle, the flash of bubbles breaking about him as though the lake were boiling, the final moon-catching disturbance of the water as they went below—seemed to make any sound at all.

I ask him if he recovered the bodies later and hid them somewhere else and he tells me no, they went down on their own and he had nothing more to do with it. But I'm asking him more things. About how unlikely it is that the bodies wouldn't have been easily found if he had just pushed them out like that without their being weighed down. About the physical difficulty of holding two healthy teenaged girls under water for that long without some kind of assistance. About whether he's sure he's telling everything known to him with regard to the circumstances of the crime. And he tells me yes, that's all. That's how it happened.

"What I need is for you to tell the court what you just

told me, Thom," I'm saying now. "But without anything about The Lady. O.K.?"

"I thought you wanted the truth."

"For our purposes, the court doesn't need to hear the whole truth. Remember what you told me? A good story should *make* you *believe*."

Tripp's head starts shaking in what I take to be the first signs of shock, but it's not. It's a laughter too weak inside of him to make its way out. My client with his head held an inch above my bare arms, laughing at me.

"I'm glad it was you, Richard," he says.

"Who told you that was my name?"

"Who do you think?"

Pull my hands away from him as though I only now recognized they were being held above an open flame. Step back until I find the table behind me and grip its edge. Even from this distance of a few feet he's suddenly smaller, his body sucked dry. Sit on my hands as much for balance as to wipe the blood off my knuckles. Tripp closes his eyes, focusing on his words.

"Can I ask you for some lawyerly advice, Mr. Crane?"

"Go ahead, Thom."

"If I plead will it stop?"

"I don't know. But I'm pretty sure it'll help."

Then he opens his eyes and shrugs. That's it. Nothing but a slight raising of sinewy shoulders to indicate his acceptance of damnation.

"Your wife steals them from you. They run off with the kid down the street. They grow up into women. They change," he says. "It's all the same though, isn't it, if the only thing you want is for them to stay?"

I say nothing to this, and in the seconds that follow he

allows his shoulders to gradually lower again. Pulls a spaghetti noodle of halfdried blood from his nose. I step forward to take hold of him under the arms and slide him up until he's standing against the wall.

When I knock on the door it takes a full minute before the guard arrives and, with a quick look my way at the sight of the blood on Tripp's upper lip, takes him by the arm. But before the two of them make it out to the hallway they stop and my client turns to face me.

"Will they let Melissa come visit?"

"Sure, if her mother will bring her. Sure thing. I'll contact her on your behalf if you'd like."

"I'm not allowed to speak to them anymore. I'm not allowed to call."

"Of course. I'll see what I can do."

I say this. I give him my assurance, promise to provide this one comfort to the man who's paying me to represent his interests. But I know at the same time that I won't see what I can do. I say this knowing that as soon as I can, I won't have anything to do with Thomas Tripp ever again.

Forty-Seven

From the Murdoch Prison for Men I head directly for Goodwin's office. Even though it's only twenty-to-nine I've learned that it's his custom to slouch downstairs well in advance of the required time in order to move at a pace compatible with the limited capacity of his butter-clogged arteries: a lumbering scuff that tips his bulging upper half to one side and then the other like a harbor buoy caught in a stiff wind. But I'm in luck. As I slide the last five feet to his door on leather soles made slick by melted snow, grab the frame with one hand and pull myself in with an accidental click of the heels I find that Goodwin's still there, putting the end to what appears to be a fried egg, cheddar and peanut butter sandwich.

"Barth! Definitely your most spectacular entrance yet! But could you just sit down for a second? I swear to God you give me an upset stomach every time you come in here sweating and panting like you just finished a marathon. By the way, has your umbrella been working out alright? Next we're going to have to get you a proper down-filled, scientifically tested, guaranteed-to-allow-circulation-to-essential-internal-organs-at-60-below winter jacket."

"Thanks, Pete. But I don't think I'm going to need it."

Goodwin lowers the last complicated nugget of his sandwich to the tinfoil it came from and takes a slurp of coffee from its accompanying styrofoam cup.

"And why's that?"

I lower myself into the chair before his desk, find Goodwin's eyes through the stacked files.

"I've reviewed the most recent DNA evidence with my client and discussed the implications upon the case for the defence in some detail. And under the circumstances, I advised Tripp to consider changing his plea."

Goodwin leans forward, his lower lip trembling outward like an unfurling tulip petal.

"And?"

"I believe he has agreed to do so this morning."

"Agreed to—?"

"Plead guilty."

"Oh."

"You won, Pete," I extend my hand over the desk. "Congratulations."

Takes the hand and gives it a limp joggle, his palm slippery with egg yolk.

"He's pleading guilty?"

"There's no point in continuing in the face of overwhelming physical evidence. I mean, as you can appreciate from—"

"But it's *not* overwhelming!" he almost shouts. "The hair doesn't end it, not on its own. Even with the other things it's not enough. You *know* that. So why are you telling Tripp to plead? Now, without even introducing the defence's case? Why plead now, Barth?"

This is unexpected. I assumed Goodwin would respond to this news the same way I would have if I were in his position: take the conviction and run to the nearest bar for a long series of libations and entertainments. But no, he's got to have it all figured out in his own mind first or else he won't get any sleep for the next fifteen years.

"I've advised Mr. Tripp in the manner that I have," I say,

working to sound matter-of-fact, "because I feel there's no longer any reasonable chance for an acquittal. The hair samples changed things significantly for us. That may not be your estimation, but with all due respect, it's not your job to judge the wisdom of strategic decisions made by the defence."

"I realize that. But this whole thing feels weird. For weeks you're hammering away at how the Crown's evidence is nothing but a load of junk, and then all of a sudden you're rolling over and playing dead. It seems to me that something's missing here."

"You're right about something being missing," I say. "The thing is I have to do this. And you have to let me."

There's a grinding from under Goodwin's chair as he leans back but says nothing. For a moment I take his silence to be an indication of doubt, but that's not it. He's listening. I take in a long breath that, held for a half-second, blasts out again. And with this banal exchange of air, the timeless *in* and prehistoric *out*, comes a sudden, devastating fatigue.

"For the first time in twenty years I'm trying to do something right," I say. "And I may be going about it all wrong, but I'm new at this sort of thing."

For a time Goodwin appears to consider my face more than my words.

"Can I ask you something? Unrelated."

"Unrelated's O.K. with me."

"You live alone?"

"You first."

"Me? Yeah. I'm a bachelor," he says, the word hanging decisively in the air as though a permanent designation.

"Me too. Why?"

"Just curious. Sometimes I think I can pick them out."

"Bachelors?"

"Lonely people."

Goodwin checks his watch again.

"We've got fifteen minutes," he says. "I'm not as fast as I used to be on those stairs. In fact I've *never* been fast on those stairs."

But neither of us moves.

"This is an inappropriate question to ask at this point, I know. But I have to ask it." Goodwin pushes his chin into his neck. "Do you really think Tripp did it? Just him I mean, all on his own?"

"I think there's evil in the world. That there has to be because nothing else can explain some of the things people do."

"That, counsel, is *not* a direct answer."

With this the big man rises, squeezes through the space between desk and wall and waits for me when he reaches the door.

"You coming down with me or is Tripp going to be without representation this morning?" he asks, turning to look back at the heap that was once Bartholomew Christian Crane, that still is, sitting in his office chair.

"I'm coming with you," I say, and with another miraculous breath manage to rise and walk myself.

Once downstairs I grab the cellular out of my bag and stand outside the doors, play the familiar tune of Lyle, Gederov's number. The snow has started again. A rustle of powder on my shoulders, collecting on the courthouse lawn even in the time it takes the receptionist to pick up and transfer me to Graham's office.

"Bartholomew! How lovely you called! This must be your breakfast break. Can I ask you something? Are you getting enough protein? Just this morning someone was telling me about the importance of protein to stimulate—oh bugger it, how *are* you?"

"I've got some news I want you to hear from me before you hear it from anywhere else. And I'd appreciate it if I could speak to you alone on this."

"What's going *on*, Bartholomew? But wait, before you go any further, maybe we really *should* get Bert in on this, because if he finds out we've been having private talks behind his back he's likely to turn extremely bitchy on both of us."

"No Bert. Can't we just have a conversation between the two—"

"Well hel-*lo*, Bert!" Graham calls too loudly out his open office door. "Guess who's on the other end of this line? Bartholomew! Would you like a word?"

In the background there's an unidentifiable barnyard sound, the passage of gas from a bull's guts

"Isn't this opportune? Bert just walked in the very moment you called!" Graham nearly squeals, an exaggerated tone from a man noted for his exaggerated tones. Then there's a click over the line and our voices expand in the vacant air of the speakerphone.

"Well now, Bartholomew, what gives us the pleasure of hearing your voice today?" Graham clasps his hands together on the surface of his desk. In my other ear a church at the far end of town ringing out the hour.

"I doubt what I have to say will give either of you any pleasure."

"Well, *tell* us then. What *is* this pleasureless bulletin?"

"I'm going to plead Tripp guilty today."

"Beg pardon?"

"It's over. I changed his plea."

Graham makes a flapping sound with his lips.

"This is something of a *shock* Bartholomew, I must say—"

"What the fuck do you mean, you *changed his plea*?"

For the moment, Bert's voice is more strangled than enraged.

"I convinced him it was the only course to take. And then he confessed."

"To who?"

"To me."

"So now you're going to fucking *give* this to them?"

"I'm about to."

"No you're goddamn not. You're off this file as of now."

"You can't do that, Bert. This is my case. You gave it to me to handle on my own and this is the way it's going to go."

"You're wrong there, pally boy. Because you're fucking done. You hear me? You do this and we'll be lucky if this guy doesn't sue us out of business! Have you forgotten how this works? You're supposed to be on *his* side, and instead you want to go and tie the bloody noose around his bloody *neck*, for God's sake! Now why the fuck would you do something like that? Why are you screwing the Crown up the ass for free? Eh? Could you tell me that, please?"

"This was my decision, Bert."

"That's where you're wrong. It's *never* been your decision, you little prick. It's this *firm's* decision. It's *our* names on the line. You're just an employee, remember? You're nobody. So whatever you do, whatever stupid decisions you make, make us look stupid. See how that works?"

"You don't know the full—"

"You don't know what your goddamn job is."

"May I interject for a moment, gentlemen?"

Graham has recovered, his voice now a controlled, theatrical baritone.

"Now listen, Bartholomew. We've been aware of the stress you've been under on this file. But after our conversation following your unfortunate press conference some time ago I thought we'd sorted everything out. And now, without any consultation with us, you wrongly advise your client on the main issue of trial. These are very severe errors, Bartholomew. *Very* severe. You of all people! He's going away for life now, you know that. And a life sentence that follows a plea of guilty is just as long as one that follows a conviction by jury. Given this, I can only conclude that you've utterly lost your capacity for good judgment."

"Actually, Graham, I feel like I'm just finding it."

"And how's that, Bartholomew? *Hmm?* Could you *explain* that to us?"

"No. I don't think I can."

"Ohh!" Graham moans. "To say the least, to say the *absolute* least, you've put this firm in a very difficult position."

"And I regret that. But there's something else I have to tell you."

"Do tell."

"I resign."

"What?"

"I'm out. After this, I'm done. I'm going to do something else."

"What *something else*?" Graham spits. "Bartholomew, you were *made* for this stuff! I know that Bert agrees with me on this, even though he's distinctly disenchanted with you at this particular moment. We've put a lot of time into grooming your talents into something that Lyle, Gederov can grow upon in the future, Bartholomew. Don't turn one mistake into two."

"It's not a mistake. And as for young lawyers to build the firm's future, there are plenty more where I came from and you know it. Go and pluck one of them out and turn them into whatever you need. I'm gone."

Surprisingly, Graham gives up. More surprising, Bert takes a stab at it himself.

"What are you going to do? Eh? You think you can just walk away from your life? You don't think we *all* haven't thought about ways to get out? Everybody wants to escape, Barth."

"I'm not escaping. I'm quitting."

"Fine. Then quit. And while you're at it, go to hell."

Then they wait. They've made the appeals they felt obliged to make, been denied as they hoped they'd be denied, and are already calculating the reputational and monetary losses that face them, recalling the names of other hot young lawyers who could be brought in to take Bartholomew Crane's place. They are practical men above everything else. Men who'd lived their professional lives knowing that their time was literally money, that in this business people frequently fall away and that the only choice is to work out the best deal you can and carry on with the dirty job at hand.

"We respect your capacity to decide your own professional future, Bartholomew," Graham begins cautiously. "But with regard to this Tripp business, we must insist that you discontinue representation of your client immediately. Do you understand?"

"It's too late."

"No, it's *not.* According to my watch you still have time to

go in there, withdraw from the case and walk away. We'll clean
up everything else."

"I know. That's why I'm doing this."

"I promise you right now that you won't *ever*—"

"FUCKING UNGRATEFUL PUNK COCKSUCKER—"

Click off the cellular and their voices are sucked away,
leaving nothing but the meltwater chattering down to the
sewer drains in the street. Look out beyond the huddled
rooftops of town at the snow falling slow and straight. Watch it
gather over the whole midnorth.

The courtroom is nearly asleep already. The clerk's head
hangs from its neck, the hacks from the Toronto dailies
buttress greasy skulls on arms sliding off the back of the
gallery's bench. Even McConnell sits folded in upon himself,
which is a change from his usual spinning turn to cast a
damning look my way. It seems that with the first evidence of
winter every vent that might have afforded the faintest lick of
circulation has been closed and the heat cranked up to a level
consistent with our sister courtrooms in equatorial nations.
The result is a haze of vaporized perspiration, carbon dioxide
and flatulence that hangs over the room in an occasionally
visible smog.

Although Goodwin and I arrive late, Justice Goldfarb is
even later. Glance at my watch but immediately forget the
position of its hands so that I have to glance again. Where's
Tripp?

Here he comes, shuffling with bird-like jerks as though
still shackled at the ankles but he's not. It takes him what feels
like the length of a foreign-language film to reach the chair
next to mine, and when he lowers himself into it his head lolls
onto his shoulder in my direction as though to receive a

welcoming kiss. Instead I lean over his way and whisper, "You ready?" into a wax-clogged ear.

"Today's the day."

"Yes, Thom. Are you O.K.?"

"I'm O.K.," he says, looking around him and behind him, moving from face to face in the gallery.

"Good. Listen, I'm going to be right here behind you when the time comes, alright? Just hang in there."

"Uh-huh."

But with the arrival of Tripp's newfound consciousness has come an aching lethargy for Bartholomew Crane. And as the clerk stands to call "All rise!" as Justice Goldfarb cuts through the jellied air in her black, funereal robes, it's all I can do to half lift myself out of my chair before the call of "You may be seated" from above permits a falling back into place.

But I'm the only one who stays up. Fingertips splayed out for balance on the table before me, my voice a sound made from outside myself.

"Your Honor, I'd like to request a change in the scheduled procedure this morning, if I could, so that my client may—"

"I'm afraid I can't permit that, Mr. Crane."

Goldfarb shaking her head, palms raised to stop me from going any further.

"I'm sorry?"

"You'll have to sit down now. If you don't mind."

I look over at Goodwin for a clue but his eyes are lowered to his lap where he concentrates on pinching at the crease in his pants. Tripp turns to me though, the taut lines of his face falling away.

"I don't understand, Your Honor."

"Your principals from Lyle, Gederov contacted me from

Toronto a few moments ago. It is their view that there is
sufficient reason to question your competence in continuing
this trial."

"But my client and I have duly elected—"

"And I felt that, given the extent of the Crown's evidence
and what I expect you are about to propose, they may well be
right."

Her lower lip pushed up into a wrinkled fist.

"No. Don't do this. Please, Your Honor, you can't let—"

"Sit down, Mr. Crane."

"—can't let him go—"

"Sit *down*, Mr. Crane."

I tumble back into my chair and almost miss the mark,
bouncing off the armrest with a metallic squawk.

"Until alternative counsel is made available for the
accused, this court is adjourned," Goldfarb is saying to the jury
now, and they look back at her with a variety of seasick
expressions. "So it's the old routine again, people. Don't
discuss any of this with anyone until we can get this show back
on the road."

Blink up to see the bailiff coming over to haul Tripp away
but taking his time about it, gut sucked in, a thumb hooked
over the butt of his pistol. Can't hear Goodwin offering an
understanding word somewhere off to the side, can't move my
head back from where it hangs over the smudge of papers on
the desk. Nothing at all but a weight on my shoulder that is my
client's hand resting next to my cheek in silent comfort.

Forty-Eight

It's hard to see Graham Lyle sitting on the window ledge of the honeymoon suite, hands gripped to his knees, eyes touring the walls of photocopied newspaper while trying to remain calm. But there he is, real as anything else. Arrived the morning after he pulled me out of court and was knocking at my door before I'd gotten out of bed myself although it's difficult to say who looks worse between the two of us. Apparently he wasn't kidding about being allergic to the country air. Pulling a nasal spray out of his breast pocket every couple of minutes to give each nostril a swift blast followed by an automatic *Pardon me* under his breath.

"Would you like some Kleenex?" I offer him from my place at the end of the bed. Graham's gaze held somewhere to my left, on the photo of The Lady possibly, although she would be too small to make out from where he sits.

"No, thank you. I think I'll just stick with the prescription drugs."

"Now there's wisdom."

"I don't anticipate being here long anyway. As a matter of fact, I'd very much like to be on the road the day after tomorrow."

"Are you going to play tag team with Bert for the rest of the trial, then?"

"It requires only *one* lawyer to deliver a motion to dismiss."

"What are you talking about?"

"The Crown is finished with its case and there's not enough to nail our friend. You know this yourself, or *would* have known it before your wits abandoned you. So I'm going to ask Goldfarb to finish this silly business right now so we can all go home."

Graham throws his head back to glance out the window and finds something on the street that catches his interest, or at least it appears he does, for he remains turned away from me for a long while.

"I hope you understand why I did what I did," I say finally.

"Well, then you hope in vain, my boy, because I don't have a clue. Although I could *guess* it has something to do with what you might mistakenly see as some kind of moral reckoning or other. But *understand?* That I don't."

"I don't believe you."

"Seems you've inherited your client's taste in interior decoration," he says, pretending not to hear and swinging his head back to show an upper lip glistening beneath his still-streaming nose.

"They're not decoration."

"Beg your pardon. What *would* you call all this then?" He circles his arm around the room while rhythmically blinking eyelids pink as hamburger. For a moment I actually search for an answer, though I know there isn't one.

"Why don't I pack all this stuff up so you can get to work?" I say instead, and for the first time Graham turns his eyes to the still largely untouched disclosure materials stacked on my desk.

"Yes, why don't you do that." Gives his nose another injection. "I'll be in Room 24 at the end of the hall."

Clips over to the door and places a hand on the tower of bedsheets that come up to his chin.

"You were the best student I ever had, you know," he says on his way out, as much to himself as to me. But by the time I think of something to say in return he's already gone.

The next morning I manage to find a seat in the gallery without meeting anyone's eyes. Focus on nothing but Graham's back as Goldfarb comes in to take her chair. Watch only his hands as they begin to dance in the air at his sides, framing his points in clean boxes and ovals. A motion to dismiss. Insufficient evidence to meet the charge. A waste of the court's resources to continue with the trial. Your Honor, the law on the matter is plain.

It doesn't take long.

Then a moment when several things happen at once:

The jury turning to each other to determine whether any of them knows what the hell just happened while Goldfarb mumbles thanks for their responsible conduct throughout the proceedings. An explosion of violent sobbing from someone in the rows behind me, followed immediately by a howl of troubled digestion and a sigh of such strangled anguish—*Oh Christ!*—it sounds like the speaker's last living breath. Tripp throwing his head around to look my way. And what he sees is a man who appears pained, though only by some minor physical irritant. A full bladder perhaps, heartburn, a pinched nerve between the shoulder blades.

Soon everyone is working out ways to leave the room, attempting to control equal urges to remain where they sit for the rest of their days or make a dash for the door. A full minute required for each of us to pull on our coats without touching whoever stands next to us.

Tripp the last one to move. And in the end it's the bailiff who has to grip him by the arm and lead him over to the side door once again. But they don't quite make it. The bailiff turning to hear something. Spinning on his heel as a matter of fact so he can put a face to the voice now booming out from the back of the courtroom. Squeezes his mouth tight at the disappointment of seeing that it's only Lloyd McConnell. And who else would it be? Shouting not in grief but a strange, giddy triumph. *You're going to burn in hell! You hear me you filthy bastard? Goddamn you to burn in damnation forever!*

Then, without turning to look, Tripp releases his arm from the bailiff's grip, pulls the door wide and is free.

I end up hanging around town for a couple of days. With Graham gone it's just me alone in the hotel again, a situation I'm starting to get miserably used to. There is, after all, nothing for me to return to in the city now except another empty room. And by that standard this one is as good as any.

But I'm staying for a reason. There's always a reason, isn't there, even when it comes to the most addled courses of action. I need to talk to my client. My former client. The trouble is he's nowhere to be found.

I've tried calling but his phone is out of service and he doesn't answer the buzzer at his apartment although I'm convinced he's up there. There haven't been any sightings of him since his last day in court and God knows the whole town's had its eyes wide open. Everybody wants to see what a man who's gotten away with it looks like.

He's up there because I can feel him up there. Then have these feelings confirmed when I go through the garbage bins in the lane behind his building and discover the teen girl magazines that I'd seen strewn across his bed. Loose clippings that sit there as a bundle of colored ribbon atop egg shells, burnt toast and coffee grounds.

The next night I stand across the street from his apartment and wait. The front windows are dark, but once or twice there's a murky brush of movement inside, a body whose shifted weight causes the glass to warp the streetlight reflected against it. Then sometime halfway to morning it comes to stand and look down at me. A charcoal outline within the window's frame.

I wave up to him. Stepping out into the street, one arm arcing above my head in what could be seen as either greeting or warning to someone far away. Don't call out his name because I'm frightened of how my voice would sound on its own in the hardened air. So I just keep waving up at him, a man caught passing through an unlit living room like a thief.

But before he pulls the blinds down for good he takes a half step forward so that there's a second when he's almost visible. The floating circle of his face. Fixed by a look of shallow horror, eyes held open to something he doesn't want to see but knew was there all along.

I'm walking out into the frigid lake with my shoes on. One minute I'm looking up at the vaultless night sky from where I stand on one of the big rocks near shore, the stars precise and screwed to their places, and in the next I'm stepping off into the shallows, the water so still my feet make a dull *thunk* as they push through. The kind of cold where the body can't decide between pain and numbness so it flashes between them. My legs could be sawed off at the hip. They could be on fire.

There is no breeze, yet the air carries a dusty half rain

that meets my face in dry pricks. It may even be snow of the not-quite-there-yet sort but it's too dark to make the distinction. Look down to watch the water creeping higher up my chest but it's me moving, not the water. Wading out with elbows lifted up in line with my ears like a beach tourist who's determined to go all the way in this time but delays the inevitable with a goofy, off-balance jig.

So cold it's clear I won't get far if I go out much deeper. More than five minutes spent up to your neck in this and it's all over.

I've got some time.

An attempt at a breaststroke at first but my arms won't go out that wide so I make my way with a kind of tadpole wriggle instead, throwing my shoulders forward and kicking legs joined at the knees. Making enough noise that I can't hear whether I'm holding my breath or not, and I'm glad for this because I know such a faltering sound would only panic me more than I already am. But greater than fear there is an idea of purpose, a grim duty that must be tended to.

The cramps start no more than twenty feet out. Glance back toward shore and I can still make out the detailed shape of the trees, the cracked trunks and nubbed crookedness of the branches. Nose kept an inch above the water. Wriggle out some more.

Then a sound I didn't notice before, an echo of the same disturbance of the water that I'm making myself. Someone swimming beside and slightly behind me. The rippling waves of our bodies meeting with tiny slaps in the space between us.

A face that cuts through the surface and stops the same time I do. And at first I see it as my own, although I realize in the same instant that it looks nothing like me aside from the blue skin and ice-crusted hair. A man with little strength left pulling catches of air through a frozen grimace. Then it becomes who it's supposed to be. My client. Working to tread water no more than an arm's length away, but going down in half-inch increments even as I recognize who he is.

He doesn't say anything although it's unlikely he could even if he tried. I know this because I try myself but without results. We are left to watch each other without any gesture of forgiveness or horror or rescue. The fact of our situation so plain there's no point even acknowledging it. We've brought ourselves out here and we can't stay afloat for much more than a dozen seconds longer and following that we'll both drown.

But Tripp decides not to wait that long. The bobbing of his head caused by whatever movement is keeping him up abruptly stops and yet for a moment he stays exactly where he is. Eyes open on mine but he's not seeing me anymore, they're just frozen that way. The grimace turned to an empty show of yellow bone. Sits like this above the waterline as though his skull were made of styrofoam.

And then he goes down all at once.

Maybe my own head goes under because my body exhausts itself at the same time he decides to give up. Maybe I go down just to watch him go.

The darkness enfolding him in the time it takes me to focus on where he is only a couple of feet below. And once he's gone it all goes with him—there's no water or cold, up or down, me or him. A dream that ends not with waking but the revelation of what it is to be nothing at all.

It's the crushing pain in my chest that brings me back. Overcoat thrown off onto the stones that glow mottled blue

in the dawn light. Shoes still tied to my feet and pants held
stiff down my legs, crisp with ice. Sitting up, clutching at my
neck and the top of my arms. First time I've ever had a heart
attack for an alarm clock.

      After a while the pain drains away on its own though, or
most of it, a weight still wrapped around my ribs like a lead
vest. The lake licking up to my ankles over the blistered sand.
There's no sign of Tripp or anyone else except for a whiff of
burning spruce that floats downwind from Helen Arthurs's
chimney. No prints left on the pebbly shore although I don't
bother to look. Nothing in my head but the idea that I have
to get up now or I never will.

      I pick my coat up and throw it over my shoulders, arms
too stiff to find the holes. Make my way into the still darkened
trees following the drifting smell of smoke as much as the
trail itself.

Forty-Nine

The following morning comes after eighteen hours of dreamless sleep. If the front desk phone rang through the night I didn't hear it, and the one in my room has been silent since I pulled its cord out of the wall and tossed it in the closet. The floor littered with folded notes from the concierge, white lilies on the hardwood floor.

There's a swelling ache I recognize as hunger, a migraine from the long denials of thirst. Scuffing along the walls, pulling on clothes as the chill requires them, I'm aware of how the movement of my body is the only thing that disturbs the perfect quiet of the room. In the air, a trace of my sweat.

Though it's with you at every moment, it's always something of a surprise to discover that you can be at once alive and alone.

"I've come to say good-bye."

Doug Pittle turns from where he stands four rungs up a stepladder replacing a book the size of a small suitcase on the top shelf of one of the stacks. A leatherbound *Gray's Anatomy.*

"Didn't know you were still in town," he says, squinting eyes still swollen from sleep.

"It's a hard place to leave."

"You're telling me."

Pittle could have been a tall man. At least his standing

above me on the ladder doesn't look wrong so long as I keep my eyes chest high. With his rich voice and beard and considered movements—he would make a better tall man than I do. It's fate, it's dumb luck, it's all in the genes. Nothing to do but blame your parents.

"So have you spoken to Tripp since the trial?" he says.

"No, I haven't, as a matter of fact."

"Well that makes two of us. I've been trying to hunt him down for an interview, but he seems to have disappeared."

"I'm sure he just wants to be alone."

Pittle heaves the textbook cradled in his fingers onto the shelf and climbs down to lean against the ladder's base. And without looking at him I realize that he knows who I am. Has known for a while probably, having done his homework— "Crane Girl Drowns in Fireweed Lake" found in an early *Phoenix* along with a photo showing Richard Jr.'s stunned adolescent face—but he's not going to ask about it. He's a historian. It's only the facts that interest him. An escaped mental patient falls through the lake ice. A boy is suspected of murdering his cousin. They're all just stories he needs to get straight.

The two of us stand there for a while, our eyes scanning the gold lettering along the uniform spines of the texts on the shelf next to us. *A Study of Common Viruses. Your Prostate, Your Health. Diseases of the Mind.* Below these a line of werewolf, demonic possession and vampire novels occupying the shelf marked OCCULT. Down another level yet, a dense row of well-thumbed paperback profiles of serial killers, all with "8 Pages of Photos Inside!", standing above the TRUE CRIME label.

"You've ordered these rather sensibly," I say. "Is it the Dewey Decimal System or the Doug Pittle Method that puts science on top, followed by black magic and ending with your old, everyday psychotic murderers?"

"That would be me. Actually, taken together this whole stack is the most popular in the joint."

We nod together at this but keep our eyes on the titles, the space where we stand too small for eye contact between parting men who have known each other for only a short time.

"Listen, Doug, I'm sorry about the interview. I know I promised, but I can't do it right now."

"Don't worry about it," he says, picking up *A Forensic Companion* from the returns cart behind him. "Give me a call whenever you're ready. And not necessarily about an interview for the paper, either. Just a call."

"Hey, sure. And look me up if you ever get down to Toronto. I'm serious. Drinks on me."

"Absolutely. Sounds good."

We look at each other directly now and there's an understanding that no such calls will be made. And not because we wouldn't want to or that, in the weeks and months ahead, the idea won't occur to us, but because we simply won't. Doug Pittle will stay here with the newspaper that's always four or five days late with the news and with the library that nobody seems to use. He won't get down to the city because he's made his own place and knows it's not much but it's his place so he'll stay. We won't call because what we have in common is the knowledge of terrible things, and why would we remind ourselves of that?

I'm pulling down the wallpaper in the honeymoon suite. Not the vines and blossoms glued to the wall decades ago but the bold headlines and columns of dried newsprint. Tearing through the same brittle photos of Ashley Flynn and Krystal McConnell that have been displayed across the country and will be recognized by hundreds of thousands for a couple of months until the next local atrocity comes along and new carelessly smiling faces are produced to replace them. At first I take each sheet and fold it back into its original quarters, but this allows too much time for every page to rest in my hands with their faces looking back at me. So I begin to rip them down instead, clawing blindly at the walls, tossing it all into a pile on the bed. When I'm done I watch the resulting cone of newsprint tremble and pitch as each of the pages struggles to open up once more. Continues this show of life until, after a time, it comes to rest as a sleeping body on the white bedclothes.

The Lady is all that's left. A face that enlarges without anything on the wall around it, filling the space as though a full-scale portrait. I pull the tape carefully away from her, hold the surprising weight of the paper in my hand before slipping it inside my shirt pocket. Feel its warm and shifting burden against my chest as I grab my bags and pull the door closed.

"Time for me to pay up," I say, keeping my eyes away from the concierge's baldness by laying a credit card on the desk and continuing to dig around in my wallet.

"Headin' out, are ya?" Taps the ancient computer to life and sets to grinding out a copy of my bill on a printer that produces a sound equivalent to the operation of a sawmill. "Thought you might be makin' this place your permanent residence."

"We can't always get what we wish for."

"No, sir, that is the truth."

He plunks the sales slip before my lowered eyes along with a ballpoint pen gnarled by teeth marks. But as I slip the credit card into the breast pocket of my jacket I feel something there, hard and slim as a postcard. Pull it out and hold a crumpled 5 × 7 below my eyes. Krystal and Ashley posing in their white lace dresses with blue ribbons tied at their waists. The one I stole from Ashley's bedroom.

I try to pull away from it but the picture holds me a moment more. Its surface gloss the silver membrane over still water. And beneath this, buried in the shallows, the reflection of those passed into the unrecoverable. Girls standing close, holding each other's hands and staring out with the faces of imagined burden and loss. Faces set by history, both the one they were acting out in the names of others and now, in death, their own. A history claiming them even as they lived. As the camera shutter clicked open to the light and their image burned itself onto the film, even in this most present of moments they were already falling away into the past.

"Would you do me a favor?" I ask.

"Ask away."

"Would you mail this to Brian Flynn for me? I think I have his street address somewhere here—"

"Not to worry," he waves his hand. "I know where he lives."

I hand the picture over to him and he finds a large enough envelope, drops it in and seals it without looking.

"Suppose I should ask if you found everything here at The Empire to your liking?" he asks after I sign the credit slip.

Then I do what I meant not to do and look at the concierge's face. A near toothless man of indeterminable age who's spent too much time out of the sun. Then I do what I *promised* I would never do. I look at the top of his head. A good long look at the bulging crisscross of veins patterned over his scalp, rushing blood around the circumference of his skull. But it's nothing more than a flaw of the body, something that proves he's alive.

"The room was very comfortable, thank you," I answer, pushing the front door open with my knee and stepping out blind into the light.

The drive back to the city is long and cold. This is mostly because the car still lacks a front windshield and the temperature, as is appropriate for the season, flirts around the freezing point. There's nothing for it but to pull up the collar on my overcoat, hunker down as low in the seat as possible and crank the heat so that, every once in a while, I feel a lick of warmth carrying the smell of burning rubber. Aside from two trucks that pass with a honk, their drivers laughing down at me to show teeth the color of diner coffee, I'm surprised that nobody seems to notice the extreme conditions under which I roll southward. Not that I'd be likely to notice anyway, eyes fixed dead ahead, my body a hunched question mark, unable to move but capable of driving straight down a four-lane highway just as well as the other unmoving shadows behind other wheels. Down past the factories, shipping warehouses and salvage yards, through the asphalt channels bordered by walls built to protect backyards from the noise their inhabitants moved out to the suburbs to avoid. Along the curving river valley, weaving down to where the highway meets Lake Ontario and dissolves.

I'm not thinking about tiptoeing around Graham and Bert as I clear out my desk, about facing the question as to whether the insurance on the Lincoln covers driver-inflicted demolition. My mind is free of thoughts on the collapsed arc of my career, how long my savings will cover the mortgage payments on the drywalled space above the rot and bustle of Chinatown, or what, if anything, I may be alternatively qualified to do. But what does occur to me, in a blink of memory that comes as I pull off the Don Valley Parkway onto Richmond Street and face the glare of sun off the mirrored downtown office towers, is the fact that Tripp's bloody shirt still sits in the trunk of my rental car.

Down Richmond, past the squinting, under-clothed tourists and teenaged runaways of Yonge Street, across Bay with its corners clotted by the ministerial faces of professional money handlers, and onto Spadina, where I make a right and head north. Making turns that take the car deeper into the cramped residential neighborhoods off College Street, one block featuring over-renovated gingerbread numbers and the next a series of brick and wrought iron squares with three-foot-high fences enclosing concrete yards. Circle back, go straight, become lost. Just driving. Not knowing where I'm going until I get there. And when I do, it's to pull over next to a parkette jammed between two blocks of redeveloped row houses, a chunk of clear space equipped with a slide and a swing and a sandbox now brimming with fallen snow like an unmarked grave.

Climb around to the back of the car and pop open the trunk. The shirt's still there, tied inside its white plastic bag. Pick it up with both hands and walk over to the garbage can next to the park's gate. On the other side, a bunch of kids playing tag. Boys and girls sent outside to burn off some after-school steam before dinner. Old enough to play together without supervision but young enough that they still love simple games like this, ones without teams or points or rules.

468 Andrew Pyper

Take the bag and bury it deep below the sweet garbage
of chicken bones, ketchupy fast food bags, an empty bottle of
vodka and today's issue of *The Star* with the front page
headline "Lost Girls' Teacher Goes Missing." Then I lift
myself straight and in the failing light of early winter dusk
watch the neighborhood kids play. Listen to the triumphant
"You're it!" followed by squeals of fresh pursuit and escape.
Children oblivious to the fact they are being watched by a
stranger on the other side of the playground fence, tagging
each other and turning hunted to hunter in regular turns,
kicking up the snow as they run so that a shimmering cloud
of frozen crystals follows each of the paths they take.

Acknowledgments

For providing the time and space to write, I am indebted to the Yukon Arts Council, Belinda Smith, Max Fraser, and most particularly Pierre Berton for my residency at Berton House, Dawson City. For my year as writer-in-residence, my thanks to Champlain College at Trent University, its students, and its Masters during my stay, Martin Boyne and Stephen Brown.

The Ontario Arts Council, the Toronto Arts Council and the Canada Council for the Arts are enthusiastically thanked for grants provided during the writing of this book.

Portions of the novel have been previously published in different form in *Carousel* and *The New Quarterly*. I am grateful to the editors there, namely Mary Merikle, Peter Hinchcliffe and Kim Jernigan at *The New Quarterly* and Daniel Evans at *Carousel* for their supportive comments.

I am very much in debt to readers of earlier drafts: Andrew Hilton, Jennifer Warren, John Metcalf, Sean Kane, and first and last, Leah McLaren. Also, to the editorial intelligence of my agent, Anne McDermid, who provided helpful focus along the way.

For the editors who have worked on this book, much thanks to Jacob Hoye, Mari Evans, and particularly to Iris Tupholme and Karen Hanson here at home.

And finally to Leah McLaren, for a whole lot of patience and various life-saving moments.

Toronto, February 1999